Cover art: Aleta Rafton
Interior Format: The Killion Group, Inc.

THE FINDER'S CROWN

THE LOST ANCIENTS
DRAGON'S BLOOD: BOOK TWO

MARIE ANDREAS

OTHER BOOKS BY MARIE ANDREAS

The Lost Ancients
Book One: The Glass Gargoyle
Book Two: The Obsidian Chimera
Book Three: The Emerald Dragon
Book Four: The Sapphire Manticore
Book Five: The Golden Basilisk
Book Six: The Diamond Sphinx

The Lost Ancients: Dragon's Blood
Book One: The Seeker's Chest
Book Two: The Finder's Crown

The Asarlaí Wars Trilogy
Book One: Warrior Wench
Book Two: Victorious Dead
Book Three: Defiant Ruin

The Code of the Keeper
Book One: Traitor's Folly

The Adventures of Smith and Jones
A Curious Invasion
The Mayhem of Mermaids

Broken Veil
Book One: The Girl with the Iron Wing
Book Two: An Uncommon Truth of Dying
Book Three: Through a Veil Darkly

Books of the Cuari
Book One: Essence of Chaos
Book Two: Division of Chaos
Book Three: Destruction of Chaos

ACKNOWLEDGMENTS

Writing is easy—take a bunch of weird ideas and mush them together. And then lie about how easy it is. Writing is hard, I love it, but it's hard. It would be impossible without a lot of other folks.

I'd like to thank everyone who has ever supported me, read chapters, edited, let me cry on their shoulder, read my books, given nice reviews, and/or bought me soothing beverages. I could never have done this without ALL of you. I can't list you all here, but you mean the world to me.

My awesome editor- Jessa Slade—thank you for keeping the mayhem under control. Lisa Andreas and Patti Huber for exceptional beta reading. And Faith Williams at the Atwater Group for proofreading. Any errors or mistakes that remain are completely mine.

Thank you to my cover artist, Aleta Rafton.

Thank you to the Killion Group for interior formatting and spine and back cover

To all my readers—thank you for coming along for the ride!

CHAPTER ONE

I ROLLED TO MY side and focused on not being sick. If this boat would just stop moving for a bit, I'd probably have a better chance. I'd avoided traveling on boats, ships, or even dinghies since I *believed* my parents had drowned in a boating accident when I was a child.

They *had* drowned. But it had been at the hands of a nasty magic-wielding syclarion who'd fought them far away from land. Exhausted and out of magic, they were too far away to fly home and dropped into the sea. Dragons were fierce fighters and most were magic users. None of them floated well. Since I was one, I was about as buoyant as a brick outhouse.

The truth of their demise had come to me not long before I almost replicated it. Luckily, getting really pissed off and having a magic sword on my side got me to safety. Along with some serious help from my faery buddies and my friends.

So the ocean didn't claim me that time.

But if it was possible to die of seasickness, I just might die anyway.

A soft knock at the door of the cabin I'd taken over was followed by Padraig. As an elf of over a thousand years old, he shouldn't look as good as he did as his long black hair was picked up by the wind, as if he'd commanded it to do so. He wasn't royalty, but I always thought he looked like he should be. He was the best friend of my missing boyfriend, Alric. And I respected and trusted him. Usually.

Right now my focus was on the odd, green-gray stick he held in his hand as he came inside.

"No drink? I thought you were working on a drink to make me better?" We'd been at sea four days out of a six-day trip to the southern continent. So far, none of the concoctions presented by my friends had helped at all. They'd moved me out of the main room that we shared to this tiny, single bunkroom for my safety. I knew it was more so they didn't have to deal with me being sick where they slept. I didn't blame them at all.

The faeries wanted to stay with me when I relocated. Until they made things worse by offering ale. Even just the smell of that was bad. The little flying nuisances were now banned from my cabin.

"This is something the captain finally suggested. You chew on it." Padraig's smile lit the cabin but didn't help my stomach.

"It's a stick." Granted, it didn't look like any stick I'd ever seen before. It was mostly smooth and that color wouldn't be something you'd see on a tree. Unless it was covered in mud.

"He's been sailing for a long time, a hundred years or more. He swears by it, but didn't recommend it earlier since he thought you'd work through it." He sat next to my bed and held it out with a smile that would probably only be given to the very old or very young. Or very sick.

"How long do I have to chew it?" I took the stick; it felt a bit gummy and slightly bendy.

"The entire time you're on the boat." And the grin went to super levels. "It won't be that bad, honest."

"I'm going to be walking around with this hanging out of my mouth for a few more days? How will I eat?

Drink?" I ignored the fact that both had been difficult the past four days. I twisted the stick in my hand. It was about four inches long. The same size as my faeries. I wasn't sure if that made it better or worse.

He looked at me with such earnestness, and I felt so horrible, that I stuck the end of the stick in my mouth. And caught it as I spit it back out.

"That's nasty. Like I'm chewing on old shoe leather." I looked closer at it. "It's *not* old shoe leather, is it?"

"Not sure, but I don't think so. How do you feel?"

"I…damn it. I feel okay…right at this moment. Maybe even hungry." I shoved the stick back into my mouth. Yep, still tasted nasty, but it was fading. Or so I told myself as I got to my feet.

Padraig handed me a waterskin, and I drank all of it.

"Thank you." I adjusted the stick in my mouth and went up on deck. I hadn't been there since not long after we first set sail.

Unfortunately, coming back on deck reminded me of my last thoughts before my stomach decided to try to destroy me—Alric. The wave of worry and grief hit me harder than the ocean spray.

Covey ran over and hugged me. "You're up! Interesting-looking snack, though."

I hugged her back. "It's an anti-seasickness stick."

"And you don't look happy about being up. Does it taste that bad?" Mathilda, Grillion, Foxy, and the two brownie constructs, Welsy and Delsy, were at the bow, studiously not looking our way. Padraig left me with Covey and joined them. Covey led me toward the back of the ship.

"Yes, it does, but it's working. Unfortunately, being sick had pushed aside my worry about Alric and it's back now." I shook my head. "And Siabiane and Lorcan as well."

Siabiane and Lorcan were both extremely ancient and

magically powerful elves. They'd been kidnapped a few weeks ago by the same people who took Alric. Three heavy-duty magic users, and all of them snapped up like someone would grab a cookie off the floor. Okay, according to Padraig, also an extremely strong magic user—and one who'd almost gotten grabbed as well—it hadn't been easy to take them. But the fact they'd been grabbed was still horrifying.

It looked like some big nasty evil magic users from the past weren't quite as dead as everyone thought. They'd grabbed the people who could best defend me to take them out of the picture and also to make me come to them. Even though it wasn't the smartest thing to go find the people who wanted your blood to control the entire world—I was already on the way to do that when they'd grabbed Alric right in front of me.

They did it for their reasons. I would find a way to destroy them for mine.

"We *will* get them back." Covey's hand tightened on my shoulder and a bit of berserker crossed her face before she tamped it down. Covey was a trellian. Almost a foot taller than me, lean, and reptilian. She was a professor of elven and Ancient studies in Beccia, and also happened to be extremely in touch with her trellian berserker ancestry. She used to fight it, but now she relished it. "I won't rest until they are back in Beccia and those grub worms have been danced into the afterlife." She grinned. "That's an old trellian curse. Sounded fiercer when I was a kid."

"I'll take it for what it was meant." I looked out over the water. "If they've hurt him…"

"They won't." Her grip on my shoulder tightened. "They need him as a bargaining chip for you, and if there's the slightest chance you'd know that they hurt him, they wouldn't have one."

War cries—or wild laughter; it was often hard to tell the difference—cut off any response I might have had as my flock of faeries, escorted by two gronking constructs, flew over the boat. The flock swarmed to the bow; then, suddenly realizing that I was on deck, swung wide and came back toward us.

As usual, Garbage Blossom was in the lead, closely followed by the other two of my original three, Leaf Grub and Crusty Bucket. Behind were another twenty or so faeries. The numbers seemed to fluctuate and some had stayed behind in Beccia. They swarmed around Covey and me; then Crusty, my little blue and often confused faery, slammed into the side of my face. "Is good!" She started kissing me, and soon I was being smothered by faery kisses.

"Okay, ladies, let her breathe." Covey laughed at them. Along with realizing she liked adventuring more than academia, Covey had come to enjoy the mayhem of the faeries. Most of the time.

"What is?" Leaf poked at the stick in my mouth.

I bit on it in case she decided to take it. I still hated the taste, but there was no denying that it worked. "It's a magic stick to make me feel better."

"Is magic? A magic stick?" Garbage flew down and shoved Leaf aside. Tiny orange hands made grabby motions toward my mouth. "Mine?"

"No, it's not yours. It's mine. So I'm not sick." I held onto it with both hands. Garbage could be an ornery one, and her little orange face was scrunched up in her thinking mode. Most likely trying to figure out how to get my stick.

"Girls, I think Foxy needs your help!" Covey put a lot of urgency in her voice. Luckily, the boat was large enough that Foxy and the others at the bow couldn't hear her selling them out.

Garbage stopped reaching for my stick, and she and the others looked up, then flew off toward the bow.

Bunky and Irving, my two flying constructs, had been

sitting on a bench. They both looked up at the faery exodus, then settled back down. Bunky was a chimera. About the size of a large round cat, with a goat face, tiny legs and wings, and a fish-like tail. He was also made of metal and shouldn't be able to fly, but he did. My people, the Ancients, had created his people eons ago. When the Ancients vanished, the chimeras buried themselves in the ruins until the time to come back.

Irving was a gargoyle construct, one made by Siabiane after the first relic we'd found, the glass gargoyle. But Irving was larger than the relic, couldn't control reality, like it had been able to, and had a love of eating relics. He hadn't gone after anything since I'd destroyed the collection of the world destroying relics that past-me had made. But I still didn't trust him around smaller objects.

The two constructs had become fast friends and both took watching over the faeries as their job. But even for them, the little maniacs could be tiring.

Both gronked at me, then went into their version of sleep mode. We had four constructs traveling with us: Bunky, Irving, Welsy, and Delsy—two brownie constructs created by Siabiane who looked so much alike I made them keep name tags on so we could tell them apart.

Which brought something to mind. "Welsy and Delsy were secretive about leaving Beccia when they joined us. They'd said they'd speak of it when we were on the water. Have they?" Like my friends Harlan, Amara, and Orenda, the two were supposed to stay in Beccia and guard the remaining scrolls from the Library of Pernasi that had been gifted to me by a mysterious benefactor. Or possible benefactor. If someone uses the line of "the enemy of my enemy is my friend," their loyalty could only go so far.

Welsy and Delsy had shown up not long before we got on the boat, claiming that elves were in town to guard the scrolls so they would join us. Considering most of the elves who even knew about Beccia were with us, I was a bit concerned.

However, I'd just seen Alric grabbed right in front of me during a battle, and then I was sick. My coping with other issues wasn't up to snuff.

"Not much," Covey said as she looked down the deck. "And not because they don't want to; they didn't have much information. The most we got out of them was that Orenda came back to town with a bunch of other elves. They secured the scrolls."

That didn't make me as happy as it once would have. As we'd painfully found out, many of the fabled elves were murderous monsters. "And Harlan went along with it?" I trusted Orenda; she was an elf from a different enclave than Alric and Padraig, but her brother was a jerk. Harlan I'd trust with my life.

"According to them." She shook her head. "To be honest, you know how Harlan can get. Those scrolls would be a big temptation for him, and an even bigger temptation would be if Orenda's people brought him relics to distract him."

I sighed and nodded. Not that Harlan would betray any of us. But if he thought he'd gained access to some hidden relics, he'd be too distracted to notice anything nefarious going on. "Has Foxy tried to reach Amara recently?" Mentioning her made me automatically rub the leaf and vine tattoo on my upper arm that she'd put on me before we left Beccia. Amara was a dryad and former tree goddess. The last tree goddess, as the rest of them had died with the other nature deities long ago in a fight to save the world. She'd given up being the last tree goddess to save Alric when he'd died during the battle of the relics. She still had some mojo, though, and put these marks on Foxy and me to allow us to communicate with her and let her see some of what we saw. Not enough mojo to spread the marks to everyone, but at least we had something as a backup.

She was Foxy's wife and stayed in Beccia because as a dryad she couldn't be far from her tree. I hadn't tried using the mark to reach her yet, but I knew Foxy had contacted her to let her know about Alric being taken.

"He checks in with her daily, just a brief 'how are things going,' etc. I'm not sure if he asked about the elves. Probably wouldn't have thought about it."

I nodded. Foxy most likely would just have asked how Amara and the pub were. The instructions for contacting her had been ridiculously simple, which meant I'd probably screw it up. But since I doubted that there was another former tree goddess drifting around to pick up my words, I tried anyway.

Amara had said that I just needed to put my hand over the mark, focus on her, and say her name.

It took three times for me to get my hand in the right spot. Hearing her voice come from the air in front of us was still disturbing, even when it had been expected.

"Taryn? Foxy said you were ill." Her voice was odd, like she was speaking through a long, hollow tube, but it was definitely her.

"I was, still am, I guess. The captain gave me some weird stick to chew on—it's helping." My stomach took that moment to growl and remind me that it was sadly empty.

"Oh! Is it a wither stick? Those do work wonders. Hard to get those roots, though; the plants are carnivorous."

She was way more excited about it than I was. I supposed a root was better than dried shoe leather. Even if the plant it came from might want to eat me for dinner.

"I guess so? He gave it to Padraig to give to me, so he might have told him. We were checking on the elves that are in town. Are they all from Orenda's enclave?"

"I believe so." She paused. "I like Orenda, but these elves are extremely snotty. They *offered* to take the chest with the scrolls off our hands. I still have enough power to point out that wasn't necessary. Along with the spell bubble, the entire cave that the scrolls are in is filled with massive tree roots. Ten more reappear for every one that gets removed. They are not happy." There was a proud smugness in her voice. Those elves weren't getting those scrolls on her watch.

Which was good, but still left a lot of questions. "What's Harlan doing?"

"He's helping keep them distracted. But there are a lot of them. I don't believe any of them are from Alric's and Padraig's home enclave."

That was what I had been afraid of. The elves had separated a thousand years ago when the Dark attacked them. They'd hidden in separate enclaves, cut off from everyone—including each other. Some had been glad about the rejoining a few weeks ago. Others hadn't been. Orenda's enclave had been one of the latter.

"Can you get a message out to an elf in Alric's hometown? Her name is Ceithera and she's the main healer there. Just pass along what you've told me, with as much information about those elves as you can gather. Does it look like Orenda is helping them?"

Amara's laugh was like a clear spring. "No. I think she hates her brother and his friends more than anyone. She's been working with Harlan. I need to go, but I will get messages sent to Ceithera, multiple ones in case one doesn't make it. Stay safe, all of you. And don't stop chewing that stick until you're solidly on land." There was a slight popping sound and her voice vanished.

"That was disturbing." Covey scowled at the air in front of me.

"The news?"

"That and the whole disembodied voice trick. My people had myths about deities who spoke from the ether. Not good ones."

I laughed. "Well, she was a goddess, after all—but one

of the good ones. I'm not happy about Orenda's brother marching troops in. How did he know about the scrolls?"

"Someone knows about the scrolls?" Mathilda had joined us without my notice. She hugged me as she stepped forward. "Good on the wither root, by the way."

Mathilda was Siabiane's younger sister. She was a few thousand years old and, with Siabiane, had come up from the southern continent as young adventurers. They were a different race of elves than Alric, Padraig, and the rest of the ones in the north. They were Alioth elves and the ones from the north were Mcallini elves. They looked the same to me, and I wasn't completely sure they could tell each other apart. Aside from the fact that there were few Alioth elves in the north.

I quickly filled her in on the conversation I'd had with Amara. Her eyes narrowed as I spoke. Mathilda was great at disguises and mostly wandered around looking like a slightly confused old elf. Right now she looked elegant, fierce, and ready to smash some heads together.

"Those sneaky rats. They must have a spy in Beccia. Not that it would be that hard to find out something happened. That fight against the grimarian and their minions wasn't subtle. But to have gotten there that quickly? Not good." She took a deep breath and settled down. "I believe that was a wise thing, having Amara reach out to Ceithera. She will get the right people down there to help keep things under control." She nodded as if everything was now settled. "We were discussing the plans for when we dock in a few days—"

Whatever else she was going to say was lost as the woman in the crow's nest yelled, "Pirate ship on the port bow! Coming in fast!"

CHAPTER TWO

I SWORE AS WE ran to that side of the boat. This was a channel between two continents, not the open ocean. I would have thought pirates would stick to larger ocean-going ships. But, there was no sign of land where we were, so maybe they figured anything in the water was fair game.

The pirate ship was still a distance away, but that black-and-white skull and crossbones flag was clear to see. I wasn't sure what the faeries' reactions would be, but squealing with delight and zipping across the waves toward the ship was not it.

"Girls! Come back!" I yelled, and Bunky and Irving buzzed around me. At least they waited for my command. Normally I would send them after the faeries, but I didn't want to risk the constructs as well. They swam about as well as I did. "Bunky and Irving, don't leave the ship unless I say so. The girls will be all right." I kept my fingers crossed that I was right.

Padraig, Grillion, and Foxy came running over. Welsy and Delsy ran in behind them.

"What are they doing?" Grillion had the least experience with the faeries, having just joined us a few weeks ago. So not realizing how pointless that question was could be excused.

"No idea, which is standard. My eyes aren't good

enough to see that far."

Padraig handed me a far-seeing glass. "Try this."

I focused it. "They're at that pirate ship…and flying around it. And now coming back even faster than they left. The pirates just fired a cannon at them." I looked around the boat we were on and handed the glass back to Padraig. "Does this thing have cannons?"

"No." The answer from Foxy was terse as he glared at the approaching ship.

"We don't swim well." Welsy and Delsy were usually extremely optimistic and confident. Right now, both looked worried. "But we will fight."

I smiled at both and ignored the slight tremble in their hands as they held their swords. They would probably sink as fast as I would if they fell overboard. "Don't worry, I won't let anyone toss you in the water."

The captain and his crew of four didn't look ready to defend anything. I swore that one of the crew was eyeing the dinghy tied to the side of the boat. If the crew abandoned the ship, it wouldn't be with any of us.

The faeries came flying back and they were pissed.

"Is not friend!" Garbage hovered in midair. She and the rest were putting on their war feathers and waving around their war sticks. Bunky and Irving hovered around them and their buzzing sound echoed the faeries' annoyance.

"Garbage? You thought the pirate ship was a friend? That flag means they are no one's friend." The faeries could and did take off for days at a time, so them knowing someone I didn't wasn't surprising. Thinking a pirate ship had friends on it, was.

Crusty flew up. "Has friend. Fly flappity flag too. Nice lady." She scowled at the ship and waved her war stick. "That not her!"

I rubbed my forehead. Sorting out when they had made friends with a pirate could be dealt with later. All of us ran for the rooms and gathered our weapons. My still-unnamed dagger crackled with green arcs of static in a welcoming manner as I put on the dagger belt. It took a few tries to get my sword to appear, but it finally dropped right into my hand. I closed my eyes to see if I felt my magic return as well. It had been blocked by a nasty grimarian troll a few weeks ago but seemed to be coming back.

I felt a slight magic tingle and could get a steady glow light to appear in front of me. But it still didn't feel like normal. I let go of the glow and shook my hand. Okay, no magic. And no changing. As a dragon, I could fly, but they had cannons and I would drown if I fell out of the sky. Not to mention keeping what and who I really was a secret was important. There were too many people looking for me and we didn't need to give them hints as to where we were.

I ran back on deck to find my friends and the small crew equally armed. Welsy and Delsy held out their swords, but they and Irving and Bunky were too close to the rails for my liking. I waved them over to me. "I need you four to guard our quarters." I held up a hand before any of them could speak or gronk in protest. They might be metal constructs but their faces were easy to read. "Seriously. If we have to fall back, we need a safe area." The truth was, if we had to fall back to a cabin under the deck, we were doomed. But if it did come to fighting, we could lose them overboard and never know. I needed them safe.

If we survived, I had no doubt they'd have many more dangers to fall into.

"We agree." Welsy and Delsy used to finish each other's sentences, but now they often spoke at the same time.

I wasn't sure which was better.

Irving looked to Bunky, and Bunky looked ready to argue. I couldn't understand him, but he was making his opinion known through a series of stern sounding gronks.

"Bunky. If things go bad, I need someone to rescue Alric." Bunky liked all of us, but he loved his faeries and Alric.

That got him. He nodded his entire body and gronked in acceptance.

"Protect this place." I nodded to all four, shut the door, and ran back on deck.

Padraig and Mathilda were our only magic users since I was out, so they were in front. Both were in the "blowing things apart" magic level and could do serious damage. He also had his sword, a spirit sword like mine that vanished when not needed. Mathilda had a large walking stick. She was actually pretty vicious with it in hand-to-hand fighting.

The ship would be within cannon range far too soon. Our boat crew was armed and trying to stay ahead of the pirates, but the other ship was faster.

"If that thing gets close enough to use her cannons, we're done for." The captain was a dwarf, rare outside of their mountain homes, and about as water buoyant as I was. I was sure there was a good story behind one of his kind becoming a ship captain; I just hoped we lived long enough to be bored by it. "You lot carrying something valuable?" He scowled at all of us. "Been out here twelve years, never once had a problem with pirates."

"Not a thing, just ourselves, our horses, and a few belongings." Padraig had spun a tale of us relocating to the south after falling on hard times. It looked like the captain wasn't believing it anymore.

"They're almost within firing range!" the woman in the crow's nest called down. She had a sword with her and looked ready to fight. At this point, we could see the ship approaching, so she came down.

The ship was about twice the size of the one we were on and appeared to be more of an ocean-going vessel.

The skull and crossbones snapped at the top of their mast but looked new. Enterprising pirates deciding to hit channel-crossing ships?

Padraig and Mathilda were conferring quietly, then turned to the captain. "We might be able to take their cannons out of the running—is that okay with you?"

I wanted to grab the captain and shake some sense into him when he paused. Dwarves were notoriously anti-magic, and whatever had caused him to break away from his people hadn't changed that.

"Aye. If you two can do that, it would help. They'll still board us, but at least we'll have a fighting chance." He held up a hand and narrowed his eyes. "No funny stuff, though."

They both nodded and turned back to the approaching ship. I looked at the back of the dwarf's head and wondered just what "funny stuff" was. From the sound of his voice, that was a broad category and might change once his ship was safe.

Padraig and Mathilda started softly chanting the spell and both raised their hands. The pirate ship had three cannons facing us as it came alongside. One by one, they imploded. Sadly, the damage was to them, but not so much to the rest of their ship.

It would have been nicer to have had them take the ship out with an explosion but judging by the exhaustion on both Padraig and Mathilda's faces, doing what they did took far more out of them than it should have. Trails of smoke coming from the other side of the pirate ship said they'd disabled the cannons on that side as well.

"That was rough. They don't have a full spell breaker on board, but they have something to affect magic. They were expecting magic users." Padraig took out his sword. "Prepare to be boarded!"

Lines from the pirate ship swung out and the first pirates over to our boat met a wall of annoyed faeries.

The pirates didn't seem surprised at seeing them but still couldn't avoid them completely. The strikes from the war sticks were causing yells but not any deaths that I could see.

Then Garbage and half of her crew pulled back. "We save!" she yelled and led the smaller group away from the ships.

"What are you doing?" I shouted back, but Garbage was using her selective hearing, and she and her group were out of sight in moments.

The faeries who stayed were still slowing down the pirates, but since there were fewer of them, the pirates were getting on the boat.

"Why did they leave? Save who?" Covey ran forward to attack one of the pirates. She had a sword but was already changing into a berserker. Her claws would do more damage than the blade.

"I have no idea!" I yelled back as a tall human-troll breed waved aside the faeries and charged for me. I blocked his strike with my sword, then pulled out my dagger. Green arcs danced along the shorter blade and into the pirate's sword. He swore as his sword was engulfed in snapping bright-green arcs and scorched his hand. He dropped the sword and threw himself over the side.

My dagger had some tricky abilities but that was a new one.

Foxy was waving around his club-like sword, smacking pirates more than stabbing them. The result was the same—they went down. His weapon was massive and would need a very strong human or elf to lift with both hands. He flung it around like it was made of feathers.

The faeries remaining with us rose in the air and started cheering and waving their sticks over their heads.

"Another pirate ship is coming in!" Grillion had been fighting more toward the back, but it put him in the best position to see the new ship. "I've never seen one move that fast."

Damn it. They were already almost overpowering us and they had reinforcements?

"The faeries are pushing the ship!" Mathilda smacked the pirate closest to her over the head with her staff and kicked him over the railing.

I looked closer as the faeries who'd stayed with us initially flew over to help their friends. Waves of faeries, far more than we were traveling with, were forcing the new ship to travel faster than I'd thought possible. It also flew the skull and crossbones but was aiming for the first pirate ship. Maybe they were warring pirate factions. It came alongside the other pirate ship first and a pair of cannons fired. Then she came around again. The first pirate ship tried to run and the pirates left on our boat scrambled to disengage and get back to their vessel.

Not the best idea.

The second ship—one *Dangerous Lady,* according to the name painted on its bow—had not only fired a second round from the cannons but had sent fighters swinging over to the first ship. The massive faery swarm dove and attacked as well.

The captain of our boat stood in stunned silence with his jaw dropped for a few moments, then started barking orders for us to move away from both ships.

The first pirate ship had lost its mast and was listing badly. Moving away was a good idea unless we wanted to be boarded again as the pirates fled their sinking ship.

Crusty came flying over with a massive grin. "Is friend! Nice lady! Save!"

"That's your pirate friend?" There was a woman in the lead, petite, with rich red-brown hair. Her grin looked almost as maniacal as the faeries' while she fought the first pirate crew. "How did you make her ship move so fast? Why didn't you help us that way?" I had to admit I was a bit jealous. Not so much about the speeding ship, but had we been able to outrun the original pirate ship, none of this might have happened.

"Is yes! Friend!" Crusty spun in the air a few times.

She really liked that pirate.

Garbage flew up just as I asked the second question and nodded sagely before Crusty could stop spinning. "You no ask. Back to fight!" She twisted around; then she and Crusty raced back to attack one of the few pirates still left on the deck of the sinking ship. The rest were either dead or bobbing in the cold water.

Covey was no longer looking berserker, but the annoyance was clear on her face. "Did I hear that right? They didn't move our ship because *we didn't ask*? Did you know they could do that?"

I watched the faeries and the new pirate crew as they abandoned the sinking ship and followed us at a normal speed. "How could I? Never seen them on the water before." From now on, I was just going to have to ask them if they could help with every disaster.

Mathilda laughed. "You have to admit, in their minds, it was logical. Twisted but logical. And something we should keep in mind when adventuring with them. I still don't think they know what they can do yet."

The captain of our ship was swearing as the *Dangerous Lady* easily caught up to us even without faery assistance.

"I think they don't mean us harm." Padraig had been studying the second ship. "They could have blasted us with their cannons at any time. By the way, Mathilda and I don't have the ability to destroy more cannons at this point."

"What? Damn it, move this ship faster!" The captain swore at his crew, but the wind wasn't strong.

Garbage looked at him, then at me. "But she friend. No hurt."

"I trust you." The faeries were frequently outrageous and often thought in ways that we didn't, but they were good judges of character. "We should let them come aside."

The captain sputtered, but the point was moot as the woman pirate swung herself over and landed gently on the deck. The extra faeries had vanished except for four, which stuck around the pirate.

"Nice wither stick—sorry about the seasickness. I'm Jadiera, and these are my faery friends Sparkle Slug, Floppy Sprocket, Tangled Ivy, and Quarkyl. You must be the nice lady I've heard about." She grinned and stepped forward, but Grillion jumped in front of me.

"See here, I can't be letting any pirates hurt Taryn." His sword shook as he spoke and she hadn't even drawn hers. But it still touched my heart. He hadn't said anything to me directly, but it felt like he had been watching me closely since Alric had been taken.

"Thank you, Grillion, but the faeries trust her." I stepped around him and shook Jadiera's hand. "I'm Taryn and if my faeries call you friend, so do I."

The rest introduced themselves, aside from the captain and his crew, who scowled from the far side of the deck.

"How did you come to know we were in trouble?" Padraig asked. He was flashing his dignified smile, and Jadiera kept staring at him with wide eyes.

She finally shook her head. "Sorry, not many elves where I'm from." She glanced to Mathilda as well. "Sort of thought you were all gone."

"We were, but we're back. It's a long story." Mathilda leaned on her staff and looked older than normal.

At first, I was concerned. Then I realized she was trying to make Jadiera feel at ease.

"I found out about you when we were restocking supplies a few days ago. Word was out about a non-pirate ship going on a hunting mission under the skull and crossbones." She glared back where the other ship had sunk. "We don't like people doing things under our flag. Makes

us look bad and it's against our code. Anyway, not only
were they fake pirates, they were specifically aiming for
a ship with faeries and heavy magic users. I didn't think
there were too many swarms of faeries flying around, so
thought it might be Garbage, Leaf, and Crusty." She held
up her hand and laughed at my wide-eyed look. "I'll tell
you the tale of meeting them over drinks sometime. But
suffice it to say that I've met your friends. They were the
ones who introduced me to my own faeries."

"That ship wasn't a real pirate ship? But was after *my*
ship?" The captain had been slowly edging forward.

"No, it wasn't. Hired by someone from the islands—
that's my home, the Sendai islands." She smiled. "But
my ship is a real pirate ship." She gave an elaborate bow.
"Some call me the Pirate Contessa."

The dwarf captain blanched but recovered quickly and
pointed to me and my friends. "These people caused the
attack? Because they were on my ship? And they brought
the Pirate Contessa here?" He spun. "Off my ship!"

His crew reluctantly drew their swords again, but mine,
Padraig's, Covey's, and Grillion's were already out. Foxy
grinned and held up his massive sword. Mathilda raised
her staff.

Jadiera hadn't drawn hers, nor did she look worried.
"These people were the victims, you dolt. And trust me,
you don't want to fight my crew and me."

I glanced over and noticed that while none of her crew
had joined her, most were near the railing and had their
hands on the ropes. They could swing over at a moment's
notice.

The captain wasn't yelling anymore, but none of his
crew lowered their swords.

"Oh, for crying out loud." Jadiera waved to her ship
and it started moving closer. "*I'll* take them to shore. It'll
be a different dock than intended, but if someone is following you, that might be a good idea." She glared at the

captain and his crew. "And if you tell anyone about this, my crew and I will hunt you down. I would strongly recommend you drop anchor for the night. Now."

It was still early enough in the day that they probably could have gotten a few more hours of travel in. But the captain and crew gave small nods and prepared to drop anchor. I'd never heard of this Pirate Contessa, and Jadiera looked far too young to have that kind of reputation—but the crew had clearly heard of her.

"We have horses." I knew we could probably buy more on the southern continent, but didn't want to lose more money—not to mention giving the captain a bonus for kicking us off.

"You have magic users, yes?" At Padraig and Mathilda's nods, she continued. "We have a broad plank, but the horses will need to have their eyes covered and have a slight sleepwalking spell to get them across."

"What about the rest of my payment?" The captain was feeling cocky now that he figured she wasn't going to kill him.

Foxy silently raised his sword as Padraig stepped toward the captain. "You received more almost the entire payment upfront for only taking us partway. I'd say you've been fairly compensated, wouldn't you?" The look on his face was to remind the captain that Jadiera wasn't the only one he had to worry about.

"I…yes. I'll be in my cabin." He nodded to his crew and vanished below deck.

Jadiera smiled. "Let's get everyone moved over!"

It took less time than expected to spell the horses and lead them across the deck. There wasn't a great area for them to stay in, so they took over a large storage section and were kept blindfolded and lightly spelled. The constructs were annoyed at being left out of the fighting but seemed happy to be moving to the larger ship. Welsy and Delsy doffed their hats to Jadiera as they came on board.

Bunky and Irving gronked as they flew past.

If Jadiera was surprised at seeing any of them, she didn't show it.

We were pulling away from the other boat when a larger ship appeared over the horizon.

"I thought most ocean ships didn't come down this channel?" Even I could see it. It wasn't moving faery-powered-fast, but it was huge and had massive sails.

Jadiera started swearing as she got a good look at it with her viewing glass. "They don't."

"Is it another pirate ship?" At this point, I wasn't sure if pirates were good or bad. Jadiera might be an exception.

"No, it's worse. That ship belongs to the company that hired that fake pirate ship." She spun around. "All hands on deck! We need to get out of here fast, people!"

CHAPTER THREE

JADIERA'S CREW WAS three times the size of the crew from the boat we'd been on, but about ten times more efficient. They had the sails adjusted immediately and I heard cannons being loaded below us.

"Um, ladies?" The faeries had been flittering about the ship, playing a game in the waves. "We could use your help?" I would have thought since they helped Jadiera's ship before, they would have done so automatically. Apparently, there had to be a request each time.

Garbage flew out of a wave, spun toward the oncoming ship, and started to charge toward it.

"No! Sweetie, help move this ship faster." I had to yell but she turned back.

Soon, she and her crew, Jadiera's faeries, and a dozen or so more were pushing at the sails. Bunky and Irving flew around them, but couldn't do what they were doing. The two constructs settled into supervisor mode.

"How does that work?" Covey asked as she watched them.

"No idea. Doesn't look like it should but we are moving faster." I wondered if I'd ever stop being surprised by the faeries. I seriously doubted it.

"Don't ask them." Jadiera shuddered as she came up alongside us and looked up as well. "I did ask once… still no idea and it took a long time to get them to stop trying to explain." She looked around the deck. Her crew was working around the faeries and the ship chasing us was dropping behind. "Why don't we go to my ready room and have a drink. I know that vessel and it can't keep up. Most likely it'll stay and have a chat with your former captain. At this pace, we should be to shore in the morning. It will be a different dock than the one I had planned."

Jadiera gave one final look as the ship following them vanished beyond the horizon. "I am a bit worried about what that captain will say to them, though."

Mathilda smiled. "He might say hello. So might his crew. I put a wee spell on them all once they set their anchor. They'll behave and seem as drunk as skunks at this point. It won't wear off for at least a full day." She shrugged. "I figured that reinforcing his fear of what *might* happen to him with the inability for him to actually do anything to stop it might be a good idea."

Padraig laughed. "I thought I felt something, but it was too subtle to pick up. Well played."

"A spur-of-the-moment spell and about all that I had the energy for at the moment. Now, where will we be going?" Mathilda asked.

Jadiera started toward the rooms below deck. "Let's go below. I trust my people with my life, but the waves can have ears."

Grillion, Welsy, and Delsy wanted to stay on deck and watch the crew, but Padraig, Mathilda, and Foxy joined Covey and me as we followed Jadiera down below.

"I like the way you work, and I'm glad I'm on the same side as you." Jadiera poured whisky. Mathilda, Foxy, and Padraig accepted; Covey waved it off—she rarely drank alcohol.

I started to nod, then pulled out the stick that was becoming a fixture protruding out of my mouth. "Probably not for me either. Thank you, though."

"Until you're on dry land, I'd say none for you." Jadiera took her glass and sat. "The place I'll be dropping you off at is in the jungle. A small fishing village that we've helped in the past. We come down the channel more often than most ships to help out a group of retired pirates." Her smile indicated that was all she'd say about that. "You don't need to tell me, but two of my crew are from the southern continent and might be able to help if they knew where you were going."

"Colivith." Mathilda didn't even hesitate, which made me more confident that trusting Jadiera had been the right thing.

Jadiera let out a low whistle. "That's a serious destination. Relic hunters? The faeries implied you dug things up." She smiled toward me.

"I'm a digger from Beccia, so they weren't wrong," I responded.

"From what I've heard, you'll love Colivith once you get down there. End of the continent, really. They don't have official dig areas, but the ruins are supposed to be impressive." Her smile dropped. "If you get there. I don't go on land much, and then mostly only the islands. But there's been some heavy fighting going on midcontinent. Government upheavals. Lockdowns."

"People having to carry papers to cross to or from the northern continent?" Padraig added.

"Aye, that too. Useless idea—the papers get faked all the time and forgeries are for sale everywhere in the islands." She laughed when she saw his face. "Yours were forged too? Not to worry. They got you on that ship and there are no checks in the village we're going to."

She went on to explain the best route past the village, then grabbed two crew members from on deck and brought them down to help. They made some serious adjustments to the map that Padraig and Mathilda had worked out. Clearly, the map we had was horribly out of date.

Mathilda scowled at the changes they'd made and tapped at an area about a fourth of the way down. A long, dark, crooked line cut through. "It's been a while since I've been home, I'll admit. But this divide right here? That was a plain before."

Kiona, one of the crew from the south, nodded sadly. "Aye, that was one of the prime hunting and farming grounds for the Losita." She looked up, and tears and fury crossed her lean face. "They were destroyed, along with their land, in a mage war three years ago. Hilstrike mages were what the rumor was. The empress did nothing during or after the attacks. The people of nearby villages had to help the survivors."

"A mage war? Did anyone see the hilstrike mages?" Most of the elves to the north were in hiding three years ago, but I was traveling the land. No rumors came north of any mage battles." Mathilda's face creased in concern. Hilstrike mages were a loose coalition of dark magic users. They were also one of the groups currently after me.

Covey leaned over the map. "Not to mention, shouldn't something big enough to have caused that have at least sent ripples through the magic world?" She turned to Jadiera. "I'm not a magic user, but elven magic theory was part of my studies. I'm a university professor."

"It should have." Padraig was now scowling at the map. "I'm not that surprised that we didn't feel it in the enclaves…but you were outside of them and should have felt it. Alric would have been going in and out of the enclave by then as well—he's strong enough to have felt something also."

"And Nasif," Mathilda said. "Don't forget that he and Dueble were out as well. Dueble can't use magic, but Nasif was extremely strong back in the day. He would have only gained strength over the centuries. If he'd felt something, he would have mentioned it when the shields around the enclave dropped." Nasif was an elven mage from over a thousand years ago. He and his syclarion partner, Dueble, were esteemed researchers but usually stayed out of things.

"Unless the southern mages were blocking like crazy, which tells me they wanted to make sure no one from the north came down." The map made no sense to me, but it wasn't hard to guess what had happened.

Kiona nodded. "Probably. The mages have run over anything or anyone that gets in their way. My village was destroyed two years ago. I left for the islands after that."

Jhori, the other southern crew member, nodded. "I left before that, but have a similar story. I was farther south, almost to Colivith. A smaller mage battle broke out five years ago. The mages didn't care that they wiped out three villages. Packed my things and left that night. Be careful as you go south. There are many powerful factions and they will destroy any who get in their way."

"What are they fighting for?" I held up my hand. "Yes, power. But there has to be something more to it than just who has the most power. This seems too secretive to be only that. And they had already sent some of their mages north to hide within the enclaves. Is this a battle of mages trying to control the Dark or something worse? And why isn't the empress getting involved?"

Before we'd left Beccia, Amara had filled us in on layers of nasty beings in the south. When she'd been a tree goddess, and her sisters were still alive, they'd taken out most of the powerful evil mages. That had been what left Amara the last tree goddess—the rest had been killed. But they believed all of the evil mages had been destroyed. It appeared that had been a mistake.

Another thought struck me as an image from our fight in Beccia popped up. "Do you have odd, throwback dwollers in the south? Small skeletal things that crawl out of the ground?" I still wasn't sure which were better, throwback dwollers or rakasas—the latter being hopefully dead and the former being new to my current world. Both of them were awful and the world would be better without them.

Both Kiona and Jhori spit to their side and made an odd motion with their hands. Sort of like leaves fluttering down. "Goddess protect."

Foxy frowned. He'd been silent this entire time and probably would have been happier on the deck with Grillion. But I wasn't the only one who caught the movement. "What did you just do?"

"An old superstitious blessing. The tree goddesses and the rest of the nature deities saved the south once, and it's said in times of death and destruction, they'll come back." Kiona gave a small smile. She clearly knew it was an old-fashioned belief but it was part of her heritage too.

I watched Foxy. When Amara was still a goddess, she hadn't wanted him to know. But she hadn't seemed as fierce at hiding it now that her goddess abilities were gone. I wasn't sure what she'd told him about how she'd brought Alric back to life.

He nodded slowly, then gave a small smile. "My Amara would be pleased to know the old ways were still held. Even if they are all gone." He looked to me with unshed tears, nodded, and blinked a few times before he turned back to them. He knew. "My wife is a dryad and held the tree goddesses close to her heart."

Jhori looked ready to ask questions but Jadiera gave a sharp shake of her head. She'd seen Foxy's reaction, just as I had.

Kiona stepped in. "Those dwoller-like creatures are called umbaji. They were nothing but myths until about ten years ago. They are mostly reported in the far south. Dwollers disavow any connection with them, although there are a lot of similarities."

"There's not much else known about them except they make rakasa look like children when there are enough of them." Jhori nodded. "And they almost always work with magic users. But if the mages fail, the umbaji eat them." He shrugged.

None of that was reassuring, except for the bad mages being eaten part.

"I can't think of anything else, unless you two have more information?" Jadiera nodded to her people.

"Not that I can think of." Jhori stopped himself. "Wait a minute. Recently, rumors came out of Whestio Valley. There's something new and ugly taking place there. The two closest villages were cleared out by monsters and no one has been close to the area in months. Steer far away around there." To emphasize his words, Jhori took the pen, dipped it in ink, and drew a heavy circle around a section of the map.

The two crew left, as well as Foxy, Covey, Padraig, and Mathilda.

Jadiera stopped me before I followed them. "I wanted to wait and speak to you alone." A deep line of worry went between her brows. "An augury had been cast back on the islands—among the people who were just chasing us. Chasing you. Whoever is in the south trying for this power grab, they are working with some unscrupulous merchants in the islands. The augury called you almost by name. Description, the faeries, it said you had great magic." She paused, and I shrugged. Right now, I certainly didn't have great magic. "But it also claimed you were from the powers beyond time. A monster so huge you could destroy the balance of the world. Unfortunately, I don't have much in the way of information about the people you are up against in the south. But their connections in the islands aren't good."

I wasn't as good as Alric or any of the elves at hiding

my feelings.

She nodded as she watched my face. "It didn't make sense to me, but I see it does to you. I believe your faeries saved my life. They at least gave me a purpose. And I believe you're on the side of right. The faeries can find me no matter where I am. If you need me, tell them to get me. My crew and I will come as soon as possible. I think you're part of something much bigger—something that could change this world for the better. My crew and I will fight to the death to save you."

She clasped my arm, and I returned the gesture. She might not have magic, but there was a lot of power behind her words. I had a feeling we were going to need as many allies as we could get. I knew there was more going on than getting Alric back. The entire bit about evil mages, both from the Dark as well as the hilstrike ones, wanting my blood to rule the world, for one. But right now, I needed to focus on getting Alric.

"Thank you. Sorry about any trouble the faeries caused."

Jadiera laughed. "They are hooligans, aren't they?"

The sound of yelling and crashing cut her off, and we both ran for the door.

CHAPTER FOUR

JADIERA WAS A step ahead of me, so she got through the door first. And was almost bowled over by a charging herd of war cats, faeries, and one wildly barking war puppy. Followed closely by Bunky and Irving in the air and Welsy and Delsy on ground support, trying to round them up. And failing badly.

"Where did these come from?" Jadiera looked like she wanted to block them and get answers, but I pulled her back into the doorway. That wouldn't have been a safe idea. Braking on the war cats was sometimes questionable.

"Garbage!" I knew where they came from and where they should still be. Garbage had promised me that the cats and dog would stay in their special bag.

The mass made another lap before Garbage flew over to me.

"They escape!"

Crusty and Leaf were right behind her, nodding enthusiastically.

"Out of your sealed bag?"

The pack slowed down on their third lap and there was less crashing as the crew and my friends had moved themselves and everything that could be moved away from the path of the animals. Welsy and Delsy started slowing the pack down, and Bunky and Irving did flybys if anyone tried to resume racing. At least they were trying to help, unlike the faeries, who had been cheering them on. It looked like some small coins had changed hands when they settled down, but they kept it hidden from me. Cat racing had been a serious issue back in Beccia. We were not having it start up again on the road.

"Might had oops." Leaf had her most innocent look on, which reinforced that no oops had actually happened.

"Get them back in their bag and don't let them out unless I say it's okay. What if one of them fell into the ocean?"

At that moment, five faeries flew up over the railing, carrying an extremely soggy cat out of the water.

"We get." Garbage smiled as the cat shook itself off. Then Garbage sighed and rolled her eyes. "Fines. We fix." She whistled, and the cats, faeries, and lone puppy all came around to where we were. The wet cat silently cleaned itself.

"Back ins!" Garbage went down to the deck and held open her green and brown bag. It was disturbing to see objects go into the tiny bags, but it was extremely disturbing seeing live cats and the puppy march inside. Welsy and Delsy looked like shepherds bringing in their extremely odd herd.

Jadiera's jaw dropped. "I'd seen them pull ale out of those bags, but animals?"

"Yeah, it's a new thing, from what I gather. Those are their war cats…and war puppy. One of the faeries is allergic to cats. They hadn't told me they had the cats and dog with them until we'd been on the road for over a week. Apparently, they are happy in the bag as it's expanded inside and quite comfortable. I have a feeling they got out because certain faeries were bored." I glared at my original three. Garbage shrugged; Leaf looked contrite; Crusty giggled, spun in a circle, and looked up at the darkening sky.

Once the animals and faeries had been taken care of, I went to find my friends. They were clustered at the aft of the ship, except Grillion, who was playing a game of cards with a few of the crew. Why he thought gambling against pirates was a good idea was beyond me. I hoped for all our sakes he wasn't trying to cheat.

"Jadiera had some more news." I quickly told the others what she'd told me. It had been disturbing to hear, but even worse was the look on Padraig and Mathilda's faces.

"An augury of that sort doesn't bode well, and it's worse that it's moved beyond the continents," Mathilda responded. "The island kingdom of Sendai isn't large, but they have connections to lands far beyond the north and south continents. This is most worrisome."

I dropped my voice. "At least it didn't mention a bunch of uses for dragon's blood."

"No, but the mages would have kept that information to themselves if they had it. They might not know specifically what you are—just that you're powerful. And unique." Padraig looked over the water. "How is your magic? I was concerned before about what we might face, now even more so."

"It's coming back slowly." I shrugged and cast my glow spell, and the resulting glow was far stronger than it had been before.

"Your dagger sparked when you just did that." Covey pointed to the dagger at my waist. My sword had gone back to wherever the spirit swords vanished to, but my dagger was entirely from this world.

"I think your magic is still connected to that dagger—somehow." Padraig held out his hand and I gave him the dagger. "Not exactly sure how, though. Robukian are rare to begin with and one actually transforming into a weapon is almost unheard of." He handed the dagger back to me.

My dagger had magically created itself out of a set of

extremely old elven jewelry called a Robukian. The faeries insisted the dagger was a he, but beyond that, no one seemed to know much about him.

"If the beings who took my magic initially were southern mages, why is my magic coming back as we get closer to them?" My dagger had proved himself helpful on many occasions, but having my magic was going to be crucial to getting Alric and the others back. And keeping those evil mages from grabbing any more of my friends.

"That is a very good question." Covey folded her arms and glared at my dagger. "We don't think he's causing it, do we? No offense meant, dagger." She winced when the dagger flared at her words.

Maybe he'd be happier once I gave him a name. The faeries said I had to pick it, not anyone else, but nothing had struck me yet.

I patted him but looked to Mathilda and Padraig. I've never heard of the weird pieces of jewelry that had combined to make my little friend but I didn't think he was bad. The faeries could talk to him, and I trusted their opinion on this.

Padraig shook his head. "I think he's acting with your magic, not taking it. I also think that once we're on solid ground and you're not having to chew on a stick to stay upright, Mathilda and I should test your magic."

"And, as the old lady of the group, I think we should get some rest for a few hours. We might not have to hit the trail the moment we land, but we shouldn't wait too long." Mathilda nodded to the crew quietly doing their jobs. "I trust Captain Jadiera, and she trusts the members of this village we're going to, but we'd do better to keep moving." She turned to Welsy and Delsy. "Can you two and your flying construct friends stand guard?"

Bunky and Irving were flying around but, unlike the faeries, they weren't going over the water. They dropped lower when Mathilda waved to them.

The four constructs bobbed and nodded in agreement. The constructs could go into a rest mode and usually did so when others were sleeping. But they didn't need to unless they'd been running for a week or more, or done some extremely exhausting things. And unlike the faeries, they were trustworthy enough to come to get us if something happened.

Foxy kept looking over to Grillion's card game.

"So where's our destination? Colivith seems pretty far down. I'd like to find out just what Qianru is up to and which side she's on." Everything pointed to Colivith being an important place, but so far no absolute proof as to where whoever took Alric and the other two were. Qianru was in Notlianda and had started all of this by sending Grillion north with a letter for me. One that led to the appearance of the Robukian pieces. Not to mention she'd first demanded I come to her in the south, then said not to. She was my former patron and quite imperious, but she didn't control me.

"The Whestio Valley is what I was thinking for our first stop." Padraig had lowered his voice. "I think any recent secretive heavy magic development might lead to something of importance for our search."

"The place we were told not to go?" Covey gave a short laugh. "That sounds like us. But since it's farther north than any other options, it probably couldn't hurt to work our way over before heading south."

I looked between them. "Yeah, it could hurt. *A lot.* They seemed pretty certain that wasn't a good place to go." I shook my head and sighed. "And rumors of extreme danger are a great way to hide things…or people."

"Exactly. I'm going to look over our modified map and find a few options for getting there. If I have questions, I need to ask them before Kiona and Jhori set sail back to the islands." Padraig nodded, then took a mage glow light and went to a dark corner of the ship.

"I'm going to keep an eye on Grillion." Foxy stretched. "He might be heading toward some trouble." He walked over and pulled up a barrel behind Grillion. The people he was playing with didn't look concerned at Foxy's appearance, but Grillion did. His pile of coins was higher than before. I hoped for his sake that he hadn't been cheating. Foxy used to run a gaming room long before I came to Beccia, so he'd spot whatever Grillion was doing if it wasn't legit. He'd also find a way to stop it without causing trouble.

I wasn't sure about sleep right now. I'd been resting for most of the past few days. But Mathilda was giving both Covey and me *the look*, so I followed them into the small bunkroom Jadiera lent us.

The faeries followed us in and set up on one of the bunks.

"Is sleeps." Garbage waited until her troop, with Jadiera's four as well, settled down, then walked in a circle and curled into a ball. "Big time tomorrow." She gave a huge yawn and crashed.

"Aw, damn it. Do you think she's seeing the future now?" If that was the case, I was going to wake her up and make her tell me everything she saw.

"Doubtful." Mathilda looked at them with a wistful smile. "But you never know what goes on in their heads. And you know she'd never explain it well enough for us to figure out. Maybe just tell her to warn us in the morning."

Covey had already dropped into a solid sleep, so I lowered my voice. "Do you miss them?"

My three original faeries had been dumped on me by Mathilda. She'd rescued me when I almost died after flinging myself into this timeline. After healing me, she took off and left me with Garbage, Leaf, and Crusty. At the time, I wasn't happy about it. Now, I couldn't imagine my life without them.

"I do in some ways, but I think they are where they belong. And I just have to find you, and I can get all the faery time I want."

"Garbage could find you some extras. It looks like she got those four to hang out with Jadiera."

Mathilda held up her hands in defense. "Thank you, but no. It's easier this way. Not as many chances of almost burning my cottage down. Or taking it for a thrill ride."

Mathilda's cottage could travel on its own. I could see the faeries having too much fun with that if they found a way to control it.

I yawned and cut Mathilda off before she could comment. "I know, rest." I took the stick out of my mouth. We were supposed to hit land tomorrow, but I didn't want to be sick while we docked. I just had no idea what to do with it while I slept.

Mathilda held out a glass of water. "It can sit in this. They only last a few days, but it should get you to shore."

I dropped the stick in the glass and went to sleep.

I immediately dreamt of Alric. Some dreams of the man you love were great, some were horrifying. This fell in the latter category. He was beaten and bruised, a nasty shiner closing one green eye, the other red-rimmed. His normally white-blond hair was matted and filthy. His clothes hung in rags and he was chained to a wall. As much as I yelled and ran, I couldn't reach him. He was directly in front of me—but I was running in place.

Two grimarian trolls—short, fuzzy-looking beings that looked like giant, malevolent dust bunnies—came to him and asked questions. I couldn't hear what they said, but whatever it was pissed off Alric. His legs weren't chained as tight as they should be and he lashed out to kick the closest one.

I screamed in my mind but also realized this was a nightmare. I'd had similar ones since Alric had been taken. But this one felt more real. It had a depth that the others hadn't.

Alric looked up as the grimarian he'd kicked got back to its feet and a troll walked into the chamber he was in. Alric looked right at me and grinned. "Take the southern road, Holen Way. They won't see you. I love you."

Then the nightmare vanished, and I was sitting upright in bed, crying. His words had been true; I felt it in my soul. He somehow knew I was there; I had no idea how I was, but I was. He told me how to get him. I hadn't seen Siabiane and Lorcan, but if they were taken by the same people, they were probably in that place as well.

Damn it. That meant what was happening to him was probably real as well.

Covey and Mathilda were asleep, but Foxy, Grillion, and Padraig hadn't come in. I needed Padraig. As soon as I put my feet on the floor, my stomach lurched. I grabbed the wither stick, stuck it in my mouth, and quietly left the cabin.

The constructs were slowly patrolling the ship, the card game was winding down, and Padraig was still in his corner, looking annoyed at the map.

He looked up when I came over and sat next to him. "I thought you were sleeping?"

"I was. Had an odd nightmare." As matter-of-factly as I could, I told him about the dream and Alric's response. I needed to keep emotions out or I'd be diving off the railing and swimming for shore. Since I couldn't swim, that would have been an extremely bad idea.

Padraig rolled up his map and leaned forward to take my hand. "Are you okay?"

I smiled. He was like the big brother I'd never had, and he loved Alric as much as I did. "I don't know. But did what he said make any sense?" I was torn between wanting to be wrong about what was happening to him and finding a way to get him out.

"It does, and it confirms Whestio Valley as their location. Holen Way is a much lesser-known path to get to there." He reached out as my amulet swung forward as I'd taken a seat. "That's the amulet that you, Alric, and Siabiane made, yes? There's a good chance that helped you two connect."

The amulets had been created in the elven enclave to help protect Alric and me and help my magic. Amara felt they might be more than that and had created different ones for the others before we left Beccia.

I grabbed mine. "Do you think this could lead us to him?"

"It might help. It's hard to say what Siabiane put in them." Padraig rolled a section of the map out again and the glow hovering above us dipped lower. "This is the valley, and these are the two roads I was looking at. Since we're coming from the north, they made sense." He pointed to a much smaller line below the valley. "This is Holen Way. From the look of it, it's not used much. If anyone is expecting us, an ill-used trail from the south wouldn't be what they'd assume we'd take." He looked closely into my eyes. "Some of your people had dream-seeing. This might be something coming back to you. Or something that happened because Alric was trying so hard to reach you."

"What if it's the enemy trying to trick us to go that way?"

"That's always a fear with seeings and sendings. But there would have been several easier routes to get us on if that were the case—including the two I was looking at taking. I believe we have to take a chance. We can't drop our guard, whichever way we go."

I looked out over the dark water. The sky was clear and there was just enough of a moon to see the tips of the waves. "I don't think I can go back to sleep. Unless you think that Alric might try to reach me again?"

"I doubt it. To speak to you like that would have taken

a lot of effort. Are you going to be okay out here? I'd like to see if Jhori or Kiona are still up."

"I'm fine. As long as I have my stick, the ride is nice. Could you tell the constructs in case they come looking for me?"

He nodded and left.

I wanted to be alone right now. The feeling of Alric's presence was still around me. He was beaten up but in no way beaten. And now we had a chance to find him. I kept looking out over the water and thought of the ways I would destroy the people who took him.

CHAPTER FIVE

———◆———

I DID FALL ASLEEP on the deck, and it wasn't a good idea. Everything hurt when I woke up.

Bunky, Irving, and Welsy watched me from about a foot away. Silently watching while I drooled in an uncomfortable chair. That I hadn't fallen out of the chair or choked on the wither stick was a miracle. I did adjust it in my mouth, though.

"How long have you three been there? Where's Delsy?" The sun was just rising, and I had to admit, pain and all, that sunrise on the water was an amazing sight.

"He's on patrol. Padraig told us to watch you, so as we shifted off patrol we did so." Welsy smiled.

I'd often wondered what would happen if only one of them was around and needed to speak. It was good to know that they functioned fine separately. Although we were going to need to work on what keeping an eye on someone meant. I doubted that Padraig intended for them to stand there all night staring at me.

"Is that land I see?" I'd been focusing on getting out of the chair and then the amazing sunrise, but there was a strip of what looked like greenery in the direction we were headed.

"Yes. We came in sight of it exactly twenty minutes ago. We would like to continue our patrols?" Welsy looked earnest, and so did Bunky and Irving.

"I'm fine. Go about your patrols." I wandered over to where the card game had been to find Grillion drooling as he slept on the table. Foxy was sitting on the deck, leaning against a barrel. His eyes opened at my approach.

"Ah, good to see you, Taryn." He stretched and got to his feet then shook his head at Grillion. "I'm afraid I didn't bring our friend here much luck. He lost almost every hand." His sideways smile told me that he figured Grillion had been mucking with the game somehow and had stopped it just by being there.

Grillion wasn't going to be happy, but I agreed with Foxy. Ripping off pirates, especially ones who were helping us, was a bad idea. Grillion snorted but was still out cold. Foxy and I went and joined the others.

Everyone was awake, and the faeries had taken off. I hoped they hadn't gone far, but knowing them, they'd gone off to see the green area.

"I filled the others in on the location of Alric, Siabiane, and Lorcan and our change of plans," Padraig said as I came in.

Mathilda and Covey both came over and hugged me.

"We'll get him back," Mathilda said. "We'll get all of them back."

"And we'll destroy the ones who took them." Covey's snarl would disturb anyone it was aimed at.

"Thank you both. I've been thinking of either ripping them to shreds, stomping on them, or if my magic is back, pushing them five miles underground." My thoughts before I'd fallen asleep had been graphic—ironically, I hadn't had any nightmares this time.

"Or all of the above? Why choose?" Covey grinned as we went back to the room we were all sharing.

"Everyone ready?" Jadiera knocked, then came in. "The faeries are back and getting into position with the sails."

"How long do we think? Should we start getting the horses ready?" Padraig looked like he'd gotten a full night's sleep in a luxury inn.

Advantages of being an elf, I guessed.

"I'd say once the faeries get going on pushing us, two hours, possibly a lot less. No signs of any other ships, by the way. But still, once we drop you off and check in with the village elders, we'll be leaving quickly. I'll be going to the northern coast and leave that way—less noticeable if they're still looking for us. I might not know who they're working with on land, but I know the ones following us on water."

As she spoke, the ship lurched forward. She smiled. "I'd say the faeries are getting us moving. Have everything ready to go." She ducked back out again.

Not much had been taken out, but Padraig and Foxy went to go check on getting the horses ready.

We had everything gathered, including a groggy and solemn Grillion, and were waiting on the deck, when the crewman in the crow's nest started swearing. "Longboat coming toward us. Fast."

Our speed was because of the faeries and there was a good wind. One that would have been pushing the other boat back, not forward. Which meant that the ones coming toward us were using a lot of magic.

"Who attacks a ship this size with a single longboat?" I could see it now. The low skimmer type of boat was used by fishing people who lived in the coastal villages.

"They're not attacking us." Jadiera had her spyglass out and was keeping up a steady stream of swearing. "They're coming to warn us off. Damn it. They don't have a lot of magic users in the village but they must be working together to get that skimmer moving like that." She turned to her crew. "Hold the ship. Faeries, stand down. Help them on board when they get here."

There were four people in the longboat, and if their speed hadn't given the magic users away, the fact that none of them were rowing would. Longboats usually only moved because a lot of people were rowing.

Only one man climbed up as the boat pulled alongside. "Jadiera, I'm glad we caught you before you got closer. The village is being watched." He clasped hands with Jadiera and nodded to the crew members. His eyes lingered on me and my friends, but he didn't say anything.

"Good to see you, Marluk. Do you know who it is or when they started?" Jadiera carefully didn't introduce us, and he didn't look like he wanted her to. The faeries dropped down a bit, but it was more likely they were waiting for the go-ahead to play in the sails, than any interest or concern about Marluk or what he might say.

"My watches say they noticed it after last night's hunt, but the tracks we saw looked at least a few days older. I'd say we were under watch a few days, then became of higher interest yesterday. No idea as to who, but we have our shields in place around the village."

"Damn. Where will you go?" Jadiera kept an eye on the shore.

"Maybe drift along with you lot for a bit? The magic users are on the inside; they sent us on our way, but I've left orders to keep the shield up until we're back—and I plan not to go back soon." The scowl on his face turned him from a kindly old man into a former pirate.

Jadiera nodded to her crew. "Get the other three on board and their boat. Thank you for the warning. We were going to drop our guests off on your doorstep. Any other ideas?"

"How hardy are your guests?" He looked us over and smiled. "I'd say not a worry. And please, don't tell me or my crew who you are. Just safer all around. I can lead you to the Devils' Path. A bit farther east than you're currently heading but no one would expect you to be coming in that way."

The speed at which Jadiera, her crew, and Marluk got everyone on board and moving again was impressive. The faeries squealed as Jadiera took the wheel and we set sail.

Padraig and I walked to Jadiera as she steered away from the coast.

"Are we going to have a problem?" He was watching Marluk and the other elders. If they were concerned about being locked out of their home, none of them looked it. I supposed that being a pirate meant you went where you went. Even when you were no longer on the sea.

"It's not good that someone knew we'd head for that village, that's for certain." She looked up at the sails. "Girls? Get more of you on the left. I'm having to fight to steer too hard." Massive giggles and the faeries balanced out on the sails. "And I won't lie, the Devils' Path isn't easy. But it's known only to pirates and smugglers. And not used much even by them. Your horses are sound but you might need to walk them through most of it as you go up the trail. It's extremely steep." She called Kiona over. "Can you get them a map for the Devils' Path? I have an extra in my room. Tell them everything you know about it."

There wasn't much to tell, and Padraig rolled up the new map with the other one. Basically, we were aiming for a rocky shore and a steep path up. The trick would be making sure we made it up to the top quickly as we'd be visible from the water until we did. And if anyone happened to be looking down from the top of the cliff.

"Can we hide ourselves with magic?" We were getting closer, and it looked to me like there were a lot of switchbacks on the cliff. We would be slow-moving and exposed.

"I wouldn't recommend it." Kiona shook her head. "I'm not a magic user, but there are enough other things to be looking out for on your way up. You wouldn't want to need your magic and have to drop the cover."

Garbage and a few of the faeries had come off the sails

as we slowed down. I waved them down to us. "Garbage? Could you and your faeries fly over us and our horses as we climb that path and block others from seeing us?" I had no idea if they could or not, but after the bit with the sails, I was going to ask every time something came up.

Garbage scowled at the approaching shore. Then conferred in high-pitched faery with her friends. "Is yes."

"You'd need to hold it the entire time up. No one can see us." I felt better that they'd talked about it, and it wasn't just her spouting off. But that was still a long, open hike.

"They see." Garbage smiled.

"That's the point, they can't see us. Or our horses." This might not be workable. But if that was the best way to get to Alric, that was the way I was going—visible or not. I could probably transform and fly up, but I couldn't take the others. I was going to rescue Alric, but I wasn't losing the others to do so.

"They no see *you*." Her smile grew wider and she winked. "See this." She closed her eyes, held out her arms, and a leaf appeared. I was standing less than a foot away, and I would have sworn that in front of me was an elm leaf someone had picked up off the ground. It was still orangish but mottled. "Is see? Up, up, up and this is what see."

"That is impressive. Have you always been able to do that?" I winced as the question escaped before I thought it through. Having her explain their tricks wasn't usually a good idea.

"Is no, then yes, then maybe." She nodded as if that clarified everything.

It didn't, but it was mercifully shorter than I'd expected, so I was going to leave it alone.

"That works for me." Padraig studied the approaching cliffs. "It might look off to have leaves moving like that but unless someone is directly below us, they won't know what it is."

"Girls? Can you make your leaves look faded?" The cliffs weren't white, but they were lighter than Garbage's change.

The faeries around us changed to faded versions of the one Garbage had shown.

"They are truly wonderful. I've met Jadiera's friends once, but to see so many is amazing," Marluk said as he watched them. "If any of your wild friends need shelter, our village will always be open to them." He gave a reverent nod to Garbage.

More surprising, she and the faeries nearby returned it.

I tucked that reaction aside for later investigation and focused on adjusting my things on my horse and our upcoming trip.

Jadiera came up to me as we were getting ready to lead the horses across. "Not going to lie, it was great seeing Garbage, Leaf, and Crusty again. And I'm glad I finally got to meet their nice lady." She handed me a bag with a smile. "Some things for you, including a few wither sticks in waterproof paper, for when you come back. And some sugar for the faeries. I'd give it to them here, but you do need them functioning, and I don't need that craziness on my ship." She clasped my arm. "Until we meet again and safe journey."

CHAPTER SIX

———◆———

GETTING EVERYONE ONTO the tiny spit of a dock that stuck out of the bottom of the trail wasn't easy, but we managed. Looking up, I knew there was no way we would be riding our horses up it at all. "Okay, ladies, do your thing." We were still fairly close together, but once we started up, seven people and horses would be a long line to cover. Bunky and Irving had wanted to fly ahead, but I didn't want to risk them being spotted. There were too many people who knew they traveled with me, and they would be too interesting to people who had no clue who I was. Either way, they needed to stay under the faery cover. Welsy and Delsy were far more compliant about sitting atop Foxy's horse as we moved up.

I kept my hand on my amulet as I led my horse behind Covey's. I wasn't sure how much it had helped contact Alric in my dream. To be honest, I hadn't thought about it until Padraig saw it. But if there was any way to let Alric know we were coming for him, Lorcan, and Siabiane, I wanted to use it.

The faeries were flying close to each other and about three feet above Foxy's head—as he was the tallest. Sunlight came through their flying, but it was like hiking up an extremely steep, tree-covered path. I tried not to look too far ahead after my first jaw-dropping gaze once Jadiera and her crew departed. It had looked long and winding from the water, but it was way beyond that looking up from the base of it.

After about a half an hour of trudging, Crusty dropped out of formation and landed on the rear haunch of Covey's horse, and faced me. The horse flicked its tail but didn't seem too concerned. I noticed about a quarter of the faeries duplicated her move, landing on various horses.

"Is break." She looked at the amulet in my hand. "Talking?"

"Just hoping this will help." I looked up as the remaining faeries adjusted their formation. "So you will take breaks? That's a good idea." I hadn't thought about it, but expending magic took energy from any magic user— even beings that actually were magic, like the faeries.

Once she realized I wasn't going to be doing any tricks with the amulet, Crusty started humming to herself and playing with the horse's tail.

After the third or sixth bend—there were a lot of them—I chanced to look down. I'm not afraid of heights, probably because of what I was, but I might be after this. We still had a lot of mountain above us, yet the channel below us looked small. I could just see Jadiera's ship fading from sight. I hadn't gotten the full story as to how she met the faeries. We had promised to catch up once we'd finished saving my friends and ending the threat to life as we knew it. But I gathered there had been some commotion one time when they had gone out wandering. Possibly when Alric and I had been hiding from them. I'd feel bad that Jadiera got them but she seemed pretty happy, so I wasn't worried.

According to the maps, it didn't look like there would be more than a few days to get around to Holen Way and sneak into Whestio Valley. I wasn't sure what our plan was once we found this fortress or whatever we were looking for. It might not have signs saying it was an evil lair, but there were often subtle stay-away spells on places like this—or so Mathilda had said. No one was talking about plans or much of anything at this point.

Grillion was leaning on his horse as they walked. He'd started drinking once he'd started losing last night and wasn't feeling very good right now. And the rest were thinking their own thoughts. Not to mention the path wasn't wide enough to risk failing to pay attention.

Another rotation of the faeries happened. This had been the third, and it still looked like it would take days to get to the top. Each time, one faery had been sitting in front of me. This time, it was Leaf. And even though I'd finally let go of the amulet and tucked it back into my tunic, she was staring at me like I was a piece of candy.

Maybe she sensed the sugar I was carrying. I'd decided to give them Jadiera's sugar when we got to the top—right now, sugar-high faeries were the last thing we needed.

"You do?" She finally tilted her head at me.

"I do what?"

"You do flappity. Zoom." She flapped her wings and pointed to the top of the cliff.

That was still an annoying distance ahead of us.

"You are watching to see if I'll change and fly up?" I laughed at her excited nod. "Sorry. If I did so right now, it would scare the horses. Not to mention you can't cover me when I change."

She sighed. "Do later? Flap-flap-flap?"

They were just waiting for me to transform. Since that was my last option, I would be too noticeable and there were too many people who wanted my blood, hopefully, it would be a long time before they saw that. After the battle of the relics, I'd been hoping to work with the elven magic users who knew what I was to help me relearn what I was.

Then everything fell apart, and I found myself back fighting and on the road. And still not exactly sure how to do most things in my dragon form. Considering that the first time I'd tried to fly, I'd shot backward into a massive clump of trees, I had a feeling the faeries were more about a repeat performance as opposed to helping me learn how to fly better.

"Not until we get our friends back. So, you have to help us rescue Alric, Siabiane, and Lorcan. Then I'll see about flying. When we're all safe." I was taking a risk of them demanding that I do it again, but I specifically hadn't said how long after we got them back and the faeries could be distracted with other things. I hoped to rescue our friends, find out what my former patron Qianru was doing—and which side she was on—stop the big bads who might be trying to take over the world, and get back to Beccia to settle down with Alric and learn how to be a dragon.

I had a bad feeling it was going to be a much longer time before any of that happened than I hoped.

"We find. Fight! Bring out the kittahs of war!" She didn't bring out her war stick, but she raised her fists in the air and yelled the last bit loud enough that all of the faeries—and we were still traveling with far more than my twenty-three—echoed the battle cry.

I winced as their yells echoed up the cliff. "Shh. We don't want anyone to know we're coming."

Leaf nodded and flew to the others, telling them to stop. Which took almost an entire minute and ended up giving away where we were if there was anyone at the top to hear it.

"Controlling them has never been possible. It still isn't. You know that, right?" Mathilda and her horse were behind me and mine.

"Logically, I know that. It's still a hope, though." I looked up as the faeries changed position again. "I don't see any giant boulders being dropped on us, which would be the easiest way to take us out right now. So that's good."

Covey glanced back. "And you're starting to think like a strategist. Which is probably a good thing. If you know how your enemy can take you out, you can stay ahead of them." She looked so serene as she spoke, I figured she must have been meditating as she walked.

The faeries settled down and while there was usually one near me, they weren't as obsessed as before. After another hour, Padraig and his horse crested the top. Covey waited a moment, then followed and waved the rest of us up. Welsy and Delsy scampered off Foxy's horse and Bunky and Irving flew up a bit, taking in the surroundings.

It had taken most of the morning to get up the cliff and my legs felt like lead. About fifty pounds of it. "Can we stop for a bit?" I knew I was whining and I didn't care. The top of the cliff was chalky and bare, but a lovely stand of tall pines stood not too far away. We'd be on horses moving forward, but I needed to rest.

Padraig had gotten on his horse and looked ready for another hour or two. He looked at me, then the rest. None of us looked ready to go except Foxy. He might not normally get out and about, but he was impossible to stop once he was moving. He wasn't fast, but he'd keep walking all day if he needed to.

Everyone else looked like I felt, and Grillion even folded to the ground.

"Let's get into the trees," Padraig said. "I can scout ahead. We have a major road to follow for a short piece before we get south of the valley. I want to know if we need to stay off it or not. It'll make our trip a lot longer if we can't use the larger road at all."

Grillion got to his feet but didn't get back on his horse. He leaned on it and followed Padraig. The trees were far enough for me to be worth flinging myself on my horse.

The animal wasn't happy, but I think it was more about having to climb up that cliff than me sitting on it. Jadiera had added some apples to our farewell pack, enough for two for each horse. She might never have gone up this thing, but she knew what it was going to take for us to make it. Once we got settled, I'd make sure the horses got their treats. Unlike us, they hadn't had a choice on this trip.

Mathilda bustled around, making a cozy mini-camp while Padraig rode off. The horses happily ate their apples and drank water we'd stored in one of the faery bags.

"Are all of your adventures this…dull and painful? I didn't mind the ride down from Beccia—at least it was mostly flat. But that was awful." Grillion stretched then sat down again, too tired to go for any food until Foxy tossed him a chunk of travel bread.

"You didn't have to come," Covey said. "You could have stayed in Beccia. You could still go back to Beccia. I'm sure someone could get you a pass to cross on one of the ships." She wasn't looking directly at him as she spoke, but I could tell she was paying close attention to him. When Alric and I had been in the elven enclave, Covey and Harlan had babysat Grillion for us. So she knew him better than I did.

And she had a point. He'd left the south to deliver a letter to me from Qianru, but he was from the north originally. He could have gone on about his life.

"I could have." He finished his bread. "Hell, the old me would have taken off a long time ago. But working with Alric for a while taught me to see beyond the next con job. Then working for Qianru added to that. From what I've overheard, you all weren't sure if she was trustworthy or not, but I think she is. And lastly, I'm not leaving, because those people took Alric. He's my friend and I don't like people taking my friends. I'm not leaving until we get him and your other friends back." He laughed. "I can't promise I'll stop complaining, though. It's kind of instinctive."

Foxy patted him on the back, almost flattening him. "Aye, you're a good man."

Grillion grinned. "See? If he says so, it's true."

Padraig rode back about twenty minutes later. "I think we want to follow alongside the road, not on it. There was no one that I could see, but there were signs of recent wagon and horse traffic." He grabbed some food and water and looked around. "Where are the rest of the faeries? And Bunky and Irving?"

Damn it, I hadn't noticed. "Welsy? Delsy?" The faeries had settled in the trees and it hadn't been clear when a bunch of them took off. More importantly, Garbage, Leaf, and Crusty were gone. That usually meant they were getting into something.

The brownies popped up from a bush they'd been studying. I'd forgotten that Siabiane built them as gardeners. "This is a very rare shrubbery."

"That's great. Do you know where the others went? We're missing a lot of the faeries and Bunky and Irving."

"They...oh dear." Welsy scowled.

"They tricked us. Said this was a hosenflower bush. Those are quite rare. We'd been telling them about these on the ride over."

I called over one of the remaining faeries. "Where are the others?"

"Outs and abouts. Things. Lots of things." She nodded sagely.

I closed my eyes and tried focusing on my original three faeries. Nothing. I added some ale to my thoughts, and sugar, even a few chunks of chocolate. Still nothing. Either my reaching them mojo had gone wonky again, they were ignoring me, or something had happened to them. I opened my eyes just in time to see something fly by me.

An arrow that missed Foxy's head by inches.

CHAPTER SEVEN

MOST OF US were already sitting. Foxy and Padraig were the only two on their feet. Padraig dropped low with his sword in his hand and the other ready for a spell. Foxy stayed where he stood but had his massive two-handed sword in one hand and a tree trunk in the other.

It might have been just a very large branch, but it was almost as tall as me.

My sword appeared in the dirt next to me. Mathilda had her staff, Covey her claws, and Grillion was also loading a small crossbow. One I didn't know he'd had with him.

Welsy and Delsy froze, then both took off in opposite directions but basically behind the shrubs they'd been investigating. The rest of our faery mass did one round over our heads, then swarmed off.

"Is anyone hurt?" Padraig said as he looked around us. We shook our heads.

"Show yourselves, ye cowardly cravens!" Foxy was pissed and ready to start smashing people. "Ye can't be shooting at my friends and live!" His mountain troll accent used to be more common for him. Being around Amara had toned it down—it was back now.

I shared a look with Covey; the arrow I saw almost hit him, not one of us. She nodded toward me and pointed down. Damn. There had been two arrows. There was one behind me with its head buried in the dirt. And to be fair, the one I saw almost hit Foxy had flown directly past me.

No one responded, but no more arrows came our way either. The wind increased a bit, but no other sound. Then Welsy and Delsy came racing back into the clearing.

"Running! That way!" They pointed in slightly different directions but both were in the direction Padraig had ridden in from. And the direction the remaining half of the faeries had flown off to.

I didn't want to be shot at, nor see any of my friends hit, but we couldn't stay down like this forever. I waved the brownies over to me and kept my voice low. "Can you sense who was shooting at us?" I wasn't certain what Siabiane had built into these two when she made them.

"Five people. Three males, two females. Two are human, three are elven. All wearing long sleeves and hoods." The two answered in sync and at the same level I'd spoken.

I had no idea how they could tell if they were human or elven with hoods up, but that might fall into the something-Siabiane-built-in category.

"Are they still here? Any of them?"

Two head shakes. "They went back down the road. Very angry at one of them. Male human. Others dragging him. Might be dead."

I got to my feet to find myself engulfed by Foxy. Not easily, what with all the weapons he held.

"Protect!" he yelled loud enough that most likely Jadiera and her crew heard him as they headed back to the islands.

I was just starting to be crushed by him when a stream of wild colors flew around us. "Is safe!" It was all of the faeries, at the least my original three, plus the other twenty we'd had, and the extras. Foxy released me, and I staggered away.

"I'm fine!" I waved him and the rest of my friends off.

My only injury was almost being squished by Foxy. My sword had vanished the moment Foxy grabbed me, so that should have been a good tip-off that we were safe.

Covey bent down and picked up the arrow that had been behind me. Mathilda went across the way and found the one that had almost hit Foxy. Covey started swearing and handed hers over to Padraig.

From where I stood, both just looked like arrows to me. A bit darker than most, and the fletching seemed to be a dark reddish-black. From their reactions, that wasn't what the others saw at all.

"Damn it, soul arrows. Don't touch the tips." Mathilda held hers up, said a single word, and it vanished in a puff of smoke.

Padraig looked at the one Covey gave him for a few more seconds, then his arrow burst into flame and vanished. "Explains the hoods. The Dark knows we're here."

"Or they just don't like strangers?" I looked around in hope, but the looks around me said otherwise.

"The Dark, as in those nasty elves and their friends who almost cost me my freedom and maybe my life?" Grillion still held his crossbow and looked into the trees around us. "Okay, and almost killed Alric?" He paused. "Were they the ones who took Alric or not? I wasn't clear on that."

"They were behind the two men you came north with. But I wouldn't think grimarians would play nice with another band of evil. Historically, the Dark only kept to their own." Covey scowled. "But it does look like they've moved beyond only elvish members."

"Go get?" Garbage had been leading her faeries in a widening circle over our heads but dove down in front of me.

"No!" It came out with a lot more force than I'd intended. The people we were up against—the Dark or some other cadre of evil—had created a powder that could ground the faeries. If strong enough, it knocked them out. I didn't want to see if they increased the strength enough to kill. "I need you to stay here with us. Where did you go, anyway?"

"We hunt." Leaf drifted down as well. "Bads out there." She nodded solemnly.

"I know, sweetie. They attacked us while you were gone. We need to stick together. If you, any of you, see something, tell us." I looked around. "Where are Bunky and Irving?"

"Guarding bads." Garbage puffed out her chest. "We caught two."

Padraig, Covey, and Mathilda had been in a quiet discussion, likely concerning the mysterious soul arrows, but all three looked up at Garbage's announcement.

"You caught two of the five Welsy and Delsy saw?" Padraig's sword had vanished but came back immediately.

Mine popped back as well. Maybe it was learning from Padraig's sword.

"Noes. Two others. With. But not." Leaf looked like she was thinking then held out her hands. Seven fingers, then she folded down five. "Twos."

"Let's go find our guests." I mounted my horse and looked at the others. "And we're going?" There hadn't been much taken out of the packs and it had been put back before our little ambush. But they just stood there looking concerned. I might not know what those soul arrows did, but they did and it wasn't good.

"Maybe you should stay here. We can find them and bring them back," Covey said.

"Look, just because they might have shot at me, it doesn't mean I'm the only target. Not to mention, *this* isn't the safest area."

Garbage wasn't listening but had already made a full loop around the clearing. "Goes now."

Patience wasn't her thing at all.

"I'm walking next to *you*." Foxy took the reins of his horse to lead behind him and marched alongside mine. "They have to get threw me first." His tusks jutted out as he glared around the forest.

I patted his shoulder as the rest got on their horses.

"Okay, girls, lead on. But don't lose sight of us."

The faeries had a different concept of leading than most people. They often forgot that there were people following them.

Garbage tore off, but the rest of the faeries drifted along in a line, each keeping the one ahead of them in sight. I felt so proud. I'd taught them that a few weeks ago in the forest outside the elven enclave. I was surprised it stuck with them this long.

"I do appreciate that you're trying to protect me, Foxy."

"Don't want you hurt. You're like my little sister." His grin still showed a lot of his tusks but his heart was in his eyes.

"That's very sweet. You're family too. But we're taking this risk together." I wasn't going to remind him that since I was technically over twenty-five hundred years old, I was far older than him. However, since I hadn't lived those years, just been flung through them, I supposed that made me younger than Foxy. Either way, he was good to have around.

Welsy and Delsy had been jogging alongside us, refusing to get on the horses. Since they'd ridden on the way up the cliff, I guessed there had to be some other reason than not trusting the huge animals. I noticed they were keeping a close eye on the lower shrubs as we rode by. Hopefully, they were looking for more unusual plants and not seeing people following us.

A crackle of light filled the air, followed by a muffled scream. Both Bunky and Irving could shock people. The chimeras came that way—something my people had done when they made them—and Siabiane had given

Irving that gift when she made him.

We picked up speed as the sounds increased.

And rode into a small clearing surrounded by faeries waving their war sticks—but no war feathers, so it was mostly for show. Bunky and Irving were slowly circling two struggling forms on the ground and with every lap, one of them would let loose a spark and a tiny bolt of lightning shot near the two prisoners. The strikes weren't hitting them but a reminder not to try to leave. The prisoners were sitting, sort of. And bound together with enough vines to tie up an army. The faeries were sometimes prone to overkill. Not to mention there weren't any vines around here.

Welsy and Delsy stomped up to the prisoners before any of us could get off our horses.

"What was your intention? Hooligans!" Both kicked the two hooded forms.

One of them kicked back, and Bunky zapped him. This one struck, and the gagged scream made that clear.

Padraig swung off his horse and pulled back their hoods. Both elves, both roughed up and gagged with vines. He turned to the brownies. "Sorry, they couldn't answer you. But your question was valid." He nodded to Garbage. "Could you remove the vine from one of their mouths without letting them free?"

I knew that Padraig easily could have done that—Mathilda too. Magic was a handy thing. But this way Padraig kept things hidden and earned some extra points with Garbage and the faeries.

"Is do." Garbage flew down and removed the vine from the tallest elf's mouth. Two faeries came behind her and tightened up the ends so he was still tied.

"Now, before we let these extremely enthusiastic faeries after you—those sticks can kill, by the way—I'd advise you to talk. The Dark, I presume?" He glanced to their arms, where the tattoos would be to confirm his guess.

They were buried under a pound of vines, but his glance was enough to show he knew what he was talking about.

"Northern scum. We've heard of you and your weak lands. You won't do anything to us."

Padraig shrugged, stepped back a foot, and waved Garbage forward. "Don't kill yet. Just make them understand what's at stake."

Garbage and about a third of the faeries dropped down and stabbed the two elves. It wasn't easy through the vines, but from the shouts, it still worked.

"Try again?" Padraig called his sword right in front of them. Northern elves and southern elves were technically different races, but they looked a lot alike. And had many of the same beliefs. In this case, from their eyes alone, it looked like they both knew what a spirit sword was and the power of someone who could wield one.

Spirit swords were a mythological sword only appearing to a few elves every generation and were well known in elvish lore. Padraig and Alric both had them at their command. Mine was one too. No one could figure out how or why an Ancient had one, but I did. Considering the look of shock on their faces at seeing Padraig's sword, I debated about taking mine out of its scabbard. Although the best impact was when they appeared out of thin air. I stood back and rested my hand on the hilt of my dagger instead.

The elf kept watching Padraig's sword, but he was less disturbed than he'd initially been. "Who are you? We were told you were a band of northern vagabonds, coming to Colivith to steal our treasures."

"Now we're getting somewhere." Padraig leaned forward. "Who told you about us? What were you supposed to do?"

Something about the way they settled back after their shock at Padraig's sword wore off made me get off my horse and take two steps closer to them. "You know who

I am, don't you? Your friends tried to kill me." I raised the dagger and green arcs danced in the air. "I took care of them. *We did*. But it turns out that we needed information I forgot to ask." I gave my best crazy grin and sent a single, low-level spell: push. Normally it could send my victims airborne. Right now I'd settle for some slight pressure. I don't know who was more surprised—me or them—when they were shoved back a foot.

I won since I recovered first.

Thanks to Alric and his con-man ways, I knew that in a con game the one who moves too slow loses. I jumped forward and dropped low in front of the first one. "Do we need both for questioning?"

Mathilda caught on first. "No, I believe we can get what we need from the one. Just don't be as messy this time."

I smiled and turned back to the two elves.

The ungagged one watched my dagger, but so far it hadn't sparked once. "Yes, we're part of the Dark. You were supposed to be captured, but I think one of the ones you killed was secretly working for the grimarians, a group of hilstrike mages. His orders were to kill. I was afraid that since your winged monsters took down me and my second, they might have succeeded."

CHAPTER EIGHT

MY BRAVADO FALTERED. A spy for the hilstrike mages had probably been the one trying to kill me. And they'd escaped. To be fair, the real members of the Dark might not have taken kindly to the spy trying to destroy me since they had different agendas. Which explained the four of them beating and dragging off the fifth that was reported by the brownies.

Grillion slouched forward with a twisted grin. He held one shoulder up and twisted his head in a very non-Grillion manner. "Yes, well, she's not dead. We're not dead. Your friends are gone. And we've got some monsters that need to be fed." He pointed up toward Bunky and Irving. Both opened their extremely wide mouths, now filled with teeth that had never been there before. I'd have to ask them about that later. "They do eat a lot, just like kids." The way he got into his part reminded me of Alric, and I tried to keep my face straight.

"Look, I don't know what else we can say. We have a drop where we were supposed to take you to. In Notlianda. They said to kill everyone else, no offense, and make sure we did it before dawn tomorrow."

"Why do they want her?" Grillion walked around them closely, still doing his lopsided leer. The change in him was impressive; he actually looked threatening. "And why before dawn? What's supposed to happen…then?"

He timed himself to spin back to the elves on the final word. If after this was over, Grillion did move back to Beccia, I was telling Harlan he had another actor for his troupe.

"She's something to someone. We don't know. We do what we're told. As for why dawn? Dunno that either but it has something to do with Dagonin Danir."

Standing out of their line of sight, Mathilda turning pale and almost shaking scared me a lot more than these two in front of me.

"Thank you." Padraig walked behind them and knocked them both out with the butt of his dagger. Then turned to Mathilda as he rifled through their packs. He took a pile of papers, but he scowled before he moved them to his pack. "Does that translate as I think it does?"

Mathilda nodded and sent a spell of silence over to the sleeping Dark. They wouldn't hear anything even if they did wake up. "Yes, it does. Dragon Day in the old tongue. A day where dragons hunt the land and cannot hide." She looked at the sky, grew more concerned, and got on her horse. "We need to get out of here."

"Aren't we doing anything with them?" Grillion seemed upset that his performance had been cut short, but he got on his horse as well.

"We don't have the time." Padraig now looked as worried as Mathilda. "If the full change happens at dawn, it's going to be a rough night leading up to it. We need shelter."

Covey shook her head. "Dagonin Danir is a myth. A folk day honored in the south, but really just a day of dressing up and eating and drinking too much food. It was a day of revealing…oh." She looked at me and winced.

Mathilda nodded. "A day of unveiling those who lived in disguise. Yes, and a chance for common folk to live out who they want to be. Fun and games, but not for us. Not for Taryn." She called down the faeries. "I need half of you to ride with Taryn, encircle her and her horse while we travel. In your war feathers. The other half of you need to find us a cave. A huge, tall cave. Safe from other eyes. I think at the base of those mountains might be the best chance to find something large enough."

The faeries buzzed in confused circles at her words, but Garbage sorted them into groups, and my horse and I found ourselves encircled by faeries. The other half, led by Garbage, shot out over the trees.

Padraig started walking farther into the woods. "We should keep moving toward the mountains. They can find us."

"Agreed." Mathilda turned to me. "How are you feeling?"

"I'm fine. So this Dragon Day?" I didn't mind a day celebrating my people. Unless that wasn't it. "It was about hunting and killing us, isn't it?"

"No, not at all. Your people left the south long before you were born, but they were recalled fondly by my people. Dragon Day was a day to remember that. A day of feasts, celebrations, disguises, and a spell that covers the south for one day to break all spells of hiding."

I blinked a few times as my thoughts didn't go where I wanted them to. "You mean I change? Whether I want to or not?" My voice went high at the end as I imagined me trying to hide as we rescued Alric, Lorcan, and Siabiane, and then went to Colivith. Not a good image. They might revere my people, but I didn't think they were ready to see one in the flesh. Not to mention I'd be exposed to the ones hunting for me.

"Yes." Mathilda shook her head. "I've lived up north for so long I forgot. And until you came along, I would have said the magic spell released on Dagonin Danir was only there to give everyone a little thrill." She frowned. "I have a feeling it's more than that. Syclarions hated that day and stayed indoors. For a reason."

Syclarions were enemies of my people. Some of their people had two forms as we did. One human looking, the other reptilian—sort of a cross between my people and the trellians. Much smaller than we were and not full dragons, but they probably didn't like being forced into a shape either.

"What do we do? Am I stuck that way?" I looked around for someplace to hide. Which wasn't a useful idea as I wouldn't fit in the same spot a few hours from now. "What happens before dawn?"

Padraig silently led the way through the trees.

Mathilda rode near me this time. Well, as close as she could with the rotating ring of faeries flying around me. "You just might have some odd quirks before you change—I've never seen an Ancient, remember. But, the feast and spell are only from dawn to dawn, so as long as we can keep you hidden for the day and night, you should change back to your human self and regain full control of your changing ability."

Her smile wasn't as reassuring as I needed it to be.

"I caught that *should*." I raised my hand before she could respond. "Don't worry, I know you've got no idea what to expect. Let's just get me hidden before I get big and scaly." I'd dropped my voice at the last bit. Mathilda had spelled the elves we'd left in the clearing, but that didn't mean the trail was safe.

We couldn't go quickly as we were still waiting for the faeries to return, but we were heading toward the base of a distant mountain. And everyone dropped into riding in silence.

I'd noticed that Grillion was still in his tough guy persona and had his small crossbow across his lap. I hadn't gotten a good look at it, but it looked extremely high-end. Which most likely meant he'd stolen it, but I wasn't going to ask. He'd impressed me with his behavior change. Maybe he would survive this trip after all.

"When we're settled, maybe we can go through some of the scrolls and see if we can find more information." Covey only had a tiny bit of drool at saying the word *scrolls*.

The scrolls in question were in one of the faery bags, along with some of Lorcan's books. They'd been in a chest that was dropped at my feet by some disembodied person from Colivith. No idea what side they were on, but Alric, Covey, and the others all went wild about the scrolls. They were from a library that was supposedly destroyed thousands of years ago: the Library of Pernasi. I'd barely heard of Pernasi and their tragic history. It had been the location of great learning for the ancient world. Until jealous tribes came and destroyed them. My friends had not only heard of the library, but they were also huge fans.

I was a digger, and I enjoyed finding relics from the past—but scrolls had never done much for me. Probably because they didn't survive long in the ruins.

"That might be a good idea, but we should only take a few out at a time. Keep the others secure." Mathilda wasn't drooling but she'd perked up at Covey's suggestion.

Garbage came swooping back with her flock behind her. "Found! Big place." She was talking to Mathilda but looking at me. She figured out why we needed the cave. She appeared to be sizing me in a much larger form as she tilted her head and nodded.

"Good job. We're going to need you to lead us, slowly. Remember, the horses shouldn't run in the forest." Padraig gestured for the faeries to lead the way.

"Not far." Crusty flew over to me, patted my cheek, and sat on my horse's forelock. The horse twitched a bit at first, then ignored her.

"Thanks, Crusty. Are you my guard?" I waved to the

faeries that were still circling me. They swapped some out with the ones who had looked for the cave.

"Yes." She grinned and waved her war stick. "I protect."

The faeries flying around me felt that was a challenge and waved their sticks and yelled as well.

"Thank you—all of you. But we need to be quiet." As I spoke, an odd feeling flowed over me. Like a sudden fever. And my hands were shaking. "How close to this spot are we? I'm not doing well." I didn't feel horrible yet, but I could see where this could progress to that point. Quickly. "If the magic whatever doesn't hit until dawn, why am I being affected now?" And who in the world cast a spell over an entire land anyway? I'd hold off on asking that one, but it was first and foremost on my mind. It seemed reckless and stupid, and I had a feeling there was a much darker origin to it than the myths implied. There might have been a reason all of my people moved away from the southern continent.

"Because of the way they created it," Mathilda said. "This was far before my time or your time. To create any long-term spell, there must be a period of lead-up. This isn't a strong spell for anyone who isn't of the shifter families, but still, it's been around for thousands of years. Even at one day a year, it's going to need to build up to function. But, like this entire thing, I'm speculating. I recalled my grandmere always shutting down her spells the day before Dagonin Danir. I thought there might be a reason." She looked pointedly at Padraig's head. "Which is also a good reason for us to watch our magic for the next two days."

Padraig nodded but stayed silent.

She turned to me and shook her head. "He can be as stubborn as Alric. I think the two of them were bad for each other."

"I heard that." Padraig's voice was neutral, but I was pretty sure he was smiling.

"Just so you know, if something weirds out your magic and you become a toad, I'm not helping you." She grinned.

Padraig just kept riding.

Intentional or not, the little interaction between the two of them distracted me long enough that the fever and shakes vanished. They'd gone for now, and thinking about them might make them worse. But knowing that my body was going to be doing weird things and betraying me for a while wasn't making for a fun ride.

We'd been going deeper into the woods and closer to the base of a looming mountain.

"How far off from that path Alric mentioned is this taking us?" I was grateful that hopefully, I wouldn't go dragon out in the open, or worse, in some village, but I also didn't want to delay getting the others back any longer than we had to. If that seeing was true, Alric was having a bad time. I hadn't seen Lorcan and Siabiane in that vision, but they were probably being tortured as well.

"We're going farther south than I'd intended, but it'll help us look like we're not coming from the north, so that's good."

Padraig wasn't great at hiding things. This was going to slow us down a lot.

"But there's no way we can hide you out here," Covey said. She couldn't see my face but knew what I was thinking. "And no, going off on your own is not an option."

There was some force behind those last words, and I couldn't blame her. The first time I'd changed had been a shock, and I was certain I was going to turn into a monster and stomp those I loved.

So, once I knew they were safe, I left them. It turned out fine, but Covey and Alric still thought of me as a flight risk.

"I wasn't thinking of it." I hadn't yet—but there was a good chance I might have. But unlike that first change, I knew what was coming and that the people around me knew as well. Taking off wouldn't help and might slow down our rescue of Alric.

I happened to reach for the amulet when I thought of him, and a shock traveled through my hand and knocked me off my horse.

CHAPTER NINE

I WOULD HAVE TUMBLED off my horse if the faeries circling me hadn't banded together to catch me. They pushed me back up, with Crusty pulling on my hair to help.

"Ow!" I grabbed the chunk of hair she was pulling on, but before I could do more, I was flung into a dungeon. Alric was in front of me, but this time he was chained to a bed. If this was real, at least they were letting him sleep.

"Alric?" I didn't want to shout. If he could hear me, I didn't want anyone else to. Although when I'd been here in my dream, there'd been no indication that the ones with him had heard him or me. At least not what he said to me.

He rolled over more, now facing me but not awake. Still beaten up, but nothing looked fresh. I couldn't move any closer to him, which made sense as it might just be a hallucination caused by the faeries letting me land on my head.

"Alric? We're coming for you and the others."

This time he twitched, then opened his good eye. "Taryn? How are you here? You need to stay away." He pushed himself up on his elbows, but the chains didn't allow for more than that.

"You told me how to come to you." It was definitely him; I felt it in my gut. But he seemed out of sorts.

Drugged maybe? Some spells could mess with a person's ability to function.

"That was weeks ago. I thought you'd gone on. Things have changed. Rescue the others. They have me too well hidden. You won't survive. Any of you."

I narrowed my eyes. Was this a trick? "It was just a day ago. And aren't the others with you?" It had been assumed that Lorcan and Siabiane were in the same place as Alric.

"Damn. They must be messing with my sense of time." He sounded more like himself and rubbed the side of his head. "But no, Siabiane and Lorcan aren't here. That information slipped out when the people who grabbed me first woke me up. They had a fight over me joining the others in the south or staying here. You need to go to Colivith. Save them. I'm gone."

First I was scared; now I was pissed. "And what happened to make you this scared? We don't leave people behind, damn it."

"I'm not fearful for me, but they've been telling me what they plan to do with you. With your blood. With more than your blood." He'd already been pale, but now it was worse. "They need more of your blood than you alone could provide. Syclarions are closely related to your people, so they will breed a race of syclarion/Ancients just for their blood."

That was a horrifying vision. "I won't let them." That wave of heat from before was back, but this time it felt good. I needed to blast something. Images from my misty past floated through my head. Dark ones. A power my people had that I'd forgotten. I wasn't about to tell Alric of it right now.

"You can't find me. They have too many traps set up. I'm too hidden. You have to forget about me."

If his face got any more stoic, he'd become a statue. I wanted to hug him, kiss him, and also punch him.

Now I saw red. Literally, my vision got a red tinge to

it. "After all I've been through to save you? What Amara went through?" I shook a finger at him. "I will tell your grandmother. I think she could bring you back without a problem!" I was burning up. Almost like massive indigestion that felt like it was going to swallow me. And I was really pissed at Alric giving up like this.

A lot happened at the same time. The door to Alric's prison opened and two troll breeds stomped in. A bunch of faeries started pulling on me in the real world, and I could feel their hands. My indigestion grew worse. A lot worse.

"Stop it!" I wasn't sure who I was yelling at, but suddenly a massive burst of flame came out of my mouth and obliterated the guards.

Alric's eyes went wide, but before he or I could say anything, I found myself on the dirt trail back with the others.

A scorched tree near me told me it hadn't been completely a dream.

"How…" I wiped my mouth. Yup, felt normal human-me mouth—not the massive-fire-breathing-me mouth. A singed branch dropped a foot away from my head.

"What happened?" I let Foxy help me up in spite of the continued faery attempts at assistance.

"You…changed…but didn't change." Covey was rarely at a loss for words, but she was now. She was looking at me like she was torn between helping me and taking me apart to see what made me do that.

"You were in the saddle, talking; then, all of a sudden, you froze. Eyes wide open. The faeries were pushing you up because you'd started falling, then you yelled for Alric." Grillion stood near me with his hands on his hips. "Then you yelled a bunch of stuff I couldn't understand, but you were mad." He looked to the others but they nodded. "Then flame. Just a bunch of flame. I thought we were under attack, but it was you." His eyes were huge but he didn't look scared.

Great. I could be scared enough for all of us.

"I somehow went to where Alric was. But he thought it had been weeks and was trying to convince me to leave him behind. Then I became *really* angry. And I think I flamed some guards in his cell. Then I was back here, in the dirt, and looking up at a toasted tree." I pointed where another bit of blackened tree dropped to the ground.

"It happened so fast," Padraig said as he and Mathilda got off their horses and started walking slowly around the burnt tree. They were doing their magic stalking thing, where they were looking for clues in the world of magic. "But it appeared that you changed and stayed yourself at the same moment. The flame here was real, and it could have been in your travel as well."

"Wait, so I was where Alric was in reality? And here? I don't think being in two places at the same time is good." Although part of me was kicking myself. Maybe I could have gotten him out of there. Aside from the fact I had no idea how I traveled there or where he really was. And I hadn't been able to move when I was there—aside from a possible flaming.

Mathilda and Covey walked me over to a rock to sit.

"I have a feeling the spell coming our way is affecting many aspects of you. Not enough is known about your people to know what abilities or gifts you might have—and have since forgotten." Mathilda leaned a bit too heavily on the word *gifts*. She was afraid whatever it was might be at the other side of the spectrum of good and evil.

"Whoever set up this spell kind of stinks." I rubbed the side of my face. I'd apparently landed sideways as there was dirt along my hairline. "But I don't think we have time to worry about me. I doubt whoever has Alric is going to be happy about what I did to those guards or his cell." If I did what it looked like I did. Which I felt deep inside that I did. Somehow I'd shot flame out of my mouth in two locations at the same time. While still a human.

What I wanted to do was get a bunch of ale, which I was pretty sure the faeries had in their bags, and get gloriously drunk.

What I needed to do was break into the place Alric was being held in, find him, and get out—all before I went full dragon. Although, in my dragon-self, those walls wouldn't be a problem. But there were enough magic users who were strong enough to take me out. And while they might already guess at what I was, showing the people who wanted my blood was still a bad idea.

What I was going to do was try to keep myself under control until the calmer heads figured things out.

"Let loose the kittahs of war!" Crusty had stayed on my horse and was jumping around on its head. The rest of the faeries took up the cry, and Garbage looked like she was reaching for her bags.

"No, no!" I raised my hands. "No kittahs…kitties…of war. Or puppy. Keep the animals in their bag."

The faeries shrugged, and Garbage put back her bags.

"How far are we from where we believe they are holding them?" Covey looked to Padraig, and he dug out his map.

I hadn't brought up that the other two weren't with Alric. I turned to Mathilda. Since this was about her sister, she needed to know everything. "If that was Alric, and the encounter was real, he said that your sister and Lorcan weren't there. He said when he woke up, the people who grabbed him were talking about them being in Colivith and some felt that he should be as well."

Her face dropped but she nodded. "We knew that might be where they were keeping them. I'd like to know why they kept Alric up here."

"Bait for me, I think." I briefly told her of their plan to make more crossbreed Ancients in the hope that their blood would prove as valuable as mine supposedly was. A source of magic-enhancing blood that could bring unknown power to the evil mages who knew how to use it.

"That's horrific!" Mathilda's staff reappeared, and she looked ready to take out an army with it on the spot. "That won't happen."

I looked around at my friends, my family. They would fight to the death to keep that from happening. There was no way I could ever repay them. "Thank you. All of you. But I won't let that happen either."

I wanted to tell them more, but I wasn't sure how to explain the images that had hit me in Alric's room. We could make ourselves explode. If surrounded and all hope was lost, we would go out in a blaze of fire and glory and take our enemies with us. My parents hadn't taken that option because they fought to the end. They also didn't have crazed mages after their blood with the intention of magically taking over the world.

Not pretty and not in any history books, but I knew it was real.

The more I thought about it, the more I knew I couldn't explain it at the moment. Maybe to Mathilda, Padraig, and Alric, one on one. At a pub. But right now, knowing it gave me strength. "We need to focus on getting Alric out. I don't think we have time to get me to a cave tonight."

It was still afternoon, but it would be evening soon. In my gut, I didn't think Alric had long. If they knew I had been there and that I'd seen him, they might believe that they no longer needed to keep him alive to serve as bait.

"We'd need to know exactly where he is or we'll be cut down as we try to find him." Padraig rolled out his smaller map. "From where we are now, we could be there within a few hours if we push hard. There's a lesser used road going up here." He pointed to a darkened section. "If I were building a fortress of evil, this would be it."

Covey scowled over the map. "I agree on both. That looks likely and we have to know where Alric is before we go in. Plus, who knows what more things will change with Taryn."

I shrugged when they all looked at me. "Not negotiable, folks—I'm going in." In a nervous twitch, I'd grabbed the amulet again and fiddled with it.

Crusty and Leaf flew close to where I held it and stared. "Is there."

"Yup."

I dropped the amulet and looked around. "What's there?"

"Pick up. That. Is there." Leaf nodded to the amulet, and Crusty started tugging on the chain. This brought the rest of the faeries in around me.

"Okay, back off." I held the amulet and thought of Alric. Nope, I was still in the woods with my friends. No images of a dungeon or Alric. "I can't get there again."

"Turns. Walks and turns." Crusty spun in a slow circle in the air.

I started walking, then turned. At about the three-quarter mark, the amulet tingled. I kept turning and it stopped. Turned back—yup, there it was again. "This thing is tingling that way. Would that be the direction you thought we should go?"

Padraig nodded. "Well, we have to veer a bit off to the right first, because of the road. But yes. If you can sense where he is once we get there, we might have a chance."

Mathilda got back on her horse. "Let's go then. Taryn, hang onto the amulet. Faeries, you just earned a pound of sugar once we're safe."

There were some issues along the trail. Padraig wanted to keep us on the thin dirt road, but the faeries wanted to go their way—straight over everything. Eventually, I convinced them to stick with us, although I did notice that Garbage sent out little reconnaissance teams as we traveled. Probably a good idea, actually.

The dirt trail vanished after about three-quarters of an hour. We had been moving at a light run, but now had to slow down and wind our way through massive trees and huge boulders. Many of the latter were closer to being small mountains.

I'd kept my left hand on the amulet the entire way, although the road seemed to be going in our direction. Then I felt the tingle disappear. I turned in my saddle. "It's that way." To our right, between two of the mountain boulders, was a small trail. If my amulet hadn't winked out on me, I wouldn't have noticed that path at all.

"That's what the amulet indicates?" Padraig looked back and changed direction at my nod. "Not going to lie, I don't like the look of that path. Everyone, be ready for an ambush."

Bunky and Irving had been flying low, with Welsy and Delsy jogging alongside us.

"Can you four venture out? See what you find? And not too far. Stay in pairs. Faeries, you too. Leave a few back here, but the rest of you do a slow check of the area." I didn't want anything happening to any of them. But the constructs and the faeries were far hardier than the rest of us.

"Do!" A mass of faeries flew off. Welsy and Delsy stuck together and ran up one of the boulders like brownie goats. Bunky and Irving flew directly over.

Padraig smiled. "Good thinking. Since it's all you and your necklace at this point, would you care to lead?" He bowed and stepped his horse back a bit.

I'd usually felt like the tagalong on our adventures. No magic in the beginning, no fighting prowess, no strategic planning. Now my magic was having problems, I still wasn't as great with a sword as I would like, and my body was looking at a serious forced change, with who knew what might happen before then. But I felt good.

My head was high as I led the others into the thin trail between the boulders. Only to have my horse rear up and dump me as a wall of throwback dwollers, umbaji, came racing toward us.

CHAPTER TEN

I LANDED HARD ON my butt and there was nowhere to go. My horse was panicking—justifiably so—but her only way out would be to trample me. Or the umbaji.

Tough choice.

I scrambled back on my horse, ignored the yells from my friends behind me, took out my feisty dagger, and charged forward.

The dagger crackled and sent out bright-green arcs toward the umbaji. I kept one hand on my horse's reins, holding them so I could touch her and send calming thoughts her way. I yelled as we charged forward.

The dagger seemed to be having a very good time as it crackled and lashed out at the umbaji. I was surprised that the arcs were hitting flesh and causing burns; it mostly had gone after metal before. Nice time for it to do an upgrade.

I wasn't as surprised as the umbaji, though. They had been charging forward but were now trying to turn away from my dagger and me racing toward them.

There were a lot of them scrambling about the boulders, and from the sounds of fighting going on behind me, more were behind us. Or something else equally fun.

Bunky, Irving, and the faeries dropped into the fray and started taking out more of the umbaji. I yelled and urged my horse to keep moving forward.

Now that she realized we were fighting back and not being victims, my horse picked up speed, even stomping the bodies a few times as we went over them. The trail between the boulders was longer than I'd thought but after a few minutes, we were on the other side. My mare stomped her feet and snorted a few times—I think she liked fighting back. Welsy and Delsy came scrambling over the boulders, looking like they'd seen some fighting as well.

My friends ran out behind me, with Foxy's riderless horse coming out last.

"Where's Foxy?" I'd turned and was ready to race back when he came out with five of the umbaji hanging on him. One by one, he took them off and threw them back into the crevasse.

"I'm here, just doing a wee bit of clean up." He smiled, patted his horse's nose, and climbed back into the saddle.

"Good fight!" Garbage came back with her flock. No war feathers, they probably didn't have time, but all were still worked up and waving their war sticks.

"That was interesting, but can we stay away from such obvious traps in the future?" Covey hadn't gone complete berserker, but her fingers were looking more claw-like than usual. She shook them out and they returned to normal.

"Sorry. But the amulet said to go that way." I looked at the wall of boulders. It hadn't been as noticeable from the other side, but that crevasse was probably the only way through for a long distance.

Padraig was looking at the same thing. "I've no idea if we'll find another way out when we come back. Can Bunky, Irving, Welsy, and Delsy stay here and cover our retreat?" He glanced at the faeries.

I knew he was thinking of asking them to stay, but it might be safer for all concerned if they were with us. As fun as that sounded.

He obviously felt the same because once the constructs nodded and vanished into the area around us, he didn't mention anything to the faeries.

"Back to leading?" There was no way to tell if the umbaji were sent out because they knew where we were or if they were just a general defense system kept in place. We had to keep going.

"Yes. And faeries, keep watching. You're our only extra eyes right now."

Hopefully, if they did see something, there would be more warning. I wasn't happy that the umbaji had popped up so fast. With a thought to any deities who might still be listening, I took the amulet in my left hand and nudged my horse forward.

This side had smaller boulders, but they were still plentiful enough to cause problems walking with horses. The amulet would get annoyed at me every time I had to detour around a pile of them and lashed out with a bit of heat.

I kept glancing back; it was odd to travel with everyone, even the faeries, being silent. But everyone had their weapons out and were keeping watch as we rode. The faeries flew in a wave above us. A few would branch off to one side or the other, then fold back in and a new group would branch out. They were becoming extremely good at formation. Hopefully, that was a good thing.

Crusty came and sat on my horse again. "Is good. Name yet?"

It took me a moment to figure out that she was pointing at my dagger, who was back in his sheath.

"Not yet, sweetie. This probably isn't a good time for naming things." I kept my voice low. Heaviness and a chill seemed to flow over me. Rather, it was there and we walked into it.

Crusty rubbed her arms, and the rest of the faeries dropped about a foot lower. I didn't blame them. The sun hadn't gone down that much since we'd entered this area, but everything seemed darker and bleaker than before.

"It's a spell." Mathilda's voice sounded like a death call. "Pay no attention to it. And keep moving."

I looked down in surprise to see my horse and I had almost come to a complete stop. A glance showed the others shaking their heads and blinking as well.

"Damn it." I wasn't sure what, if any, of my magic was back, but an old spell song hit my memory. One from when I was a kid. My mother sang it to me when I had nightmares.

I closed my eyes and softly sang. My horse moved forward at its prior pace, and I heard the rest doing the same. A faery patted my cheek. "Is goods." Crusty switched over to my shoulder and stayed there, humming the lullaby as I sang. Soon, all of the faeries were softly humming. Interestingly, they actually could carry a tune well. Maybe humming worked differently for them than singing. Their singing was horrific.

My horse got us through the weird miasma within a few minutes, and I risked opening my eyes. The trees were lighter, the air fresher, and we were still going the right way. I stopped singing the lullaby and after a round or two, the faeries dropped their hum-along.

"Another not-so-fun thing." I sent a silent thank-you to my mother. I'd forgotten so much about her and my father when I'd flung myself forward, that everything I recalled was new and wonderful. But this had been extremely helpful as well.

"What was that you were singing? I thought I knew all of the spell songs; they are as rare as they're hard to use. That one was subtle but definitely powerful." Mathilda kept her voice down.

"My mom used to sing it when I had nightmares. Didn't remember it at all until now. Glad it worked." I glanced back. The area we were coming out of looked dark and menacing, even from here. "What kind of spell is back there?"

"A Jhea. Old, old spell. Basically makes people, horses, even faeries, too depressed and tired to go on." Padraig had dropped back so he was right before Foxy at the rear. "It starts subtle and people either turn back or give in and just sit there until they die. When things are settled, it might be a good thing if you could teach young spell casters that song."

I nodded. The big issue was when things got settled. I had a bad feeling that this was a much larger problem than just getting our people back. Too many not-very-good groups were involved. While it did seem that they didn't get along with each other, it would be too much to hope for that they'd wipe each other out. At least not without some help.

The boulders shrank in size and the trees grew wider apart. A huge rock-strewn mountain sat ahead of us, though.

"My amulet is getting tingly. I'm thinking that's what we're looking for?" It didn't look like a fortress to me, just an almost black hill.

"That's what was on the map. If your necklace thinks so as well, that's where we go." Padraig rode up to me as we moved closer. "I was hoping that maybe you'd get a feel of where he is in there?"

"Inside that lump of rock?" The amulet was leading us directly to it, but I figured the fortress must be on the other side.

"There's a fortress there but you're not seeing it?" He turned to Covey, Grillion, and Foxy, all of whom shook their heads.

Mathilda nodded—she saw it.

"Interesting. Your magic is playing games, Taryn." Mathilda gestured toward the rock. "The song, which is very hard to pull off, worked. Yet you don't see through that glamour. Try seeing it with the eyes of your Ancient self. I know the human form is true as well, but your other form might see things differently. Don't change form, but just use your eyes."

Great idea but she, like me, forgot that I might be having some weirdness based on the closeness of the Dragon Day. I took a breath, closed my eyes, and focused on seeing things as a dragon.

No one was screaming, but muffled oaths made me open my eyes. I was currently flying above everyone, including my very confused horse. She hadn't run off, so that was good. But there was a definite look of wondering what I was doing on her equine face.

I didn't feel dragonish, and a quick inventory revealed only human parts. Aside from some scaled-down dragon wings coming from my shoulder blades. They didn't hurt, just felt extremely odd. I flapped them a bit more and rose into a swarm of faeries. All of whom thought my new wings were amazing and kept darting forward to touch them.

"Yay! Play!"

"Flappity!"

"Boom!"

Garbage, Leaf, and Crusty made sure they were the closest to me. I wanted to ask Crusty what she meant by boom, but they never gave a clear answer and she looked happy about it. Hopefully, it was a good boom and not a bad one.

"What do you see ahead?" Mathilda asked.

I looked over to the giant rock and sucked in a breath. As I watched, it changed into a low-slung fortress. No soaring turrets here. This thing was no more than three stories tall, wide, and low to the ground, its structure reflecting the black rock it was built into.

"I see it now." I wasn't sure how to go lower or retract my wings. I stopped flapping and dropped quickly. Not a good idea, so I flapped again slowly. "Can someone take the reins of my horse? I'm not completely sure how to control these. It's different than when I'm changed." I still wasn't good at flying when I was in my dragon form, but it felt more natural than this.

Covey took the reins to my horse and tied them behind her own. "I don't know that having her or the faeries up there is a good idea. We still have some cover, but the last bit leading to that rock is open." Even though she personally couldn't see the fortress, she was willing to accept it was real. That was a massive change from the book-bound professor I used to know.

I waved over to the faeries. "Can you show me how to land?" I might not be able to wish these wings away, and there was a possibility that having them was letting me see the fortress, but I felt like a target up here. I didn't see any siege weapons around the fortress, but that didn't mean they weren't there.

Garbage flew closer, carefully inspected my wings, rubbed her chin a bit, then nodded. "Goes down."

"That's what I'm trying to do, sweetie. But I either fly higher or drop like a stone."

"This." Garbage held up both hands, then flipped so she was upside down and dove for the ground. She pulled up and flew back to us.

"Oh." That made sense, but if I missed, I was going face-first into the dirt.

CHAPTER ELEVEN

I FINALLY GOT MYSELF flying down and managed to pull up before I crashed. Well, mostly. I sort of used a shrub as a landing spot.

I pulled myself free of it and shook out my wings. They were pretty, actually. Mostly light green with dark patterns on them. A lighter version of my full dragon wings. I could fold them up against my back, but couldn't get them to vanish.

Great.

I waddled over to my horse, rubbed her nose, and undid the reins from the back of Covey's saddle. There was no way I could get up into the saddle, though. I finally admitted that after three failed attempts.

"I think this is as good as I can get it. The flame issue went away on its own; hopefully, these will too." I grabbed my amulet. The tingle was stronger this time. I grinned. "He's that way." It wasn't just sending me toward the fortress; it was focusing on a specific section of it.

Padraig studied the fortress for a moment, then turned back to me. "I know you're afraid of what is happening to him, but I think we might want to wait until dark. Even if they are counting on their spells and creatures to stop people, they'll notice us crossing that open space."

The amulet flashed hot, almost searing my hand. I thought I could hear Alric yelling but it might have just been in my mind. "No. It has to be now." A sudden stabbing pain hit my gut. It felt so real I expected to see blood when I pulled my hand away. I didn't see any. "The connection between the amulets is stronger—they're stabbing him!" That red film from before covered my eyes, and my body felt huge and bloated. I looked down. Not a full dragon, but not fully human either. If I was going to change anyway, I tried to force it. Go full dragon.

Nope. My wings were now full-sized, my body a bit larger than normal, almost like a syclarion size. And I really wanted to destroy something. But I hadn't gone full dragon.

"I'm sorry, I have to get him!" I took off, flying toward the wall where the amulet sent me. I wasn't holding it, but the chain had adjusted to my size, and I felt its vibration as I flew. Faeries in war feathers surrounded me, and they weren't smiling anymore. They didn't even chant but silently raised their war sticks as we flew.

There were guards, and I felt crossbow bolts fly around us. Magic, or something, kept them from hitting any of us. So much for a stealthy attack.

The amulet pulled toward a lower wall. "Hang back. Wait until I hit it." I turned so my powerful back legs—still not full dragon, but much stronger than my human ones—were coming up to the wall. And I kicked, spun, and flew through the hole I'd made. That was a serious kick.

The faeries flew in alongside me, swarming two grimarians, an elf, and a full dwoller. The dwoller was fast and casting spells, avoiding the faeries' strikes. I followed her to a corner and flamed her. Not as much as what I'd used before, but it worked. She ran out of the room, smoking, if not completely in flames.

Alric was slumped in a corner. The blood on the floor around him wasn't good. I reached down and started crying when I felt his pulse. It was there. Weak, but there. Scooping him up wasn't easy, but I managed.

The faeries were yelling and striking everything. The elf and one grimarian were down; the last one was a strong magic user and managed to get his shield up in time to block them.

My hands in this form weren't great, large and claw-like. But I was still able to keep Alric over my shoulder between my wings and draw the dagger. The dagger crackled with enthusiasm and let out huge arcs of green flame, obliterating the shield and the grimarian. I wasn't sure who was more shocked, me or the grimarian as he exploded. The dagger seemed happy, though. Once the grimarian was obliterated, he settled down and I put him away.

The faeries started to fly off through the doorway the dwoller had fled to. "No! We have to leave." I had to yell twice before Garbage whistled and got her flock moving out of the hole I'd made. Crusty was the last one out.

We made it to the others, but people were coming out of the fortress. Heavily armed people on horseback.

"How much weight can you carry?" Mathilda yelled as I lowered myself to hand Alric over to Padraig. Plus side: I had more flying maneuverability in this form. The downside: my skin wasn't thick enough to hold off a successful strike if any of those arrows or crossbow bolts hit me.

"I can't take you on my back." That would have been impossible in full dragon form, let alone whatever form this was.

"No, but if the faeries help, Padraig and I should be able to use a spell to get us up in the air a bit. If I magically connect us and the horses with some enhanced vines, you should be able to grab the end and haul us all along."

I wanted to be shocked at the suggestion and I was sure

once I wasn't pulsing with adrenaline I would be. Fact was, we were out of options.

Mathilda, Padraig, and the faeries got everyone up in the air. The strain on their faces wasn't good, and I began to worry if we could even do this. The horses were not happy, but Padraig kept murmuring to them as they slowly rose.

Crossbow bolts tore through the air as I grabbed the end of a long vine Mathilda and the faeries created, and I flew off.

We'd gotten just past the crevasse from earlier when I felt myself changing. At first, I thought I was just losing strength from pulling so much weight, but then I realized that I was shrinking and my wings were vanishing. I tried to drop lower so we'd have less distance to fall, but control wasn't happening.

"Hang on! I'm not going to make it!"

Padraig, Alric, and the horses had been the lowest, so they hit first. He quickly led them out of the way. Foxy had been next, and he rolled then bounced to his feet to try to catch everyone else. Which might have worked if the rest of them hadn't all pretty much come down at once.

The others dropped with a range of successful landings. Mathilda was the best but I think she was using magic to slow her descent. I was the last, and Foxy did catch me.

We still stumbled a bit but I patted his arm and ran over to where Padraig was laying down Alric.

Mathilda was right behind me. Her healing magic came as a wave around her. I dropped to one side and took his hand. Like everything else, it looked bloody and bruised. But unlike the two stab wounds in his stomach and chest, the injuries to his hands weren't fresh.

"Alric? Can you hear me?" I brushed aside his hair but his eyes didn't even flutter. "You have to save him." There was a flash of red across my vision as my fear tried to take over, but I squashed it. I hoped this angry/flaming issue would vanish after Dragon Day ended.

"I'm going to do my best." Mathilda squeezed my shoulder. "I might need some help, though." I looked around, figuring she was looking at Padraig, but she was looking at me. "Nothing too hard, just keep holding his hand. Think of how much he means to you, and sing your lullaby." She looked up. "Ladies, you are welcome to join in, but softly."

"I'm going to spell the other end of the crevasse and guard it with the others." Padraig looked down at Alric. "But if I can help magically, tell me."

For a few moments, I'd forgotten that we were being followed. My flying out got us away faster than horses could travel, but they still had to have known which way we were going. If anyone could keep that crevasse closed, it would be my friends.

Mathilda's spell grew stronger, and while it was focused on Alric, I felt refreshed as well. His grip on my hand tightened, and I started singing my song. I closed my eyes and put every happy memory of us into my thoughts. I heard the faeries drop to the ground beside us and start humming.

Alric was fighting back but against the healing, not the injuries. He'd accepted death. I tried sending more memories, happy ones, and tying them to my song. The spell they'd worked on him was stubborn and not giving up.

That was fine—neither was I.

I stopped my song long enough to lean close to his ear and whispered, "Damn you. I told you, you're not dying. We're not leaving you. And I will go to the gates of death to bring you back. Stop fighting us, you stubborn elf!" I added the weight of my fear to my words, then went back to singing.

His hand squeezed mine again, and his face relaxed as Mathilda's magic started healing his wounds and my song chased away the last bit of the Jhea spell.

The yelling coming from the crevasse told us the fighters from the fortress had hit the other side and weren't happy. We needed to get moving quickly.

Finally, Mathilda rocked back on her heels. "He should be able to do the rest on his own. But he'll need to take things easy for a day or so."

Alric winced and opened his eyes. His smile was a wonderful thing to see. "I thought I was dreaming."

I bent down to kiss him repeatedly. Then smacked him lightly on his shoulder. "Don't you ever give up like that again. *Twice.* Twice you tried to give up and just die. Not on my watch!" If I stayed angry enough, hopefully the tears would stay away.

Mathilda watched us. "They might have been using the Jhea spell on him too. Especially if you thought it had been weeks since Taryn reached you the first time?" She directed the last bit to Alric. "You were grabbed just over two weeks ago. She reached out to you a day ago."

He nodded, then winced. "Yeah, it felt like I'd been there for months. Everything hurts, but I feel more or less intact."

Grillion came running up. He had his sword this time. "Padraig isn't sure how long he can hold our friends. How long before we can move?" He flashed a smile at Alric.

Alric rolled to his side and his sword reappeared. "I can fight."

"Against what? Small bunches of flowers?" Mathilda got to her feet. "I just spent a lot of magic making you not leak. Taryn here sang to keep you stable, and the faeries helped. You're not undoing that. Put your sword away and get on a horse." She looked ready to tie him on one if he didn't move fast enough. Alric's horse had been tied to Padraig's for most of the journey since he'd been taken.

"You can ride mine; he's steadier than yours," Foxy said

as he and Covey came running back. "I move faster than it if I need anyway." He clapped Alric on the shoulder, then picked him up and dropped him on his horse in a single move. "Padraig is setting up something, told us to get out, and be ready to run."

CHAPTER TWELVE

THAT GOT EVERYONE moving. Bunky and Irving had been hovering over the crevasse but flew over to us. Bunky didn't do a head bump to Alric, but he did buzz around him excitedly.

Welsy and Delsy came scrambling over the boulders. "Very good to see you! We should be moving now." They didn't wait for a response but took off down the trail. It was amazing how fast those little legs could go.

The faeries swarmed Alric, giving pats and kisses, then took off after the brownie constructs.

"We should be going!" Padraig raced toward us, leaped on his horse, and started after the faeries. The rest of us were right on his tail, with Foxy bringing up the rear by choice.

We were riding as fast as possible, but the heavy tree growth was going to slow us down. A massive explosion shook us but didn't knock anyone over.

"Keep running!" Padraig yelled.

I looked behind us and saw a plume of smoke and dust rising high in the air. Right about where those massive boulders had been. He'd blown them up? That reminded me to never make Padraig angry. I hadn't been planning on it, but that was a serious amount of magic if he did what I thought he did. Hopefully, we were right about that being the only nearby way to get through. None of us were up for a fight right now.

Alric kept looking back and his sword had reappeared after vanishing when Mathilda threatened him. We'd forced him to ride behind Padraig and his own horse, so there was no way he was getting past all of us. First, he gives in and just wants to curl up and die. Now, barely snatched from the jaws of death, he wants to go fight. I loved him, but we were going to have a serious conversation when this was over.

"Send that sword back where it came from." Mathilda was behind me and saw what I had.

A second later, his sword vanished and he bent down low over his horse. Foxy's horse had been a draft animal due to Foxy's size. He was used to hauling much heavier people than Alric—and it showed. He looked to be watching for an opportunity to pass Padraig and Alric's horse. Alric was an excellent horseman and he slowed the huge animal down.

I'd figured that we'd slow down once we were free of the explosion Padraig had caused, but he kept going as fast as possible until the trees slowed us down. I wasn't the best at maps but it looked like we were roughly heading for the base of the mountain we'd been trying for before our detour to get Alric. The location of the giant cave the faeries had found.

A familiar nasty feeling started building in my stomach. No wings yet, but I might be shooting off flames soon.

"Umm, I think I have a problem." I slowed down enough to safely turn my horse down a thinner side trail. Alongside the one they followed, but not on it. I felt like I was about to cough, but instead, a belch of flame shot out and hit a tree. That could have been Alric or his horse.

"What was that? Taryn? Were you hit?" Alric twisted around, but as I kept riding, so did he.

"Long story. Not a lot of control. How far are we from

the cave?" I felt better but more flames could be coming so I stayed on the side trail. I had no control over anything involving my dragon-self at this point.

"Damn it." Padraig glanced over to me. "You're looking a little green and scaly too. We still have at least another hour, more if the forest gets thicker and we have to slow down."

Garbage flew over to me. "Flappity. Easier." She pointed to the top of the trees where the faeries, Bunky, and Irving were flying.

"Nice idea, but I don't have any control." I tested it, trying to start the change, but nothing happened. Which was probably good since changing on top of my poor horse would probably have given her a heart attack. Or squished her if I couldn't get up in the air in time. I was not a huge human woman. A bit taller than average, but that was about it. But dragons were big. At least I was, since that was the only reference I had.

"Flappitys!" Leaf came down to join us and was grinning like mad.

"No, sweetie, I can't—" My words were cut off as that weird feeling came back. Yup, those mini wings were there. I tried to fold them back down but it was hard. Not to mention, if I was still flaming things, being away from my friends and our horses might be a better idea. But I didn't want to leave my horse unattended. I rode her back into the line with the others; handing her off while we were running wouldn't be easy.

"We's steer." Leaf and a dozen other faeries landed on the reins and saddle. Crusty went to the forelock and made clicking sounds. The horse looked back briefly, then just kept jogging along.

There wasn't time to sort it out, as I was feeling another belly of fire building. "Stay right behind Alric. No funny stuff." At all of their nods, except Crusty, I stood and jumped up. There was a gap in the trees where the trail went, so I shot up and out over the treetops. It was honestly quite lovely; twilight was starting to fall and the forest below me was a gorgeous carpet of greens and golds…then I burped. Singed a few treetops, but the fire immediately went out. I mentally sent an apology to the trees.

I looked down; I'd gotten ahead of Padraig by quite a distance. A little ahead wouldn't be bad, but honestly, if something was waiting to attack them on the trail, I probably wouldn't see it anyway. Too far ahead and I'd miss any turns they made. I knew in general where we were heading, but not the specifics. The weird changes so far had been problematic, but it would be best to get me hidden as quickly as possible before they got worse. The fewer people who saw me in that form, the far better.

I dropped back a bit and kept as close to the trees as I could without smacking them. An escort of Bunky, Irving, and about half the faeries flew alongside me.

When I wasn't overwhelmed by fear, this was an amazing way to travel. I almost tumbled as a memory of learning to fly with my father flooded my mind. It was so real; I felt like I could reach out and touch him. I embraced the memory, then focused on not crashing into a tree. Which was pretty much what I'd been doing in the memory as well.

Things were great until a crossbow bolt missed my right wing by inches and scattered the faeries. Bunky and Irving gronked and spun back to where the bolt had come from, with the faeries right on their tails.

My friends had slowed down and were engaged in a fight with people on the ground. I reassessed the situation—they were fighting a group of syclarions. Not all of that species could transform into their dragon-like selves. But at least one of the fighters below me could. He'd spotted me and was flying my way.

I felt my body change again and was hoping for a full

transformation. Nope, it was the weird halfway-there version. I shuddered to think what I looked like but didn't
have time for that as the syclarion flew right for me.

The last time I'd faced a syclarion in the air, it had
been Edana, and she was trying to murder me over the
ocean just as she had my parents. It felt like a lifetime ago,
even though it was less than two months. I was tired and
frightened at that time, but I still managed to win. This
time I wasn't a full dragon, but I was seriously pissed. I
let loose a roar—never done that and not trying it again
until I was in full dragon form. The result was odd, to
say the least. But it was very heartfelt. My eyes did that
weird red thing, and I felt nasty-looking spikes come out
on my arms and legs. So far the weird body issues had
been aspects of my dragon-self, but I'd never had spikes
as a dragon.

They were handy, though. The syclarion flew at me as
I swung out with one spiked leg. Sliced his thigh nicely.
Slowed him down, but didn't stop him.

"Who are you? We want the dragon spawn, not you.
Whatever in the hells you are."

Then I noticed he had a net in his hands.

I narrowed my eyes, and he tried to get closer to me
again. Either he wasn't the brightest of the bunch, or I
looked even weirder than I felt. Possibly a combination
of both. The pressure in my stomach and lungs built up,
and I let loose a massive flame. His net and a harness
he wore caught fire, and he swore and tried to swat the
flames out as he tumbled out of the sky. No idea where
he landed, but hopefully he wasn't coming back.

That flame business could be handy if I could control
it. Like everything right now, I had no control. And I
couldn't easily get down to my friends. Along with the
new spikes, I'd grown again and the trail wasn't wide
enough for me to land. My mouth also felt odd, although
it could be due to all the fire going through it.

The faeries and flying constructs flew up to me. "Gets?" Garbage pointed over her shoulder. It looked to be roughly where the flying syclarion had landed.

"No, I need you to go help our friends. Fight off those other syclarions." I caught a glance below us of Alric leaning to one side as he fought. He was going to undo everything Mathilda had done to save him. "Use your war sticks."

All of them flew down except Crusty.

"You pretty." She patted my forehead, and I realized I had spikes there too. "Now look like old—is way it was." She kissed me on the cheek and flew down after the others, yelling and waving her stick.

I had no idea what she meant, and the quick survey that I could do while still staying in the air and lacking a mirror showed me lots of spikes, thick, short legs, a wide tail, and if my transformed hands were correct, large ant-lers…they could be horns, but it felt like they branched off. They were also longer than I could reach. This was not my standard dragon form.

The faeries swarmed back to me, laughing and cheering. "We wons! All go bye." Garbage hovered in the air with her hands on her hips, looking as if she'd saved the day by herself.

I started to answer, but pain tore across my body as I felt myself shrinking. Unfortunately, the wings were shrinking the fastest. Damn it, the abilities were handy, but they needed to be controllable. "Clear the way!" I yelled as I tumbled toward the ground.

Things suddenly slowed down as dozens of tiny hands grabbed me, and Bunky and Irving pushed me up from underneath. I was still shrinking, still falling, and a tiny flame escaped when I opened my mouth. But I was fall-ing slower. I had no idea how well I'd land even with the assistance I was getting.

The faeries pulled harder as we dropped through the

trees. And Foxy was right below me. "Coming down!" I waved for him and the others to stand back but of course, he didn't move.

He caught me and grinned. "I'm getting good at this." He set me on my feet with a smile.

"Thank you." I smiled at my friends. There were no injuries from their most recent fight that I could see, and I felt back to normal as I took two steps toward my horse and collapsed.

CHAPTER THIRTEEN

I N MY DREAM, I was fighting off an army of leaves. They weren't attached to trees, or any plants, just racing for me with tiny swords. Then a bunch of squirrels appeared and started fighting the leaves; then they were fighting me. Only I was the same size as the squirrels.

Then one of the squirrels started shaking me. They somehow knew my name and wanted me to wake up. *Oh.* I pried open one eye. Alric's face hovered over mine and odd, scary shadows flickered behind his head.

"How do you feel? You've been out for a few hours." He held up a water bag and helped me drink. Then a second water bag when I finished the first.

Flame-throwing must leave one extremely thirsty.

I handed back the second bag. "Where are we?" I looked at my hand. It was dark where we were but it looked normal to me. I checked the top of my head. Hair, not spikes or antlers. "Do I look like me?"

"Yes. Although the faeries were trying to explain what happened to you in the air. We still aren't sure what they're talking about. Once Mathilda determined you'd just collapsed from exhaustion, she started trying to sort them out."

He slowly helped me sit up. He'd found a place to clean up and had changed into clean clothes. Aside from a few lingering faint bruises, he looked fully recovered. He looked wonderful.

We were in a cave or a really cave-like building. I couldn't see the ceiling, but the sides looked almost like walls; old and falling apart, but walls. "So, where?"

"This is the *cave* the faeries found." Padraig came up, shaking his head. "It's not a cave at all, but a ruin that might have been old when your people were still around. It was created inside the mountain but shows no signs of collapsing."

"Thoroughly ransacked, though." Grillion sat on the other side of the fire. From the tone of his voice and the disappointment on his face, he'd done a thorough check. Diggers were good at assessing a find quickly; ruin thieves were even better.

"But it's amazing that it's still here. The carvings in the side chamber are stunning." Covey had her lost-in-academia look, and I wondered if we were going to have to drag her out when it was time to leave.

Probably.

"Do we know who made them? Ancients?" I couldn't see much, but getting on my feet right now wasn't going to happen. My legs felt like jelly.

"Not a clue." Covey's face grew more blissful. "In the daylight, we should be able to see more. There are magically enhanced mirrors to send sunlight from the entrance through to the back rooms—and they are intact. It's amazing."

"We can't stay here, you know." I was beginning to get worried about her staying behind. I hadn't seen her this extreme in a long time.

"Actually, from what they tell me, we will for at least a day." Alric brought me some packs to lean against, then handed over dried meat and travel bread. "Something about Dagonin Danir?"

"Oh. Yeah." I bit into the bread savagely. "If it's as much fun as this lead-up has been, then I can't wait." I told them what happened to me in the air, at least what I knew. I still was only going off what I felt to determine how I'd changed.

"Are you sure it wasn't just a full transformation?" Covey was forcing herself to pay attention but she was still trying to see where the flames from our fire illuminated the walls past us.

"I couldn't see myself, but no, these spikes and horns were new."

"And not what we've found in descriptions of your people," Padraig said.

"Crusty said I was old, and the way I had been. But it didn't feel right. I'm getting more of my memories back, and none of the Ancients I've seen looked like what happened up there. The flying syclarion who was trying to capture the 'dragon spawn' didn't recognize me as one."

"It could be the change the Dagonin Danir spell is bringing. Mathilda wasn't sure what would happen, but she knew the magic would affect you." Alric still looked tired as he sat next to me, and if I knew him, he'd been watching me the entire time I'd been out. And nagging him to rest would do no good.

"Where's Foxy?" I finished my meal and looked around.

"He and the constructs are on patrol. He isn't a fan of our cave. I also think he might have wanted to reach out to Amara," Mathilda said as she came to sit by me. "The faeries were very impressed by your changes, by the way."

"Did they say what I turned into? Because I don't think it was just an Ancient."

"Only that you were showing the past. That it would be gone soon, so it went to you." She sighed. "They also said it was something new. None of them could agree on anything except cool spikes." She looked over to where the faeries were playing a drinking game. "I have a bad feeling they're going to try to grow some themselves."

"They can't do that. Can they?" They had enough

new/old tricks that kept reappearing. The idea that they could change their bodies on a whim was terrifying.

"I honestly don't know. They did want to talk to you about how you made them, so I think we're safe." She patted my arm. "Don't worry. I told them until after you've changed and recovered, you need peace and quiet." She looked around. "That goes for everyone. We need to rest."

"I'm staying with Taryn." Alric only limped slightly as he got up and grabbed some blankets. He looked a lot better than when I'd rescued him, but he still wasn't recovered. I knew he wouldn't discuss much of what happened to him beyond anything of strategic importance, but I knew they'd tortured him.

"Grillion, Covey, and I will be swapping off with Foxy on guard duty." Padraig held his hand up to hold off Mathilda's comment. "You need to get some rest. I might not be a healer, but I know how hard healing Alric had been. We can't afford to have you exhausted if we face another battle soon." He turned to Alric before he could jump in. "No. You also need rest and to keep an eye on Taryn. We can argue about it later."

Alric rolled his eyes but gave up easier than I expected. I feared he might be more injured than we believed, but then I saw a flash of worry as he looked at me.

Mathilda, however, still looked feisty, but even in the thin firelight, her face was drawn.

I reached over and took her hand. "I'd feel better with you in here as well. I know the major change is supposed to be at dawn, but who knows what will happen to me before then?"

She sighed and patted my hand. "Fine, no guard duty for me or Alric. But the rest of you need to get rest when you're not standing watch. And if you do have to fight, Padraig, I would strongly suggest using your sword. You've been using a lot of magic lately."

Padraig gave a perfectly reprimanded bow and went back to the other side of the fire.

Alric built a spot for us with blankets and packs close to the fire, but I shook my head.

"That would be lovely, except we're not sure how large I'll get—or what new parts might start." I looked around at what I could see of the chamber. "Maybe over there. Far from the others and fire." My skin as a dragon was tough, but the forms I'd been switching in and out of didn't have the same skin and hadn't been as thick. I had a vision of me changing and squishing my friends and landing myself in the fire.

Alric looked torn.

"It's not that cold in here, and I think it's safer." Being alone with him right now would be wonderful and even more horrific than rolling into the fire if I changed. I laughed and choked at the same time as some extremely inappropriate images hit me.

He pounded my back but I waved him off. "It's okay, just a horrific visual." That I was never sharing with any-one.

With help, I was able to get to my feet, and we shuffled back away from the others. I noticed that Mathilda took up a spot a few feet from the fire and partially facing our direction. Probably a good idea in case I spent the night flipping through different forms.

Grillion made some stew and brought us each a bowl. He watched Alric for a moment, then hugged him fiercely. "I'm glad you're back." He seemed embarrassed as he nodded and walked away.

I smiled. I'd seen the tears he'd been trying to hide. I waited until he was back at the fire comparing recipes with Covey, and even then I kept my voice low. "I think you're his only real friend." I looked around the group. "Until he dropped in with us anyway." He was one of us now.

The memory of the smile that Alric flashed was what kept me going the past two weeks that he was gone. "I never thought of it, but I think you're right. He was sort of like an annoying little brother."

"One who you took the fall for and made sure he got out of Beccia with enough gold to be able to comfortably support himself." I winced. "For a while, anyway."

He laughed. "I should have known that enough gold to set up any normal person would be spent quickly when left to his own devices. He loves women and he loves to gamble. Not a good combination."

It seemed so normal to be sitting here chatting with him. I'd been angry and numb when he'd been first taken, then shoved aside the terror in my mind and focused on getting him back. But now my fear, worry, and loss came slamming back and hit me hard. I felt like someone had hit me in the gut.

He took my hand. "What's wrong? Are you okay?"

I leaned forward and hugged him as hard as I could. I didn't care that I was sobbing or making hiccupping-crying sounds. "I lost you. They took you. *They. Took. You.*" My tears were over me, him, and possibly on my friends back by the fire. I didn't care.

"Deep inside, under that Jhea spell, I knew you'd come for me. I just couldn't reach past the spell." He pulled back a bit and gently brushed aside the tears. But he was holding me tightly. "I will always come for you, and I know you will always come for me."

"Even when you tried to give up." I poked him in the chest. "Don't do that again!"

His answer was possibly the most intense kiss I'd ever had. We were far enough from our friends that while they probably knew what was going on, they didn't have a front-row seat. At this point, I didn't care about that either.

The kiss finally ended—this wasn't the time or the

place for anything more—and I leaned against him.

"How did you find me so fast, anyway?"

"We owe Siabiane big time. As we got closer, this indicated where to go. I'm pretty sure it was also how I reached out to you in my dream."

I could see his amulet reflecting the firelight as he reached to lift mine. "All those changes and this didn't pop off?"

"Nope. Like my clothing, thank the goddess. Even though these changes aren't controlled or normal, this necklace, like my clothing, must vanish and reappear. This last change even kept my clothing and my dagger in place. I'm trying not to think about it too hard." I nodded to his amulet. "And they couldn't get that off?"

"No, they tried. I do think it partially protected me. Aside from that Jhea spell, they couldn't do much against me magically. Just physically."

He'd almost died, but he brushed it off.

"That. Right there. You almost died, but because it wasn't magic, it wasn't worth worrying about? If I didn't love you, I would hit you right now." I was full of too many emotions to be rational—not to mention that the weird spell designed to force me into a change might be messing up my emotions.

"And if you weren't exhausted." He kissed the tip of my nose and rubbed my back. "It was thinking of you that kept me going. They were trying to get intel on the enclave and our fighting ability, as well as holding me to drag you to them. Trust me, that Jhea spell was what got to me. It removed all hope for survival and even realizing it was a spell didn't help. That first time you appeared gave me hope—then they increased the spell and messed with my head. I heard you sang your way out of that spell. Spells like the Jhea are old and not commonly used. But if they're being brought back, your lullaby spell could prove vital."

"That's what I'd mentioned to her."

Padraig had approached so silently we didn't notice. Or I didn't. Alric didn't look startled.

Padraig turned to me. "How are you feeling? It's fully dark outside, but we have no idea what will happen before dawn."

"Tired, achy, annoyed." I leaned into Alric as he rubbed my back. "Thinking of never letting him out of my sight again. No weird dragonny things, though." I looked around. "Any place I should aim if I get flamey?"

"Actually, yes. Grillion and Covey collected a bunch of rocks, with help from Foxy and the brownies. If you feel like you're about to flame, aim that way." He pointed to a dark corner away from the fire and the entrance.

"I wish we had a better idea of what to expect. The last few hours have been all over the place." I smiled as Alric increased rubbing my back.

Padraig nodded. "I'd heard of Dagonin Danir before Mathilda mentioned it, but it was just a folk festival, not revealing for anyone. Of course, with your people gone, the syclarions hiding, and changelings clearly doing the same—not many people would notice it happening. Try to get some rest, both of you. Once you change completely, we'll have to stay here."

"For only a day, right? Wasn't that what Mathilda said?" I ignored the tinge of panic in my voice. A day was annoying. What had already happened was also annoying—but helpful in some ways. If I had to travel in my regular dragon shape, that wasn't going to be annoying; it could be catastrophic. Having the people after us think I was a dragon, and knowing I was one, were two different things. Right now, the risk was too high if I exposed who and what I was to others. I'd have to hide out while the others rescued Siabiane and Lorcan and found out what Qianru was up to.

Worse, Alric would have to go with them.

"I'm sure it will just be the day. The festival always went from dawn to dawn; there's no reason to think the spell went longer." Padraig smiled, but I wasn't sure I believed it. None of them had a clue. "Now, if you don't mind, I'll be sleeping, as I have first watch after Foxy. Good night, you two." He went back to the rest and set out his bedroll.

"You didn't even ask again to be put on guard rotation? Giving up after one attempt? Who are you and what have you done with Alric?" I studied his face in the distant firelight. Less than two weeks and yet in my heart it felt like months.

"Even I know when I need to rest." He frowned as I started laughing. "Sometimes I do. Fine, they already told me I wasn't going anywhere before you woke up. Mathilda pushed me over when I tried to show them I was fine. The time in front of you was the second time."

I grabbed his face and turned him to look at me. "I know what you were like when I pulled you out of that dungeon. I wasn't sure if you were alive or not. So, healing spells or no, you're not going anywhere."

"Yes, ma'am." He smiled and gave me a gentle kiss. Then I yawned and ruined the moment. "I'd say we both need to sleep. And don't worry, I'm a light sleeper. I'll get out of the way if you transform in your sleep."

"It's not proper to remind a lady of her size." I tried to look haughty, but another yawn ruined that too. We ended up cuddling into each other to go to sleep. Having him near me was comforting but also nerve-racking. Joking aside, I was terrified of changing in my sleep.

Crusty and three other faeries came flittering over as we settled in. "We watch." She gave me a serious smile, which for her was terrifying, and she and the others settled on a bit of broken wall near us. They didn't even have an ale bottle.

"Thank you," Alric said before I could. "And thank you

and the others for keeping her safe. And for helping to rescue me."

All four faeries came flying over and started giving him kisses, and then hopped over to me and did the same. Crusty did her best imitation of Garbage and put her hands on her hips after they flew back to the roost. "Is goods. Now sleeps. Or I sing?"

I was pretty sure she meant my lullaby, but normal faery singing was horrific. We both shook our heads and lay back down.

Alric fell asleep before I did, and I let myself enjoy just being next to him and him being safe. Somewhere between his soft snoring, the faeries telling some wild tales, and our friends laughing quietly by the fire, I dozed off.

Until the screaming started.

CHAPTER FOURTEEN

THE SCREAMING SURROUNDED me, and at first I thought it was another dream. Especially since my friends looked to be running away from me and they looked exceptionally small. Then I realized they were running toward the entrance, where a group of people were trying to get in. Mathilda and Padraig were supposed to have been holding off on using magic, but someone had put a spell shield at the entrance. The people on the other side were trying to get through, but Grillion, Covey, Mathilda, Foxy, and even Alric were there waiting in case that happened. The fire inside was reflected by torches being carried by those outside and lent an odd cast over everything.

I swore and tried to go over as well. Sadly, I was my dragon-self, so movement was not easy nor fast. The ceiling that had been lost in the darkness when I was human-sized was now a few feet from the top of my head. That didn't appear to have horns or antlers. Yet.

"You stay. We save." My faery guard had changed out and now Leaf, and three other faeries I only knew on sight but not by name, flew up to me. "Nice lady stay here. Others outside—they protect too."

A glance around showed that along with Padraig, the rest of the faeries and all four constructs were missing. They must be on the other side of the shield but waiting to circle our attackers.

"Who is out there?" My attempt at moving forward to help was cut off by faeries in my face again.

"Back. Go back." Leaf looked concerned as she shoved me.

They might have a point; whoever was out there was likely looking for me. Between the murky spell shield, distance, and my being mostly in the dark, they might not have seen me yet. Could be best to keep it that way as long as possible.

But if that shield fell, all bets were off.

Once I focused, I could see the front line of people trying to get in—all human or elvish. Most had hoods up. I couldn't see their arms but I was pretty sure I knew what would be tattooed on their inner right wrists: the dagger and the circle of the Dark.

I leaned closer, making Leaf fly up to my face again when she thought I was going to move. As far as I could see, there were no syclarions, dwollers, grimarians, or any other non-elf, non-human people out there. My guess was at least three distinct groups after us: the Dark, the syclarions, and the hilstrike mages: dwollers and others who were working with the grimarians. My late and unlamented patron, Thaddeus, had been a powerful high-caste syclarion who had been working with a pair of grimarians when he took the glass gargoyle relic and tried to change the world. So there might just be two groups. The Dark seemed to mostly stick with elves, although they'd been recruiting others as minions lately. On average, neither syclarions nor grimarians were good followers. There were good syclarions out there; our friend Dueble was one. I'd yet to see a non-homicidal grimarian, though.

The shield was holding but seemed thinner. Or my trying to see through it made it look that way to me. The people trying to get in yelled and turned as something from behind attacked them. Hopefully, it was Padraig and a bunch of faeries and constructs. And not one of the other groups fighting for the chance to bring me in. It was extremely disappointing to be a huge, powerful being and be forced to hide in the corner. I fought as a red film drifted over my eyes. Not now. I needed to stay back. No matter how much I wanted to charge out there and stomp them all.

Great. Forced changing made me violent. I took a few calming breaths and watched as the attackers outside fought back a fleet of dive-bombing faeries. Then one of the cloaked attackers pulled out a pouch.

"No!" My yell was more of a bellow, and everyone both inside and outside of the cave froze. We'd seen the enemies use a powder against the faeries before—varlick powder mixed with a sedative and who knew what else. It knocked the faeries out, and the fear was it could do more. My yell made everyone look up. "Girls! Hold your breath!" Not much of a defense but it seemed to stop the powder from working since they wouldn't breathe it.

They heard me and, as a bonus, some started flashing colors. I still wasn't sure what the evolutionary benefit of flashing colors when they held their breath was, but it seemed to make them happy.

More importantly, none of them fell when the tall man released the contents of his pouch into the air.

"Good spotting. Now, stay back." Alric turned to me with a stern smile.

Considering he shouldn't be up there either, he didn't have room to talk. I had to admit he looked more recovered than he had before we went to sleep. Which couldn't have been that long as it was still dark outside.

I wasn't supposed to change until dawn, yet here I was. I looked down at my dragon form. That it took me this long to make the connection with the time of day wasn't good, but it had been a hellish few days. This felt and, from what I could see, looked like my normal dragon form. I didn't change myself, nor could I change back.

And to make things worse, the spell shield was collapsing. The Dark we'd run across so far had some heavy magic users with them. Either they'd been late to the party or capturing the faeries had also been part of their plan. With the faeries removed as an option for grabbing, the ones attacking us decided to bring in the heavy hitters.

The faeries made one more dive, all blinking brightly at this point, when a cloaked person shouted spells and flung up an arm. The faeries were slammed back as a massive wind hit them. Lots of tiny bright lights, all shining as they vanished into the distance.

Leaf tilted her head as if listening to something and then patted my shoulder. "Theys okay."

Bunky and Irving came down toward the attackers, and each got a few arcs of static out and struck a few people, but the same mage pushed them aside. They weren't flashing but also vanished from sight.

The spell shield faded where it was touching the mouth of the building. My friends braced themselves.

And I stood there, hiding in the dark.

The shield collapsed completely as the first sign of dawn lightened the sky. And every part of my body started screaming at once. Whatever I was changing into, it wasn't a dragon.

"Clear the way!" I yelled but almost didn't recognize my voice as it was low and gravelly. The feeling in my stomach was not good. Luckily, my friends got out of the entrance just as I let loose the largest flame yet.

The people trying to get inside didn't fare so well and ran back into the forest, screaming. The red film on my eyes came back even more so, and part of me really wanted to chase them down and stomp them.

"No, calm." Tangle Morning Glory, a lovely lapis-blue

faery, came to me. She folded her legs in midair and closed her eyes. "Calm." She started humming a song similar to my lullaby but in a slightly different pitch. She was quickly joined by a dozen other faeries as they came into the building.

The red film faded.

The rest of the faeries were swarming back from wherever they'd been sent. They looped through and then went after the fleeing attackers.

"Keep holding your breath!" I'd noticed that less than half were brightly flashing. If one attacker had a pouch with varlick powder in it, more of them could. I think my burst of flame scared the attackers more than hurt. I hadn't been that close.

My friends obviously felt the same and took off running after the attackers as well. Except for Alric. He stood at the entrance, sword high and hand couched for a spell like an elven prince of old. He wasn't going to let anyone near me.

Or he was making sure I didn't go out. Not that I blamed him. Tangle Morning Glory and the other humming faeries were helping, and still humming, but I still felt the need to go stomp some bad folks into the dirt. I also wondered what my fallback spell, push, would do with this much power behind it. We hadn't had a chance to test my magic, but I felt like at least some of it was back.

I also wondered what I looked like. Pretty sure the antlers were back—I could see the spikes on my legs—and my tail was long and snakelike this time, with cruel-looking barbs on the tip. The faeries were looking at my spikes with too much longing even as they hummed to keep me calm.

The sounds of fighting grew distant as morning came into being. Welsy and Delsy came trudging back, with Bunky and Irving flying low over them.

"We're here to protect."

"To back Alric up."

I smiled. Not that I doubted their fighting prowess, but they were clearly being escorted out of the fighting. Probably by Padraig.

Another half hour passed, and I moved closer to the front of the cave. Still out of the way, but where I could talk to Alric. "This is something like what I turned into before when I was in the air. Only it appeared in pieces last time." I shook my leg as Leaf began sizing up a spike on it.

"Very impressive. And not what you looked like before when you changed." He grinned. "I still love you, whatever you look like. Spikes and all."

"Thank you." I fought off the chill that hit at his words. What if I couldn't change back after this? Being able to change forms was one thing; being forced into it was another. Not to mention this wasn't even my dragon form.

"Calming." Tangle Morning Glory and her choir of humming faeries started up again.

Nice to know it worked with anxiety as well as anger.

The sound of voices came from outside. I assumed it was our people, or the Dark were even bolder than we thought. Sure enough, Padraig, Mathilda, Covey, Grillion, and Foxy came inside.

"They created a chawsia path from here to escape. Just as Theria used when we were up in the enclave." Padraig reached for a waterskin. "They might have come in that way too. Their trail started and ended about a mile from here." He looked over to me. "How do you feel?"

"Thanks to my humming faeries, better. Sorry about the flame, everyone. Once I changed to this, it needed to come out." I supposed part of me was grateful for the earlier partial changes since it made this one a little less shocking for me. Or maybe it was just that I felt calmer because a few more faeries had joined in the humming. "Was it the Dark? How did they find us? Were they the ones who grabbed Alric?"

"Yes, not sure, and probably not." Covey came up, walked around me, and whistled. "You know, you have some familiar attributes. But I can't remember the source." She tapped her chin and narrowed her eyes as she tried to recall what I reminded her of. Which might be nice to know.

Mathilda came up closer as well. "She does...oh my. That Dagonin Danir spell was trickier than I thought. I wish Amara was here." She walked around me slowly, shaking her head with a look of shock on her face.

"And?" I stopped following her after her second round.

"And, I want to confirm something first." She turned to Foxy. "Can you reach out to Amara? Let her see what you see?"

He scowled. "I can reach her, aye. But to see what I see?"

"It would be on her end. I need her to see what Taryn has changed into. It's not going to last and next time she changes, she'll be herself. Both selves."

Foxy shrugged and put his hand on his vine tattoo. His was on his leg. A moment later, Amara's voice came out from the air in front of him. He quickly explained what happened and what Mathilda wanted her to do.

There was silence once the spell was cast as Foxy walked slowly around me. It lasted so long I wondered if we'd lost contact with Amara.

"How is this happening?" There were a dozen emotions in her voice, ranging from confusion to hope to fear. "Those are attributes of the ones who fell in the final battle, which also took my sisters. And the rest of the lost deities."

CHAPTER FIFTEEN

―――――――

"GODDESSES? GODS? DEAD deities?" I was impressed at how my voice didn't rise. But panic was in my head. How and why did I transform into a bunch of deities? Or rather, how did some of them start showing up in me? There was no way this was going to be good.

"They were lost, but their bodies were never found. The final battle that we won, but from which their bodies were never recovered. But I felt them go. They ceased to exist." She paused. "We searched for them in all the realms, but they weren't there."

"How are their attributes appearing now?" Timeline issues were being forced aside by my growing terror, but I was pretty sure all of the gods and goddesses were long gone by the time I'd been born. The ones on this plane, anyway.

"I don't know. Foxy explained about Dagonin Danir and maybe that gap in the worlds at this time is doing it? Aside from Taryn, can any of you draw well? Very well?"

Only Grillion kept his hand up at the second comment.

"He draws scarily well." Alric nodded.

"Good. Draw as much of Taryn's current form as you can. Even if you don't think it's something new, draw it. Then make copies. I'll find a way to get a copy to me.

But each of you should carry a set." She left the "in case not everyone makes it back" part out, but it was there.

"It's that important?" I knew it was to me because I had been freaked out even before I found out these were things that had come from a bunch of lost deities. But not sure why this level of information protection needed to be taken.

"It could be far more important than any of us know. Combined with the parts of the seeker's chest that those umbaji stole from Qianru's former house in Beccia? There might have been many small things going wrong for thousands of years and no one knew. The word of this change needs to get out. Make sure a copy gets to your two friends in the south, Nasif and Dueble. They will get the information to the right sources." Again a pause, and when she came back, she was annoyed. "I must go. There is an issue in the bar. No, Foxy, I'm fine. Don't worry. Dogmaela even brought some of her cousins to town to help. But I need to go deal with things. Keep me apprised of the situation." Her voice popped out.

Alric dug out some charcoal and paper from his pack and handed it to Grillion. "Use your ill-gotten talents for good, my friend."

Grillion grinned and set himself up in front of me. "Just don't get mad that I'm drawing your girl, Alric." He winked at me. "Nothing personal, you know."

Of course, as soon as I knew I needed to hold still, all I wanted to do was move. I tried to keep my twitching down to a minimum after a few narrow-eyed stares from Grillion.

The others were mostly standing off to the side, talking, but Covey was fussing with a large rusty mirror on a heavy stand near the entrance. It took a bit, but she managed to angle it right and it sent a beam of sunlight back into the corridor behind this massive chamber.

"Ha! Now I have you!" She ran after the light beam

into the back, adjusted another mirror left by the original builders, then tore off to an unseen chamber.

Grillion stopped drawing and watched her leave. "You don't think she'll take any treasure, right?"

"I thought you searched everything? Covey just cares about what's on the walls…or if there are any surviving scrolls." In my mind, we had enough scrolls and none of them had come in terribly handy as of yet.

"I did. But it was very dark back there." He gave the back corridors one more glance, then sighed. "But I have an important job first."

He returned to his drawing with a bit more motivation than before, but he was doing it. We were going to make a functioning member of society out of him eventually.

"I hate to be nosy, but I did miss everything that happened out there. Could you folks move closer to me so I don't have to disrupt the artist to hear you?" Padraig, Alric, and Mathilda had been talking in low tones just far enough from me that I couldn't hear them clearly. Foxy was whittling a stick as he sat by the front entrance. He appeared to be telling a story as the four constructs and a dozen faeries were all sitting at his feet, listening to him.

Alric smiled as they all came closer. "They were just filling me in. It did look like the Dark and they had at least one magic user strong enough to create that chawsia path. But they took off too quickly to find out more."

"But if they knew we were coming, couldn't they have come up more safely?" The tunnel remains I'd seen outside of the enclave had left a lot of damaged trees. Since the person who created it was a necromancer, there was also speculation as to what else he'd killed to create his tunnel to the south. The idea that he might have been outside with those others almost made me ill.

"I don't think they were behind the ones who grabbed me," Alric said. "Theria was with the Dark, and I don't believe the people in that fortress were from the Dark.

Which means, the ones who attacked us here weren't expecting us."

"So they were working with the syclarions?" I turned slightly when Grillion motioned for me to do so.

"I seriously doubt that." Mathilda was gathering food for breakfast but stayed close enough to remain in the conversation.

Because that's what you do when you've fought off a bunch of bad guys. Make breakfast for everyone. My friends were odd. Amazing, but odd.

"Actually, we found the formerly surviving syclarions who had attacked us. They'd been killed. But they weren't killed by a necromancer, so that was good. It means the two groups aren't working together." She scowled. "Or three. The ones at the fortress could be a completely separate group."

Her comments echoed my thoughts and that was before I'd known that the syclarions had been killed. I knew some had died while I was up in the air fighting their leader, but they'd said at least five ran off. Not far enough, obviously.

"And everyone is after me? That's so reassuring." I looked down at myself. I was probably the best fighter among us in this current condition. And the one that couldn't go out and fight.

"We'll get through this. Honestly, this additional change you've gone through makes me think you will return to yourself with the coming dawn. And gives me an insight into why the Dagonin Danir spell was created." Mathilda just sat there with a huge smile until even Padraig couldn't take it anymore.

"And? The reason?"

She laughed. "Sorry, was just thinking of the academics who'd ignored the harmless folk festival for eons, and it might hold some serious secrets about the lost goddesses and gods."

"That's what I don't get. So did everyone think they were dead or just missing? I'd think people would have been looking for them." How did they misplace them?

"That final battle was before my time. But the tales we grew up with said they defeated evil but at great personal cost and all were lost. Dagonin Danir appeared a few years after as a way to unify the people of the south. Everyone was to drop who they pretended to be and simply gather to share food, stories, meet other people. Now I think it was something else entirely."

"Am I going to have to force this out of you, word for word?" Padraig was joking, but this kind of information was right in his area of research.

"Sorry, pausing for dramatic effect. I theorize, that when that last battle ended, not all of the deities were lost. They were trapped somewhere that no one could sense, so they were presumed dead. The day was made to disclose them if they were hiding. And it sort of did." She looked up at me.

"They're inside me? Not just aspects showing, but *them*?" Panic was going to be coming and no amount of faery humming was going to stop this freak-out.

"Easy there. I should have made it clearer. I think they are using this day, and this change, to let us know they still exist. Somewhere. Maybe someplace where time is frozen. They might not even know who they are."

"Are you talking about people trapped in a *tir cudd*?" Covey came back and caught the end of Mathilda's comment.

The *tir cudd* were pockets of reality protected and hidden from the world, created long before I was around and not made by my people. We'd found one of my missing relics in one—the diamond sphinx. It wasn't a place I'd want to spend much time in. Certainly not centuries.

"That does sound like one of those, doesn't it? Or many of them. They are almost impossible to track, but

Nasif told me his theory was that there could be dozens of them. He was working on a way to predict where they were and how to get into each one." Mathilda nodded to Covey. "I think there might be some lost deities trapped in *tir cudds*. And I think that this festival day was created in the hopes of exposing them."

Covey's face dropped. "And they're *in* Taryn?"

Mathilda looked between us and smiled. "You both have the same thoughts far more times than you know." She explained her theory and instead of rejecting it, Covey nodded as she went along.

"That would go with the chamber I found in the back. Most of the walls are too damaged to see much of the designs on them and sorting them would take a full digger crew. But one small chamber in the back seems fairly well preserved. It looks like a lot of goddesses and gods are depicted."

I got excited until I looked at the size of the archway and corridor. Yeah, not going to fit.

"I've got most of Taryn drawn; do you want me to switch to draw that chamber?" Grillion stood and stretched.

"Yes," I responded before anyone else. "Look, I can't get back there, and knowing our luck, the moment I change to normal, we'll have to be off on the run again. I'd like to see these drawings." If I had to, I was putting my oversized foot down on this.

Both Padraig and Mathilda looked ready to say no, but Padraig glanced through the drawings Grillion had already done.

"He has done a great job here. A quick sketch of that chamber couldn't hurt, and we might need those drawings as well if they're connected to this," Padraig said.

"Agreed," Mathilda said as she, Alric, and Padraig started walking back, with Grillion almost running alongside them. Foxy and his listeners were engrossed in his story and didn't look up once.

Covey waited until the others left before speaking. "How are you doing? I mean, all of this—finding out who you are, Alric, magic, no magic, now somehow you're a beacon for deities who we thought were dead, but are trapped in odd pockets of reality?"

"When you put it that way," I laughed, "I don't know. I think after hunting down those relics, I'm becoming the queen of denial. Just keep shoving things aside to deal with later. But since everyone else, including a spell that's thousands of years old, is interested in who I am, I guess this is one I can't ignore."

"This isn't how life was going to be, that's for sure." She rubbed the side of her head, spiking up her short hair. "Don't take this the wrong way, but when I saved you from that mugging all those years ago, I had no idea it would lead to this."

"Sorry." I shrugged. Or what felt like a shrug—this form was hard to gauge what I was doing. "Save a stranger's life, have yours messed up beyond belief." When I'd first come to Beccia, after being ditched by Mathilda after I'd flung myself into this time, I'd almost been mugged. Covey had saved me, and we'd been friends ever since.

"Oh, don't be." She laughed and folded down to sit where Grillion had been. "You changed my life for the better—far better. Now, my life has been in danger more times than it would have been, I've had to kill to defend myself and my friends more than I would have had I stayed teaching at the university, but better than dying of boredom. I love academia, don't get me wrong. But it leads to a boring existence sometimes."

"Boom!" Foxy, the constructs, and a lot of faeries almost made me jump through the ceiling when they all yelled at the same time.

Foxy looked over to us and shrugged. "Sorry about that. Thought you'd all gone to the back."

I lifted my front foot/arm—whichever it would be called—and waved it around. "Can't fit into much this way. What was going boom?"

Covey shook her head and hadn't turned toward them.

"Ah, we can't share that with those who don't know the power of boom." He shook his head, with his ears flapping. He also winked.

Sneaky. He probably didn't understand boom any more than I did but was playing along like he did.

"Okay then, if that's the case, we'll just keep talking about our stuff." I would understand boom someday, but clearly, not today.

Covey waited until Foxy started telling another tale before leaning forward with something else to tell me.

Just then, my height dropped to only a foot above her. And I felt impossibly wide. "Ahhh!" My front hands were now flippers, and I was definitely feeling dried out. Massively so. "What in the...look at me!" I'd just meant that as a general statement of fear and panic. I was changing into some sort of sea monster. My yell had been loud enough that Alric, Padraig, and Mathilda came running out with weapons up. All three raised them and ran for me.

CHAPTER SIXTEEN

COVEY CAUGHT ON before I did as they charged us—they thought I was a monster. She drew her sword and jumped between them and myself. Honestly, I wasn't sure that I could fight in this condition. My body was heavy and floppy.

"Stand back! It's Taryn," Covey yelled.

They skidded to a stop and stared at her, then me, then her again.

"It's me. And I don't know what I turned into, or why, but this form needs water." I swore I could hear my skin starting to crack.

Mathilda didn't even question things, just called up a massive amount of water and dumped it on me. "I have a feeling you regressed. Not you specifically, but before we realized that the Ancients were dragons, a creature very much like how you look right now was seen as the dragon of myth. We got a lot wrong with that." She walked around me, shaking her head and tossing more water on me with her spell. "That is not a creature designed for land at all."

Padraig came forward, minus his sword as well, with Alric standing there, looking stunned, behind him. "That definitely looks like one of the Tragleani sea monsters. And agreed, it can't live on land. All of those theories were wrong." He sent the same spell that Mathilda had been sending and more water flowed over me. The ruins were tilted so it ran off into a corner.

"The water is great, thanks. And so is speculation that my appearance will change academic scrolls everywhere. But how do I get out of this? It's not just the water—this body needs to be buoyant. Seriously. Things being squished inside." I was feeling pressed into the ground like a boulder was sitting on me.

Before anyone could respond, the world shrunk again. Or rather, I went back to almost hitting the ceiling again. "Antlers?"

Covey looked up. "Yup. You look the same as before."

"Did anything trigger that response? Either of them?" Padraig stepped closer.

"No, we were talking to Foxy about boom, and then I changed." I looked over to the faeries still clustered around Foxy. Interesting that none of them had flown over when I changed. "Girls? Did you boom me?" I folded my arms as best I could and glared.

Silence from some beings was good. From faeries, it never was.

Foxy stared at them. "Ladies? What did ye do?"

Garbage flew up from the front of the group and came to me. "You not stable. We push. You BOOM!" She grinned until she saw that none of us were smiling. "Fines. You mushy right now." She patted her hands together, then pulled them apart. "We change you to old. Only now. No hurt. Fun."

"You were able to change who she was to an ancestral form? Can you do that to anyone?" There was a tone of panic underlying Mathilda's question—one I extremely agreed with.

That would be a terrifying power for anyone, let alone a bunch of faeries.

"Yes. No." Garbage sighed. "Air unstable. She not stable. Until fixed, can change."

"Can you change me back to my human shape?"

"Noes. Only other shapes."

"And it goes away tomorrow at dawn?" Alric moved closer to me.

"Guess so?" She shrugged. "No more booms. Promise. For now." With a smile and a nod, she spun away to rejoin the rest.

Foxy looked over, but at my nod went back to telling them stories.

"I know this whole Dagonin Danir spell is what let them do it, but is anyone else disturbed by that new ability of the faeries? I might be more concerned since it was me they did it to, but that could be bad, right?" Never mind fighting off killers; we now had to deal with a new power for the faeries. Who knew what was next?

Mathilda was still watching the faeries but finally turned back. "When I first found the three faeries, I thought they were a group of odd little throwbacks, creatures of myth who brought candy to good elven children. They are so much more than that, and I don't think we've seen it all. So, yes, this could be bad. If we were home, I'd say we get to the bottom of these changing abilities. For now, we just need to watch them."

"Where's Grillion?" I hadn't noticed his absence before but I was trying to keep from dying.

Alric looked around. "He said he'd be right behind me. Let me go see how he's doing with the drawings."

Covey saw me watching him run off, then nodded to me. "I'll go, too. There were some parts I wanted to see again." She took off before anyone else could question her.

Good thing, because she was a bad liar. I'd had a flash of panic as Alric took off and she'd seen it on my face.

A crashing sound came from the corridor and Padraig ran after them. Mathilda stood between me and the corridor, and Foxy joined her. Both were ready if something other than our people came back down it.

A weird calling hit me. There was something back there that I needed to do. Aside from the fact that I was too large to fit, I needed to get back there. "Garbage? Can you ladies boom me into a throwback small enough to fit in those corridors? Preferably not water-born?"

Her tiny face lit up and before Mathilda could shout, I was about two feet high. Still on all fours, I felt like a goat, but it looked like I had claws. Big ones. "Thanks. I think. Stay here in case someone tries to get in." I tore off after the rest, with the constructs and half of the faeries flying behind me.

I followed the light mirrors down a few corridor changes. That and the sound kept me on track. There was no yelling, but it did sound like a fight was taking place. I didn't know what I was, so no way to assess my fighting skills, but I had claws and it felt like my magic was kicking in.

The final chamber was easy to find as the sounds were louder. Still no cries of help, but lots of crashing and smashing. Welsy and Delsy had taken the lead and skidded to a stop just inside the door but moved to each side. Bunky and Irving flew over them but split up and stuck to the sides as well. The faeries and I came charging in, with me trying to figure out how far this form could jump as the combatants came into view.

Padraig, Alric, and Covey were fighting off a large rug that had pinned Grillion in the corner of the room. I wasn't sure what to expect, but that wasn't it.

As soon as I came into the room, everything froze. Literally. In mid-swing. The rug pulled away from Grillion and reshaped in front of me into a tall, bipedal form. The faeries flew through the image, so even though it had been holding Grillion in place, it wasn't solid now.

I took a step back as the shadow formed into the vague shape who'd given me the chest of scrolls from the Library of Pernasi. Of course, all vague smoky forms mostly looked the same.

My friends unfroze.

"You're looking a bit different today."

Yup, that was the voice that I'd heard before. I held up a paw to indicate to Alric that it was okay.

"But it's good to see you again, Taryn. I'm sorry if I scared your friend. You're in such proximity to each other that I thought you were in here." The form glanced over to where Grillion was looking wide-eyed and starting to slide to the ground. His drawings were scattered around his feet. "Sorry about that." The shadow looked back at me. "You need to get down here as soon as possible. The forces that I thought were still weeks behind are active now. But, you also can't take a direct route. They have watchers everywhere. Fast, but slow enough to be cautious." The form nodded but it was to itself. "Yes, side trips might work. Confuse the watchers. But you still can't dawdle. They will be coming for you."

The shadow person just gave me a massive headache.

Alric came up behind me but didn't touch me or the smoky person I was speaking to. "They already have been coming after us. How will going farther south help?"

I knew there was no way he would think of leaving Siabiane and Lorcan behind and they were to the far south. He wanted to see what this person knew.

"High lords. Always so presumptuous, even when they're not." The weird figure gave an odd laugh and moved closer to Alric. The usually invisible elven high lord mark on his cheek flared into existence, then vanished. "Taryn's power originated in the south. All of her people did, and yours as well. The original home of all sentient beings is in the south. And it is fighting to stay alive." The shape turned back to me. "The relics you created were a sign of power misused, but a sign of power nonetheless. The type we will need. Take what you can from here, but use it wisely." The shape turned to the faeries. "Thank you for leading them here." The form turned shapeless as it drifted toward Grillion, then vanished into the walls.

The faeries shrugged and flew back out of the room.

I'd have to talk to them about what led them to this ruin—aside from the size. I still hoped the smoke-entity-shape was on our side, but we needed to be aware if it had power over the faeries.

"Who…what…was that?" Grillion got to his feet and gathered his drawings. He looked more rattled than usual but better than he had when I came in.

Covey and Padraig walked to the wall he'd been leaning against. Unlike the other three, it was mostly covered in geometric shapes but no people or animals.

"I don't get what it meant about taking what we can. There's nothing here." Except for some detailed drawings. A goddess with small wings and a nice set of antlers caught my eye. Probably what mine looked like when I got them. I'd have to look up who she was.

The plain wall started rumbling, cracked down the center, and we stepped back as a pile of relics tumbled out. Weapons, armor, books, and scrolls. And a few odd trinkets that I had no clue as to what they were.

The others started walking forward slowly.

I stayed where I was. "Are you sure that's a good idea? We don't know where that person really came from."

Padraig nodded. "Good point." He closed his eyes and sent forth a spell. It was subtle, and I felt it drift around the room. It settled in on the pile of items that came from behind the wall.

"The rest of the room might be questionable, but these are safe. Or at least not directly targeted against us." He turned to me. "Didn't you say the voice said the enemy of my enemy is my friend when they gave you the scrolls?" At my nod, he picked up a delicately engraved helmet.

"The feeling from these is the same. For now, they are on our side as we're all against the same evil."

CHAPTER SEVENTEEN

IT TOOK THREE trips, even with Foxy and the rest of the faeries joining in to move the newfound treasures into the front. It probably could have been done in one, but Padraig, Mathilda, and Covey didn't want them being jumbled until they were looked at. I held back from mentioning that they'd been jumbled up behind that wall for thousands of years.

I got one round of viewing the drawings on the other three walls before they chased me out. Covey pointed out that the faeries change hadn't lasted long last time, and did I really want to be trapped here if I resumed my full size?

I ran out to the main room as fast as my little clawed feet would carry me.

Good thing, too: I poofed out into my more recent larger form as soon as I cleared the archway. Still the odd me with antlers, spikes, and whip-like tail. I noticed that my wings had small feathers all over—my normal ones were sleek and had tiny scales instead of feathers.

I stood back and watched them bring out the items and place them carefully in order. Covey insisted on spreading blankets around to put them on. I again bit my tongue about where they'd been. Academics could be dangerous when focusing on something interesting. And Covey was more focused than I'd ever seen.

The faeries flew over to me as apparently they weren't seen as trustworthy to help carry things out.

Probably a good idea.

"Girls? Did you recognize that smoky person in the other room?" I watched as the others sorted items and found my hands itching to jump in. Old digger habits die hard.

"Your friend." Garbage was also watching them organize the stuff, but I think she was looking for anything sparkly to grab. The faeries had a thing for pretty rocks. In fact, their former collecting habits had been what gave us the first glass gargoyle relic. It had been disguised as a pretty rock that the faeries had stolen from a pack of possessed squirrels.

"My friend, *who*? Do you know them?" Someday I hoped to get the faeries to start using names. Probably on my deathbed.

"Friend-not-friend from elf home. Still okay. Show us here." Garbage didn't want to carry on this conversation; she was almost doubled in half with the urge to charge forward and play in the relics. I wasn't going to get much out of them—even if they knew about the smoky person, which I doubted. She'd confirmed what I believed: that was the same being who'd appeared in my room in the healing house in the elven enclave.

"Grillion? Can you get something from my pack?"

He had put down the items he brought out but was lingering over them. He finally looked up at my call.

"A small bag from my pack." I'd held off on giving the faeries the sugar because we'd gone from bad to worse once we made it up that cliff. But right now having them sugared-out might be the best idea.

He shrugged, got it, and brought it over, all while never taking his eyes off the collection of items. He and the faeries had a lot in common.

"Thanks. I'll need you to open it and pour it out."

The faeries were looking ready to charge the collection. "Girls! Sugar!" I yelled as Grillion poured out the bag onto a large rock. Unfortunately, he hadn't had time to step back and ended up being in the middle of a faery swarm.

"Argh!" He yelled and stumbled backward as he covered his head and dropped to the ground.

The faeries grabbed the sugar, crammed as much as they could into their mouths, and settled in near the entrance of the ruin to soak up the sunshine. All the faeries got some and there was still a bit sitting there. Leaf came back, her cheeks bulging with sugar, and scooped the rest into one of their black bags. "Fos lathers." Then she joined the others.

"Are they always like that? Because that was horrible." Grillion was still curled in on himself.

I recalled Alric saying they'd had an issue with some wild faeries before I brought him in as my bounty two years ago. From the wild look in his eyes, Grillion just had a flashback to that.

"They wouldn't have hurt you. I should have warned you to step away quickly after you poured it, though. They really love sugar."

"I gathered." He stood up, but it looked like everything had been brought out as everyone except Foxy and the constructs were muttering and sorting the items in a dedicated frenzy. I knew those things would be traveling with us—in faery bags, most likely—so I wasn't sure why they were so frantic about sorting the items now.

With a nod to me, Grillion went and joined them. Alric wasn't the only former relic thief who knew a lot about artifacts.

I moved a bit closer, but I had to lower my head a lot to be able to see anything. My neck and head took up too much space around the items. So I stepped back and watched from higher up. "Do we know anything about what these are?"

"Not yet. But they are old, extremely old." Alric wasn't drooling as excitedly as the others, but he was looking to be joining them soon.

I couldn't blame them; had I found these items on a dig, no one could have pried me from them for at least a week.

Watching them move things, debate placement, and speculate on the meaning of minute details wasn't fun when I couldn't be involved, nor see anything well. The eyesight for my current form wasn't great. Probably a tradeoff for adding all the weird additional parts.

"I'll be over here, near the front, napping." I tilted my head toward Foxy and the faeries. "I won't go outside." That none of them had jumped up to say that immediately told me how far hooked into the relics they were. With a sigh, I went to join the others.

Foxy was telling another story, but whatever it was, it didn't involve things going boom. It was calm and soothing and somehow involved fluffy clouds and open meadows. The faeries were drifting into a sugar-filled doze, the sun was showing through the trees, and I settled my head down with a sigh.

And an earthquake jostled the faeries, Foxy, and me.

Oops. In all the excitement, I hadn't had breakfast. Not an earthquake, but my stomach, my quite large stomach, complaining that it needed food.

"Anyone know what I eat?" I was fairly certain that as my normal dragon-self I ate what I did as my normal human self. No idea whatever I currently was ate.

Mathilda pried herself away from the relics long enough to bring me a pile of carrots, an apple, and a mass of traveling bread. She also brought water. "I'm not sure what that body will take, but many of the deities have restrictive diets. I know you haven't turned into them, but you're carrying their attributes, so who knows what effect that will have."

None of it looked appealing, but once I started in, it was good. And reminded me I'd missed dinner too.

Foxy's voice had been getting softer, and he eventually extricated himself from the faeries to come around to my side. The faeries were out like tiny drunken sailors and snoring almost as loud. "I'm going to go tell Amara about what happened. You're okay watching them?" His nod encompassed the faeries and our friends in their relic-frenzy.

"Yeah. I know I need to stay hidden but if someone finds us, I'm pretty certain this body can defend our friends. Give Amara my love. And ask her if she's seen Harlan or Orenda and what's the news about the elves; if Ceithera came down or sent anyone."

He nodded and vanished into the woods.

I knew we had more than enough things on our plate, but I was concerned about the happenings in Beccia. The fact that Dogmaela brought in family members made me extremely nervous. Amara had played it down, and Foxy wasn't concerned. But I knew most trolls didn't like coming into town. Dogmaela loved the city, but I doubted her family did or we would have seen some before. I might have to try to contact Amara myself when Foxy wasn't within earshot to get some more information. Dogmaela had a reason to bring her relatives down.

I finished my odd, yet filling, food and repositioned myself so I could see out better but most of my body was hidden behind the wall. My new eyesight adapted to the different levels of green far better than looking at the golden relics, so I looked out over the forest. I was full, comfortable, and the sun was shining on my face. I let my eyes drift shut as the faeries kept snoring around me.

As my thoughts drifted around—ignoring the sound of the faeries—I felt part of my consciousness go out along the forest trail just beyond this building. The sound of birds singing in the distance drew me in. I knew that song—the kit sprite; small native songbirds who loved dense forests and lived in huge nesting compounds high in the trees.

That was weird. I didn't know what birds lived outside my house in Beccia, yet I knew these immediately. Maybe one of my tagalong deities loved birds. I thought about my now feathered wings. Maybe one of them *was* a bird. Or bird-like. Or was a bird deity. I'd heard of the tree goddesses, but not much beyond knowing they existed and had died. The only thing I had heard about the other deities who fought down here was that many were nature spirits.

My contemplation was cut off as the kit sprites all went silent. Even just plain me knew that wasn't a good sign in the forest. I strained, but there were no other noises to be heard. In a forest that had been bursting with sounds a second ago. A predator of some sort was out there. And we weren't lucky enough for it to be a bear or a big cat.

I opened my eyes, but everything looked the same. The forest was now just silent. Then I heard the distinct sound of heavy horses on a packed dirt trail. The kind of massive horses used for people in armor.

I pulled back into the ruin and started nudging the faeries awake. Sugar had kept them from harassing the others, but we needed them sober, fast.

I didn't want to do it, but they were extremely sleepy. "Do we have any tea to wake the faeries?" I stomped over to my friends. "The forest is silent except for some heavy-shod warhorses. I have no idea how far away they are, but one of the deities inside me has really good hearing."

"Damn it, we need to spread these out. I don't want one person to have them all in case we get caught. Does everyone have a bag?" Padraig already had three tiny black bags out, but after a quick glance inside them, put two away. I knew there were some questionable things in some of those bags. Obviously, he didn't want to contaminate anything. Covey, Mathilda, and Alric were already putting stuff in their faery bags.

Grillion looked around. "Any way that I could get one of those?"

"Don't worry. They are stingy with them." Not that I could have put anything in. My normal dragon-self had hands I could use. This form had oddly shaped claw hands, not unlike the ones the little me had. I'd be good in a fight, I supposed, but it was hard to pick things up.

Mathilda had a kettle of tea ready. She'd used magic, but I needed those faeries awake fast. "I made a weak infusion. From what you've told me, tea gets them a bit too hyper." At my nod, she walked over and started giving the faeries tea in a huge bowl. They were up and buzzing around, but not on full tea-overload, in seconds.

"Where's Foxy?" Alric finished putting away his stash and even had both our packs loaded and ready.

"He went to have a private chat with Amara. Where are the horses?" I couldn't use one right now, but we'd need them. I hadn't heard a sound from them if they were tied up out front.

"I'll get them." Grillion gave up trying to get a faery bag and walked to the back of the massive hall. A small room held the horses.

"I convinced them to relax when we brought them in," Alric said. "Well, that and Mathilda slipped them a spell. They needed a rest and we weren't sure when they'd get one. They should feel like they've had a week on a farm."

"Goes?" Garbage flew up to me, looking far too enthusiastic. The tea might not have been full strength but she was definitely perky.

"I think so." I looked to the others. Everyone was packed and ready, but Foxy hadn't come back yet.

"Let me see if I can tell how far they are." Alric started

for the entrance without his horse. "I'd rather not go on the road just yet unless we have no choice." He gave me a nod and took off.

I didn't want to leave in this form either, so I completely agreed.

I watched him go and forced my worry for him aside. I couldn't lose everything the moment he went somewhere without me. He was a powerful magic user and swordsman—and had fallen a few times. The last time could have been his death.

"He'll be okay." Padraig stood alongside me.

"I know. It's just..." I shook my head.

"I know." He patted my shoulder and went to stand by the entrance.

"So, what's the plan if we do have to run? Or in my case, fly? I just take off and hope they don't see me?" I looked down; I would be extremely hard to miss.

"Maybe she should leave before us?" Covey was scowling in my direction. "If she took off before they get too close, they might not notice her."

Not a great idea, but better than me sitting here, waiting for whoever was after us. That they might not be enemies didn't pass through my thoughts long enough to be considered. "I could take some of the faeries and Bunky and Irving with me to keep in touch with you. No idea where I'd go, though." My sense of direction had improved with our travels, but that was in my own country. I couldn't be certain that I wouldn't be going back toward the water until I saw it.

"We're going south."

"And that helps me how again?" Of all people, Covey knew I had a bad sense of direction. But just as I said it, a tingling sensation hit me. I lifted my arm and pointed to the left of the building. "Is it that way?" That was not coming from me. I had no idea if there was a deity of direction, but someone hanging around inside knew their north and south. Might be the bird goddess; birds were usually good at that.

"Exactly." Covey smiled.

Alric came running back in. "They are a few miles away, but there are a lot of them. The entire forest is still silent. I think we need to leave as soon as Foxy gets back. There's not a single direct trail here, but they're on the main one we followed. The odds of them just passing through aren't great; they have to be after us."

I let out a breath. "I'm taking off then?" Flying off had been my idea, sort of, but now I was having second thoughts.

"We's helps." Crusty zipped over and patted my cheek. "No lost." Then she settled on my head and hung onto an antler. I appreciated the thought, not sure about her up there steering, but couldn't be worse than her steering me by my hair.

Garbage carefully split up her gang of faeries. At some point, I'd ask if the new ones were staying. We'd had twenty-three, added another two dozen wilds when we were crossing the water to the southern continent, and they were still with us. They were still wearing leaves, not overalls—yet.

Garbage, Leaf, and Crusty were with me, along with a dozen more and Bunky and Irving. The remaining faeries flitted around Mathilda.

"Shouldn't Foxy be back by now?" I knew he loved chatting, and even more when it was with his beloved wife, but he'd been gone half an hour now.

"He should be." Covey stalked toward the front of the entrance. "I'll bring him back. If I'm not back in five minutes, assume the worst. Get Taryn out." She took off at her extremely fast run before anyone could stop her. Five minutes wasn't much time, but she had a point. Foxy might like to chat, but he wouldn't have gone far to do so.

"I didn't see him the way I went, but I didn't go off the trails," Alric said.

Bunky buzzed close to me, with Irving next to him. They both gronked. I looked to Leaf. Some people could understand Bunky; no one aside from Bunky and a few of the faeries understood Irving. I didn't understand either of them.

"They say protect you. Fly below and keep eyes from you." Leaf nodded.

"We surround. No eyes." Crusty patted my antler as Leaf joined her on the other side. Faeries had an on-again, off-again ability to hide people if they sat on them, but only sometimes. And only if the person didn't move.

Five minutes passed and still no Foxy or Covey.

"You need to go." Mathilda waved to my faery escorts. "Keep her safe, keep going south, and if you find a safe place she can hide in, do it. We still have most of a day and all night before that spell breaks."

"Maybe I should wait a bit longer?"

Even Grillion shook his head—along with the others—at that. The faeries weren't sure what they were shaking their heads at, judging by the giggles.

"Go, now." Alric put his hand on my face when I lowered it down to him. "We will find you."

Damn it. They were right but it still didn't make me happy. "Fine. If you need me, send some faeries. Stay safe, all of you." I waddled to the entrance with my flying entourage and took off.

Not a graceful lifting into the air; there were a lot of trees near the entrance and this form was even more unwieldy than the other one. And those feathered wings were weird. But I got up in the air. I glanced toward where I heard the horses coming from, but the tree coverage was too thick and I couldn't see anything.

I felt tapping on my antlers and turned south with my escorts. After saying a silent prayer to any deities traveling with us to keep everyone safe. What was the point of manifesting some gods and goddesses if I couldn't ask for help?

Getting into the air might have been problematic, but once I was above the treetops, flying was amazing. The feathers took some getting used to, but my wingspan was massive and I got a nice speed going. Bunky and Irving did as they'd said, taking up positions under me. I wasn't sure how two constructs, neither much larger than my current foot, could protect something my size, but it was nice to have them around.

The faeries were spreading out, mostly chattering as they flew around me—clear sky, nice breeze, and a massive bank of darkness speeding our way from the west.

CHAPTER EIGHTEEN

"DAMN IT, GIRLS, what is that?" It looked like a quickly moving rain cloud heading our way. Aside from the fact that there weren't any clouds out, it was moving against the wind, and it was moving far too fast. "Is it a flock of birds?" Whether it was from me or from that bird deity inside me, a coldness hit as I sorted it out.

My vision was much better up here and when I focused, I saw individual birds. They were massive, about twice the size of a raven, but still all dark. They also had gigantic beaks, and I could see their razor-like claws from here. Murlin. I didn't know how I knew them, but I did. And knowing what they were made me change course as fast as possible. Those were hunter birds and always worked for someone—usually a powerful mage not on the side of good.

"Is bads. We got fix!" Garbage had her war stick out and the others were doing the same.

"No! You can't go after them. None of you can. That goes for Bunky and Irving too." The part of me that recognized the murlin knew the faeries wouldn't win this battle. These weren't just birds; these were birds trained with one purpose—kill whatever they'd been set loose to get. They supposedly didn't exist anymore, having been destroyed during the mage wars a long time ago. So much for history.

"But—" Garbage wavered.

"No. You must stay with me." I banked hard and headed lower over the treetops. Through that weird repository of knowledge crammed into my head, I knew murlin had bad eyesight, and they might not have seen us yet. But I also knew they were looking for us, or at least me. They might not have known I'd be airborne, but they could have helped those soldiers pin down my friends if they stayed on their current course.

New plan.

I flew higher again, where I had a better line of sight with the murlin. They might or might not have seen us, but they were definitely heading toward the ruins we'd just left. I may not be able to fight against the soldiers unless things were hopeless, but I wasn't going to let these things help the soldiers either.

"Bunky? Are any of your chimera buddies in the south?" There had been flocks of the chimera constructs, and while many had fallen during the final battle, I knew a lot had survived and left the area.

He flew up to my eye level, glanced at the murlin, then gave a rough gronk.

"He say those bads, and his people coming." Leaf leaned closer to my ear. "Can't we go fight?"

"No. Stay with me, all of you." I had no idea how Bunky communicated with the other chimeras, but I was extremely glad he did. I'd seen them destroy dozens of sceanra anams, long snakelike flying bundles of teeth with the sole purpose to destroy. Hopefully, they could do the same with these murlin. "How long until the chimera can join us?" I was formulating a plan, mostly focusing on keeping those birds away from my friends and not dying or getting those with me killed in the process, but timing could be important.

Bunky bobbed then gronked.

"He say ten minutes." Leaf leaned in closer. "Bad fly-ers."

"That's longer than I hoped, but we need them. Thank you, Leaf—we know they are bad flyers."

"Is no. *More* bad flyers." She pushed my head to the right. Sure enough, another smaller dark cloud was head-ing our way. Belatedly, I recalled that a group of faeries coming home from the far south a few weeks ago had run into a flock of sceanra anam. I had a bad feeling that the town they'd come out of was to the west of us. And far too close.

I took a few deep breaths, then a few more. Nope, still terrified. Focus. I needed to focus. I was an Ancient, one of the most powerful beings in the world. I was cur-rently packing along some missing deities. Or at least their attributes. I just needed one of them to come up with an idea.

I paused mid-flap, dropped for a moment, then started flapping again. I'd never tried seeing if any of the deities were actually inside my head. The whole bit with their physical attributes was odd enough, but what if more than that was in me?

"*Hello? Is anyone else here?*" I asked it in my head. Felt a bit foolish, but either a flock of killer birds and sceanra anam attacked my friends or I found a way to take them on. I didn't get a verbal response, but my added parts all tingled. Antlers, spikes, feathers, and a whip-like barbed tail: all suddenly acutely aware. "*Okay, so any powers? We've got backup coming but we need to get those things to follow us now. And not kill any of us in the process.*"

Crusty broke in by tapping the antler she was hanging on to and then swinging down where I could see her. "These comings. Antler not happy."

I looked over to the west. "Yup, the sceanra anam are heading this way now." I glanced over to the east. The murlin still seemed to be heading toward the ruins, but a few in the lead were starting to turn our way. Both groups would get to us before the chimeras could. I picked up speed and kept flying south. I knew they could catch us, but I also felt a thrill. I hadn't been challenged like this in the air for ages. Part of me freaked out as I realized it was the bird goddess who felt that. She wasn't really with me; it was as if a memory of her was tied to the attributes.

Thinking of her increased my speed. The constructs could keep up but some of the faeries were struggling.

"Girls, can you pop out for a bit?" I never knew where they went, but they ofttimes vanished.

"Nos. Not nows."

"Bunky and Irving, you carried them inside you once—can you do that now? I need to go faster."

Bunky and Irving both opened their mouths wide and at my urging, all of the faeries, except my original three who were too stubborn and stayed sitting on my head, flew inside. Bunky and Irving picked up speed and flew alongside me. I sped up.

We'd been racing for a few minutes but there were still a few more minutes before the chimera appeared. I was impressed with our speed, but the two groups were still slowly gaining on us. If Bunky's timing had been right, we'd be caught before the chimeras arrived. The sceanra anam were going to hit us first, but the murlin wouldn't be that far behind.

"Bunky and Irving, I need you to stay by me. I'm going to count to three, flip in midair, and flame those things. Stay back and after the flames, let the faeries out. Garbage, when that happens, you lead your faeries and attack." I hoped to destroy as many sceanra anam as possible, get everyone back together, and outfly the murlin long enough for the chimeras to show up. And actually be able to pull this off.

I counted to three. My flipping in the air was awkward as I flailed about, overcorrected, then spun in the right direction finally. But I did it, then flamed. That would have worked better if I hadn't been dizzy from flipping and hit the group of sceanra anam in the middle as planned. But I did take out their entire left side. The survivors weren't as impressed with my maneuver as I was and after their initial scatter, they flew forward again.

Bunky and Irving hovered in the air, opened their mouths, and the yelling faeries charged out. Garbage took half and swung out and to the left. Leaf took the other half and swung to the right. It took the sceanra anam precious seconds to realize who they were up against, but their retreat was blocked. The faeries charged forward, with their war sticks stabbing at the sceanra anam. I swore more faeries were popping in as the battle continued but they were darting around so fast, I wasn't sure.

Crusty pounded on my antlers for emphasis and yelled encouragement, but hadn't gone with the others.

"Why aren't you out there?" I called up to Crusty. Mostly the constructs and I were watching for escapees; it was safer than taking the risk of being accidentally poked with one of the war sticks.

"I guard you." She swung back down so I could see her, kissed my cheek, then swung back. "Use zaps later."

That was odd on a few levels. Nothing against Crusty's fighting—she could jab with the best of them—but I did feel better having her with me. "What do you mean zaps?" That was worrying.

"These zaps zaps!" She tugged on the antlers, then swung around them. "But no now. Needs wait."

I kept an eye on the faery battle. They were winning, but it was better to not count on that. "Honey? How do they work? Are you going to do something?"

"Nos! You think hard—zap zaps!" She laughed so hard I felt her lift off my head. She was back a moment later.

So, my temporary antlers could zap people. I was so looking up these lost deities when we got back to Beccia.

Zapping people with your antlers was fairly amazing. I had no idea how to do it, but it would be awesome.

"I have no idea how to think hard enough to zap someone." We had to get moving again; the murlin were getting closer and there was still no sign of chimeras. "Bunky? If I call the faeries back, can you and Irving finish off those few sceanra anam?" This was taking too long, and I was beginning to think the faeries were drawing it out.

Bunky gronked and bobbed his head. Which moved his entire round body, but it got the point across.

"Faeries! Fall back!" My bellow had a lot more power behind it than I thought and at least five faeries tumbled out of the way just from that. The rest moved when Garbage echoed my command. The remaining sceanra anam charged forward just as Bunky and Irving circled them and let loose with their odd shocking arcs coming from their mouths.

The chimera constructs had been created by the Ancients to fight the sceanra anam. Bunky was living up to that and soon the sceanra anam were gone.

And the murlin were almost upon us. There wasn't time to get the faeries back into the constructs' mouths, and I wasn't sure how much farther I could fly at my prior speed anyway. I think something more substantial than carrots and bread was needed to fuel this body, and I was functioning on adrenaline alone.

I flapped my wings to stay in place and yelled for everyone to get behind me. I already knew my flame wouldn't be as big as that last one; it took time to recharge and this hadn't been near enough. But I'd do what I could. "After I flame, fight them as best you can—but stick together! Bunky, if you can hurry the rest of the chimeras, this would be the time."

Bunky's responding gronk was lost as the first wave

of murlin came into range and I flamed. I got some of them, but not nearly enough. This flock was huge. The bird goddess aspect of me flared, and I felt fury flood my system. The goddess didn't like them at all. They came closer and I saw at least one reason why. All of the ones still in the air after my flame had harnesses on, with familiar-looking flashing red gems.

I swore as I saw them. We'd faced squirrels with those same gems. They were a spelled control trick used by some nasty magic users. Murlin weren't nice birds; they were ruthless predators. Now they were ruthless predators with magic superpowers. Great.

Once I saw the blinking gems, I tried to call the faeries back, but they were still riled up from their successful fight against the sceanra anam, so they didn't listen. They charged forward, only to be rebuffed by the murlin staying next to each other and projecting a red wall.

The faeries were flung back but didn't appear to be injured, just stunned. Bunky and Irving flew down and met the same resistance. The murlin were focusing on me.

Crusty was still on my head. "Zap zaps! Now!" She kept yelling like a deranged little general as she pounded on my head.

"I don't know how!" The murlin were coming closer, still keeping their line as they flew when Crusty pinched my head. Hard. Considering the size difference between us, I shouldn't feel a pinch. Then she did it again, and I realized that she was poking me with her staff. Near the base of the antlers. I was about to say that wasn't going to work when my head felt like it exploded. An arc of electricity larger than any lightning I'd ever seen shot out through both antlers and into the birds.

They weren't expecting that any more than I was. One by one, the red gems in their harnesses winked out. If it had only been those spelled gems that were controlling them, they could take off.

They started cawing horribly and flew toward us.

CHAPTER NINETEEN

BUNKY AND IRVING recovered faster than the faeries, or they hadn't been flung as far since they were heavier. Both came racing toward us, gronking as they came. They flung themselves into the middle of the flock, scattering the birds around.

I was about to see if I had any flame left, when out from the forest below us, dozens of birds, all types except for murlin, were flying up toward us. At first, I thought something below us had scared them. I had no idea where I was in relation to where my friends should be at this point; they could have been fighting for their lives right below us.

Then the birds started harassing the murlin. The ravens were the largest of the new group and even they couldn't take out a murlin, but they could bother them, especially when there were about five times as many smaller birds as there were murlin. I saw the faeries in the distance making their way back to us.

I also saw a bunch of familiar black, round, stubby creatures appearing in the air. I'd seen faeries pop in and out of places before, but never chimeras. I wasn't going to argue. At this point, they could have appeared however they wanted—the important thing was they were here.

Crusty trilled some odd call, still standing on the top of my head, and the smaller birds pulled back and went back to the trees below us.

And the chimeras charged forward. I called for Bunky and Irving to stay back as well as the faeries as they caught up to me. There were a lot of chimeras and they didn't like the murlin any more than they did sceanra anam. The murlin were gone within a few minutes.

Bunky flew to the chimeras and bumped heads with a few. Then he flew back to us. The chimeras did the odd whole-body nod, then vanished.

"They took off before I could thank them."

Bunky gronked and Leaf translated. "He told them. They glad to help. Had fun."

"Okay. Well, then." I was still flapping to keep myself in the air, but it was getting harder to keep it up. My energy was gone. Those zaps might have come from the attributes of a goddess, but the force behind them came from me. "Um, I don't feel so good."

Garbage flew in front of me and looked closely at my face. Then she put her hand on my snout and scowled. "Not good."

"I know that, sweetie. I think I need to land." I was slowing down and dropping lower no matter how hard I was trying to pull up. A black cloud appeared over my eyes. I blinked rapidly and it vanished, but I was now almost skimming the treetops. A meadow was just ahead but I was a bit too large for it; however, I didn't have much of a choice. I was going down somewhere.

The trees would have hurt more if I wasn't on the verge of blacking out. But I made an almost-not-crash-landing and collapsed in the meadow and on the trees that didn't make it.

I shut my eyes, only to have them forcefully opened by a dozen tiny hands.

"You no sleeps." Garbage's scowl said there would be hell to pay if I didn't obey.

"I can't help it. I'm exhausted and need food. Water,

too. Just let me rest a bit." My entire body ached. We'd been in the air and fighting longer than I thought. It was late in the afternoon, judging from what I could see from the sunlight around me, but right now I felt like I wasn't going to make it to dawn. I wondered if my body would change back if I died before the spell broke.

My eyes shut again and this time the tiny hands brought something that smelled wonderful to my nose. Hay? I opened my eyes, looking for what was making my mouth water, and saw a mountain of hay in front of me. No idea how the faeries brought that much, nor why it smelled so good, but I took a bite. Tasted amazing. I ate the entire thing and the next pile the girls brought. Myths were that dragons ate only meat. As an Ancient, I knew we were omnivores. Apparently, the deities were herbivores and had taken over my stomach as part of their shenanigans.

"Come. Water." Leaf motioned to me like she would a stubborn horse.

Didn't have to tell me twice. And I could stand and walk now, so that was a plus. The pond wasn't that far and only one tree got knocked down as I waddled to it. I finished off half the pond.

"We need to find where the others are and hide me somewhere until they get here." If I had my regular hands, and pencil and paper, I could write a note and have the girls or constructs take it back to Alric and the rest. As I was now, I had nothing. The amulet trick I'd used to find Alric might work, but I wasn't sure if it was still with me, or completely vanished along with my clothes. I couldn't access it, regardless. It would come back when I changed, but I'd rather find out how they were doing and where they were before I changed back in the morning.

If I changed back.

The fear that Mathilda was wrong and I would be stuck this way kept kicking around the back of my mind. "I need you to send a few faeries to find the others. Send ones you trust. They need to find out what's happening back at the ruins and how our friends are." Communication by faery was dicey but better than nothing. "Tell them we stayed due south. There's a meadow and a pond, but I might have to move if there are people nearby." I hadn't seen or heard any but the faeries had stolen that hay from somewhere. Since they were now popping back and forth again, I was hoping it was somewhere far away.

Garbage yelled for five faeries to come over and she spoke fast in native faery. Part of me wanted her to go with them, but I also felt exposed out here and wanted her to stay. The faeries would more or less listen to me, but she was their leader and could get results faster than I could. I was able to walk, but something told me any attempt at flying right now would end badly. My energy was still too depleted.

Trying to find a larger meadow, I went back into the trees but I couldn't fit between most of them. So, I returned to my pond. Bunky and Irving were on patrol, flying through the trees in a widening circle. Most of the faeries were playing in the water.

"Ale?" Crusty had finally climbed off my head and was looking up at me as she went to pull out her bag.

"No, sweetie. Not now." Being lost in a forest with a bunch of drunken faeries was a horrible idea.

"Other bag?" She leaned forward to whisper but it was loud enough that anyone within a dozen feet of us would have heard it. Luckily, the other faeries were too busy screeching and chasing each other in the water to notice.

"What other bag?" I was pretty sure that Garbage or Leaf carried the bag with the war cats and war puppy, and we didn't need those running around right now. The other faeries should be only carrying more ale.

"Is founded." She reached into the tiny pocket in the front of her overalls and pulled out a black bag. With a huge grin, she reached inside and tugged things out.

"Scrolls? Where did you get these?" It was hard to unroll them with my current hands, but some bored faeries came over and used their bodies to keep them flat. They fell asleep as soon as they took the position of weighing down the edges of the papers. I'd expected to see elven words, maybe Ancient—which I still couldn't read as well as I'd hoped, considering it was my native tongue—but the pages were filled with glyphs. Symbols were used instead of letters.

I blinked as I found I understood the symbols and the words they conveyed. This page was from a diary explaining what happened when the southern continent fell. I pulled back and shook my head. Fell? The battle all those centuries ago had been to keep it from falling— and they'd succeeded, for the most part.

This was written by a man—he didn't say who he was, just that he was the last man in his city. All the others had been destroyed and the city was completely engulfed in flames. The dragons were coming and they were going to destroy everything before continuing to engulf the world.

Dragons. Ancients? Finding out what I inadvertently had done to both my own people and the syclarions had been a horrible shock. But that my people had willfully tried to destroy the world? That I couldn't believe.

The two faeries helping with this page turned it over at my request, then went back to napping. The back of the scroll had a drawing of a large, scaled being. They weren't Ancients. If the drawing was accurate—and this person's art was extremely detailed, so it looked like it was—they were giant constructs made to resemble my people, but clearly were not them. That the pieces were metal and had been soldered together was clear in the drawings. It partially reminded me of the construct dragon head we'd found in the Ancient aqueducts outside of Beccia. Only far nastier looking. This was made to terrify people.

I looked to the next scroll. The same type of writing, but different hand. And appeared to be dealing with crops. The third was almost as exciting, with what looked like a report of a bar brawl that had taken place a few thousand years ago.

"Crusty? Where did you find these?" As I read them, she'd been pulling more out. There were dozens.

"In place." She pointed north. "Way in backs. In box."

Maybe it was exhaustion on my part, but the faeries had never taken to scrolls before. "Can you read them?"

"Noes." Her grin was wide.

"Then why did you take them?" Somewhere in that mess, there might be more about these giant constructs, but I didn't have the focus to wade through them now. Not to mention that the faeries holding the scrolls flat were losing their interest in napping and kept sitting up to look at the pond.

"Told me to." She nodded as if that said everything.

"Who told you to?" I loved my faeries, couldn't imagine life without them, but they could be exasperating at times. Many times.

"The rock." With the flamboyance of a magician revealing their greatest trick, she reached deep into her bag and pulled out a stone.

One that someone had marked with a single word: Taryn.

"There are other people named Taryn. It's not that uncommon of a name."

"Is for you. Feel." She put the rock on the ground and rolled it toward my hand.

I touched it to humor her. And fell back on my haunches as images flooded my mind. All of the images were of me. I wasn't certain how I knew, but they were me. The chimeras had been made by my people to combat the sceanra anam but also to store memories. I still couldn't touch Bunky without a glove because the images of other Ancients would slam into me. This felt the same. I moved away from the stone that wasn't just a stone.

Someone thousands of years ago, most likely before I was born, had wanted me to find these scrolls. Yet they managed to have images of me as a child? I didn't think they were thinking of my using the lists of crops—there must be some important information on many of those scrolls.

The faeries who'd been holding down the scrolls finally scrambled to their feet and ran for the pond.

I watched Crusty. "Did you find anything that isn't a scroll, besides your rock with my name on it?" I needed to go over these scrolls but not out here, nor as I currently was.

Her eyes went wide and she shook her head.

I sighed. "Crusty? If you found something in those ruins, you need to show me."

"Only if from place?"

She was too happy about that.

"Anywhere. If you have anything that is currently in this bag that you found since we left Beccia to come down here, you need to show it to me." I raised my hand. "Except for odd leaves, twigs, or nuts that you might have found." I'd sat through some of her collections before. They were a great sleep aid.

She seemed pleased that I wasn't going after her nature collections, then almost crawled completely into the bag to drag out a collection of large jewels. Eight, to be exact.

"Do *they* say anything?" I didn't want another memory flood; those things were uncomfortable.

"Noes. Pretty." She patted a large green one that wasn't much smaller than her.

I looked closer. They were serious precious gems, professionally cut and removed from settings a long time ago. "Where did you find these?" Whoever they belonged to was probably not happy about them being taken. The last thing we needed was more people after us.

"In bad place. We chase. You call back. These in corner."

The bad place was most likely the fortress we'd broken Alric out of. I seriously doubted they had valuable gems just lying around, though.

"Just sitting there?" If I'd been in my human form, I would have crossed my arms and glared. I had to settle for narrowing my eyes.

She started to nod, then shook her head instead. "In wall. Shiny. I grab. You call, we leave."

"You pried these out of the wall?" I looked closer at the green one without touching it. There was a bit of dust and mortar on the sides. I didn't recall seeing gemstones embedded in the cell they'd had Alric in, but he'd been dying at the time, so I was focused on that. I couldn't figure out why someone would take valuable stones out of their setting and put them in the wall of a cell.

I touched the green stone and felt myself change.

CHAPTER TWENTY

C HANGE WAS A mild word.

I flipped through about a dozen shapes in a matter of a minute. I finally stopped at my human form, held it for thirty seconds, and then crashed back into my antlered modified form. "That wasn't fun." I felt vaguely ill but fought it down. If I was going to recover enough to fly out of here, I couldn't throw up what I'd just eaten.

The rest of the faeries continued to play in the water and didn't notice a thing.

"Stones magic." She grinned, wiggled her fingers, then shoved them back in her bag.

Probably a good idea. The rest of the faeries were ignoring us, but the way she'd hid the stones when she showed them to me said she hadn't told the others about them.

"You should have told me that before." Great. Magic-imbued, valuable gemstones. That my faery stole. At least she took them from people who were already after us, so this didn't increase the number of people chasing us.

"Surprise?" She put the scrolls back in her bag as well, then tucked her bag away, and flashed me her best smile.

"When our friends join us, you have to show them the scrolls and the gems. It could be dangerous for you to keep them." There was no way to know what spells those stones held, but there must have been a reason that they were embedded in a prison cell wall. I gave her my best earnest and concerned look. I wasn't sure how it looked on my current face, but she didn't seem impressed.

"I found." She did a Garbage impersonation, with her lower lip stuck out and arms folded.

"You stole."

Before she could respond, Leaf and two other faeries flew over to us. "Who stole? We steals!"

I closed my eyes and let a breath out slowly. It was better to leave everything with Crusty for now than have the faeries fighting about it. I opened my eyes again. "Nothing. Just talking about her stealing my sleep. I was going to rest."

Crusty played along, twirling in a circle before plopping down to sleep. She was my goofy and often confused faery, but I'd been noticing a change over the past few weeks. She was more aware of things than I thought.

Plus, she probably didn't want anyone taking her pretty stones and for now she got to keep them.

Bunky came flying in, escorting the five faeries we'd just sent out. My guess was they popped out and reappeared there and here to be back this fast. It would be a great skill if it could be counted on.

Garbage flew over from the pond and the faeries circled me. Irving flew by, but then continued his rounds. Bunky gronked once, then went off as well.

"We sees!" Penqow, a black and white faery, jumped up and down. She'd been one of the five and seemed happy even though she was covered in dirt. They were all covered in dirt.

"That's great. Did you tell them what I told you?"

"Did. They say stay."

"No notes?" Of course, if they were on the run and possibly fighting, writing a note to me wouldn't be high on their to-do list.

"Noes."

"Why are you covered in dirt?"

"Flame stick get too close. We dive." She didn't seem upset about herself and the other four almost being shot by a flaming arrow. Even Garbage didn't look concerned.

I was, though. A flaming arrow meant my friends were either fighting or running. While I knew that was likely the case, seeing evidence was worse.

"No other information? Were they running? Being attacked? Injured?"

Penqow threw back her tiny shoulders and nodded. "Noes. Yes. Yes. Noes." The faeries clapped at her recital and she bowed.

The five returning faeries looked longingly at what was left of the pond.

I sighed and waved them on. I trusted that they got to Alric and the others, and as of now, they weren't hurt. But it wasn't as helpful as I hoped.

Without a clue as to how long my friends would be and no idea where they were—or, for that matter, where I was—I looked around for a place to hide. I could try to see if Garbage and the faeries could make me small like they did in the ruins, but that didn't last long and at this point, I didn't want to do anything that might mess up my returning to normal in the morning.

I was mostly dark green so the trees would help hide me. Except that to get far enough into them, I'd have to knock a few over. Which would be noticeable.

My choice was made for me when I heard voices yelling and horses running through the woods across from us. I called the faeries to me. There was no way to call Bunky and Irving back, but I got the girls to come in close as I backed up into trees on the other side of the pond from the yelling.

"Can you pop out?"

Garbage shook her head. "Is no, too many pops."

"Any chance you can make me invisible?" That ability seemed to come and go, but right now would be a great time for it.

"No." She wiggled her fingers. "No ompf now."

I was afraid they had a limit of how much they could do that at a time. "Okay, all of you hide under me." The way I was crouched, there was a gap under me about two inches higher than they were.

Garbage looked ready to fight, but letting them draw attention was going to bring it to me as well. Our best bet at this point was to hide.

"I need you to stay with me. We hide." I might have regained enough energy to fly away. But I couldn't chance that and if I tried and failed, we'd be worse off.

"For yous." Garbage patted my nose, then led her troops to hide underneath me.

I nestled my head in the leaves and mostly shut my eyes. I didn't want them reflecting anything and bringing those riders closer. I hoped whoever was coming our way wouldn't come over to this side; if they got too close, there was no way they'd miss me, even hiding.

I felt some scurrying and a few faeries darted out, threw leaves over me, and then ran back under. Not sure that was going to make a difference at my size, but I appreciated the help.

The horsemen and horsewomen charged through the woods across from us. They looked more like game hunters from some village than people coming to kill me. None were wearing armor and they didn't appear to be the overthrowing-the-world type. But I did have my eyes partially closed, so who knew?

I thought they were going to pass us when they slowed down and started pointing at the ransacked pond. Damn it. It looked like an army of faeries had a water fight—which they had. I had no idea what the riders thought had happened to the pond as they slowly approached the churned-up mud.

Then Bunky and Irving dove out of the sky, gronking and bleating. They buzzed the riders, then took off north.

The riders turned and raced after them.

I didn't want to move yet, but the faeries could get out from under me. They just needed to stay nearby at least until Bunky and Irving came back. "Girls? You can move now." No movement. I rose enough to see that all of them were sound asleep. The familiar dusting on their wings told me what it was. While I'd been watching the human riders, someone had snuck up and dusted the faeries with varlick powder. While they were hiding under me. How in the world could that have happened? I heard a low cough and turned. A pack of feral brownies stood there, grinning. Then a huge bag of powder exploded in my face.

I reared back, or tried to. My limbs were made of jelly and the world spun around me. This could be varlick powder or something else. But it was messing up my ability to focus.

"Wha yous do?" Great, that powder made me speak like the faeries. My tongue felt like it had been covered in heavy rags and tasted about the same. "Powder ick." Wow, I was really not working right.

"You just stay right there. We get a fine bounty for you!" The lead brownie was far scruffier than most of his kind—definitely living in the wild. His clothing was old and worn, and most of his companions had outfits and hats made of grasses and tree bark.

I wondered if they made dollies out of pine needles. A small burst of flame shot out as I tried not to laugh at my own joke. I didn't hit any of the brownies, but I scared them.

They stayed farther back now and didn't look quite as cocky.

"Looks…" I shook my head and gave up trying to

speak. My mind was muddled, my body was numb, and I had a feeling that had been my last flame for a bit. Not to mention the sedative effects of the powder were hitting me, and I'd already needed a nap.

"Shouldn't it be sleeping now? Maybe just reach under and grab the little ones. Make money from them. Leave this one behind."

That must be the second-in-charge brownie as his pine cone hat was taller than the others.

The one in charge lowered his brows and glared. "We need the money from this big one. Now, tie it up." His command did nothing as the rest stood back and watched—unmoving. My flame-laugh had at least slowed the process down. "I'll feed you to the great beast! Now move!"

I had no idea what this beast was, but it was obviously scarier than me as the brownies raced around, tying me up with ropes and vines. Within minutes, I was tied in place, still hunching over the sleeping faeries. And another bag of powder was thrown at my face. If this was going to become a thing, they needed to work on the taste.

I hovered on the edge of falling asleep. I needed to, but I had to watch what these brownies were doing. I might not be able to fight back now, but I might be able to later.

"Attacks!" The yell came a moment before the buzzing sound.

Bunkie and Irving darted into the forest, knocked off a number of brownie hats, then flew off. I knew they could shock the brownies, but like me, they might have to recharge whatever it was they used.

Odd shapes and colors started drifting around the forest as the brownies yelled, the constructs dive-bombed, and the faeries snored. I was almost willing to just pass out. Then a shape appeared that seemed more structured than the rest of the odd hallucinations I was seeing. Still transparent, but tall and…Siabiane? The shape looked like her. But I was also hallucinating. However, if I was going to dream up anyone, it would be Alric.

"Siabiane?" I blinked and tried to focus. If I paid close attention to my mouth, I could speak almost normally.

"Taryn! Oh stars, you did change. And you have spikes and antlers. Probably not a worry now. Where are the others?" She looked around.

I didn't know if anyone else could see her, as I wasn't completely sure I was seeing her. Turns out, the brownies could see her.

"A ghost! Run!" They threw things at her visage, which, of course, passed right through her, which led to more running and yelling from the brownies.

"Not here. Hit us with varlick powder…I think." Those words took so much out of me, I felt ready to fall over. If I wasn't already sitting down.

Siabiane's form expanded in size, and she towered over the brownies. "Who do you think you are?" Her voice was deeper than normal, and she shook her arms.

That did it. The brownies tore off in multiple directions, running into trees along the way. Within a few moments, they were gone.

She shrunk and smiled. "That was fun. I've forgotten… how it is out there." Even transparent, it was easy to see the sorrow on her face.

"You've been gone less than a month." She looked the same, aside from the transparent part, but she was acting as if it had been years.

"Only that long? Seems so much longer. When the others find you, tell them you all must go back to the north. Lorcan and I are lost, and so is the southern continent. No one can stop the fall." She looked to her left. "I had more to say, but they are here." She nodded and vanished.

Unfortunately, my alertness had been tied to focusing on her; once she was gone, I started fading out.

Bunky and Irving came back and buzzed around me. Neither had hands so I couldn't have them undo the ties nor grab the faeries.

"Get water." I tried to point to the pond. "Water all of us." If it had been varlick powder that had been used, washing it off would work. If it wasn't, it couldn't hurt.

Bunky and Irving nodded, then took off. I fought to stay awake but it just didn't happen.

CHAPTER TWENTY-ONE

M Y DREAMS WERE wild. Huge brownies stomping around a color-filled land, chewing on trees.
Fish swimming through the air, and faeries living in the
ocean. And something was pulling me.

It took a while but then I heard Alric's voice. "Taryn?
Are you okay? Get some more water on her."

"We's helps!"

Garbage's voice was right next to my ear. At least the
faeries were okay. My eyelids were too heavy to open
and see.

A cooling splash of water dumped over me, and I
cracked my eyes open. Now that I could feel my body, I
could tell I was still in my gigantic form. But it was night,
so there was hope I just hadn't changed yet because it
wasn't dawn. Or I'd been stuck here unconscious for days
and was never going to change. Even I gave myself an eye
roll at that. I was still tied up, though.

"Alric?" My voice sounded rusty.

"Thank the stars. We couldn't wake you. The faeries
woke up an hour ago."

I looked past him and saw a small fire with Grillion
standing by. The others were working on the vines still
covering my body.

"I think those brownies gave me a double dose."

Welsy and Delsy popped around from where they were

chopping at a vine. "Some of our kind did this?" Granted, they were constructed brownies, not biological ones. But even though they disagreed with most of the biological brownies they'd met so far, they still considered themselves true brownies.

"A bunch of your kind. Feral, living on the land. They were going to sell me and the faeries to someone, but Siabiane scared them off."

Mathilda stopped magically dumping water on me and turned my way. "You saw Siabiane? She's here? With the brownies?"

"Unless it was a hallucination, she sent a visage right before I passed out. The feral brownies could see her, too, and ran off." I paused. "She wants us to turn around and said she and Lorcan are lost. Also that the entire south is lost. It looked like her, but I was seeing a lot of strange things thanks to that dust."

Mathilda scowled. "That is *not* my sister."

"No, but our enemy has been using Jhea spells a lot," Padraig said. "It's a good way to keep powerful magic users from finding a way out. Let's face it, keeping Siabiane, Lorcan, or Alric caged would take a lot of magic. But if you take out their hope for escape, make them believe all is lost? They don't even try."

"When we find them, I get to hurt the people holding them." Mathilda folded her arms. "But I am glad she showed herself and was able to help."

"We would like to hurt the ones holding her as well," Welsy and Delsy said. "And find these feral brownies and have a discussion with them. A most stern one."

I stared at the fire for a few seconds, then shook my head. "Wait. There was a hunting party near here. They might come back."

Alric cut through a vine, then swore as it grew back almost as quickly as he cut it. "We already met them. We explained we were magic users on a seeing voyage. They left quickly."

Seeing voyages were trips into the wild and often involved hallucinogens. Which, combined with magic users, could have some nasty results for outsiders. It was good thinking on his part and would make the hunters sure to stay far from us.

I knew my friends were talented, strong, and had a lot of magic. "Why are the vines taking so long? Not that I don't appreciate the wash-off and all, but I really want to move."

Foxy called out from somewhere behind me. "Sticker weed vines. They are beasties. My Amara could get rid of them with ease but it's slow going for the rest of us."

"And they're spelled against magic," Covey added. "Your brownie friends might be living off the land but they have someone behind them with power."

"I wonder...everyone stand back." I waited until I heard them say all clear, then I stretched. I was stronger now and my friends had weakened the vines. Sticker weed vines were nasty things and extremely hard to remove as they could grow back together almost as fast as they were cut. But if I shattered them? I fought the bindings to get to my feet, stretched my back, legs, wings, and then I stomped.

I was feeling better, apparently, as the ground shook and Grillion almost fell over. Our horses glared my way from their area but didn't run.

"Sorry." I shook myself to get the last broken pieces off. No longer connected, the vine pieces turned brown. "Look at that."

Padraig bent down to pick up a piece. "That's a unique way to stop them, but I've never seen them turn brown like that. Whoever spelled them didn't do a great job."

"Those brownies couldn't have spelled anything, even badly. There's still got to be someone behind this." I thought back to my encounter. "They seemed more opportunistic than actually looking for me specifically, though."

"They were not adhering to the brownie code. We must speak to them." Welsy and Delsy looked more likely to go smash heads than speak, but whatever worked.

"You have a code?" I'd never heard of one. But my encounters had been limited and often confrontational.

"We do now." Welsy beamed.

"We created it." Delsy looked proud enough to burst. "Once we get Siabiane back, we will spread the word."

That had a faint religious doctrine tone to it, but on the whole, brownies were disliked because they tended to be violent, greedy, and self-serving. Maybe this would help change that.

I'd have to warn Siabiane once we freed her.

"It looks like everyone made it out of the ruins intact? The faeries I sent said they had a flaming arrow shot at them?" The faeries were now sitting by the fire with a few bottles of ale. We were still in danger, but that was probably going to be the case all of the way down, and they'd worked hard today. They had earned some downtime.

"Yes, although we almost lost Grillion," Alric said. "He'd gone out to find Foxy after you left, but Foxy came back on his own. Grillion was about to be attacked by two of the knights when Covey grabbed him and pulled him to safety."

"I would have noticed them." Grillion seemed a bit put out, but he gave a sincere smile to Covey.

She just shook her head.

"What were knights doing out here? Shouldn't they be jousting around a city somewhere?" Alric and Padraig were technically elven knights, but I'd only seen them in armor once. The day Alric died. If I had my say, he'd never wear that stuff again.

"Knights do ride patrols, you know," Padraig said. "But

these were far from any city that we know. They didn't seem to want to chat, however."

"We outran them." Covey brought over a pile of assorted food for me. "They probably could have kept following but they turned around at a wall. It was nothing more than ruins and wouldn't hinder them, but they spun back as soon as we passed it."

I looked at her carefully not looking at me. "If you outran them, how did you see where they turned back?"

Everyone looked to Covey at my question, even the faeries.

"Two of the faeries with us got knocked out of the air with an arrow, not a flaming one, but they were both down. I was riding in the rear so I went back for them."

"Without telling any of us, by the way." Padraig was trying to look stern but couldn't hold it.

"I sent my horse to follow you." She shrugged. "The faeries were stunned in the road, and I know they're tough, but still, warhorses with armored knights are heavy. I darted out, grabbed the faeries, then went back into the trees. I was just past the wall. The knights slowed down and at first, I thought they'd seen me. Then they stopped, turned around, and rode back. It was odd."

"Next time, please let us know." Mathilda added more food to the pile in front of me.

I hoped it displaced itself when I changed back.

"It's a good thing you're a fast runner. We were ready to charge back for your rescue."

"To nice lady! Save our friends!" the faeries yelled, and blew kisses at Covey.

She looked a little awkward but waved back. Far cry from two years ago when she could barely tolerate them. Now she was risking life and limb to save two of them.

I kept my grin to myself. "Oh! Before I forget, we were attacked by a pack of sceanra anam who came from the west, and some murlin birds with spell crystals—not unlike the ones those squirrels had." It was hard to eat daintily as I was, but I tried. In between bites, I told them of the attacks, the chimeras, and my antlers.

"That's fascinating. So many details of the lost deities had vanished over the centuries." Mathilda peered as closely as she politely could at my antlers. "Too bad this will be gone in a few hours." She quickly pulled back. "From a scientific angle, of course. I wouldn't want you to have to keep going around like that. But it would be so helpful for researchers."

I narrowed my eyes but I understood. If it hadn't been my situation, and if I were someone who studied the deities as opposed to relics, I would feel the same. "And there's more." I wouldn't make Crusty take the items out, we were still very exposed here, but I wanted the others to know. Everyone was sitting around the fire as I explained about Crusty's finds. I made it sound like she was collecting the items at my request so that Garbage didn't give her too bad of a time if she heard. But the faeries were working on ale bottle diving, so they didn't even notice what we were talking about.

There was a lot of muttering and discussion after that. Clearly, everyone except Foxy, who had no interest, wanted to see those scrolls but agreed on waiting until we had a more secure location. Grillion was more interested in the jewels.

"She got them where Alric was held? What were they there for?" He leaned closer to me.

"That's a darn good question. Alric? Did you notice them? The only one I touched changed me a dozen times—and not gently. She said they're all magic."

Alric shrugged and threw another stick on the fire. It wasn't cold but it felt nice to have the cheery flames. "I hadn't been in that room for long—at least not from what I could tell. But when done right, spelling gemstones can be extremely powerful. It can also blow up spectacularly and the best ones are done with expensive stones. Most people who own them won't give them up."

"Maybe we should check, just to make certain..." Grillion let his words drop as everyone looked at him. "Or not. They're safest where they are." He grinned extensively at everyone, including the constructs.

Padraig watched him for a few moments, then shook his head. "I think we'll want to get on the road quickly after dawn. I want to get as far as we can from those knights. They might have turned back, but we can't be sure that they don't cover a southern route as well. It might just be this part of the road that they don't cross into. I didn't recognize the banner they flew."

"I did. Sacrit. It's a small principality to the east." Mathilda managed to make the word sound like a swear word. "When Siabiane and I came north, they were many weeks' ride from here. They must have spread out, but I didn't see anywhere near here that looked like it had a large population. They were not nice people back in the day, but that was a long time ago. They were marginally enforcers for the empress at the time." Her voice indicated that she doubted they'd changed.

"Could just be defending their border territories," Alric said. He brought over my bedroll, then looked around after comparing it to my current size.

It might make a nice pillow.

"I'm fine with just the ground. My skin isn't bothered by pine needles, rocks, or small animals. I'll just stay here. But I can take a watch shift." I gave a huge yawn right after I spoke.

"I think you probably need to sleep." Alric came to the same conclusion I had about the bedroll and did make it into a pillow instead. "You're not used to flying or fighting in the air." He then set up his bedroll next to me.

I was touched. But also concerned. "You know I roll about in my sleep. I'd be extremely upset if I squished you right after rescuing you."

He kissed me on the cheek but didn't move his bedroll. "I won't let that happen. Now sleep."

I had been serious about taking a watch shift and planned for just a few moments of shut-eye.

My body had other plans. I woke up to a warm body draped over me and snuggling me close.

My eyes flew open, and I looked to see Alric next to me. As in a normal-sized me. I rolled onto my back and stretched. The size, flying, and other weird talents had been great, but I couldn't express how glad I was to be in my human form again. I was still getting used to my dragon form and being locked into that odd version of it hadn't been fun.

"You yous!" Leaf flew down onto my chest and beamed as if it had all been her doing.

"I am."

Alric stirred next to me. "I felt you change and you sang a song as you did. A sad song, but beautiful."

I rolled onto my side to face him. "I don't sing, aside from that lullaby, which is more of a chant with humming. I have a horrible singing voice. Were you helping the faeries with their ale?"

Mathilda and Grillion were stirring in their bedrolls but not sitting up yet.

Padraig had been on watch and was looking off toward the pond, but turned at my comment. "I heard it too. Short, just a snippet, but you sang an elven song of farewell."

"That was it. I knew it sounded familiar. Haven't heard it in ages." Alric stretched.

Foxy had been missing but came back into our camp. "I went back north a bit. Didn't see any signs of anyone."

Covey came jogging up. "Nothing to the south either. I think we need to get moving, though."

Alric gave me a quick kiss and got out of his bedroll.

"Your pack is next to you. Let's eat and be off."

I inhaled Mathilda's breakfast, drank about an entire pot of tea, and said hello to my horse. The faeries were flying around, playing games with Bunky and Irving.

Welsy and Delsy came back into camp and both looked vaguely disappointed. "We scouted for the feral brownies you encountered."

"Alas, they have fled the area."

"Ah. Good of you to look, though. They were quite disturbed by Siabiane." I hoped that meant my new friends wouldn't follow us south. With everyone together, the brownies wouldn't be a serious threat, but they could be a nuisance and cause problems if we were under attack from a serious threat.

"Are you sure you're all right?" Alric steadied me as I tipped a bit to the left.

I shook my shoulders out and held my head up high. "I'm fine. Just a wobble." Then I almost fell over. "Or not." I'd felt okay when I got up, but to be honest, I had only gone to my horse and was focused on being me again. Now I was thinking of walking on two feet instead of four and my mind got confused. I looked to Mathilda and Padraig. "Could this be from the powder they gave me? I feel off."

Both came over, sat me down on a boulder, and looked into my eyes. Then shook their heads.

"There's no spell residue." Padraig stood back.

"Could be from that change you went through." Mathilda shook her head. "We've nothing to base anything on since as far as I know you're one of a kind."

"Or it could be from her flying around in dragon-with-extra-parts form for twenty-four hours and having had odd portions of that for a while before," Covey said from behind them both. "Trust me, it takes time to get adjusted to adaptations in your body if you're not used to them." Covey had some serious issues when she first started switching into her berserker mode. She'd even tried running away to a convent for a while to make the urge go away. Came back more in tune with herself, with a fondness for meditation, and an appreciation for what she could turn into.

Maybe when we got back, I should try that.

"She might be right. When in doubt, look for the simplest answer." Mathilda smiled. "But tell us if it develops into anything else."

I nodded and slowly got back to my feet. The rest loaded their horses, but Alric had already packed his and mine.

Covey finished adjusting hers and came back. "If you need to talk about the transforming business, come to me."

Two faeries that I didn't recognize came flying up, a lavender and green one and a bright-pink one. They flittered around behind her.

"Thanks. Um, you have some friends?" I noticed that they both had on overalls—the way to tell the difference between Garbage's expanding crew and the wild faeries was whether they wore leaves or overalls. The clothing on these two looked new, so possibly recent converts. Still no clue where the overalls and flower petal hats came from, but Garbage kept clothing them.

Covey sighed but didn't even look back. "Yes, Middle Leaf and Gopher Rocks. The two I saved. They've more or less joined your pack, but have told me that they will now watch over me for saving them. Can Garbage order them to relax a bit? They are following me *everywhere*."

I fought to keep from laughing as the faeries in question started playing with Covey's short hair. "I can ask her, but most likely you're stuck until their attention span fades off. Usually, it's not that long." I'd had my faeries swear to guard me with their lives forever and forget about it a day later. They meant it when they pledged, but there were a lot of things going on in those tiny heads, and intentions and promises sometimes got pushed out.

"It's going to be a long couple of weeks." She reached out to help me as I got on my horse.

"You'll be fine. Harlan would be proud of you for risking your life to save them." Harlan might not know these faeries in particular, even their names weren't familiar to me, but he adored all of the faeries.

She nodded. "I hope that old cat is staying out of trouble. I agree this trip would have been too hard on him, and he hates water and ships, but I find myself missing him."

"Me too." I looked around for Foxy, but he was discussing something with Grillion and Alric. I'd ask if there were any updates from Amara about Beccia when we got back on the road. I trusted that he would have said something if anything bad happened, but I'd like news anyway. I hadn't liked Orenda's brother when I first met him. In my mind, the sooner he got out of Beccia the better.

We headed out and I pretended not to notice how I was strategically placed in the middle of our line with Alric behind me and Covey in front. Always guard your weakest piece. And even though Alric had recently almost died, I was their worry.

I'd protest if I felt better.

When we'd been on the water, my focus had been on not being horribly sick and worrying about Alric. Once we got him back, there was the entire changing issue. But now I could look forward to our long, boring trip south. The southern continent was longer and wider than the northern, and I'd never seen all of that one even though I lived there. Now we got to see way more than we wanted to of the south.

"I know we bypassed the checking of our papers coming into the south by our unusual entry, but from what it sounded like, they were preparing for an attack from the north?" I tossed my question out in general, but Grillion was the only one who'd been down here recently. Or in most of our cases, at all.

Alric coughed. "I'd like to know that too, Grillion."

"What? Yes. Well, you're going a different route right now than we did when we went north. We were farther to the west. But this way is fine. Although…" He broke off, muttering to himself until Padraig, who rode ahead of him, turned and glared. "Sorry. I was just thinking about those knights. Did anyone notice if they had a pair of stars, good-sized ones, up near the neck of their armor? I didn't get a good look."

Covey snorted at that, but I saw her nod. "I had an excellent look. Yes, the ones I saw did have those marks, one dark and one light. But don't the military have things like that?" Beccia had no military, and her people, the trellians, were recovered berserkers—also no military.

"Those weren't military; those are directly from the empress," Grillion said. "Dang, they moved fast if they were carrying Sacrit banners. They have control of the entire strip of land along the channel—or most of it. They're the ones behind the travel bans, too."

Before he could continue the discussion, and figure out how screwed we might be with those knights behind us, a swirling tunnel appeared in front of us. Or rather, me. My friends riding in front of me scattered as it appeared but my legs wouldn't nudge my horse, and she froze. The world slowed down as my faeries tried to fly to me, my friends turned to me, I heard Alric yelling my name behind me, and I found myself facing Theria, the troll necromancer we'd fought in the elven enclave, as he rode through the tunnel right for me.

CHAPTER TWENTY-TWO

THERIA WAS STILL just as big and nasty as he'd been when we last saw him up north. A troll necromancer was almost so rare as to be unheard of. Grillion had come north with a letter from Qianru for me with two people he believed were just normal guys, but who turned out to actually be thug followers of the Dark who had secret instructions to free a changeling and Theria from the Beccian jail.

Lucky us, we now got to run into him again.

The tunnels, chawsia paths, he was using took massive amounts of magic and were tricky to maintain. We'd used a small version to get from Beccia to the elven enclave and back, but Theria had destroyed things and murdered people to get his to the far south when he'd fled the elven enclave. Who knew what he did to create this one.

"Taryn!" Time snapped back into place as Alric yelled my name, charged his horse forward, jumped off it, and rolled us both off to the side of the trail. Both our horses took off running to safety.

Theria kept charging forward, riding one of the armored licten beasts—massive, thick-skinned animals with short, sturdy legs and strong enough to plow through a horse. When trolls did go to battle, these things were their rides. They also were found almost exclusively in the extreme northern tundra—except now that Theria had somehow brought some to the south.

Alric leaped to his feet and had his sword raised before I even got off the ground. Theria was still charging for us, and Padraig and Mathilda were trying to do something to the tunnel—close it, hopefully; there were more dark shapes in it coming our way.

I scrambled to my feet; fear was a great motivator. But my off-again, on-again sword wasn't playing and hadn't appeared. I still had my weird and cranky dagger, though. Hopefully, he hated evil troll necromancers as much as he hated evil grimarians.

Theria veered around Alric to try to get me, but Alric sliced Theria's leg with his sword as he passed and threw a spell at the licten beast. Its back legs collapsed as they were stunned, and it dumped Theria to the ground as it rolled over. The animal didn't look happy, but would likely recover. It wasn't its fault an evil troll used it for a ride.

Theria was far more limber than the average troll and quickly got to his feet. He didn't even look down at the blood pooling at his feet, and it wasn't slowing him down. He had a nasty long sword and was muttering a spell under his breath.

Foxy roared and tackled him from the side, with Grillion and Covey right behind him. They were trying to keep him down, which was their best hope of defeating him. But as good as they were, I knew Theria was stronger.

The faeries swarmed the licten beast, then Garbage patted it on its head. I think I heard it purr. It seemed content to stay on its side.

Alric joined in on the fight against Theria, but Theria threw Covey and Grillion high in the air and even Foxy got knocked out. I couldn't run, but I could move closer so my dagger could reach him.

Alric and Theria locked swords, and both were muttering spell words.

Damn, too bad I didn't have flame abilities anymore. I was close enough for my dagger, and he went to town sending green arcs into Theria. He twitched but wasn't going down.

Theria kicked Alric closer to the still open tunnel and turned to me. Holding my dagger as high as I could, I added my push spell. And focused all of the anger and fear I'd felt in the past few days into it. My record for the push spell had been sending my very late and extremely unlamented ex-boyfriend, Glorindal, thirty feet or more underground. This time I made a three-foot-deep trench with Theria and slammed him up against a tree a few dozen feet away. I didn't think I'd killed him—trolls were extremely difficult to kill—but he was done for now and didn't get up.

Padraig and Mathilda were still fighting the tunnel, but it appeared to be pulling back on its self. And sucking me along with it. Alric grabbed me, but we were both pulled in. The good thing was that the dark shapes I'd seen in it before were gone; the bad thing was we couldn't stop what it was doing. All of our horses except for Padraig's and Mathilda's came running into the tunnel with us, with Welsy and Delsy riding the first two and calling the rest to follow. Bunky and Irving herded the horses from the back. Mathilda was on her horse still but lifted Foxy, Grillion, and Covey into the air with a spell and brought them into the tunnel as well. The faeries swarmed inside, bouncing along the waves that created a chawsia path. Then Padraig rode his horse in and pulled the tunnel closed behind us. The chawsia paths still took time to travel, just not as long as walking or riding the distance would. Or should. The entire tunnel spun around us too fast to see more than a blur once our end closed and we were flung out the other end. Somewhere far from where we started.

Alric and I had come in first so we landed first. Either that was a badly made chawsia path, or being taken over by Mathilda and Padraig had messed it up. It still sat there but was whirling faster and making odd keening sounds. Alric was still holding me and quickly got us to the side as everyone else came out. No one except for the flyers and the horses came out okay; everyone else was beat up or exhausted from heavy spell use.

"Stand clear!" Padraig yelled as he helped move our unconscious friends off the trail. The tunnel whooshed out a mass of air, knocking down a few trees in the process, then fell in on itself and vanished.

"What…What just happened?" Covey asked as she regained consciousness and looked around. She and Foxy were near me, and both were groaning but looked okay.

I helped Covey up and together we got Foxy up. Mathilda pulled Grillion up as well. No one looked great, but we were alive and that necromancer was hopefully trapped up north for a while.

"Was fun!" Crusty and a bunch of faeries came zipping over. "Do agains!"

"No. Hopefully never again." I shuddered. That had been too close. I turned to Mathilda and Padraig. "Why did you all come through, though? We have no idea where we are or if Theria can follow us."

Mathilda and Padraig had the annoyed parents' look. She wagged a finger at me. "We're not separating again. It grabbed you; Alric followed—so did we. We need to stick together down here, no matter what happens."

"Where are we?" Grillion rubbed his head.

The trees were more spread out here, but massive. They were larger than even the Gapen trees back home but had odd bulbous bodies and their roots were below ground more than the Gapens. The grass was long and wispy, but the horses loved it.

"I'd say farther south?" Like Grillion, Covey was rubbing her head. Unlike Grillion, she looked like she was ready to find a way to get back where we had been and have another try at beating up Theria.

"Mathilda? I'm thinking this doesn't look familiar to Grillion. Do you recognize it?" Padraig rode closer to the nearest tree.

Grillion just wandered around, shaking his head.

"I'm not sure." She also walked around but appeared to be looking for something specific in the grass. Small yellow and orange flowers were hidden among the long grasses. She lifted a strand of them. "This is good and not good. These are fox blossoms and only grow near the far south." She turned to me. "You said your former patron, Qianru, lives in Notlianda? I'd say we're only a few days' ride from there." She glared at the flowers, but I doubted it was their fault.

"We were only in that tunnel for a few minutes." Alric sounded shaken also. "How much power does Theria and whoever he's working for have if they can create a chawsia path that powerful and that fast?"

"The better question is how many people did they kill to do it," Padraig said as he came back. "And where did they start from? That tunnel kicked us out before it terminated and collapsed on its own, and hopefully, there's no way for Theria to find out where it dumped us. But I still think getting away from here is a good idea."

We made certain all of the horses were fine, then got on. Padraig had his map of the south, so after a brief consult with Mathilda and Grillion, he started leading us to the right. Or west, if we were still facing south. I had to say, I missed my brief ability to immediately determine direction.

I'd glanced at the map and wished I hadn't. If where he'd marked as our current location was accurate, we'd traveled three weeks' worth of riding in a matter of seconds. What was worse was knowing how a necromancer got that power.

Foxy was walking and leading his horse again and kept near me. He'd recovered from being knocked out by Theria but was oddly subdued.

"What's wrong?" Our line had spread out a bit since for now we were crossing a plain. But Covey and Alric were still near me. Foxy seemed to be alongside me because he wanted to, not that he felt I might come under attack.

"I'm not used to losing a fight. And I'm feeling sorrow at being this much farther from Amara. I figured it would take time so I'd get used to being away." He waved one giant hand around us. "This happened too fast."

"But at least we're not near Theria anymore." I kept the "for now" in my head. I didn't know enough about chawsia paths to know why that one broke down so quickly. But I had a bad feeling that if Theria found us once, he could find us again.

Foxy nodded and went back to his thoughts. He had a point about fighting; before the relics came into play, he didn't have to fight for his life, just to toss annoying drunks out of the Shimmering Dewdrop. And he never lost. Now the stakes were higher and he was dealing with that, too. I left him alone; if he wanted to talk, he would.

Covey's two faery friends were buzzing around her, trying to put the little yellow and orange flowers on her head. With almost no hair, it wasn't an easy task. Finally, they recruited friends and made a tiny crown of the flowers, then dropped it on her head. "Queen Covey!" They flew around her, singing.

I'd had faeries in my life for over fifteen years and they'd used my name once, maybe twice. They didn't use anyone else's either. "They must really like you."

Covey slightly turned, rolled her eyes up at the crown, but didn't remove it. "I told them that they had to use my name or go away. They did it."

I grumbled under my breath. I should have thought

of that when I first got my three. There was no way to enforce that at this point. But at least it showed that they could do names beyond "nice lady" if they needed to.

Grillion rode up to us from where he'd drifted toward the back with a bunch of faeries. "There's a group of riders coming this way. We outrun them?"

The horses seemed rested—we'd only been riding for a short bit—but Padraig looked back and shook his head. "They aren't heavily armed. I don't want to keep running and hiding if we don't have to. Plus, I'd like to get a feeling for the area. Probably should have come up with a cover before, but for now, just go along with what I say." He turned about so that we were all facing the approaching horses. He was smiling and appeared relaxed, but his sword was still in place at his side and he had his hand on the hilt. "The constructs and faeries might do best to stay out of sight, though."

The faeries made a low swoop, then they and the four constructs seemingly vanished.

"How did they do that?" I knew the faeries could pop out sometimes but to take the constructs with them?

Mathilda smiled. "They're off to our left about a hundred yards. I've got a spell on them that they need to hold still for." They must have stopped moving because she nodded. "Better. I can't hold this long, so let's not chat."

Alric's sword hadn't vanished yet, and he was likewise resting his hand on the hilt. My sword still hadn't popped up, which could be good or bad since it had already ditched me during Theria's attack. Obviously, it was back to being stubborn and obtuse.

Everyone else stayed behind Padraig and looked relaxed. Forcibly, in the case of Covey; she needed to vent some frustration soon and it showed on her face. I almost felt sorry for the first person to cause us trouble.

"Hello!" The group stopped a few lengths away from us. Fifteen or so, all dressed in dark greens and browns.

The one who called out to us was a tall human woman, but there were a few elves of both genders in her group. They looked like hunters, but disguises would be easy.

I looked forward to the day when my first thought at meeting new people was no longer wondering how they were going to kill me.

Padraig nodded as they rode closer. "Hello. We're travelers from the north, on our way to the village of Solts for some work."

I kept my face neutral. Good thinking about changing our destination. Hopefully, there was something a group like us could do in that village to not make it seem weird.

"Aye. Thought you didn't look to be from here." She rode forward with a smile. "And well-armed too. The north is still bad? Are you refugees?"

Padraig shrugged. "Just adventurers looking for a new way of life. It's been a long road, though, and we've not been staying in towns. A rest would be good." That hadn't been our plan, but something about the group led to Padraig changing things.

"Didn't come through the Nerlin Pass then. The fighting has been horrible. Supposedly attackers from the northern continent are invading."

"I came up the pass a few weeks ago. It was fine then." Grillion spoke without thinking but Padraig didn't look concerned at his involvement.

"It's not now. Completely closed. Supposedly a rockslide, but I say magic was involved." She looked us over. "Three elves, two humans, a trellian, and a ..." She paused, tilted her head, and studied Foxy. "Troll-faril-gots breed? An unusual grouping."

I looked to Foxy as he smiled. In all the years I'd known him, I never knew what his heritage was. Always seemed impolite to ask. Farils and gots were both uncommon in our kingdom; I'd heard of both but never seen one. But now that she called it, I could see it. The long floppy ears were a trademark of gots but they were far shorter in stature than him and extremely solitary.

"We're just a band of adventurers who have found work due to our unique abilities," Padraig said. "I am Elfren. Pleased I am to meet you." He gave an elaborate bow. Tricky from the back of a horse, but he made it look graceful.

"Larisona. I am likewise pleased to meet you. We're rangers and ride the lands outside of a group of villages, providing protection. I can recommend a good pub and inn in the village of Hassi."

"That might be what we need. We are tired." Padraig smiled.

None of us were that tired, and if the hunters looked at our horses, they'd note they weren't either. Then I looked down at my mare. She was now covered in trail dust and the other horses had mud on their legs.

Mathilda's smile told me that was her trick. Either she knew why Padraig was changing plans or she was just going along for now.

"Excellent. As it happens, we were changing the guards, so to speak. I and half of my people were going back into the village. Rollen and the rest will continue the circuit. We can ride in with you. It's less than half an hour, but you would have missed it had you kept going in your current direction."

A chill went up my back at that, but there was no indication that she or her people were anything other than what they said they were. I knew we'd planned on riding at least a few hours today so this change in plans made me wonder what Padraig had seen or noticed that I hadn't.

CHAPTER TWENTY-THREE

———◆———

THE RIDE TO the village was quiet. Padraig rode
up front next to Larisona, and the rest of her people rode behind us. I kept my hand on my dagger and
noticed that the others were similarly prepared. It was
hard to appear relaxed and yet be ready to fight to the
death if needed. Especially when I wasn't sure why we
were taking this detour.

Foxy continued walking his horse next to mine. He'd
seemed surprised when Larisona guessed his heritage but
not upset. Something else was bothering him, though.

"Are you okay?" I kept my voice low. I wasn't sure how
much we were hiding from Larisona and her people, but
Padraig's fake name gave a clue to be cautious. None of
us had terribly uncommon names, but if someone was
looking for all of us in a group, not giving our real names
was probably a good idea.

"Something is tickling my thoughts about the leaves
they wear on their shoulders. But I can't fix on what it
is."

I hadn't even noticed leaves, so I had to pretend to
adjust something on the back of my saddle to take a peek.
Small tree leaves adorned the left shoulder of the two I
could get a look at. They weren't real but looked like
extremely detailed metalwork. I turned back. "Maybe it's
a club of some sort? Maybe these rangers wear those to

identify themselves?"

"Aye, could be the right of it. But there's something specific about them. Something just past my thinking." He nodded to himself. "I'll sort it out eventually."

When I'd glanced back, I also looked for any signs of the faeries or the constructs. I knew that magically hiding anything was hard and far worse if they moved. Those spells were on my to-be-learned-at-a-much-later-date list. I couldn't recall having mastered the spells in my prior life either. But we were moving, and I didn't see any of the faeries or constructs. Nor heard them. I knew all of the constructs could be silent—I doubted the faeries' ability to do so. Which probably meant they'd taken off as soon as we all left the area.

The trail to the village was wide and well used, most often by carts if the ruts were any indication. The trees grew denser here, a patch of oak forest on a plain, but it was nice, if odd.

Foxy started muttering as we passed under the trees. "That's what they are. Alitian oaks. Don't grow this far south normally. Same as Amara's tree."

"That could be good, though, right?" My voice had risen a bit, so I smiled at the closest ranger and dropped it. "I mean, her tree is good. So these should be good?"

His scowl deepened. "Aye. But her original tree was destroyed. And she came from down here somewhere. Keep a hand on that dagger and a wary eye around us."

I nodded and looked around. The trees seemed happy if they could be seen as such. They were healthy, that was certain. As we passed under them, I got a better look at their leaves. Yup, Foxy had spotted it. The decorative leaves worn by the rangers were these. Which supported the idea that they wore them as identification. This was a noticeable forest because of those trees and a good way to identify locals.

Then why was Foxy still scowling about? Nothing

could ever be simple, but I didn't want to ask him where I might be overheard.

The village itself was rustic and had a nice distance between the houses. Rather, homes were built around the trees in such a way that it was clear the forest was here first and that unlike in most areas, no clearing had been done to put the village in. They worked the buildings around the trees.

To me, that sounded hopeful. Good trees; people protected the trees; hopefully, they were good people? Or just evil people with a love of oaks. I sighed and leaned back as we rode through the village. A few locals looked up but didn't seem concerned. Probably because of the ranger escort we had. All in all, it looked like a smaller, more rustic version of Beccia, with far more trees and far fewer pubs.

Larisona led us to a large building with a sign of the Ox and Cow. If this was their only pub and inn, which it appeared to be, at least it was huge. Three stories high and twice as wide as the Shimmering Dewdrop. She stopped and gestured with her right hand. We were surrounded by the original group of rangers, as well as more who must have been following us as we rode in. They'd filled in slowly and I hadn't noticed them.

"I wouldn't be reaching for your weapons or magic, my friends. But I would be talking quickly and explaining where the tiny demons who follow you came from." Larisona motioned again and more of her people came up from behind. They had us well surrounded and if we had to fight our way out, things would get ugly. "I have a spell breaker, although I don't have magic, and it showed you hiding them. Speak quickly."

Padraig looked at the crowd around us and slowly removed his hand from the hilt of his sword. "We mean you no harm and asked our friends to stay hidden so as not to frighten you. They aren't evil nor are they demons."

"They are demons! Small, flying dangers to us all!" an elven ranger yelled and looked ready to attack us until Larisona glared him down.

"We do not follow the dangerous ways of the north, nor will we allow you to bring them down here. There is more than one way to invade a land, and using a kind voice and handsome face is not uncommon." Larisona was upset but rational.

The people around us were becoming less so.

"Foxy, you're certain these are the same type of trees as Amara's?" I didn't move and kept my voice low.

Foxy had excellent hearing. "Aye."

I reached my hand up my sleeve and touched the vine mark. "Amara, look through my eyes." I looked at the trees around us and the closing-in crowd of rangers.

It was a long shot. I couldn't tell her what to do, nor explain our situation. Hopefully, she'd figure it out.

"What are you doing to my friends?" Her voice came out loud and strong in the air in front of me. Which caused the rangers to raise their swords and move closer.

"The trees?" I looked up to the trees again. She'd worked with other plants before she lost her goddess-hood, but if there was any connection between her tree and these? Maybe she could do something. These people had a connection with the trees, and they were ready to tear us apart right now.

I felt a flood of unnamed emotions crash through me and all of the oak trees around us started swaying. Arcs of green light, far less aggressive than the ones my dagger made, bounced between each tree.

"Let them go!"

This sounded like it came from the oaks, but I recognized Amara's voice. She might not be a goddess anymore but she was still a powerful dryad.

Even Larisona turned pale as the words and movement continued. "Who are you? The goddesses are gone. Only they could give the trees such movement. Show your-self!"

Amara didn't appear, but the faeries all flew in with Bunky and Irving. Welsy and Delsy came scurrying in as well.

"I was the last tree goddess. My tree was murdered and the remains won't let anything grow. These beings are all dear to me." Amara's voice settled and now appeared to be coming from in front of Foxy. The tears in his eyes were balanced by his smile.

"I...I apologize. We didn't know." Larisona dropped off her horse and looked ready to kneel.

"I am beyond worshipping now. But I admire the grove you have made and offer what blessing I once held. Treat my friends well. Protect them as you would my memory."

There was always an odd popping feeling when contact cut and I felt it now.

The elf ranger who'd wanted to destroy the faeries was seriously conflicted. They were keeping high in the air, but seeing them flittering about had him reaching for a bow.

A sword appeared at his throat. He'd been closest to Alric, but Alric had moved so smoothly even I hadn't seen it. "I'd not be doing that. Those faeries are watched over by a goddess—one who saved my life."

Larisona regained her composure. "They are welcome here. No one will harm any of the beings blessed by the goddess." She gave a glare to her people around her but most had already backed down. Three stayed near the one that Alric was a hair's breadth from decapitating.

Alric nodded and lowered his sword. "No harm given if none was meant."

The ranger rubbed his neck but stood down.

I held up a hand to the faeries to come down. If the people who feared them were still going after them, I wanted to know before we got comfortable. Garbage flew to me. "This is Larisona. She and her people follow Amara. They are friends."

Garbage flew to Larisona, who looked more curious than frightened, and studied her for a moment. "You goods?" She tipped her head. "Amara is friend."

"Amara? Do you mean Amaraili? The lost tree goddess? The remains of her tree were what this village and two others were built around. But if that was her spirit who spoke, how can she be your friend?"

Padraig rode forward; this was going to be complicated. "She survived but is changed. She is a friend of all those who follow the path of good. As our small friends do."

There were times that he really looked like royalty. This was one of those times. I knew him well and I almost felt like I should kneel.

Larisona looked the same. She also looked a bit smitten.

She nodded and smiled at Garbage. "I declare these people, *all of them*, to be our friends. Harm them, and I will retaliate." Her words ended right as she looked at the elf who'd been anti-faery.

He met her eye for a moment, then bowed. I had a feeling she was more than just the leader of some rangers.

"Now that that's taken care of, please, the first round is on me." She led her horse around to the back and everyone followed her.

The one who'd protested and his three friends hung back and were gone by the time we went into the pub. I made a note to tell the others. It might be nothing or a big pile of bad something.

The Ox and Cow was as massive inside as it looked outside. The ceilings were easily about five feet taller than Foxy. The wood used was old and well worn. And noticeably not oak. These people took their goddess worshipping seriously, even though the tree goddesses had all been gone for over two thousand years. It was still early, so it wasn't crowded. There were mostly humans, but a few elves. All of whom watched Padraig, Mathilda, and Alric closely. I noticed they all wore long sleeves, but so did many of the humans. The weather was noticeably cooler than the area we'd come from. Still, the elves behind the Dark and a lot of pain and suffering had come from the south. And they carried tattoos of a circle and dagger on their right wrists.

Either the ones in this town were also followers of the Dark and hiding here, or they were concerned that our three elves might be.

Alric found a table large enough for all of us. "What's the odd look about?"

"Just thinking about Jovan and his friends." I nodded to the elves across the room. Then noticed that Alric, Padraig, and Mathilda all had long sleeves on too. "Dang. They might be thinking the same thing because all of your sleeves are down." It was a hard one to call. If my friends rolled up their sleeves, it would show their lack of a Dark alliance if the ones around us were actually part of the Dark. But if they didn't, good elves might think they were with the Dark.

Alric didn't pause but rolled up both sleeves as if it were nothing. The waiter came by and we ordered ale, as did our friends. Padraig noticed Alric's sleeves and did likewise. Mathilda was busy getting some faery attention for something, but when they flew off, she rolled hers up as well.

Our ales arrived, and I took a long sip while I looked around the pub. After the past few days, that was possibly the best ale I'd had.

"Now to see if they attack us or talk to us." Alric lifted his ale glass.

Mathilda sat down next to me. "So, have we seen anyone running out to tell the evil ones that we're not one of them?"

"Not as of yet. But Padraig has a good eye on that door.

I wish they would roll their sleeves up, though."

As Alric spoke, I noticed that his sword was across his lap. He was tricky. I was sitting right next to him, and I hadn't noticed him do that.

Mathilda nodded and sipped her ale. "I sent the faeries and the constructs away. I'm glad that the general population no longer wants to destroy them, but I think it best if they stay out of sight and mind. And we don't want to answer questions about the constructs."

"Was this like where you and Siabiane grew up?" I was still watching the elves in the pub, I think we all were, but this village didn't look like something a young Siabiane would be in. Mathilda either, although she liked living out in the wilds more than her sister.

She laughed. "Not at all. We grew up far farther south than here in a large elven city named Tarlinca. We didn't see humans until we'd started our journey north." She hit my arm with her elbow to make me look over. An elf at the bar casually rolled up his sleeves but started with his left. The Dark's mark was on the right wrist of all of the members. He then rolled up the right sleeve and turned to face us.

He smiled. "Fear not. We don't abide by the Dark in this village, or either of the two villages near us. It's good to see our cousins and our sister." He nodded to Alric and Padraig at the first reference, then to Mathilda. There were two races of elves; the ones from the north were the Mcallini, and those from the south, the Alioth. To my eyes they all looked the same. But clearly, the difference was noticeable. Mathilda was Alioth, and Alric and Padraig were Mcallini.

"It is good to meet our southern cousins." Padraig had been up at the bar and two waitresses followed him with platters of food. "Please, join us. I am Elfren, and I lead this group."

"I'm Halor, honored to meet you. I'd say from your

speech you're more than just a leader of some adventurers for hire."

"Aren't we all more than we seem?" Mathilda batted her eyes and extended her hand. "I am Janil, very pleased to meet you." She wasn't using magic to glamour herself, it could be too noticeable, but she changed her stature and bearing almost as well as a spell could have. She also had wrapped a long, bright scarf over her head and reminded me of an old soothsayer Alric and I had met in the past.

We all introduced ourselves with fictitious names except Foxy. But being as his given name was Foxmorton, Foxy was a name change anyway.

I picked Kiltia just as it popped into my mind and then had to look away from Covey as she almost started laughing. Kiltia was the name of a regional wine I'd once sampled. Nice to know when trying to come up with something exotic, my mind went for the booze.

And that Covey caught it before I did. Too late now. Hopefully, that wine never made it this far south. Considering that Halor didn't blink when I said it, it must not. I forgot everyone else's fake name pretty much as soon as they said them. Something was making the hairs on the back of my neck rise, and I looked around the room, trying to figure out what was wrong.

Not a thing appeared off. Beyond my sword suddenly popping in at my feet.

I tried to remain calm but it startled me.

"Are you okay, Kiltia?" Halor asked when I jumped.

"Your sword fell off your pack." Alric reached down, lifted my sword, and handed it to me. "My fault. I should have tightened it."

"I didn't see you with a sword earlier." Halor's eyes narrowed but he still smiled.

There had been a number of us, and he'd noticed everyone's weapons? I hadn't noticed him in the group of rangers and he'd been in the pub when we came in.

"Yes, I've had it for a while. But you might have seen me with my hand on my knife and not noticed my sword." My sword had appeared with its sheath, but I'd take it out if needed.

"Halor is exceptionally good at riling people." Larisona came over and joined us.

She seemed genuinely glad to speak to us, after the blessing and all, but something was still causing the hairs on the back of my neck to stand up. And my dagger was starting to spark from within the sheath. He didn't normally do that until he was out, but something was bothering him.

Foxy got to his feet. "I'm going to check on the horses." That was extremely unusual, but if his furrowed brow was any indication, he was feeling ill at ease as well. He'd been gone less than a minute when the doors to the pub all slammed shut and the smell of smoke started coming in.

CHAPTER TWENTY-FOUR

EVERYONE JUMPED TO their feet and ran for the doors. Larisona might not have magic, but there were some magic users in the village. Four of them took formation in front of the double doors and started sending spells.

That did nothing.

Even I could tell that while they had magic, none of them were strong—but they still should have been able to do something to those doors.

Padraig turned to Larisona. "Mind if we step in?" His being polite was nice, but there was no way any of us were going to stand still for whatever was happening.

Larisona nodded, then grabbed Halor and two others and ran behind the bar and into the kitchen. There should be a door there too, but I doubted that it wasn't also blocked.

The windows were all high up but Covey climbed up to the largest one. And started swearing. "It's that elf you pulled a sword on, and a bunch of friends. The flames aren't on the building yet, but they will be."

Padraig, Mathilda, and Alric all threw spells but the doors wouldn't move.

"They have a spell breaker hanging in the closest tree!" Covey called down from her perch.

Damn it. It would be close enough to cover this entire

pub. I could sometimes get the faeries to come by mentally calling them, and I tried it now. It took three tries but about half of the current flock, including my original three, popped into the pub.

"Bads! We gets!" Garbage yelled and shook her war stick in the air. No war feathers yet but they all had their war sticks out.

"Not yet! We need all of you, Bunky, and Irving to destroy that spell breaker out there. The one in the tree. Then you can go after them."

"Goods!" Garbage and her faeries pushed their way through the wall and vanished. No matter how many times they did that, it still was disturbing.

People started coughing as the smoke grew worse but there were no signs of flames in the windows. Yet.

"Cover your mouths!" Larisona and her people came running back, along with the staff. They all had wraps of cloth around their faces. "The back door is even more well barricaded than the front." She looked around. "Damn it, he has a spell breaker, doesn't he?"

"That's what it looks like," Padraig said. Like all of the magic users, his hands were twitching from not being able to cast spells.

Covey was still up in the window. "That elf has ten others with him, all elves and all in long sleeves. I hope you're not attached to any of them, especially their leader." Covey transitioned into berserker mode so fast that everyone on the ground below her stepped back. Probably a wise precaution, but as long as none of them tried to stop her, they were fine. "The faeries are having trouble and it looks like the elf out there tied up Foxy. Hope you don't like this window." Before anyone could respond, she reached a clawed hand through the window and shattered it. Then she jumped out.

She must have either needed or wanted to take out a few of the ones outside before destroying the spell breaker as I heard yelling and fighting, but Padraig shook his head when he tried to use a spell against the door.

Then I heard the crackling that Bunky and Irving made, followed by gronks, and more yelling and screaming from the bad people.

Then the shattering of glass and triumphant faery yells.

"Try the doors again!" I yelled.

With the spell breaker out of commission, the combined effort of Alric, Padraig, and Mathilda blew the double doors to splinters. The locals all went rushing out and immediately attacked the elf and his buddies, and I ran to free Foxy.

He was bound and gagged but awake and furious. As soon as I freed him, he grabbed two of the enemy elves and bashed their heads together. It was a move often used by Dogmaela in the pub and it worked well here. Both of them collapsed into a boneless pile.

He looked ready to go for more, but the others were all down. Larisona had a group going around and pulling up sleeves. A steady stream of cursing followed her. Her people tied up the survivors, including the initial faery-hater, but they were all unconscious.

She came over to us. "Sorry about that. We were afraid there were some of the Dark here, but with specialized theater makeup, the tattoos can be hidden. It's cool enough now that long sleeves are common, so I'd hoped they wouldn't still be hiding them. I was trying to figure out how to reveal all of them when you came around." She rubbed the back of her head. "I didn't think they would act so quickly."

"You took a huge risk," Padraig said and folded his arms. "Something that a simple leader of some rangers probably wouldn't have taken."

She smiled. "Aye. I'm the leader of this village. Not a huge place, but we keep an eye on things, along with our two neighboring villages. Halor is the leader of Licoln,

the next closest village. Tricera, the third leader, is over
there helping load them on that cart to drag to jail." She
looked up to the faeries flying around in circles. "Your
friends there were extremely helpful. What happened to
the other two larger flyers and the brownies? I've never
heard of brownies working with others."

"Those are our companions, but I'm afraid they aren't
fond of strangers. I'm sure they're off hiding somewhere."
Mathilda smiled but kept watching the skies.

I watched the ground but neither brownie was in sight.
I agreed that we really didn't want to have to explain
the constructs to strangers. Such beings were rare in the
world, and we didn't need someone mentioning they saw
some to the wrong people. They were usually far better
behaved than the faeries, and while I did appreciate their
help just now, I hoped they were staying out of sight until
we left the village.

I was still curious about whatever Padraig's plan was for
bringing us here.

"I'll understand if you no longer trust our hospitality,
and again, I apologize for using you all like that." Larisona's face said that if it was helping her village by using us,
she'd do it again.

He nodded, with a glance at all of us. Everyone's face
was neutral. "I understand. We have had some issues with
the Dark ourselves. I believe we were about to have an
early supper?" His smile could have taken out a licten
beast at ten paces. It was a good thing he didn't use his
charm for evil.

They walked back into the pub, but I noticed Foxy was
still standing near where he'd been tied up and glaring at
the pub. Alric and I walked to him.

"How did they grab you?" Alric got his question out
before I could say something nice and caring. But from
the look on Foxy's face, Alric's question might be the
better choice.

"They used oakweed. Aye, stunned me enough for them to grab me and tie me up."

He looked like Covey when she was about to go berserker. I hoped he didn't have some trellian buried in that mixed heritage he had.

"But oakweed isn't a sedative. Why would that hurt you?" Oakweed was a common plant and pretty much ignored by most people.

Alric shook his head and started swearing. "It can be if they steam the roots and you happen to be part faril."

Foxy nodded. "They brought in a steam pot, had it behind the tree. I destroyed it, but it already hit me."

"And how many people down here know he's part faril? And they had it ready?" I shook my head. "There's no way they could have known you would go outside, though." The only person who mentioned knowing what Foxy was had been Larisona. But she'd been in danger with us in the pub as well.

Foxy didn't blush much, but he got a pinkish tinge. "They called to me. I was standing near the door. The pub made me homesick. Then they imitated Amara's voice, calling me. Neat as that, they got me."

"It's not your fault on any of it." Alric looked to where the remains of a steam pot were smashed against a tree. "I don't know that we can assume that all of the Dark were captured. We need to stay on guard."

"Wouldn't it be better to just leave?" I wasn't happy about being a target in a strange village.

"*Elfren* has his reasons for staying. Hopefully, they'll prove helpful." Alric dropped his arm around my shoulder. "Come on, Kiltia and Foxy, let's eat and rest a bit." He raised his voice just enough that I knew he'd seen someone watching us.

I slipped my arm around his waist and nodded. Foxy trailed behind. We had a lot to think about and discuss, but it wasn't safe anywhere out here. I agreed with

Alric—I hoped this gave Padraig what he was hoping for. Whatever it was.

The inside of the pub was quieter than before but had more people now. And most were drinking. Foxy went to join Grillion at our table. Since the gambling issue on the ship, they'd formed an odd bond.

Covey walked up to us. She jutted her chin at a group of locals. "Apparently, no one could get out of their houses or businesses when the attack came. They found some people unconscious outside but most were just trapped inside their places."

I'd seen that look on her face before—when she was discussing a student who dared to cheat in one of her classes. She'd changed back from her berserker self, but I noticed that both her hands kept twitching. And that the locals moved away from her when she came over to us. A good idea on their part. Trellians weren't common in the south, but their reputations were fierce. Her showing how easily she went berserker was giving them pause. Regardless of whether they were up to no good or not.

We quickly filled her in on what happened to Foxy.

"That's very bad. *I* wasn't even sure he was a faril breed. He doesn't fit them at all." Covey watched Foxy. "How did they know quickly enough to prepare something just for him?"

Padraig joined us. "Come on up. They are giving us rooms for the night." He kept a straight face so I knew he wasn't joking. "Here. Upstairs."

All three of us looked at him in varying degrees of confusion. Alric added concerned, Covey added annoyed, and I was sure I just looked lost. We'd had a rough time lately, and I would be the first to welcome a night of sleep in a real bed. But at the best, these people risked our lives to use us as bait. And it could be far worse than that.

"I believe a rest would do us all a world of good."

His smile was so fake I almost reached for my sword,

which had hung around this time. I'd given up trying to sort out why it did what it did.

There were still too many people in the pub for a real conversation. It appeared that while Padraig wasn't sure how safe things were at the moment, he wanted us to play along for now. He then suggested that we all go to our rooms to freshen up before trying a meal again.

Once we were all upstairs—we had four rooms between us—he motioned for all of us to go inside the largest one. Alric shut the door and leaned against it. Padraig cast a spell and a glittering blue light covered the ceiling, floor, and walls.

"We can talk now and I'm adding color to my spells while we're here to be aware if another spell breaker appears." He took a seat, so the rest of us did as well. "I know all of you are wondering what I'm up to and why we're not leaving."

All of us slowly nodded, although Mathilda looked like she was in on it. Or at least had a good-sized clue as to what he was up to.

"There were at least two other members of the Dark in the group of rangers who left. Larisona knows it and knows that they weren't outside the pub just now. There might have been more; she's not sure, and I couldn't see all of them to tell. I didn't know we were going to be bait, but when I saw the marks, I thought this would be a good way to get information concerning the level of Dark activity down here."

Grillion rubbed his face. "So these members of the Dark are evil, nasty killers and you decided we should hang out with them?"

"They are evil, there's no way around that. But I thought it was worth the risk. There are too many evil factions down here, and it could be deadly if we misjudge them. Larisona wasn't one, so I took a chance." He gave a weak shrug.

Now it was Alric's turn to give Padraig the look. "I've known you most of my life, and you are by far one of the people *least* likely to take a chance on a whim. You're an alchemist and a researcher—caution is what you do." He folded his arms and glared at his friend.

"I know. But…logic and reason aren't holding out well right now. The attack on Siabiane, Lorcan, and myself should have been impossible. What happened to Taryn drove that home as well. The way we always thought the world works is wrong."

Covey nodded. "I'd agree on that. Especially what I've seen these past few years. But you can't become rash simply because you feel logic isn't working. It's the views that are at fault, not the process."

Padraig and Covey were the most academic of us. Mathilda studied things, but it was more within the realm of nature. I knew things were topsy-turvy in my world, but it was disturbing to realize that our resident smarties were having issues too.

Alric sighed. "It turned out okay this time, but mostly because of the faeries and Covey. And the constructs. They use spell breakers with too much ease down here, and I think one thing we have to do is not count on being able to access our magic when figuring out what we're doing."

"In other words, I was too cocky and assured when I led us to this village." Padraig grinned. "I was too much you."

"Exactly." Alric grinned back.

I felt that Alric had been becoming more cautious as of late but wasn't going to say anything since they were both trying to make a point.

"So, the plan is that now *we're* using ourselves as bait to catch these other members of the Dark?" Covey narrowed her eyes. "Which assumes they didn't all run off as soon as they heard what happened here. And that they don't have another spell breaker."

"I wouldn't say bait per se. Did you notice that they didn't try to grab Taryn? They went after Foxy. The Dark we know and hate wanted Taryn," Padraig said.

"Two groups of the Dark?" Grillion still looked confused, and I agreed.

"Why not? We know other people are fighting them, not necessarily good people, but the Dark has enemies. Why not some from within?"

"But it still doesn't explain why they lured Foxy out. Yeah, he's a big guy and a fighter, but no one in this group is weak," Grillion said.

Foxy had been silently watching as everyone spoke, then finally nodded to himself. "Might be from a long time back. Before I moved to Beccia. Had some issues in the capital of Lindor and came south for a while. Had some problems here and went back north to Beccia to settle down. But I'd swear I never was near any of these villages. I didn't bring it up as I didn't think they'd still be looking."

"You have a bounty on you?" That was shocking to even ask. Although, I met Alric from bringing him in as a bounty, so you never knew. Except that Foxy was pretty straight in his thinking. He sometimes skirted laws—like providing hidden gambling dens during a brief no-gambling law time in Beccia long before I arrived there. But he was otherwise forthright.

"That might be the case." He nodded thoughtfully. "It was a long time ago."

"I don't see the Dark hiring out as bounty hunters," Alric said. "Unless…just what might they have a bounty on you for?"

"I didn't know they were the Dark. Never heard of that until you people told me about them. But some people had captured a bunch of trolls and were trying to make them work in the lava beds way down south. They weren't getting paid, not being treated right, and being held against their will. So I freed them and we took off north."

A few pieces clicked into place. "Dogmaela and her family?"

He grinned. "That would be the right of it. Her cousin Theagan is a mage, book learning mostly, but can cast some mean misdirect spells. The group I freed them from wasn't happy, and I might have made a mess when we left."

"How long ago was that?" Mathilda asked.

"Near on twenty-eight years this spring."

"Would someone have a bounty outstanding for that long?" I'd been a bounty hunter whenever my digger patrons died or vanished. But bounties didn't stay active long in Beccia.

"Could be." Alric watched Foxy. "Just who did you take them from?"

"The Klipu mob." He looked around and shrugged. "They weren't being nice. So I freed their prisoners. They might not have taken it well."

All of us went silent, and Grillion looked ready to faint. The Klipu mob never went north, but there were rumors that they ruled the south—it wasn't clear if the empress over the south knew it, but it was common knowledge to everyone else.

And Foxy had broken in, liberated a group of trolls, and then ran across the entire continent—and survived. I wasn't certain whether to be impressed or terrified. I settled on a cross of both. From the looks around me, I wasn't the only one.

Aside from Grillion—he looked ready to be sick. Or pass out. He blinked a few times, then fell off his chair.

"That still probably wouldn't explain the Dark trying to grab Foxy." I checked on Grillion but he'd just passed out.

"Unless the mob has something the Dark want and would be willing to trade for the right price." Alric looked down as Grillion started stirring. "I'd say their presence is still extremely strong down here."

"Not good." Grillion sat up but stayed seated on the floor. "The mob have been encroaching on Notlianda the past few months—working with a tribe of change-lings was the rumor. Qianru was trying to keep an eye on them. She thinks they want something she has…wouldn't tell me what it was, though." He sighed. "They're bad news."

That was an understatement. "What do we do now? I mean, after we leave this village? We still need to rescue Siabiane and Lorcan. I know Qianru didn't want us to come south, even though she asked me to under duress, but we should check on her. Find out where the Robukian she sent to me came from and what she thinks the mob is after, if nothing else." I looked down to Grillion. "Does she still have a man named Locksead with her?"

Locksead had been the leader of a gang of relic thieves up north. Alric had been working for him in disguise for a few years off and on. He'd gone with Qianru to the south a few months ago when she went to report what had been happening with the elves in the north. Although he'd been a thief, I trusted him about Qianru. If she was on the wrong side of things, he would have left. Or been removed.

"Yeah, tough bastard he is. He's her foreman, tries to keep things running smoothly." He laughed. "Which isn't easy with her poking her nose into everything."

That made me feel a little better about Qianru and her loyalties. But that would have to wait until we got there. A more pressing concern was right in front of me. "Can we send Foxy home? Use one of the chawsia paths or something?" I looked at him. "It's too dangerous for you to be here, let alone going farther south."

"I need to face my past. Amara knew of what I did to free Dogmaela and her family."

When he stuck his heavily tusked lower jaw out like that, I knew arguing was a moot point. The only thing harder than his head was his determination. I might assign a few faeries on him just to keep an eye on him, though.

Amara being so adamant about Foxy having to go even though it tore her up was a bit clearer now.

"That's one mystery solved. Do we hit the road now, or wait to bait Padraig's trap?" Alric asked. "Knowing that the Dark might be more interested in grabbing Foxy than doing anything else."

Padraig nodded. "Larisona said I and two others can question the ones they have in lockup. Like me, they want answers before killing them. I say we stay the night."

He was our de facto leader with a strong assist from everyone, but unless any of us objected, we'd follow his lead.

"I don't like it, but I think we can stay." Mathilda held up her hand. "But I want to add a spell to the amulets Amara made us back in Beccia. Not to Taryn and Alric's, since I wasn't there at their making. I don't want to disturb anything Siabiane put in. Not to mention we might be able to use them to find her and Lorcan when we get closer. But for the rest of us, if you could pull out your amulets?"

The amulets were similar to the ones that Alric and I had, but had the image of an oak leaf on them. Amara had seen mine and determined that the others needed something similar. So far I hadn't noticed anything coming from their amulets, but then again, I wasn't wearing them.

They hadn't glowed the last time I'd seen them, but they were now.

"Oh, that tricky tree goddess." Mathilda smiled as she

looked at her own, then the others. "Coming this way might have been more than just to follow the trail of the Dark. These are now charging from the oaks around this building." She smiled to Padraig. "You might have had more reason than you realized to lead us here. A slight nudge from a former goddess."

Everyone held their amulets and smiled.

"It feels like a hug right now." Covey laughed. "As odd as that sounds."

Foxy took out his amulet. It was larger than the rest; Amara had crafted it separately. But it also glowed. When he held it, all the tension that had etched its way onto his face faded away. "It didn't do this before."

"I think she knew there were oaks like hers down here and that they could charge these." Mathilda called up her staff, which, like the spirit swords, seemed to appear and disappear on her command. "This will just add a layer of protection and connection to what is already there." She held her staff in front of each then stopped in front of Alric and me. "I know I said that I don't want to mess with my sister's magic, but I believe your amulets will make anchors for the rest of us."

Alric seemed to understand what she was doing. I had no clue, so when he nodded, I did as well.

A green light flowed over all of us. Warmth, safety, and family were all inside it.

Then my dagger started crackling violently in its sheath and the door busted in.

CHAPTER TWENTY-FIVE

I GRABBED MY DAGGER and my sword, and everyone else grabbed weapons as well. Mathilda stopped her spell but kept her staff raised. She could cast spells without it, but I'd noticed that it seemed to give her spells more power. Not to mention it was great for bashing people in the head.

The leader was that damn elf thug who hated faeries. He had one eye swollen shut and looked worse for wear, but he wasn't locked up or dead. Both of which were better options. I only recognized half of the men and women behind him, and fighting could be heard down in the pub.

Apparently, when the other members of the Dark in the area heard what happened to the ones in town, they hadn't run away. Unless it was to gather reinforcements. If the other two towns were the size of this one, I'd say the entire area had an extremely large problem with members of the Dark.

The leader stopped at the shattered door and held back his people. "We only want him." He pointed his sword at Foxy. "I don't know or care who the rest of you are. If you stay out of our way, we'll take him and leave."

All of us moved in front of Foxy.

"Or you can back off and leave before we kill you." Alric was in front of everyone.

I knew he was fast; I'd seen him fight for years, but even so, when the leader and two others leaped forward, Alric's blade was nothing but a blur as he blocked them and pushed them back.

The blue light that had been on the room vanished. They had another spell breaker. Didn't slow down my dagger, though. He was crackling worse than I'd ever seen. I stepped forward but Covey shoved me aside as she went into berserker mode, roared, and flung herself at the group blocking our door.

My dagger was not to be held off, though, and it crackled over the heads of my friends and right through the elven leader's chest. Alric ran him through at the same time, then continued fighting the others.

Foxy tried to run forward to fight but Padraig turned to block him. "Stay back! Grillion, stay with him."

I did a double-take at Padraig. Grillion was a good fighter, but not great. If the attackers got through he couldn't stop them. Then I saw the look on Foxy's face as Grillion stepped back to him. He also knew Grillion couldn't fight against all of them, and so he stepped back to keep Grillion safe.

Damn, Padraig was good.

The three Alric had challenged were all dead and the rest trying to survive Covey's rampage. I took out my sword but was mostly giving my dagger free range as I moved forward. Mathilda dropped back to stand in front of Foxy and Grillion, and the grin on her face said she was fine with stopping people the old-fashioned way. Her staff was twirling and looking for heads.

The attackers were backing away from the door but were trapped with Covey still in their midst and Alric, me, and Padraig coming down for them. I wasn't the swordsperson they were, but I was counting on my cranky dagger to even that score.

The door to the pub was still shattered so I had a great

view as a massive flock of faeries tore inside. They'd even taken the time to don their war feathers. And find more friends. There were probably close to a hundred now.

The fighting in the pub was still going on, and aside from a few people that I recognized, there was no way to tell friend from foe. We needed a way to knock them all out and sort them later. "Garbage!" I had to yell a few times; the faeries were having too much fun poking people to bother listening to me. I doubted that they were able to tell friend from foe any better than myself right now. They were mostly doing annoying pokes rather than trying-to-kill-people pokes.

"Is whats?" She finally flew to me but kept watching the chaos below us.

"I need your faeries—all of them—to go find the new spell breaker outside. Destroy it. Don't fight—go destroy." Spell breakers were glass and they needed to be hung high to work properly. This village was lovely with all of its massive oaks, but that gave a lot of places to hang those things. Considering how dangerous and difficult they were to make, I wondered if someone was mass-producing them for the Dark down here. Might be another thing to add to our list of things to hunt down.

Garbage whistled, and all of the faeries stopped and then followed her out the door.

I shook my head as they left, then ran back to the room we had been in and grabbed a section of the shattered door. Padraig's spell should still be there once the spell breaker was destroyed and that would tell me when we could use magic again.

Padraig and Alric had cleared the stairway and were now blocking it. Covey was bouncing from table to table, smacking select people with her clawed hands. Maybe being a berserker gave her a way to tell them apart. Or she was just too wound up to stop at this point.

I felt a tingle in my hand and looked down. The piece

of wood glowed blue. So did the rest of the room when I stuck my head back in.

"Mathilda? Ya have anything like a giant sleeping spell on hand? No way to tell who's good and who's bad down there."

"I think I can modify one. They aren't a good idea in most battles, and they can cause a serious backlash. But just might be the thing in this case." She smiled at the light blue appearing on the walls and ceiling. Then gave Foxy a stern glare, and marched to the stairs and raised her staff. A few spell words later, everyone collapsed where they were—except for our people.

"Oh good, it did work." Mathilda went downstairs and then picked her way across the floor around unconscious fighters. "I had hoped that my upgrade of the amulets would let me exclude our people from the spell."

I followed behind her. My dagger stopped crackling so I put both him and the sword away. "You could have knocked us all out along with them?"

"Possibly. And there could be far worse outcomes with this spell. It worked this time, but I wouldn't recommend it for normal fighting." She narrowed her eyes as she looked at me. "So, if you do learn it, do not think it can be used like this. Trust me." She stopped in front of Larisona and tapped her gently on the shoulder.

Larisona groaned and slowly got up. Then she saw everyone had collapsed where they'd stood. "Is everyone dead?"

"No. Most are simply in an assisted sleep. There was no way for us to tell which were your people." Mathilda waved her walking stick around. "If you tell me who should be woken up, I can wake them like I just did you. Otherwise, the spell should lift in about five hours."

Larisona kept shaking her head as she looked around the pub. "You got everyone in here?"

"Possibly in the village as well. At least anyone close to

the pub. I needed to make sure I stopped the Dark—this did seem the best way."

"Okay. I'm fine with that." She looked up toward Padraig and Alric. "Just don't ever get mad at me, any of you." She walked a few feet over to Halor. "Him." Then a woman elf three feet from him. "Her." One by one, the villagers or those visiting from other villages to help were woken up. Including their two healers who had been right outside the pub door when Mathilda's spell put them to sleep.

Padraig and Alric came over with Covey and stood by Foxy and Grillion. The faeries had taken off after destroying the spell breaker. I hoped they hadn't taken my order to destroy things to heart.

"Do you recognize them?" Padraig pointed to a pile of still unconscious people in front of them.

"Some, not all." She pointed to a wide human male. "Halor? Isn't he the baker in your village?"

Halor bent down and rolled up the man's right sleeve. "Damn. Yes. Didn't suspect him. Been there over two years and made the best buns during the holidays." He shook his head. "Are we killing them all? Doesn't seem fitting, but they were trying to kill us, and holding them didn't work."

"No, it didn't work. But you had a larger problem than you thought. They were expecting you to keep them prisoner." Padraig looked around. Some people would not be getting up. "How many people did you lose?"

"Five villagers, and Tricera, the leader of the third village." One of the healers had been near us and answered. "Three more are seriously injured."

"Tricera? Damn. Too many good people lost and it could have been worse. We have to destroy them." She didn't sound happy about it but there was no doubt that she would do it.

"We'd like to speak to a few of them first." Padraig

nodded to Alric and Mathilda. "We have questions."

I was on the verge of including myself, then kept quiet. I could kill to save myself or others. I knew all of the members of the Dark would not hesitate to kill me, or if this group figured out who I was, kidnap me for their leaders. But I still couldn't sit there and watch what they might have to do. Nor what they would be doing to the rest.

Covey came over to us but the signs of her berserker change were slower to leave this time. She looked mostly like herself, but her shoulders were still wider than normal and her hands were still closer to claws. "I'd like to sit in." She looked at her hands. "Either like this, like me, or full berserker, whichever you feel would be the most helpful. I have done some recent research into the Dark."

Jovan, an elf who had secretly been one of the Dark's leaders, had captured about half of the Beccian population to use as feeders for his plan of dominance. Covey had been captured and a spell on the prisoners meant they were aware but couldn't do anything more than stand in pens, awaiting their fate.

Her interest in the Dark had expanded after that.

Larisona nodded to all four of them. "The village commons is probably the best place. We can get enough armed people to watch the doors. And you will be undisturbed."

"I can help with guarding." I raised my hand and saw Grillion and Foxy do the same, but Mathilda motioned for them to stay, then went over to talk to them. If we had all of the Dark, then Foxy was safe. Until we met other people after the same bounty. Once they finished with the Dark, we needed to find a way to disguise Foxy. Not going to be an easy thing—he was extremely noticeable—but we needed to try.

They used some process to determine which ones they wanted to talk to. I had no idea what criteria they were using, but they tied up the five they picked and dragged them out.

Mathilda was almost to the door when she turned. "I have an idea for the rest of them. Could you tie them up and bring them to that big oak out front? Trust me, that spell won't fall for another few hours. Even if someone brings another spell breaker." At Larisona's nod, she followed the others out.

Besides me, Larisona sent ten other villagers she obviously trusted to stand guard outside of the village commons. She and Halor were going to oversee the binding and dragging of the ones remaining.

"You trust her, right?" Larisona asked as we were about to leave.

I'd forgotten Mathilda's fake name but smiled. "With my life. If she has a plan, it'll be a good one." I hurried up and left before she asked me anything that involved me recalling any of my friends' fake names.

The village commons was larger than I'd expected but looked like one of those halls used for everything. Beccia used to have one of those but it was never used much and got destroyed in the last battle near the town. It got replaced with a new pub. I took a look inside; the others were just setting up their questioning area. I smiled at Alric, then took a stance outside the main door, facing the pub. We had one person on each door. The rest stood between the doors, looking tough. It was starting to get dark but lanterns were lit across the village and smaller ones, probably mage lights, twinkled high in the trees. It was a cute little village if you overlooked the people trying to kill or at least damage you.

I had a direct view of the others when they started bringing the unconscious and tied-up bodies out of the pub and dumping them at the base of the giant oak. I had no idea what Mathilda had planned but many things on this side trip had made no sense. Once they finished bringing the bodies out, Grillion and Foxy went back to the pub. I almost called out to them as I was getting a bit lonely, but they were laughing and chatting and I knew both of them could use a good friend.

I jumped when the door at my back opened, and Covey slipped out.

"I thought you were one of the Dark. Warn a person before you come out like that."

"You thought five tied-up and groggy followers of the Dark overwhelmed the four of us and then would politely exit the building?"

I rolled my eyes. "No. I wasn't sure what I was thinking. It's been a long day, and I just want to grab something to eat and go to sleep."

"Okay, I'll agree on that." She folded her arms and stood next to me, looking out across the village as I was. "What are we looking for?"

"I'm watching in case the Dark has yet more agents out here and they are going to try to mount a rescue. I thought that you were going to help inside with the prisoners?"

"Eh, they didn't need to be scared. Those are not the type of Dark we faced in Beccia, let me tell you. Maybe these were junior ones. They are babbling and selling each other out faster than Mathilda and Alric can write down notes. Padraig is asking the questions, but they're answering before he finishes. I almost want to check to see if those tattoos are even real." She was calming down but still sounded disappointed at not being able to rough up any more bad people.

"I wonder if you've hit on something? Fake tattoos. Judging from the way Larisona just set us up as bait, the Dark are a problem here too. What better way to gain respect if you're a thug than pretending to be them?"

"That would be…odd. But it might be the truth of it, as Foxy would say." She looked over to the unconscious pile. "But they still killed people."

"I know. Can you keep an eye on the door for me? I'll sneak in and wave Alric over; we should check those tattoos." I wasn't sure what difference it would really make—they were still killers—but it might help figure out who was after Foxy and who was after me.

Covey nodded and bumped up her glare as she folded her arms.

I silently went inside and waved down Alric. He was mostly standing there looking fierce, with his sword ready to chop heads. He gave a short nod, then came over and we went into a small side room and shut the door.

I told him my theory about the tattoos.

He scowled. "That could be what's going on, fake Dark. Four of them are tripping over themselves to talk and contradicting each other on every word. But one is silent. He also doesn't look scared, angry, or worried."

"Dark recruiting people on the road? Why would a real member of the Dark work with fake ones?"

"Good question. Also, how many of each are there? If it's simply makeup, then concentrated alcohol should remove it. See if the pub has a bottle of Lizon. I'll let Padraig and Mathilda know about it."

I went outside, left Covey still standing guard, and went to find Lizon. I was mostly an ale drinker myself, so aside from knowing to stay away from dragon bane, I didn't know a lot of the harder alcohols.

There were fewer people inside the pub now and they were busy cleaning things up. Grillion and Foxy were eating some sort of stew. My stomach growled as I went toward the bar. Then detoured to Larisona. Asking for a bottle of booze and not paying for it might not go over too well. Neither did explaining our suspicions about the fake Dark.

She stood there for a moment, almost waiting to see if I was kidding. She finally shook her head. "That makes no sense, especially if you're right and there are some true Dark in the bunch. But I'll get the Lizon." She went behind the bar and grabbed a small glass bottle with clear liquid in it. Then a second one. "We will have to check all of them. Good thing they'll be out for a bit."

My stomach growled again. The last meal I'd had eaten had been the vegetables and hay Mathilda gave me before I changed back. And it had been a long day.

Larisona laughed. "Hold on." She ducked back and came back with a plate of cheese, cold meats, nuts, and fruit. "To keep you going."

I inhaled half of it before we got to the village commons, then after the fact, held the remaining out to Covey.

She smiled but shook her head. "I'll keep watch out here, but scream if you two need help."

The scene was mostly the same as before, except this time Alric was at the other end. My guess was the one he stood closest to was the one he suspected as being a true member of the Dark. He also was letting his facial mark, a stylized horse in a faint white-blue line that showed him as an elven high lord, show slightly. It was spelled in such a way that even a spell breaker couldn't reveal it. But a strong enough magic user had forced it to show before—Jovan when he was torturing Alric. He didn't seem concerned, so I figured he was letting it show for a reason.

"Ah, thank you." Padraig smiled at Larisona and me. "Now, if you could hold out this first one's wrist?"

Alric left his sword on a table behind him, then pulled out the first wrist. An elven woman with long, dark hair similar to Padraig's. She squirmed a bit, but to me looked more confused than concerned.

He poured a bit of the Lizon over her wrist and wiped it harshly with a rag Larisona brought.

I was close enough to see the Dark tattoo fade as he wiped. A fake.

CHAPTER TWENTY-SIX

THE WOMAN TRIED to twist away. But Padraig grabbed her as Alric stepped back with the Lizon.

"What did you do? It's sorcery!" She looked to the one at the end of the row, and her face was complete terror. She was far more afraid of him than any of us. "I don't know how this happened!"

The next three had the same results, although they'd fought more now that they saw what was happening.

Alric stood in front of the last one and smiled. "Should we even bother?"

"Do what you want. I'm like them. We thought the marks were real. We've pledged to serve the Dark." He had medium-length red hair and looked to be a human-elf breed. He also looked far too calm.

Alric braced himself as he held out the man's wrists, then nodded to Padraig. "Would you like the honor?" He sounded as calm as the prisoner, but I saw the tension in his face as he held tight. There was no idea what this one might do.

Padraig poured the liquid, scrubbed, and stepped back. "And yet, your mark is true. You've been exceedingly quiet. Want to share with us?"

Mathilda stepped next to Alric and Padraig, and before the prisoner could finish speaking a spell, they had him gagged and bound. Then Mathilda magically pushed over his chair and added a bag over his head.

"He wasn't going to talk and was starting to annoy me. He can't hear or see anything now either." She glared at the remaining four.

Larisona turned away but not before I saw her smile. "She is fiercer than she looks."

"Oh, very." I kept watching the other four prisoners. All still looked exceedingly upset but were trying not to move.

"I'm going to try this again, without your leader listening. Talk now and fast, or we let her fix you. You won't like what she can turn you into." Padraig stepped back a bit and Alric reclaimed his sword.

The mark on his face had vanished again. I wished I knew what they were doing. He'd shown it to the true member of the Dark, but if he was killed, as per the plan, his knowledge about Alric's status wasn't going to do anything.

Which meant they had other plans.

The four non-Dark were silent for a few moments, then all started talking at once.

At the same time, four popping sounds came from behind me, and Garbage, Leaf, Crusty, and a bright-yellow faery swarmed in front of me.

"What dos? We smash all bad balls." Garbage was smiling, but the look she gave our prisoners was definitely not a friendly smile. I was pretty sure she was wondering if the destroy orders could be extended to them.

"How many were there?" I winced as I said it—numbers and faeries weren't as bad as them and names, but they usually weren't clear. I should have told them to tell us where the balls were before smashing them. Why would the Dark have so many here in a small village, though?

"This many." Leaf flashed both her hands quickly.

"Slow down." I couldn't tell if there really had been

that many or if she was repeating things.

Leaf slowly flung up her fingers, then held them. Nine. They'd had eleven spell breakers in this one village? I nodded to Leaf and turned to Larisona. "Did you know about those? You said you had one?"

She shook her head. "Mine is just a charm. It showed your flying friends briefly before they vanished but couldn't break spells. I'd like to know where these others were, though."

The yellow faery flew to her. "I show. They beat up now." She grinned at Garbage.

Larisona shrugged. "Okay, let me grab Halor, and you can show us. You'll all be okay?"

"We will. They might not be." I nodded toward our four prisoners. "Garbage looks annoyed and likes to get that feeling out of her system."

Larisona and the yellow faery left, and my original three buzzed closer to the four prisoners.

"Ours?" Garbage waved her war stick toward them.

"What are those things?" The one she was closest to didn't look happy about her hovering there. Smarter than he looked.

"Your worst nightmare." Alric grinned. "Why don't you show them what you will do if they don't tell us the truth immediately?"

Garbage zipped forward, poked the man a few times, and flew back. He'd bitten his lip to keep from yelling, but I knew how painful those little stings could get.

"And they can call in a few hundred of their friends." Mathilda smiled at the faeries and then turned back to the prisoner. "Please speak slowly and start with you. The rest of you will get your turn."

The man who'd been poked nodded but didn't stop watching Garbage. "We were hired by the one on the ground—his name is Dhalin, by the way—to pretend we were in his club of the Dark. It seemed like a good way to make money. We set up those balls, reported what was going on in the villages, and made sure his people had safe passage."

There were a lot of questions to ask.

"Why the mark? Couldn't you have helped him without it? How many others like him were there?" Alric leaned against the table but still had his sword out. The faeries hovered menacingly close. Except for Crusty. Even with her odd new insightfulness, she was still flying around upside down, poking the walls with her war stick. The walls didn't react.

"He said we needed to make it seem like there were a lot of Dark agents, but we were also to keep it hidden. We just started wearing them two weeks ago. Itch something awful."

Two weeks ago. When Alric had been grabbed. I didn't know if there was a connection, but I scowled at the man anyway.

"We didn't know they were going to kill people."

Garbage flew within an inch of his nose. "Is lies."

I agreed with her; he probably was still lying about a few things. I hadn't noticed the faeries developing an ability to tell truth from lies, but they were usually a good judge of character, so that could fall under the same mindset. Even though these four, and probably many of the ones under the oak tree, weren't actually members of the Dark, they still weren't nice people.

"Our friend here believes you're lying. One chance or you'll be the first to demonstrate what they can truly do." Padraig stepped back, and more faeries started popping through the walls.

"I'll talk!" A human woman next in line would have leaped out of her chair if she hadn't been tied to it. "I know we're not on me yet, but I will talk. He is lying. We knew people might die. It was to be avoided if possible, but if not?" She shrugged. "We were promised not only money, but that we would be given jobs with the Klipu mob once we proved ourselves. Bringing in that bounty was going to secure it, he said. They're waiting for a bigger catch who won't be here for a few more weeks, but our leader got greedy and said we should get this one first. Take him in to the bosses. Show them what Dhalin was good for. That's what he said." She spoke so fast that the faeries looked impressed.

"Them who?" Padraig turned his smile on, and the first guy yelled and tried bouncing out of his seat. "Who is the bigger catch they are waiting on?"

"It's my turn! They didn't tell us what the other prey was. Something big and powerful that will change everything—that's all they said." The man who'd been first in answering jumped in his seat. "Dhalin's worried that the other Dark don't respect him and his crew. They're working with the Klipu mob right now. He has five other buddies here, unless your people killed them. Maybe more. Wipe their marks—you'll see." He glared at the woman.

Mathilda nodded to Padraig and Alric. "You go, I'll stay here with our friends. Garbage? Could you call some more faeries in?" The words were barely out of her mouth when twenty faeries came racing in the main door to join the ten or so already there.

Covey had opened it for them and stuck her head in. "Everything okay in here?"

"Yes. If you don't mind keeping guard still, along with the others, our friends will be checking the tattoos on the ones on my pyre." Mathilda's eyes darted to the prisoners at her words.

They all flinched except for Dhalin, who couldn't hear anything.

"Not a problem." Covey held open the door as the three of us went out. "Good luck. They haven't moved at all. Even when the logs were added." She grinned as she added that for the prisoners' benefit.

"This is going to take a while; should we split up to get them all checked?" There were only two bottles of alcohol, but I could get more.

Foxy and Grillion came out of the pub at that point, each with a small, clear bottle.

"The barkeep said that you'd be wanting these. Thought we could come out and help," Foxy said.

Grillion held up his bottle. "You're not drinking it, are you? Because they have far better things behind that bar than this. My old man used to use this for taking off paint."

"No, but we're getting rid of some of the Dark," Alric explained, and we soon split up and checked everyone's wrists. At Alric's suggestion, we started moving the real Dark from the not-so-real ones. There were only three real Dark out of the twenty lying here.

"Damn. I don't get why they have those marks anyway. Then to give out fake ones? And they're master criminals?" Grillion peered down at one of the real Dark. "If you're a secret society, wouldn't it be better to be secret? Stay hidden?"

Padraig nodded. "It's attached to how they get their power. Whoever began them—and it's been lost in history, if the person was ever known—wanted to control their minions. The mark gives the individuals more power, but leaves them open for being revealed."

"It doesn't hurt that it is small and unless you know you're looking for it, you wouldn't notice it." I walked over to one of the real Dark. "Are they all connected somehow? To each other? To their leaders?" I was thinking of how Mathilda's spell connected all of us. Hopefully, something done against one of us wouldn't impact the others. And we'd killed a few Dark and I didn't notice anything among the survivors. But there might be something.

"Not that I've read," Padraig said. "But we might want to look into it. And whatever we do to them, we should keep the two groups separate."

"It might be best if they didn't wake up, any of them." Alric looked up into the giant oak they were piled under. We'd been joking about lighting a pyre, but Mathilda had wanted us to leave them here for a reason.

"Gonna just kill them right here?" Grillion shoved his hands in his pockets and nodded as if that would be his idea too. Of course, he also took a step away from Alric.

"No." Padraig had been slowly walking between the two groups, making observations and nodding to himself. "But I am also interested in Mathilda's plan. Especially for Dhalin since he knows we have an elven high lord with us." He laughed and shook his head. "You were just doing that in case he got away?"

"Wait, what?" Grillion looked back and forth until Alric explained what he'd done.

"Mostly I was looking for a reaction. There are high lords down here, or used to be. He's a half-breed but few people can tell the difference between Mcallini and Alioth elves. I was hoping he'd slip up and give away something."

"Not sure that it worked. But it's something to keep in mind." Padraig started back for the common house. "Let's find out what Mathilda has planned."

Covey wasn't at her door.

CHAPTER TWENTY-SEVEN

———◆———

A COLDNESS HIT ME as we ran for the door. Had we misjudged the Dark again? We flung open the door and raced inside.

To find lots of faeries, Bunky, Irving, Welsy, and Delsy all helping Mathilda fight off some monster. Correction, two monsters. Three, if we counted the one on the ground being destroyed by Covey in full berserker form.

They were each taller than Foxy by at least three feet, and twice as wide. With overly long arms that ended in thick curved claws. They were covered in an odd gray fur and their faces were things only a mother couldn't hate. Tiny brutish eyes, almost no nose, and lower jaw tusks that made the two Foxy had look like toothpicks.

From what I could see, Dhalin was in pieces across the floor, and a dark hole in the wall near him was probably where they got in. Two of Larisona's people had been watching that side; most likely they were in the same state as Dhalin.

"Why didn't we hear anything?" I felt my mouth move but didn't hear the words come out.

Alric turned and grabbed my arm. He spoke but too fast for me to read his lips, and again no sound came out.

The faeries and constructs were diving down on the creatures but with that fur, the war sticks didn't make an impact. Bunky and Irving were more successful and a few of their arc strikes caused the creatures pain, judging by their open-mouth grimaces. But on their second pass, the larger creature swung out both arms and smacked Bunky and Irving across the room. Neither got back up.

Welsy and Delsy yelled—or so it looked; no sound came from them either—and charged the monsters but were kicked aside with ease. They flew across the entire hall to land near us but stayed down.

Alric still had my arm and pulled on it to get me to look at him. He spoke slowly, over-emphasizing the words. "Tjolia mountain dreks."

My stomach wished I hadn't had anything to eat when I finally figured out what he was saying. Like the licten beasts, mountain dreks were from the far north, not the south. They were also the reason we couldn't hear any sounds. Because being highly efficient killing machines wasn't enough, they also could silence their prey and themselves during a hunt. Great.

I pulled out my sword and dagger. I might not be able to yell about it, but I was going down fighting. A nice push spell might be handy as well.

Alric took my arm again and pointed to the door.

Damn him. Someone had to tell the others about this, not to mention that Foxy and Grillion had gone back to the pub. I shook my head, but the rest were already fighting, and I knew he would be the better choice to stay, being both a better fighter and a better magic user.

It didn't make it any easier, though.

I sheathed my weapons and ran back out. The sudden ability to hear almost knocked me off my feet. I ran to the pub.

"There are monsters attacking everyone in the common house! They're dreks and are swallowing all sound with magic. We need fighters!"

Foxy and Grillion had been sitting at the bar, but Foxy was on his feet immediately. "They shouldn't be down here." He ran for the door with a confused Grillion jogging behind.

Larisona and Halor were right behind them, along with a few dozen villagers.

I almost beat Foxy and Grillion back at the speed I ran.

The constructs were still up against the walls, but it looked like the rest of my friends were still fighting. I saw more injuries than I'd like, but they were up.

Covey had finished off the first one, but couldn't get close to the other three. Wait, there had only been three total; one was dead and now there were three fighting?

I ran around behind the fight to what had looked like the way they busted in. A stench of rotting meat hit me as I got closer. That was a corrupted chawsia path, and at least one more of the monsters was running down it toward us.

I wasn't sure how to shut one of these down, but I sent a heavy push spell, followed by a hard direction of down. The tunnel folded into the ground, then vanished. I didn't know if I'd closed it or shoved it deep underground. As long as the things on the other end never got here, I'd call it a win.

I spun just as one of the monsters got hold of Alric and lifted him like he was a child's toy.

I didn't plan on exposing what I was to anyone else if possible, but there wasn't a choice. I transformed faster than ever and reached a clawed dragon hand out for the drek holding Alric. I shook the monster until he released Alric, then snapped the drek in half. No red film over my eyes this time. That attribute probably belonged to one of the deities, but I was pissed and scared.

The other two dreks saw me kill their companion but kept fighting. So be it. I roared even though no one could hear me, and attacked them.

The fight was over in moments as I killed the remaining two. Then I changed back to myself.

Alric ran to me, one arm hanging brokenly, but he was alive and moving. Unlike me. As soon as I'd changed back, my legs gave out on me.

I felt oddly weak and there was something wet along my right side.

"Taryn! You were hit." Alric's face was pale as he tried to stop the blood loss. I glanced down and turned away quickly when I saw too much blood.

That was something to keep in mind. Apparently, when in my dragon form and mad as hell, I didn't feel really bad injuries. Damn. I tried to say something to Alric and then passed out.

———

There were voices and sounds around me, but I wasn't sure if they were in my head or actually around me. A crackling feeling came from my right side. It seemed like my dagger but I couldn't open my eyes to see. I was dying but my dagger was still defending me? That was a stubborn hunk of metal.

An unfamiliar voice was near my head. "We need to stabilize her. And we're going to need whatever healing magic you people have. Neither of us are strong magic users."

"Whatever she needs, we're here." That was Alric, only sounding a bit hysterical. I knew he wasn't a healer, but he'd give whatever he had.

I smiled but still couldn't open my eyes.

"She smiled." That was Mathilda, also quite close to me.

"That's good. If you can hear me, just save your energy." A pause. "What's her name again?"

I'd expected to hear Kiltia but Alric's voice was loud. "Taryn. She is a magic user and stubborn."

I tried to smile again but the energy wasn't there.

"What's this powder on her and all of you?"

"A spell bomb the attackers had. Caused some mild

hallucinations. I thought I saw a dragon, for one. No idea what others thought they saw." Mathilda was rubbing my left arm gently. She was also sending cooling healing magic into me. She wasn't a true healer like Ceithera but this helped a lot.

There hadn't been a spell bomb, not before I'd collapsed anyway. After I'd turned into a dragon…oh. My brain was extremely sluggish. One or more of my friends had cast a spell, with powder, to hopefully confuse the villagers who'd seen me. Nice thinking.

I screamed as someone touched my right side. My eyes flew open at the pain and my dagger, next to me on the bed I was in, crackled warningly at the friendly-looking healer woman next to us.

She took a step backward.

"It's okay." My voice sounded like I'd been doing a lot of screaming lately. The dagger settled down.

"He wouldn't let us take him from you. He's a feisty one." Mathilda patted my hand.

"They're going to have to put you under now. There's a lot of work they need to do." Alric's glorious green eyes shone with unspent tears. "You're going to be fine." If he gripped the hilt of his sword in its sheath any harder, he was going to break it. Or his hand. His injured arm hung in a sling.

Padraig was there as well, and his face looked carved in marble. His eyes were also exceedingly bright.

I was obviously not in good shape.

"Dagger? I need you to let them work on me. Please. Let Alric keep you safe." I had a feeling working around a crackling dagger for surgery wasn't a good idea.

The dagger stopped crackling, and Alric took it. He gently touched my arm. "I love you." It was little more than a whisper; he was fighting not to cry.

"I love you too." Great, now I was fighting not to cry.

"We need to operate now. She's lost too much blood.

I need the strongest magic users to stay over there." The second healer, a male elf, smiled and put a mask over my face. "You need to sleep now. Not everything can be healed by magic."

CHAPTER TWENTY-EIGHT

I'D LIKE TO say I had wonderful dreams from whatever they knocked me out with, but I was awake one moment and then waking up again obviously a while later. I was in a different room than before, and no one was in my range of vision. Lifting my head to look around was too hard. The room was dark, most likely to help me rest, but a low rumbling sound came from along both sides.

While barely lifting my head, I was still able to see two rows of bright wings lying near me. The faeries were purr-snoring in their sleep.

A louder snore came from the corner near the only light source, a small glow. Alric still had his injured arm in his sling but had fallen asleep in a long chair in the corner.

I tried to see if I could feel whatever had been done, but all I could tell was that my side wasn't leaking blood anymore and I was safe. I might ask to find out what they'd had to do at some other time, or I might not. Part of me didn't want to know how close I'd been to dying.

I was closing my eyes—sleep seemed like the best idea at this point—when I heard a soft voice near my head, calling my name.

"Amara?" I kept my voice low. My throat still hurt and I didn't want to wake anyone else.

"Foxy told me what happened. From what I can sense, you'll be fine. If you still feel a bit off, go sit near one of the large oaks when you can get up." A feeling not unlike a mental hug flowed over me and the voice vanished.

"Is okay?" Crusty disentangled herself from the other faeries and crawled over to my head.

"I think I will be. Are all of you okay? What about the constructs?" All four had gone down hard and not gotten up.

"Is all good." She pointed to the open door. The brownies stood in military precision in the doorway facing out, and Bunky and Irving sat on a chair next to them.

Crusty patted my cheek and kissed it. "Sleeps. Need sleeps." She snuggled in at the base of my neck, and I fell asleep.

The next time I woke up, it was daylight and I heard people walking around out in the hall. And smelled stew.

"Food?" My voice croaked and immediately Alric helped me sit up and gave me water.

"Foxy said that would wake you up." His injured arm wasn't in a sling anymore and he seemed fine. There were still some bruises and fading cuts, but they looked like they were healing.

"Thank you." I finished the water, then sat up even more and started in on the stew and fresh bread. "They fixed your arm?"

Mathilda came into the room. "It was an easy fix, just a bone break. But he wouldn't let any of us touch him until you were done and recovering. They had to take one of those creatures' claws out of your side, by the way."

I felt a lecture from her coming on, but I just nodded and kept eating.

"We have to work on controlling your change. If you had stayed in dragon form, the injuries wouldn't have been near as bad."

"I didn't want the villagers to see me." It sounded more

logical in my head before I said it. They'd already seen me at that point. Based on my size and movements, I seriously doubted that the common house survived dragon me. "Okay, I wasn't thinking. Is everyone else okay? Did the chawsia path open back up? More monsters were coming through it. Did I hear something about a spell bomb?"

Alric walked to the door, said something to the constructs, and shut the door with them outside. The faeries had taken over the small table in the room and looked like they were listening to a story.

"First, yes, everyone is fine. Foxy and Covey both got knocked out right before you destroyed the drek holding Alric. Everyone has some bumps and bruises, but you were the most injured." She nodded to Alric.

"The chawsia path they used to get in is gone. Not sure where it went, but it vanished. The bodies of the dreks vanished as well. Padraig is checking the area. Something had to have pulled them back. Mathilda was the one with the spell bombs. You'd passed out, but the villagers were looking at you and talking among themselves. Mathilda released a few powder spell bombs and we pretended to have seen a dragon and other things."

I finished my stew. Thought about asking for more, but wanted to give my stomach a chance to adjust. "Can I see the claw? The one from my side?" Morbid curiosity, but since I hadn't died, I'd like to see it.

"I told you." Mathilda laughed as she took it out of her bag. "He didn't think we should keep it."

It was huge. Granted, everything had happened so quickly, and I'd been dragon-sized for most of it, but the claw was longer than my hand by a few inches. "That was in me?" I wasn't sure whether to be impressed that my dragonhide was tough enough to not notice a thing that big, or horrified. I stayed somewhere in between. "Oh, where's my dagger?" I figured that my sword had jumped ship as soon as I'd changed.

"Right here." Alric handed it to me.

It felt like it purred as the faeries did.

I looked down at it and a thought hit me. "What's the ancient elvish term for warrior?" This dagger was one for sure.

"Rhyfel. That has a nice ring to it. For both of you." Alric's smile was for me, not my dagger.

I picked up the dagger. "Do you like that? Rhyfel?" I tested it out and the dagger—Rhyfel, I corrected myself—seemed to glow.

"Rhyfel! Rhy! Rhy!" The faeries immediately started yelling and singing his name, and he glowed brighter.

"I'd say we have a name."

It took an hour for the two healers and Mathilda to declare me healed. The two healers had been in surgery for quite a while getting me put back together; then Mathilda, with magical reinforcement from Alric and Padraig, had sped up the healing process. They didn't want to release me too early and have that hard work undone.

Covey, Foxy, and Grillion made their way in as everyone was discussing if I was fit to travel. I kept trying to talk but they were talking over me.

Covey gave a huge whistle—which the faeries applauded—and she then pointed to me when everyone else finally shut up.

"Thank you, Covey." I was wearing a long nightgown, not something I owned, so I swung my legs over the edge of the bed. "Everyone did an amazing job fixing me. I think I'm fine. Aside from it being too crowded in here."

Mathilda chased everyone out, even the faeries, so I could change. I'd just gotten into my normal clothes and shoved the drek claw into my pack when a soft knock came.

Larisona stuck her head in when I called to come in. "You are okay? I am so very sorry that you and your friends went through that. I wanted to chase out the Dark members, but not at such a risk."

"I'm fine." I smiled. "Odd question, but I noticed that your healers weren't strong magic users. Do you have many here?" Something had been drifting around my brain as I was sleeping. Why so many spell breakers? A bit that I'd read during my attempts at relearning magic bounced around my head.

"Actually, we don't anymore. We never had a lot, but those we had have been moving on in the past few months. Same with the other two villages. Why?"

"Spell breakers can be used to disrupt magic users if they are on a low level. They can make it difficult to be in the area after a while." I shook my head. "I have no idea what the Dark is, or was, planning for these villages, but it wasn't good."

Larisona nodded. "Halor and I were coming to the same conclusion. He went back to check his village early this morning. Not as many spell breakers as here, but enough. They were so high no one would have noticed them. He's checking the third village now." She paused. "I heard you being called a different name than Kiltia when you were attacked." She held up a hand to stop me before I could respond. "No. I don't want to know who you really are. It's probably safer for all of us. But we appreciate what you've done on a level I can never express." She came forward and grasped my forearm. "You and your friends will always be welcome in the three villages and will be called friends. Even your odd little faeries."

"Thank you. We have some things to take care of, but when we're done hopefully we can come back for a bit. Oh, what happened to the Dark under the tree?"

She shook her head and opened the door. "It's easier to show you. Once word gets around of the protections we have, hopefully, no one will mess with us again."

I followed her outside and stopped in my tracks. The ground where the stunned bodies had been placed was now filled with statues. Of the Dark. All were posed in fighting stances and looked to be made of stone. As I watched, Foxy and a group of workers came up with a large cart and loaded a few of them into it.

"Ai! T— Kiltia! Good to see you up. We're relocating our friends to the edges of the three villages. Fierce looking, ain't they?"

"They are interesting, for certain." I walked up to one of the statues still standing there. Only a few remained, so they must have been setting them up for a bit. Even close up, they still looked like stone.

Foxy waved, then they left with their cart.

Mathilda came up next to us. "That was Padraig and Alric's doing. Those people aren't dead, but so slowed down that it will be eons before they break through the stone. A creative spell, if I dare say so."

"I've never heard of anything like it."

"They won't admit it, but I believe they made it up."

That was shocking. Alric was faster and looser than Padraig, but even he got annoyed at me for making up spells as I went. Maybe I was rubbing off on them. Or things were so messed up, they were coming over to my confused and make-it-up-as-you-go side of things.

Larisona nodded across the village. "I need to go deal with the rubble removal. We're going to build a new common house with a dragon motif. Our story will be that a dragon turned the evil ones to stone and will come back if needed." She grinned. "Hallucination or not, the dragon mythos will come in handy." She patted my arm and ran off.

I wasn't sure how I felt about being the source of a new myth, but as long as no one believed that they saw a real dragon, it was fine. I turned to Mathilda. "Are we leaving today?" It was late morning from what I could tell of the sun between all of the branches.

"Alric would like to. I'm thinking another night of rest might be better, and Padraig is undecided."

That was disturbing. "Is he okay? He's been acting oddly on this trip."

She sighed. "I think it's just the researcher in him finally feeling overwhelmed—he's spent a few hundred years in his study and is now finding many things he knew to be true, aren't. Give him time. He'll recover."

"I would rather get on the road sooner rather than spend another night here. Nothing against these people at all, but I'd feel better sleeping on the trail." I laughed. "And I never thought that I'd say that." Which was true. But as much as I hated sleeping on the trail, I didn't want to be here any longer. Who knew what might be next to attack us.

Mathilda laughed as well. "Okay, I'll tell them we'll head out once they finish what they're doing. Padraig and Alric are helping with the common house."

"Great. I'm going to go sit by this tree for a bit." I didn't feel sickly but figured that if Amara was counting these trees as friends, then visiting for a while might be nice.

"Ah, Amara." She patted my shoulder. "Sit as long as you like. You know they won't leave for a while." She headed over to the remains of the common house.

I walked past the remaining statues and sat down against the massive oak's trunk. Rhyfel gave a soft glow from his sheath, and I took him out and placed him against the tree. His glow steadied. "Hello, tree. Amara sends her best." I kept my voice low; there were still enough people walking around that I didn't want anyone noticing that I was talking to a tree.

But the tree noticed.

It wasn't words so much as feelings. The first rays of a spring sun, good fresh rain, the gathering of squirrels in its limbs: all those feelings flowed through me like a warming cup of tea.

"Thank you." I leaned back and just listened to the leaves and enjoyed the peaceful feelings. For about five minutes, until a flock of faeries swarmed me.

"Found! Bad!" They circled me, yelling about bads, but none of them seemed that upset. Of course, faeries were weird and what was bad for others might not be bad for them.

With a sigh, I put Rhyfel back in his sheath, patted the tree trunk, and got up. "What's bad? Where?"

Garbage flew off, then returned with her trail of faeries when I couldn't go as fast as her. Magically sped-up healing was great, but it still took more than a few hours for a full recovery. I just needed to not show my stiffness in front of the others. I really did want to get back on the road.

"Is this! Come!" She waved her arms like a tiny windmill, then flew ahead. And back. I thought about telling her to wait, but it wouldn't do any good.

Eventually, we got a distance into the trees and the faeries clumped around a massive boulder. One that looked normal to me, at least from this side.

"See!" Leaf flew in circles, pointing; even Crusty was waving to the other side of the boulder.

I came around, the faeries flew up and away, and I froze. It wasn't just a boulder. It was a mass of dreks all embedded in the stone. Unlike the stone statues Mathilda made, these were dead. Their faces were even nastier in death than they had been in life. And they were real stone.

CHAPTER TWENTY-NINE

———◆———

"WHERE...HOW DID YOU...DID you do this?" If the faeries had discovered a new-old trick of turning creatures into boulders, we had a serious problem.

"You do!" Garbage looked ready to burst with pride. "You go boom! Make them go rock." She hugged my wrist. Which she'd never done before.

"I did this? How?" The how hit me a moment later. "When I pushed away the chawsia path. Damn, there are at least five of those things in there." I was impressed and horrified at what I'd done.

"Is mores. This many." Leaf focused and held up eight fingers.

"There were eight more in that tunnel?" Talk about overkill. "Can you get Alric, Padraig, and Mathilda and bring them here? They need to see this."

Garbage, Leaf, Crusty, and three more faeries hugged my wrist and forearm. "Yous good!" Then all of them flew off.

Leaving me to look at my creation. I'd only seen one more in the tunnel when I spell pushed, yet there had been seven more behind it? I walked around the entire boulder. The back side had moss growing on it and the dirt at the base looked undisturbed. I hadn't turned them into the boulder; it had been there. But I'd forced them into it. And I had no idea how.

I was still slowly circling it and thinking not great thoughts when the others and their faery escorts arrived. I'd only asked for the magic users in hopes they could tell me what I did and how to keep from accidentally doing it again. But Covey, Foxy, and Grillion were here too.

Like me, everyone looked at the boulder in confusion—until they came over to my side.

"What happened?" Covey got the words out first, but the question was the same on everyone's faces.

Except for the faeries. Once the excitement of showing their find faded, they were getting bored. "Things! Need to do things!" Garbage yelled, circled us, then led her flock off somewhere.

"Don't go far! We're leaving soon." I shrugged. They'd find us.

"Did this just happen?" Alric stepped closer to the boulder to look at the dreks.

"No. I think these were who was coming down the chawsia path when I did whatever I did to it." I shuddered. "I'd only seen one of them coming. And before you all ask, no, I have no idea how I did this."

The three magic users started examining the boulder, making soft comments mostly to themselves as they did so.

Covey stepped over to me. "That's extremely impressive."

"Thanks. The faeries thought so too. It's scaring me, to be honest. I have no idea how I did it. I guess this is what happens if you shove a chawsia path underground?" I was hoping one of my brilliant magic-using friends would confirm that, but the looks they gave me said they were as confused as me.

"If that many of those things had gotten through…" Grillion had stayed back after his first glimpse of the front of the boulder.

"Not only would everyone in this village be slaughtered, but so would everyone in the other two," Covey said.

"Is it just me, or does that seem like massive overkill? Even if someone knew we were here. I couldn't have fought more after that thing got me."

Padraig had been taking a long study of the boulder but looked up. "I'd say they were planning on making this area impassable for some reason. We need to tell Larisona. And tell her about the two villages Jhori mentioned when we were on the ship as being destroyed by monsters. They wouldn't have been near here, but there might be a connection."

It took another fifteen minutes for them to study, comment on, and crawl over—in the case of Covey— the boulder. We were silent as we started back. Mathilda would bring out Larisona and Halor to show them while we packed to leave.

Alric came alongside me as we got to the village. "Are you sure you're up to travel? I know I wanted to leave, but if you need to rest?"

I smiled. "Thank you, but I want to get on the road." Which sounded better than wanting to specifically get out of this town.

We were packed and ready to ride within the hour. Larisona and Halor came back from looking at the boulder grim-faced but determined. There was still no idea why these villages were under such a heavy attack, but they were aware now. Neither had heard of the two destroyed villages Jhori mentioned, but they were going to look into it. And work on getting former residents of the villages who were magic users to move back.

Larisona also loaded us down with enough food and supplies that we almost needed a pack pony. Foxy put most of the food on his horse since he still preferred walking to riding.

"Thank you, but we've only a few days left on the road. A week at the most." Whatever had thrown Padraig off before, he was back to his charming and gracious self. Larisona simply smiled and refused to take anything back.

I wasn't sure about this week business he was talking about. According to the maps, we should be hitting Notlianda in three days at the longest.

Once we got back on the road, we needed to discuss Padraig's secret plans.

We headed out, passing my modified boulder as we went. A few of the villagers were removing tree branches, shrubs, and small rocks around it as we rode by. Padraig nodded as we passed and they waved to us.

I waited until we got out of earshot. "What are they doing?"

"They want to make it a shrine. Like the stone Dark members, they want people to see what they can do." Alric frowned. "The problem is they didn't do either of those things. While that might keep some folks away, there's always some fighter who wants to prove themselves. I tried telling Larisona that, but they were determined."

"Hopefully they'll be okay." I looked back but we were already heading out of the oak forest. "How long will it really take us to get there?"

Alric and I were side by side and right behind Padraig.

"I said that just for a bit of misdirection. But we might work in a few detours." He seemed too happy—he had something planned.

"We need to find Qianru, see whose side she's really on, then get down to Colivith." I wasn't up to more detours at this point. I didn't feel as panicked as I had about reaching Alric, and Siabiane seemed fine, even if she wanted us to turn back. But we needed to get her and Lorcan back and get off of this messed-up continent.

"And a detour might help with that. But we'll see as

we get farther down." He picked up the pace.

"Easier to just let him have his game. He used to do this when we were younger," Alric said as he raised his voice. "He likes keeping secrets. Makes him feel special." The teasing in his voice was nice to hear.

Padraig continued riding and didn't look back.

The massive odd trees we'd seen when we first arrived here were back in force. They were so spaced out, though, that I found myself wishing for the oak forest we just left.

"Any ideas how both licten beasts and those dreks are living down this far south? I've never seen a drek, and hope never to again, but I know they live even farther north than the licten beasts." And I really wanted them to go back and stay there.

"They shouldn't be able to survive in this warm climate, neither species should," Mathilda said from behind us. "Someone might have held open a path from there down here, but I don't know any magic user, now or in the past, who could have done that. And keeping them alive would be a major undertaking."

"Could they have changed what the beasts need to live? Modified them enough to stand the warmer areas? I can tell you, that took some getting used to." Grillion had ridden up to the other side of Alric.

"Did you see that fur on the dreks? There's no way they have been modified," Alric said.

"Then how are they living down here? Granted, the ones that came after us didn't survive, but there could be more. If someone is setting up chawsia paths and sending those things through to kill and maim, they could destroy more than just outlying villages." I was looking at the big map as we rode. Well, parts of it. "The only things the two villages that Jhori mentioned and the ones we left behind now had in common are that they're out in the sticks and easily avoided." I knew the speculation was that whoever sent them was trying to block the area from travel, but neither location would be that hard to go around.

"Which sounds to me as if someone is testing strategy for a larger attack." Covey was taking advantage of the wider spaces and was riding alongside us, close enough to hear the conversations, far enough away to ignore them if she wanted.

"That was my thought once we started looking at the other two villages." Alric reached over, and I handed him the map. "They could be tests, but if both areas were destroyed, they are closing the number of paths down farther south. They're trying to remove options as well as testing their abilities."

"The members of the Dark in the village were unaware of who I was but were after Foxy. Yet Theria obviously was after me. Do we still think multiple groups? Although, how and why would they have known Foxy was coming this way?" There were too many moving parts, and I didn't like any of them.

"I'd say there are at least two groups within the Dark with different agendas," Covey said. "The ones in that village could have been a sleeper group. Lying in wait for specific orders from their leader. The fake ones got their marks two weeks ago? Add a few days and it's when the grimarians and crew attacked us up north and grabbed Alric."

"And they saw me." Foxy had been sauntering along, seemingly lost in his thoughts but he was listening. "They are either part of the Dark, or working with them."

"Weren't we going to try to hide him somehow?" I still had no idea how they were going to do it, but he was unique and too easy to recognize. Another thought hit me. "Did you used to mostly stay in your pub because of what you did down here?" I'd known him for fifteen years and he'd rarely left his pub until all of the trouble with the relics started. I'd just figured he was a homebody.

"Aye. I didn't think that mob would send folks up. The

kingdom of Lindor has its own gangs and isn't all friendly to outside ones. But I wanted to stay low just in case. Dogmaela and her family did as well, for the same reasons."

Beccia was an ofttimes ignored part of the Lindor kingdom, but he was right about the gangs.

"What are you expecting to resolve by going back?" Covey rode a bit closer to the rest of us. "If they try to take you, I'm not even certain Taryn and the rest of our magic users can stop the Klipu mob."

"And I don't want them to." Foxy leaned over to make sure I saw him. "You can't risk yourselves trying to protect me. Promise me you won't."

I looked at him for a few moments. Along with Covey, he was one of my oldest friends. Not going to happen. "I can't promise that. Not to mention, like Covey, I'm not sure what you're doing. I get not wanting to live in hiding or feeling bad about what you did—which you shouldn't because you saved Dogmaela and her family— but I get it. I don't get how sacrificing yourself to the Klipu mob is going to help anything." I didn't think that Amara would have let him go if he was planning on giving himself up to the mob.

"Nah, not going to hand myself over. I'm going to remove the leader of the mob. I should have done so when we escaped, but I didn't. He's a bad person and is still taking troll slaves. And hurting others. I intend to fix things." He said it so calmly, it was as if he were stating the specials at the pub rather than announcing killing the leader of one of the most feared mobs in the known world.

Luckily my horse kept walking because I certainly would have stopped. Success was already a massive long shot because of the people we were going after, and now Foxy announced he's going after the Klipu mob. With the same tone he'd use to order more beets for the weekly stew.

The disbelief and shock I felt must have shown on my face, or maybe it was everyone else who was looking the same. Foxy waved his hand.

"I'll be doing it after we save your friends. Don't worry."

He didn't really know Siabiane or Lorcan but they were our friends, which meant they were important to him as well. His smiles always looked more like he was thinking of tearing your head off but I knew he meant them as smiles.

"We might be able to help you, but first we do need to hide you." Mathilda shook her head. "Had you told us that you were a wanted man sooner, we could have worked something out." She rode closer to where he walked and tilted her head. "Any heavy magic glamour will be picked up by other magic users to some extent. But maybe a light glamour and some makeup? Larisona gave me a bunch of the heavy theatrical stuff she gathered from the homes of those fake Dark."

I looked at Foxy. "He's seven feet tall, with long floppy ears, and tusks. How is makeup going to help?" It wasn't like we were just changing his hair color.

"You have a point. I'd be hard to hide." Foxy didn't seem concerned about it but I knew that none of us wanted to be fighting off bounty hunters along with everyone else.

Except that no one was following us.

"How come no one is following us?" We weren't going to be able to modify Foxy's appearance until we stopped and this was also an issue.

"There's no one left in that village to come after us?" Grillion had been riding alongside us silently.

"Not from there." I held up one hand. "We were attacked before we rescued Alric." One finger. "Then the people we took Alric from. Then the syclarions, which yes, looked to be all dead, but they could have friends."

Two more fingers. "Those knights. Those inane brownies. Whoever sent the birds and sceanra anam after us." On to my second hand. "And Theria. He might not have known where his broken chawsia path left us, but you know he could build another one to try to find us." I left the "if he found enough people to kill" part off. "None of them are after us. Why?"

Covey nodded. "They have their own territories. Common among my people until we became civilized. That odd turnaround from the knights, for example. They could have possibly run us down. But they stopped and turned back—why?"

Padraig hadn't joined in but turned around now. "My thoughts exactly. There seem to be people against us wherever we go. They aren't following, really, but it appears that they know where we'll be. That's why I'm making a detour. There are some springs down here—in theory, anyway—and they might help us sort this out. And give us a place to hide for a day."

Grillion gave a laughing snort before he realized Padraig was serious.

I was fine with water, as long as I didn't have to cross an ocean of it. But I hadn't heard of water stopping people from knowing where we'd be going.

Before much more thought could be given to Padraig's newly mysterious ways, we were invaded.

CHAPTER THIRTY

F ROM THE SOUNDS, which we heard before we saw anything, I really did think we were under attack by evil forces. For a brief moment, I thought maybe I'd jinxed us by pointing out we kept getting attacked but not followed far.

Then Bunky and Irving came into view. They were flying high and a mass of faeries was under them, carrying something below them in the air. Welsy and Delsy were harder to spot, running along the ground as they were, but they also had something with them. Their something was also covered in cloth and trying to fly above them. The thing the faeries held seemed to be fighting back as it was dragged through the air.

"I recommend everyone have weapons and spells ready." Who knew what those hooligans had captured. And, more importantly, how whatever it was felt about being captured. I shaded my eyes to try to see better, but whatever they were bringing in was wrapped too well in that fabric. Bunky and Irving were clearly flying escort but started to come lower as they reached us.

"We gots! They gots! We all gots!" Garbage came down with her flock and their bag of whatever. It wasn't a bag really but a large sheet and the clothesline it had probably been hanging on before the girls grabbed it. Whatever they had in there could definitely run, and Foxy and

Alric had to jump off their horses to grab the rope as the faeries began to let go and the sheet started to run off. There were some serious knots in the line, so at least whatever it was couldn't get out that way. But the things inside were pulling hard to run once they hit the ground.

Welsy and Delsy were smarter as they didn't release their flying bag—also a former sheet—but looked like they would like to hand it over. "We have found some beings of interest. Don't worry, we took off their harnesses." Welsy dumped out a faery black bag, and a bunch of broken spell harnesses with no longer bright-red gems tumbled out.

Crap. "You found more of the murlin? What do the faeries have?"

Delsy bounced a bit as the birds inside their bag started squawking and hopping. He smacked down with his fist and they stopped. "They have the brownies." He looked around the open trail. "We had hoped you would have found shelter by now."

Padraig rode up. "Thank you for bringing these to us, but you're right, out here isn't the best place." He grinned. "Which leads us to my secret location, which should give us shelter and room to investigate what they have brought us." He turned to Mathilda. "Could you quiet them down for now?"

She gave him an odd glance—something like that would be easy for his magic as well—but nodded. One swift bop over both bags with her staff and both groups went still and silent.

Of course, the faeries felt that meant they could take off.

"We gets mores!" Garbage was heading into the air.

"No! You need to stay with us now. Secret things. We need your help." I added a note of concern to my voice on the word *secret*. Padraig wasn't the only one who could use secrets to keep people moving.

Garbage turned back to me. "Importants?" She narrowed her eyes as if forcing me to tell the truth.

"Extremely." I kept my face somber.

"We does. Where go?" She flew over to Padraig.

"Thank you all. Now we need to gather closer together." He motioned for all of us to form a circle around him. We kept the four constructs and the captured birds and brownies in the center. The faeries hovered low over us.

Padraig waved his arm and the trail vanished. For the blink of an eye, I was nowhere. No sight, no sound, no smell, nothing. Then we reappeared in a small clearing. Not too surprising, the center of it was a lake with a waterfall coming off a cliff at the far end. And a suspicious lack of a defined sun, although the area was bright.

"Is this a *tir cudd*?" The only time I'd been in one of these odd places was when we were trying to find the diamond sphinx relic. And it had taken a lot more effort and magic to get inside it. Not to mention that it had almost killed me.

Alric looked around slowly. "How did you know it was here? And get us in so easily?"

"Yes, it is a *tir cudd*. It was on an old map within those scrolls in the ruins we were in, and it wasn't easy. That took all of my magic reserves." Padraig looked around. "Also, I believe the other *tir cudd* had stronger defenses due to the relic and the creatures it was protecting. The note on the map said this was an abandoned one, so I took a chance." He was getting paler as he sat there.

Alric and I jumped off our horses and ran over to him just as he started to fall.

Mathilda came over as we lay him on the ground and looked him over. His eyes were still open but his breath was in rapid, short gasps. And his skin was turning gray.

"Damn it, you overdrew, didn't you?" Alric looked ready to choke him. "You could have asked us to help." He sat back as Mathilda pulled out a small vial of a swirling blue liquid.

"I'd have to agree with Alric. That's the kind of move a child would make, not someone of your age. Now drink this before I hold your nose and force you to."

I'd learned to watch my friends' faces and actions more than their words. Mathilda had been frantic when she ran up but now looked annoyed more than concerned. That was a good thing.

He grimaced but allowed Alric to lift him and took the bottle from Mathilda. He drank it in a single gulp but didn't look happy about it.

"That was as nasty as some of Ceithera's creations."

"Where do you think I learned it?" Mathilda rocked back on her heels. "I swear, I know you're having troubles with the world being upside down from what you knew. But knock it off. You're our leader on this adventure, and I need you to snap out of this funk. Now."

Mathilda or Alric easily could have taken over as leader; Padraig had simply been our automatic default. But they both looked like they weren't going to step in. Yet.

"He needs to rest. My potion will help but he needs to sleep." She glared down at him. "Or do you need help with that too?"

Padraig was a little older than Mathilda, but he'd been in a spell-induced coma for over five hundred years, so in many ways he was much younger. Right now, she looked ready to put him over her knee.

He waved a hand with more strength than before. "I'll sleep. No more potions." Alric had Padraig's bedroll set up next to him and with help, Padraig flopped into it. He rolled away from us and—judging from the snoring—fell asleep.

We went a distance away, closer to the lake and the sound of the waterfall.

"You put something in that potion." Grillion grinned. "Something to sleep."

"Aye. He's a stubborn man, so I thought it best to take the option of not resting away from him. Now, shall we work on our guests? My spell won't hold them long."

Garbage flew up. "We go explore. Be back!" She waved and took off, all before I could respond.

Bunky buzzed in inquiry, and I motioned toward the mass of flying faeries. "Yes, please go after them. Welsy and Delsy can help us with the prisoners." With an agreeing gronk, Bunky and Irving flew after the swarm.

"Which bag to open first?" Covey and Foxy stood over the two sheet bags.

"The brownies," Welsy and Delsy said at the same time. "They have much to answer for."

"Might as well," Alric said. "Not to mention the murlin were most likely magically controlled. We might want to wait to deal with them." He'd scooped up the harnesses and gems when they'd been dumped out, and I knew he wanted to take them apart before dealing with the birds.

It took some work to get the clothesline unknotted, but eventually, seven sleeping brownies appeared amid the flowered sheet. Mathilda held her staff over them, said a few soft words, and the closest one stretched its arms.

Then screamed when he opened his eyes and saw us. "Stay away!" He started patting his pockets.

"We removed your pouches." Welsy leaned forward to sneer at the brownie, then held up another black faery bag—or the same one he'd had the harnesses in. "They are inside. Nasty powder."

"Used by cowards." Delsy stomped to the other side of the brownie. "Have you no honor?"

"I...I...you're not real brownies." The brownie on the ground narrowed his eyes.

Considering that Welsy and Delsy had appeared as if they were biological brownies to the ones we captured at Siabiane's cottage, I found this odd.

"We are exceedingly real. Shall I show you?" Welsy grabbed the brownie and flung him so high in the air that he was lost from sight; then Delsy caught him right before he splattered into the ground.

"Aieee! Brownie guardians come from the original home to smite us all!" The brownie dropped to his knees and bowed.

I looked to Welsy and Delsy, and they shrugged. This could work. I nodded as the brownie continued to prostrate himself.

"Yes! And we are not pleased with any of you!" Welsy's voice was booming and over the top.

I lowered my hand.

"You have much to answer for." Delsy got it a bit better, imperious, but not too much. "Speak now or feel our wrath."

The brownie looked up slowly. "We are a hunter tribe and sometimes find things of interest to bounty hunters. There was a large bounty on that massive beast you had with you. But the wee ones are also valuable, just not as much money." He looked around, even though all of us were standing nearby. "It could mean a lot of money if you could find that creature again."

"That isn't honorable behavior. How sad the brownies have fallen so low," Welsy said. "Tell us, who gave you the powder? Who were you supposed to bring the beast back to?"

I wasn't happy about being called a beast, but it wasn't far off, technically.

"The powder was made by a witch in the south. A cruel one who has been causing problems. She appeared before the beast when we tried to take it and tried to get us."

"Siabiane? She is not evil." It looked like Delsy was going to say more but a sharp look from Welsy stopped him.

Siabiane was trapped; she wasn't out roaming the countryside. But that did explain them running off as they did when her visage appeared. Damn it. Who was using Siabiane's likeness?

"Where were you to take the creature when you captured it? To this evil witch?" Welsy recovered first from the shock of them trying to blame Siabiane. Delsy still looked like he wanted to throttle the brownie until he admitted he was lying.

I'd expected him to say Colivith since our mysterious watcher said we needed to go there. I was extremely wrong.

"Notlianda. Lady Qianru. She is expecting us and those we bring back." He looked up eagerly. Whoever these brownie guardians were, they were beings that caused a lot of worship and fear among brownies—something to keep in mind for future encounters. "There is a rather large reward for the beast. We could split it, you know."

True brownie: even scared, he was looking out for the money. I briefly wondered what he'd do if he knew I was the beast.

"That is not appropriate behavior from one of our kind. If you wish to be protected by the guardians, you need to stop grabbing innocent beings for your gain." Delsy looked sternly at the brownie.

"Yes, your guardianship. But the beast isn't innocent. We were told of its crimes. It destroyed a ship at sea. It damaged a classic stronghold that was thousands of years old. It stole the magic gems of intari. It is a danger and a menace."

I assumed that the magic gems of intari were the gems Crusty stole. By the nodding and looks from Alric, Covey, and Mathilda, they had heard of them, even if I hadn't. When we finally got through all of this and I could settle down with Alric in Beccia, I would start reading more history books. Or at least try.

The brownie was about to continue when the faeries and Bunky and Irving came swooping in. At first they were just a mob, but once they got close enough to see what they were, the brownie yelled, ran off, and managed to slam into one of the few trees in the area.

Welsy and Delsy ran over. "Knocked himself out. Should you wake another one?" They came back, dragging the unconscious brownie between them.

"I think we got what we can out of them." Alric looked at the pile of brownies. "But I don't know if we want to go through the entire brownie guardian routine again. I am concerned about Qianru, but at least we're aware." He looked up as the faeries landed. They looked worked up about something. That could range from a sadly deceased mouse or an artifact that could destroy the world. "But maybe we should wait until we sort out what's up with them. Can you put this one separate from the others?"

Welsy and Delsy dropped him where they stood.

Mathilda went over to look at the brownie. "He didn't hit his head terribly hard, but we don't want him waking up until we're ready." She waved her staff over him. "Let's keep him asleep a bit longer."

Garbage came zipping down but the rest of her flock stayed airborne. "Not empty hide-hole. Bad things."

CHAPTER THIRTY-ONE

"WHAT BAD THINGS, sweetie?" A chill went down my back at some of the bad things that we'd encountered in one of these *tir cudds* before. As far as I could tell, there were no killer rocks, murderous trees, or dangerously unfinished but transformed male faeries.

"Big things, little things, all bads." She folded her arms as if that explained everything.

I took a deep breath. It had taken fifteen years but I'd finally learned that dealing with the faeries took different angles sometimes. "What would *we* call those things?"

"Bad."

"Are they all the same type of thing?"

"Small. And big."

I would be willing to ignore the headache she was causing, but the rest of the flock were still circling above us and had donned their war feathers. This wasn't good. Bunky and Irving were circling the flock of faeries but appeared to be on the lookout.

"Do we need to fight or hide?" That was as basic as I could get.

She paused and looked out across the plain to a clump of trees. When she turned back to me, her tiny orange face was serious. "Hide. That way." She pointed to the waterfall. Faeries did fine in water but they weren't really aquatic beings. The horses and the rest of us definitely weren't.

Welsy and Delsy bundled the unconscious brownies back up in their sheet. And Foxy picked up the still unconscious Padraig. Alric tied Padraig's horse behind his, and Foxy's behind that.

Damn it, whatever these bads were, everyone believed Garbage. So did I, but I did wish we knew what we were hiding from.

"Maybe there's a cave near the falls. That cliff dips back a bit to the right." Covey had better eyesight than me, so I took her word for it. We were far enough away that it all looked like one giant rock to me.

Foxy started jogging in that direction, the weight of Padraig in his arms not seeming to slow him down at all. Bunky grabbed the bag of brownies, and Irving grabbed the bag of birds. The rest of us got on our horses and followed.

"This! Move faster! This way!" Garbage and her flock stayed right in front of Foxy but kept pointing to the waterfall. We were already riding along the water's edge and the lake looked fairly deep.

"Sweetie, we can't go into the lake." As we got closer, I kept looking at the cliff face for any breaks but it still looked solid.

Alric and his string of horses passed Foxy and started veering closer to the waterfall. Those sharp elven eyes picked up something that we hadn't seen. The faeries hovered near the cliff, yelling about going faster. I hadn't seen anything behind us but the hair on the back of my neck was rising.

"There's something dark behind the fall. There's a walkway to it." Alric picked up more speed.

I'd become jaded over the past few years of relic mayhem. My thinking was that something large and dark with a convenient path leading to it was most likely a cave monster waiting to swallow us all. I kept my cheery thoughts to myself but kept my hand on my dagger. My sword popping in and almost falling to the ground as we ran didn't make me feel any better.

Before I could yell for him to wait, Alric vanished into the waterfall. Foxy followed without pause, but I slowed down.

Alric stuck his head out of the fall, yet he didn't look wet at all. "It's safe. Come on!"

I charged ahead, with the others on my tail. Even though Alric had appeared dry, I still flinched as my horse and I ran through the fall.

Not a single drop of water on me or her. There was water, I felt the spray, but there were two layers and the real water was farther out over the lake. We ran through an illusion spell. I kept riding into the cave as the others followed with Bunky, Irving, and the faeries bringing up the rear.

I wasn't sure what I'd been expecting, but the cave was massive. Alric had already sent up some glows toward the ceiling and the back, which made me feel a bit better that something probably wasn't going to pop out and eat us. Or if it did, we'd see it coming.

The faeries tore around the cave, flitting about everywhere. Irving and Bunky dropped off their sheet-wrapped cargo and joined them.

"I still don't know what's after us and if we could get here, what's to stop them?" Grillion had stayed near the waterfall and kept looking out.

I nodded in complete agreement. There was nothing but some water overlying an illusion spell of water between us and whatever the faeries had seen.

"Bads no see now," Garbage said as she, Leaf, and Crusty broke away from the mob and flew over to us.

"Is goods," Leaf added.

"Old hides. Noseeum no gets," Crusty said.

That sounded disturbing. "Noseeums? As in whatever

is after us is invisible?" The last thing we needed were invisible foes. How would we ever leave this place?

"They be seen, but not here. Some see here. We see. He see." Garbage pointed to Foxy. "You see. Others no see." She'd pointed to me as her "you see." But I was clueless as to why Foxy and I could see things that the others couldn't.

"How can Foxy and I see them?" I looked out through the water; the area we'd raced through looked empty to me. "If something was following us, I don't see it. Foxy? Did you see anything?" I came away from the falls.

He'd carefully placed Padraig down but shook his head. "I wasn't looking on the way in to be truthful, but when I did, I didn't see anything."

Garbage flew over and tapped my tattoo from Amara and then Foxy's. "This make see." Amara's tattoos gave us some power in the *tir cudd*. "But need more." She scowled. "We fixes." Before any of us could yell no, Garbage zipped to everyone except Foxy and me, and stabbed each person once with her war stick. Judging by the lack of yelling in pain, the stick didn't hurt this time.

Grillion was still the only one close to the falls, and his yelp and jump back told me that Garbage's poke had worked. He stumbled back toward the rest of us. "You have to see this." He looked around. "Can they hear us?" Whatever *they* were, it was clear he hoped that answer was no.

"I can make sure they don't." Alric released a spell and the interior of the cave dimmed. Then he walked to the waterfall. "Damn, narbeasts. I'd say someone else found this abandoned *tir cudd* before we did. They have harnesses on."

Narbeasts weren't unusual. But like so many creatures we were coming up against, they didn't live this far south. Massive armor-skinned animals with three nasty horns on their broad, flattish heads. They were used as draft animals by trolls and northern gnomes. A quick peek told me they looked just as I'd imagined. Terrifying.

They thundered past the lake, giving no notice to the waterfall or us hiding behind it. Good thing, too; although they looked like plant eaters, they apparently ate anything they could find. The ultimate omnivore. Like the licten beasts, they lived in the tundra. There were too many far northern species living down here for it to be a coincidence.

"Big noseeums." Crusty waved goodbye to the passing herd with a sad look.

"Honey? You know those things are dangerous, right?"

She sighed. "Is yes, but want to pet."

Even Garbage yelled no at that.

The rest of the faeries went back to investigating the cave, and my original three started to join them.

"Wait, those were the big ones, but you said there were also little ones?" I expected smaller vicious beasts to be out there, but I saw nothing.

Garbage stuck her tiny head out of the not-water waterfall, then pulled it back in. "Not there."

"I gathered that; do you know where they are? Can we see them?" I waved her stick away. "Without help from your gang, and not counting Foxy and me, could we see them if they came by?"

She tilted her head, went into a low-pitched discussion with Leaf and Crusty—neither of whom said a thing—then turned back. "No." I think she'd seen us have discussions too many times but had no idea what they were.

"So, the noseeums, both types, are hidden to anyone without that mark from Amara or a stab from your sticks?" Covey was still peering out through the fall, but she seemed more focused on the water, or whatever was pretending to be water.

"Or other marks. Those see too."

"Other marks? What kind of marks?"

Leaf did a fast movement in the air; at a look from me, she slowed it down. Way down. A circle and a dagger.

"This *tir cudd* is being used by the Dark?" We needed to wake Padraig up and have him get us out of here. Now.

Garbage shook her head. "Wrong marks." She drifted down to the dirt, grabbed a twig—her war stick had already been put away—and drew a semi-circle, another semi-circle, and a jagged line on top of the two.

My stomach dropped as some part of me recognized the symbol. "I don't think that's much better." I chewed on the side of my thumb and told myself that there was no way I could recall something like that after twenty-five hundred years. The cold horrified mass in my stomach said otherwise. I knew that mark.

"Taryn?" Alric appeared right in front of me, which probably meant he'd spoken my name a few times already.

"What? Sorry. That just triggered something. The syclarions like Edana and Nivinal pretended to be part of the Dark as long as it helped their agenda. But that was what they belonged to. An old syclarion group that focused on the evil arts. I forgot about them." My voice trailed out at the end, but it was all I could do to not run away screaming and keep running until I hit the end of the *tir cudd*.

"You mean the Paili? Are you sure?" Mathilda walked slowly around Garbage's drawing. "That does look like their mark. But they were only rumors when Siabiane and I moved north, and nothing more." She must have noticed my face as she came closer. "They're gone. Any who remained were destroyed when you used your staff twenty-five hundred years ago."

"Edana and Nivinal were both Paili. I remember now. That group was who killed my parents. They took credit for their deaths." I couldn't decide if I was going to get sick or have to go out and kill something evil to vent my anger. Maybe we could get the narbeasts to come back and I could beat up a few. A laugh escaped at that thought.

"What's funny?" Alric was close but aside from Padraig, who was still unconscious, all my friends were. And they all looked worried.

"Just had an odd visual. I'll be okay. But if those two survived, we have to assume that others did as well. Someone set this up and hid these animals inside a hidden pocket of the world. Who does that?" I put my arms around myself tightly and forced calming thoughts.

"Garbage? Are there other marks that can make someone see the noseeums?" Mathilda asked.

"Is yes." She was still on the ground, so she pushed people away from her area and started scribbling quickly. When she stopped, there were fifteen symbols there, sixteen if you counted the Paili.

"I'm not picking up anything from any of the others." I walked around them slowly, waiting for any sort of recognition to hit. Nothing.

"They are all from the old deities. Seven goddesses, five gods, and three ascetics. They were all lost in the great mage war that destroyed Amara's sisters." Mathilda squinted at the drawings as if they could tell her more. "Yet none of these were tree goddesses. They were all nature deities, but none of Amara's sisters."

Grillion was looking at the marks, but staying back as far as he could. "These nature deities set up those narbeasts in here? Why? Thought it was abandoned?"

"It was abandoned. But I don't think any nature deities would have brought narbeasts to a place like this. Nor do I think any animals have been in here for a few thousand years until extremely recently." Padraig had gotten up and walked over so silently that both Grillion and I jumped when he spoke. The others didn't seem surprised at his sudden appearance. "Thank you for the sleeping addition to your potion. I feel remarkably refreshed." He flashed Mathilda a smile. "What do we have here?"

Garbage flew up to his face and pointed back toward her symbols. "Those can see noseeums. And the plant lady friends. Big noseeums run. No littles yet." She nodded slowly and pointed to her eye. "But wes saw littles. They there."

I had to give him credit: he'd overdrawn his magic to a point of collapse, just woken up, and yet he nodded and smiled as if Garbage's statement made perfect sense.

"Is okay." Garbage patted Padraig's cheek, then flew off with Leaf and Crusty to join the flock.

Padraig walked closer to Garbage's markings. "The Paili and a bunch of nature deities? Missing and presumed dead, if I know my theology."

"Those are the ones, along with Foxy and I, who have Amara's mark, who can see the noseeums that apparently live here. Well, everyone in here now can see them since the faeries did something and poked everyone. None of them are good and the big ones were narbeasts. Still waiting on the little ones." Talking about things other than directly discussing the Paili and their possible continued existence helped. So did Alric wrapping an arm around my shoulder.

Padraig took another long look out through the fall, then came back. "Let's move farther away from the edge. Magic seems to be distorted here, and Alric's sound spell might not hold as well as it should."

I'd been standing there when Alric cast his spell, and once the glow had faded I wouldn't have been able to tell that he'd done it. Padraig's magic was recovering at least.

Alric pulled in some more glows and set them together so we could see each other as we moved deeper into the cave.

"I'm sorry I have been acting odd, even pulling everyone here as I did…I should have told you that was my plan. But I knew if I did, certain other magic users would insist on joining in and there was a chance that it was a trap."

"So it was better for you to sacrifice yourself instead of asking for help?" Mathilda was seriously pissed. "Who gave you that right? Together, we might have been able to determine if it was a trap. Instead, you drained your magic and risked your life." She started to say more but closed her mouth.

I'd known Mathilda longer than I'd known anyone here aside from my three faeries. And I'd never seen her so furious.

"What's happened to you?" Alric almost seemed hurt more than mad, but he could pull a stoic look when he wanted to and he was doing that now.

"I just didn't want to risk anyone else…"

"No." Covey watched him carefully. "There's more than that. I'm not a magic user like our friends here, but you are acting reckless because you feel lost. You were fine before Alric was taken. Your behavior has been slowly changing since then." She hunched forward to watch him better. "That was your point."

"His point?" Covey was dangerously smart in many disciplines, but I wasn't following her on this.

"His breaking point." Her lean face softened as she turned back to him. "You never had a real chance to deal with losing your wife and friends. Then the enclave fell. Then Alric, your brother in all but biology, was taken. And you couldn't stop any of it. Not to mention your friend is an actual Ancient, you ran into a former tree goddess, and there seems to be a new world order trying to break through." She smiled. "We live in interesting times and it's terrifying."

Padraig kept his face still as she spoke, and I was afraid she'd insulted him by bringing up his lost wife. He hadn't had time to grieve over anything.

Finally, he sighed. "I was trying to see if there was a polite way to point out how horribly wrong you were but I can't. Hells, I never dealt with being struck down right before the Breaking and waking up five hundred years later. I've developed a great skill of avoidance."

"The more things you ignore, the more problems they cause." She gave him a crooked smile. "My life is nowhere near as messed up as yours or Taryn's has been. But I found meditation, solitude, and reflection helped a lot."

"None of which we have time for right now." He held up his hand as all of us protested that. "But that doesn't mean I'll ignore things. I'll work on small sections; maybe with Covey's assistance?"

Covey nodded and patted his knee. "Much rather that than you doing something irresponsible." She looked around. "Actually, too late for that. I'm not a magic user, but even I know coming in here was an absurdly reckless move."

"Incredibly reckless." Mathilda looked less angry but it was clear that her anger had been driven by fear for her friend. It was also clear that she'd be watching him closely. "For good or bad, we are together on this. I believe all of us," she looked over as Grillion turned away, "including Grillion, are facing things we didn't expect. We need to tell each other if something is wrong. This is looking to be a much more important trip than getting back my sister and Lorcan."

Everyone was silent for a bit, so I jumped in. "Any idea what we do next? How long are we staying here? Why did we come here?"

Padraig laughed. "I did have a legitimate reason. Two, actually. Something followed us after we left the village. They started tailing us about an hour before we got here. I couldn't see them, but I could sense them."

"What were they?" Grillion shook his head at himself as soon as the words left his mouth. "Never mind, you couldn't see them."

"No, and that disturbed me. Whatever they were, they were being magically shielded."

"Noseeums!" Crusty had drifted over to us and popped up next to Padraig. "You no see."

"Those narbeasts, the big noseeums, were behind us?"

"Nos. No get out. Same." She wiggled her fingers.

The faeries *were* magic, so they didn't use it really. But I'd noticed that finger move when they were talking about other magics.

"Someone used magic similar to what was in here on things out there?"

"Yup!" Satisfied that she'd sorted us out, she flew off.

"Does that help at all?" There was no way I was asking her for more.

"Yes, it coincides with what I felt not long before I brought us here, but it didn't seem right as it was magic that should be gone from this world. With this information, I believe my feeling was correct. I don't think you're going to be happy about it." He was looking at me, and a sick feeling hit my stomach.

"Paili magic users." Alric tightened his grip on my shoulder as I said the words.

CHAPTER THIRTY-TWO

———◆———

"I BELIEVE SO," PADRAIG said. "The taint of it was weak; other magics were included, which diluted it. But their magic is distinct. They aren't full necromancers, but they are closer to them than any other type. Nivinal successfully hid his Paili magic when he lived in the enclave as one of us. I never ran into Edana directly, or I might have noticed it."

"Why didn't they attack, though?" Grillion asked but Foxy nodded in agreement. "Why just follow? I'm not saying that I wanted to fight off nasty magic users that make our lady dragon go pale, but we were in the middle of nowhere—that's when I would have attacked."

I wasn't sure how I felt about being called a lady dragon—it was technically true, but still.

"He has a point," Covey said. "The Paili were known as brutal and opportunistic. That Nivinal had been able to hide who and what he was for a thousand years inside your enclave was unheard of."

"He didn't have a choice," Mathilda said. "That shield went up fast and there was no in or out. Siabiane was going to make them let me in, but I refused. He *couldn't* get out. She was furious when she realized that he'd been right in front of them all that time. As for not attacking us, they most likely had a better spot for the attack planned further up the trail."

The sheet bag that held the brownies started twitching. It was near the entrance to the cave, and I didn't think letting a bunch of brownies loose in a *tir cudd*, semi-abandoned or not, was a good idea. I was closest, so I grabbed the bag and dragged it back to where we were sitting.

Covey followed suit with the bird bag. They weren't moving yet, but they would be.

"Not to change the subject, but what are we doing with these?" I wiggled the brownie bag and their movement stopped.

Welsy and Delsy had been sitting under the illusion waterfall but came running over. "We can take care of them."

I didn't let go of the bag; I had a bad feeling that taking care of them involved the lake outside.

Alric opened the bag, peeked in, and then shook his head. "They're not awake yet, mostly trying to shake off the spell. I don't know how much more we can get from them. But I don't want them or the murlin following us."

His main concern with the murlin had been the harnesses they'd worn and the now dead spell gems. I'd noticed he'd kept those in his small black faery bag, most likely so he could take them apart later.

"I'd like to question the brownies more thoroughly, but we don't have time. We do have something I want to find here. Then we need to get back on the trail to Notlianda." Padraig started to cast a spell, then looked to Alric and Mathilda with a wince. "Still recovering. Might you two freeze those bags for now?" As he spoke, the brownie bag started moving more. Until Alric spelled it. Mathilda did the same with the birds.

"That's not permanent." Alric stepped back to me. "They will wake up eventually. Might take a few days, but they're still alive."

"But they can't hear us now and we can dump them outside of the *tir cudd* once we leave. However, as I said,

I came here for more than just to escape. This place had an odd symbol on it on the map. A fractured crown." Padraig gave a dramatic pause. His smile dimmed a bit when none of us responded.

I was glad I wasn't the only one looking at him blankly. Even Covey and Mathilda had narrowed their eyes.

"None of you know the myth of the golden canfydd crown? Alric? Mathilda? Didn't you hear it as kids?"

They both shook their heads, which prompted Padraig to rummage through his pack and drag out the map. "In the tales, there was a magic crown worn by a queen of old; one which gave great powers to its wearer. But it could also bring great sorrow and madness. I won't tell you the entire tale, but suffice it to say, it was found to be bad for all beings and destroyed." He grinned like a five-year-old on naming day. "The symbol on the map matches the one given in the stories precisely."

"You brought us here to find another dangerous relic? Didn't we have enough of those with the glass gargoyle and crew?" In my opinion, lost mythological bad things were not a good idea and should not be found.

"I think it actually belonged to your people. There were some references to it and the missing Ancients in some of those scrolls from the Library of Pernasi that you got when we were in the enclave. Many myths are created to keep people away from powerful objects."

The way he nodded, I wondered how many myths he'd created just for that same task in the past.

"Thank you, but I'm not sure how finding a dangerous crown is going to help me. And the rest of my people are still missing." I didn't say that out loud often. Nor think it. But those words haunted me. My people were missing because of me. That was not something to get over quickly and my gut tightened every time I thought about it.

Padraig watched me for a moment. "Based on what I

read, I believe we can use it to at least find what period of time your people were sent to. Given enough research and time, we might be able to bring them back to our current time." He looked around the cave. "Sorry. Getting us out of harm's way was the main focus of my pulling us here, but I will admit I was intrigued by the crown and had been thinking about diverting here. It won't help us right now, not to mention its jewels were all destroyed so it doesn't have the power it once did. But I couldn't pass up this chance. After we rescue the others and are safely back in the north, we can work on finding your people."

I wiped away the tears that caused. He was thinking more about my people than I had been. "Thank you."

"We're a family, Taryn. Family helps family." He rolled up the map. "Now, it might not seem like it, but it is night. My plan is to rest here tonight, find the crown tomorrow morning, and head out after. I might need some spell support on the getting out part. I want to put us far south from where we went in to throw off whoever was following us." He looked to Alric, Mathilda, and me at that. It was nice to be included in the magic user's status again. I hadn't pushed my magic, but it hadn't failed me since we'd gotten on back on land.

"So we can just find this crown, just like that? Why not get it now?" Grillion was becoming less of a relic thief as we traveled together, but it was still in his soul.

"Yes, we can. Rather, our tiny flying friends can." He nodded to where the faeries had gathered in a circle near the front of the cave. "But we need to be well-rested when we go for it—them too. Taryn, can you get them to rest? Tomorrow will be trying for everyone."

I looked to the giggling faeries by the waterfall. The last thing we needed right now was to have them take off exploring. I sighed. I needed to think of something that would make them stay and sleep.

"Girls?" I rummaged through the bottom of my pack.

Harlan had given me a chunk of chocolate for the trip, and I still had about half of it. I would be sad not to eat the rest but it was for the greater good. "Girls? I have chocolate." As I spoke, I went farther into the cave. When they passed out from the chocolate, they would pretty much drop wherever they were. Having them not under-foot would be helpful, even if we weren't planning on staying up late either.

A third call to them and all of the faeries swarmed me with hands out. I kept the chocolate hidden in my bag. "I need all of you to settle down. I have some important things to say."

Garbage finally had to whistle to get them settled.

"Thank you. Now first I want to thank all of you for working so hard lately. We all appreciate it greatly. As a thank-you, I am giving you all a bit of chocolate. You'll share it." I looked around to see all of the faeries watch-ing me and nodding. Except for Crusty. She was looking at the ceiling. She did nod, though. "Secondly, no one goes out of this cave until we're all ready to go out. This is important." Even Crusty flipped around to nod this time.

"Okay, here you go." The chocolate piece was still fairly large and I thought about saving part of it for myself. But better that they were all taken care of. I needed them to sleep.

The faeries were controlled chaos as they each broke off a piece and flew off to cram it in their mouths. By the time the last faery had taken her piece, the first ones were already sitting on the floor, ready to pass out. When I walked back to join the others, all the faeries were either curled up into happy little balls, asleep or nearing there.

"That was well played. I wish I'd known about their reaction to chocolate when they first came to live with me." Mathilda had a fond look as she watched them sleep. "Would have come in extremely handy."

I smiled as the group settled in for the night. Padraig was at the farthest end of the cave, going over meditation with Covey. I nodded in his direction as Alric and I set up our bedrolls together.

"Do you think he'll be okay?"

He watched them, then turned back. "I believe so. It's not going to be easy; he has a lot to work through and we're likely going to add more before this is over."

I snuggled into his side with my arm around his torso and his arm in my hair. It would be nice to have some private time, but after having him taken like that, I was currently just happy to be near him.

I fell asleep almost immediately and woke to faery yelling. Always a nice way to start the day.

"Bads!" All of the faeries were stomping on the brownie sheet bag. Considering that the brownies should have still been frozen, I was at a loss for the reasoning. I was also groggy. I'd fallen asleep as hard as they had. Alric looked more awake than I felt and helped me to my feet.

"What are they doing?" He didn't go closer to them.

"I have no idea." I walked over. Garbage was doing most of the yelling and stomping but the rest of the flock was joining in. My non-faery friends were in a variety of stages of waking up.

"Girls? What are you doing?"

"Stomps!" was yelled by more than a few of them.

"Bads moving." Garbage held back from stomping long enough for me to see movement under the sheet.

"Folks? Shouldn't that last spell have left them frozen still?" I didn't hear any noises coming from the bag, but there was no doubt there was movement. "And what is that smell?" A nasty rotting odor drifted my way.

"Bads! Nasty bads!" Garbage yelled.

"Go bads." Crusty wrinkled her nose and a number of the faeries flew away from the bag.

"Can I look?" Alric walked over. "I will spell them if

they try anything." All of us moved closer.

"Fines. But bad." Garbage led her crew up in the air where Bunky and Irving hovered.

"We could do that for you, if you'd rather," Welsy said.

"We're not able to be killed," Delsy added.

"I think I'll be fine. But please jump in if they try to get out." Alric appeared more concerned as the rotting smell increased. He cautiously untied the knot holding the sheet closed, peered inside, then frantically tied it back up. His sword appeared and he stood back, ready to use it.

"They've become zombies."

The bag twitched still but his knot was holding. Until small claws started working their way through the sheet. Brownies didn't have claws. Apparently, the zombie version did.

"They weren't dead!" Grillion looked groggy but at the word zombie, he'd grabbed his sword.

"A strong necromancer helps that process along." Padraig also had his spirit sword. "I'd say these brownies had been working for the wrong person."

"They're in here?" Foxy had his massive sword and moved toward the cave mouth.

"I'd doubt it." Mathilda walked around the twitching bag slowly. "My guess is these brownies had a spell attached. One that was triggered when they failed their job or in this case, vanished." She poked the sheet bag with her staff as a zombified brownie arm came through the sheet. "They aren't very strong, though."

"Let's keep it that way. Does anyone mind if I do the honors? Learning from them is impossible now." Alric was already working through a spell in his head.

I could tell when his left hand started twitching.

"By all means." Padraig gave a small bow. "Given the situation, you won't mind if the rest of us stand by?"

"Of course not." Alric smiled, then stepped closer.

Bunky charged down at his approach and looked to be

trying to bump heads. It was something he used to do with Alric whether Alric liked it or not. But this wasn't the time.

"Not now, Bunky."

Bunky dove around and put himself between Alric and the bag.

"Why is it doing that?" Grillion asked in a loud stage whisper.

"Bunky?" I stepped forward. "Alric has to take care of the zombie brownies. He can play later."

He gronked and made another pass for Alric's head. Bunky was a unique creature but he'd never done something like this. Meanwhile, a second zombified brownie arm ripped through the bag.

"Alric, touch him. The chimeras hold memories, right? He might have something that could help." I couldn't understand Bunky's gronks, but others could.

"He's saying this will help." Alric reached out his left hand, touched Bunky, and froze. He stepped back, shaking his head. "Damn. Had I used the spell I was planning on, they could have increased. The one behind this is tricky. Change of spell." He put away his sword and wrapped the bag in a spell bubble, a strong one if the opaqueness of it was any indication. Then he motioned for everyone to stand clear as he magically lifted it and moved toward the cave mouth.

We followed as it went through the waterfalls, both illusion and reality, then kept going higher.

I had no idea what to expect. Before being captured, Alric had been working on my spells but we hadn't gotten far. I knew there was plenty he hadn't taught me yet. And there were a lot of images, thoughts, and spells stored in Bunky.

Alric spoke a few soft words that vanished the moment he said them. The spell bubble kept rising but was starting to glow red. A moment later, it exploded.

CHAPTER THIRTY-THREE

ALRIC HAD BRACED himself for the explosion but none of us had. "Sorry. A new spell. No idea it would hit that hard."

The faeries were even affected and tumbled around in the air above us, laughing.

"Do again!" Crusty yelled out from somewhere in the mob.

Foxy shook his head and nodded to Bunky. "Not sure what you told him, but thanks to you for saving us. I really don't like zombies." He shuddered and put away his massive sword.

I didn't think anyone other than their creators actually liked zombies, but I knew what he meant. Glorindal had secretly raised a troll zombie to attack the Shimmering Dewdrop to impress me when he defeated it. It had. Until I realized he'd created it and was basically a soul-sucking follower of the Dark. Up until Alric, my choice of men wasn't great.

Mathilda scowled out of the cave at the tiny bits of zombie and sheet that drifted down. Extremely tiny. It was more like a brownie zombie dust than anything. She cast a spell and the dust dispersed. "I'd rather those particles were never near each other. Ever."

I turned back to the bird bag. It wasn't moving and we weren't sure if the birds had been sent by the same people as the brownies, but better to be safe.

"Girls? Are the birds zombies too?"

Garbage flew over and sniffed. "Nope. No more go-go."
She shrugged.

Covey was closest so she cautiously undid the knot.
"Are they supposed to be blue? I thought murlin had
black feathers."

Yup. The pile of birds was blue and they didn't look like
they started that way.

"Oops. Too much mojo. Broke now." Leaf flew over
and before any of us could say anything, broke off the tip
of a feather. "Nope. No workie."

"That spell of mine shouldn't have done that." Mathilda
looked into the bag and frowned.

"Mine shouldn't have triggered a zombie response
either," Alric said. "I'd say this place has an odd impact
on spells."

"Are they dead?" I was guessing so, as pieces shouldn't
just come off live birds. But they were also extremely
frozen.

"Yes." Padraig turned to Alric. "Did Bunky give you
any insight as to what to do with these?"

"No, it was only about the zombies. When things have
settled, I think we need to have a long chat with Bunky
and his chimera friends. I've never had something like
that happen before."

I had. Every time I tried to pet Bunky without gloves.

"Feed noseeums." Garbage flew forward and poked
one of the frozen birds. "They yum."

I hoped Garbage was saying the narbeasts would think
they were yum and not the faeries. Better not to ask
sometimes.

"I'm fine with that. Maybe it'll keep the narbeasts away
long enough for us to find the crown and get out of
here." Padraig had packed away his things, but had the
map and a small scroll out. "I didn't want to read this pas-

sage last night because I believe it will trigger the faeries. But there was a section of the scroll that pertained to the faeries and the canfydd crown. Sometime long ago, I believe the faeries were involved with the hiding of it. Probably not these ones specifically, but the passage speaks of a genetic aspect connecting them all."

We'd run into things like that with them before. No one knew how old the faeries were, although from what they'd told me, they were the oldest people.

"Let's get everything together, then we can offer the birds to the narbeasts and you can set your spell." Mathilda looked around the cave for anything we forgot.

Things took a bit longer than expected because we kept chasing off the faeries when they wanted to jump on the dead and frozen murlin. But eventually, we got on the move, away from the cave. The horses had been quiet during their time in the cave but nickered softly as we got out, clearly happy to be in the fresh air. Crusty flew to my mare and patted her head. "Good horsey." That was one of the few times I'd heard any of them use the correct name for something—aside from the kittahs and puppy they traveled with. Then she smiled at me and tore off after the others.

"Don't we need them here to find that crown thing?" They and Bunky and Irving were flying around us but slowly lifting higher as they went. I didn't want to be in this place any longer than we had to and searching for them could prolong it.

"I think the passage I read will bring them down to us and where they need to go. The magic contained in the words almost leaps off the page." Padraig kept switching between keeping an eye on the faeries and his scroll.

Foxy and Grillion moved the sheet bag with the murlin in it a distance away, then came back. Grillion got on his horse. At first, Foxy didn't; then he looked up into the sky. "I know I can walk faster than him, but I have a tingle that says we might be running." He climbed awkwardly into the saddle.

Padraig read from his scroll. Like the spell Alric had used, I heard the words, but they didn't stay in my mind long enough to process them. I'd sort of hoped my Ancient brain would catch them and give me insight, but nope.

The effect on the faeries was immediate, however. They stopped in midair, swarmed over our heads, then took off across the plain. The ground started shaking, and at first I thought it was part of the spell. Then I saw the herd of narbeasts coming our way.

Padraig yelled to his horse, and we ran away from the narbeasts and after the faeries. Welsy rode with Padraig and Delsy rode with Grillion, and both looked far too excited. Siabiane might not be thrilled with the changes in her serious brownie constructs. The adventure bug had hit them hard.

I glanced back and sure enough, the narbeasts detoured to the frozen bird offering. One problem avoided.

The faeries didn't look back at us but seemed to know we were there as they'd loop around us from time to time. Bunky and Irving flew on the outside of the swarm, but they were following them just as we were.

I had a lot of questions but as everyone else was silent, I felt it best to stay that way too.

The faeries were heading toward an old gnarled tree just inside a small grove of regular pines. It was so massive in size that at first I didn't recognize it. Then I started swearing. It was a sycubian tree. A much larger cousin to the one that had trapped almost all of the faeries back at the elven enclave a month ago. Lorcan might have said that these trees were more populous in my time, but my only memory was of Alric, Garbage, and me tricking one so we could get the faeries out of it.

The same faeries who were flying directly into the

maw of this giant one. "Padraig! That's a sycubian tree! What was in that passage?" We'd used honey and a large stick to get the faeries out of the last one. We'd need gallons of honey and a ten-foot stick to do that this time.

"It shouldn't hurt them." He stared at the tree as the faeries approached. "The passage was for them to go to where the hidden stay and then away. I'm hoping the crown might be in that tree."

I wasn't sure if I believed the bit about this random crown helping me get my people back, but I knew what those trees did and that one wasn't taking my faeries without a fight. I rode after them as the others slowed down. I didn't want to stop the faeries; I just wanted to make sure they were okay.

I heard the others yelling but I jumped off my horse and threw myself into the tree just as the faeries did. The snap of the formerly open tree mouth slamming shut was not what I wanted to hear.

"Tricked!" Garbage shook herself and looked around the hollow interior. "Bad tree!" She kicked the side, then started squirming as her foot stuck.

I pulled her free.

"What should have happened?" The interior was like a sappy, sticky, tall, and narrow cave. I motioned for the faeries to gather closer to me and freed five more from the goopy walls.

"Come here, get old hat, leave. Bad tree!"

I was still holding her so she couldn't kick the goo again but she swung a bit in my hand as she spoke.

It could have been me that set off the tree. Maybe the tree would have allowed the girls to get the crown and leave if I hadn't been with them. I let that thought settle a bit, then laughed inside my head. Right. A magical and sentient tree with a taste for mayhem and faeries, in a pocket reality, not intending to eat the faeries. Yeah, no.

Sentient. Lorcan had once said these trees didn't think

like we did but were sentient. Maybe I could use that.

"So this tree lied. It doesn't have the hat." I faced Garbage but the words were aimed at the tree. "It's not as powerful as it pretends." My words worked a little too well. The tree shivered and a golden tendril reached out to grab three faeries. I was waiting for it and pulled out Rhyfel. The golden tendril dropped before I had to touch it with the dagger, but it didn't give up. A few more tendrils tried to appear but crackles from Rhyfel sent them back into the goo.

"Tree, we can keep doing this or you can give us what we came for and let all of us go." A feeling came from around me. This tree was older than my real age, extremely aware, and snooty. All communicated without words.

Did he want snooty? I could do more than that. I sent back feelings too. The crown, the faeries, and me free, and what I looked like in my other form. This was a big tree, but my full-sized dragon-self was much larger. With my magic protecting me, I'd shatter this tree from the inside if I had to.

I felt the tree pause as it tasted my words. Then fear. Not from me—of me. I didn't like scaring things but he wanted to eat my faeries. That wasn't going to happen, with or without the crown.

I sent back the image of the crown, the faeries and me free, and a happy, intact tree.

There was a serious slap of hate-anger-fear flowing my way, then the mouth opened again and I, the faeries, some metal objects, and a lot of tree sap went flying out and it slammed shut again.

CHAPTER THIRTY-FOUR

———◆———

ALRIC WAS AT my side in an instant and his sword vanished as he grabbed me. "Are you okay? Why did you do that?" He was hug-chastising me and his voice reflected both feelings.

"That tree was tricking the faeries and intended to keep the crown and eat the faeries." I looked around at all the goo-covered faeries and objects. "Garbage, can you make sure that all of your faeries are here? Can someone check for the crown? I have a lot of flame built up if a certain tree lied to me." I growled at the tree. It looked like a few limbs shook, but nothing more came out.

"Alls here!" Garbage had her goo-covered faeries all standing. "Too ick." She pulled at her overalls. They were filthy. Before I could answer, she spotted something and grabbed it, then rolled it my way. It was a very gooey crown.

"Let me help with all of that." Mathilda pulled up her water spell. "And I might suggest that we take the other items it threw out as well. Never know what they might be." She let loose her water spell, then dried us all with wind.

I had the crown, nothing fancy, just the standard points, and places for eight missing gems—ones smaller than the ones Crusty found. And while it was large, it wasn't something that could fit on my head if I were in dragon form. The other items, no longer goopy, looked to be a random assortment of gold jewelry. I was just reaching down to grab another piece when Irving started gronking, came racing toward me, and ate all the gold. Including the crown, which he snapped out of my hand. He then raced up high and stayed there. Bunky followed him up.

"Irving! Give those back," I yelled at him, but he didn't appear to care. "Anyone have an idea how to get him to give those back?" Like all constructs, Irving didn't have to eat. But he'd developed a taste for relics when we were trying to gather the ones from my staff. Apparently, old gold was good too. I was about to yell again when a rumbling shook my feet. I turned around to see six narbeasts, clothed in far fancier harnesses than the ones we'd seen before, racing for us. And they were being ridden by pixies garbed in leaves and metal.

Garbage and her flock all pulled out their war sticks and swarmed down. "Noseeums! Bad!"

Thanks to Amara and Garbage, we all could see them running for us. But they were so loud there was no way anyone could miss that something was coming even if they couldn't see them. Not sure what the point of not being seen but being that loud would be, but they went with it.

The irony of the faeries calling the pixies *little* was something I'd deal with later. Faeries were, on average, four inches tall. Pixies had disproportionally long legs and arms and were closer to ten inches tall. They looked like clothed sticks with sharp, cruel faces for the most part. We didn't have them in Beccia but they'd had infestations in other parts of the kingdom.

The narbeasts ran directly through where the gold pieces had been. I'd never question Irving's eating habits again. We wouldn't have been able to get the pieces up in time before they would have been stomped.

The rest of my focus was on the narbeasts and their pixie riders.

Mathilda put up a shield that bounced the narbeasts back. She'd been using her magic a lot lately and I knew that barrier she just threw up should be farther away than it was. She was holding back because her reserves were low. Another item to deal with later.

"We can't hold them; we have to fight," I said to the others.

Mathilda was shaking, trying to keep the shield around all of us and our horses.

"I agree. Mathilda, drop your shield." Padraig sounded like his old self.

We were all armed when she dropped the shield. She was leaning more on her staff than usual but stood strong.

The faeries held back when Mathilda raised her shield but now continued their attack. The pixies pulled out wicked little crossbows and started firing. Like the faeries' war sticks, the bolts stung more than anything. But the faeries' war sticks could kill if enough of them were involved. I didn't want to see if that was true with the pixies' bolts as well.

I pulled out Rhyfel and green static filled the air. It seemed thinner than normal, but it was the right size for the pixie riding right for us. Rhyfel blew the pixie off the narbeast with a barrage of green static, and I used magic to push the narbeast toward the sycubian tree. I didn't think swords would do much to that hide.

The narbeast slammed into the sycubian tree and its largest center horn stuck. The tree flung branches at it; the narbeast bellowed. I hoped they'd be extremely happy together.

The pixie that Rhyfel had brought down didn't get back up and crumbled to dust. "Good work, Rhy." I'd ask later if that often happened to pixies or if that was just here. My friends were taking on the remaining pairs, and

I noticed that Welsy and Delsy stood back but watched the fighting carefully. Bunky and Irving stayed high enough that the tiny bolts from the pixies couldn't reach them. "They came for the gold." My brain took a bit to connect things, but I *had* been in a tree today. That could mess up anyone. Not to mention I was used to people going after us just because—the fact that these wanted to rob us was new.

"That would be a good guess," Alric said as he swung at a narbeast. His sword did nothing to the hide.

There was no way to get all of them to run into a tree, not to mention only the sycubian tree was large enough to not be destroyed if one of them hit it.

The pixies were falling, but like the one Rhyfel took down, they crumbled to dust immediately. Then more appeared. They were definitely tied to the narbeasts. Even Foxy couldn't take the one he was fighting down.

My magic-using friends weren't able to get much strength behind their spells. Even for me, that first one was a fluke and I couldn't pull in enough mojo to even get another good push spell.

Well, damn.

I stood away from my friends and the trees, and changed. It was nice to do so because I wanted to and did turn into my normal dragon form. No wings, but those were tricky and I didn't need them right now.

The pixies and narbeasts didn't even notice.

I gave a roar that shook leaves off the trees. Flame would be more noticeable, but I liked normal trees and didn't want to toast them.

The roar worked. The narbeasts spun toward me, ignoring the commands from the pixies to stay and fight my friends. I ran farther out into the plain. Sadly, that was as far as my plan went. I was still relearning being a dragon and while I knew we could fight on the ground, the exact things to do were lost in memory.

The narbeasts charged toward me, and I spun around as fast as I could and slammed into the first two with my rather substantial tail. Pixies exploded and the narbeasts went tumbling. One got to its feet slowly; the second didn't.

The one that got up narrowed its eyes at me, snarled, and then ran away. A pixie reappeared on its back as it ran but it shook it off and kept running. The one that went down was still breathing, but not moving even when another pixie came. Aside from snapping the pixie in half when it got close to its face. Smart narbeast.

The remaining three charged toward me, and all of them had multiple pixies this time. I focused on my wings appearing and rose just as they got to me. Then I dropped back down after they charged past and swung my tail again. Two narbeasts went down this time and the remaining one was covered in pixies shooting their bolts at me.

"Look. I can stomp on you, or you can take off and live. It's your call." I was speaking to the narbeast but the pixies reacted with an increase in crossbow bolts. Unfortunately, Rhyfel disappeared when I changed form this time. He would have loved going after them.

Luckily, so did the faeries.

My swarm came forward, yelling war cries, and attacked the pixies. There was a brief skirmish as more pixies kept popping in. The narbeast finally shook its head and took off running. The pixies soon lost the fight and vanished.

My friends were riding my way—I'd gone a bit farther away than I'd thought—so I walked toward them in dragon form to cover more ground, then dropped back into my human form. That was still a jarring change, but hopefully, I'd get used to it soon.

"Nice job!" Grillion got to me first.

"A bit of a warning next time might be nice." Covey didn't appear upset, but there was concern in her voice.

Alric didn't say anything but handed me the reins to my horse. His eyes said enough.

"Yes, I took off, but in the middle of the battle I couldn't stop and explain myself." I saw all the looks of concern. "I know you're worried given my unique situation. But you all have to start trusting me." I'd never been the one to charge forward into trees or battle, but I was now. I was touched by their concern, but they needed to understand that I'd changed.

"She has a point." Alric grinned. "Any of us would have done the same. If we could."

Bunky and Irving had flown over but were still staying extremely high up.

I watched them as they watched us. "Padraig, we can't do anything about that crown yet, right?"

He looked up at the constructs and nodded.

"Maybe Irving could just hold it and the other pieces for us?" I noticed that both constructs drifted lower. "Until we get somewhere safe to deal with them? It would keep them safe, and he did save them from being stomped on just now." They both came even lower.

"I'd say that's a good plan." He looked up. "What say, you two? Irving keeps the gold and Bunky protects Irving?"

Bunky gronked and the two came to hover right above us. Hard to tell with construct faces but they both seemed quite pleased with themselves.

"Okay, so now can we leave?" I swung up on my horse and patted her neck. "Please?" I knew the connection, whatever it was, of the lost nature deities and this *tir cudd,* was something that Padraig, Covey, and even Mathilda would love to dig into. But it would have to wait. If there was a chance some of those presumed dead deities were trapped somewhere and had been that way for thousands of years, they could wait a bit longer.

Padraig studied the area around us and then nodded.

"Agreed. I will still need some magical assistance to get us out. My issues notwithstanding, there seems to be a strange magical drain in here. The way out should be just to the south of us." He turned his horse and led us across the plains.

Maybe it was because of all the damage that I'd just inflicted upon trees and beings that lived here, but I felt a brooding animosity rising around us. The odd light in the sky now dimmed and the air grew cooler. "I think the *tir cudd* would like us to leave now as well."

"Agreed." Foxy was on his horse again but watched the sky carefully. "I don't like those clouds."

I hadn't seen clouds earlier; the sky was just a vague murky blue as always. Now it was an annoyed murky gray and getting darker. The mass of clouds heading our way was so dark that it was almost black.

Padraig looked up and urged his horse to go faster, and we followed quickly. The faeries were staying lower than normal, and Bunky and Irving stayed on the edges of them but were also flying low. Those clouds didn't look friendly to anyone.

We raced to what looked like a cliff, and Padraig turned to us. "I need Alric, Mathilda, and Taryn to all focus on a chawsia path spell at the edge of the cliff. I'll be running a calming spell on the horses and that's about all I can focus on at this point. Our flyers need to stay extremely close to us when we go in."

I joined the others but wasn't happy. If something went wrong with our spell, we'd go straight down and the cliff was so high I couldn't see the bottom. The faeries and constructs hovered around us, with some of the faeries landing on horses and riders. Alric and Mathilda came on either side of me, and we joined hands. I'd never done a group spell before but obviously, they had. I might have held their hands a bit tight but neither said anything.

"Now!"

My horse had been trembling but she now steadied at Padraig's shout as his calming spell flowed over her.

I pulled in magic for a chawsia spell and felt the same on the other side of me. The chawsia path opened and I wondered if we could have the same calming spell as the horses as Padraig ran into the tunnel, followed by Covey, Grillion, and Foxy. It looked like they vanished into the air. Better than going down, but still unnerving.

The three of us were just riding into the tunnel when a massive crack of lightning snapped behind us.

"Run!" Alric pulled on me, and I tugged Mathilda as we ran for the path. The thunder that followed the lightning was just two seconds away and another lightning bolt lit the sky behind us.

The path was starting to close as we rode in and a lightning strike hit the edge of the tunnel.

CHAPTER THIRTY-FIVE

A MASSIVE FORCE OF air crashed into me as we rode through the tunnel and the entrance slammed shut behind us. Visions of us being flung miles away from the rest of our friends hit me, and I focused on stabilizing the path. I recalled little of my past in terms of magic but a spell for this jumped up and smacked me. I sent out a spell to calm the tunnel. It worked but the tunnel wasn't stabilizing as well as I'd hoped. Then Rhyfel started crackling in his sheath.

We'd had to drop hands as we rode in, so I grabbed him and asked him to help stabilize the tunnel. Well, I asked him in my head. There was no way to talk in the massive windstorm that engulfed us.

He crackled and sent arcs of green to the walls. It was still wildly windy but the tunnel seemed calmer. I couldn't see beyond Alric and his horse, but it felt like there were only the three of us in here. Could be good, could be bad. I was focusing on the good.

Luckily, our horses had great balance, as the tunnel vanished without warning.

We landed near a swamp with massive trees covered in vines and moss. I'd say we were a lot farther south than we'd started. That was good. Unfortunately, our friends were nowhere in sight. Actually, there were no living beings in sight.

The three of us didn't have any of the faeries with us, so there was no way to send one of them to find our friends.

"Does this look familiar?" Alric asked Mathilda as she pushed back her wind-tossed hair.

Mathilda tilted her head as she glanced around. "It's been a long time, but judging by the landscape, I'd say we're not far from Notlianda. Probably only a few hours or so. I don't see our friends anywhere."

"Me either." I knew elves had better eyesight than me, at least in this form, but there was nothing to be seen but more swamp and more swamp trees.

And a ten-foot-long log swimming our way. "What's that?" I kept my voice steady, but normal logs didn't move like that. Expecting the abnormal was becoming my way of life.

"Damn, we need to get out of here. That's a long-strike and those things are killers." Mathilda started backing her horse up and led the way at a jog.

Alric and I followed but the log creature kept coming. It was still mostly in water so I couldn't see much of it. I had a feeling that might be for the best.

"Maybe let's get far from this swamp and then find our friends?" Alric stayed behind us, but we were all riding close together.

The creature got out of the water. It still looked like a log, one with short, stumpy legs and a long, nasty-looking jaw. Sort of like a water-based sceanra anam.

We eventually left it behind but it took a full sprint from our horses. Rhyfel didn't react once—he must prefer magical enemies.

"Please tell me those things aren't common down here?" We'd stopped running but I kept looking back the way we'd come. Things like that shouldn't be able to run as well as it did.

"They weren't when I was growing up." Mathilda

scowled at the trees around us. "But the swamps weren't this large either. Things have changed."

"How are we going to find our friends? Could they be in Notlianda?" I wanted to get as far from these swamps and those long-strikes as I could.

"They could have come out anywhere. Can you try calling the faeries?" Alric asked once we slowed down, but he took the lead and kept the horses walking quickly. The direction he was heading appeared to be away from the swamps, so I was fine with it.

I closed my eyes and tried calling. On the fifth try, I thought I felt something from them, but they didn't show up. I opened my eyes. "Nothing. Not like before when I was blocked from them and lost my magic—I feel fine right now. But they aren't responding." While the faeries could be unpredictable, they would have shown up by now. If they could.

"What's that?" Mathilda pointed to a thin column of smoke in the distance. It was away from the swamp, and the trees blocking whatever was causing it were of a different type.

"Maybe a village? Notlianda shouldn't be this close, though." Alric shaded his eyes as he looked. At least we were back in normal sunlight again.

Mathilda nodded. "And that would be too small. Shall we go see if perhaps our friends landed there and set up camp, waiting for us?"

I had a bad feeling that our friends weren't just sitting around a campfire waiting for us to catch up but I'd found voicing these concerns just made them more real to *me* and didn't help anything. And I knew that we needed to check out the smoke anyway, so I kept quiet.

It seemed painfully silent without the chatter of the faeries and the rest of our friends. As we rode, I kept trying to call out in my head for the faeries. Still nothing but a faint feeling that they heard me. Which meant they were possibly trapped. Faeries were difficult to trap, but it had happened before. Usually using one of their vices against them, like chocolate or alcohol.

Both Qianru and Locksead knew about the faeries. I'd been on the fence about Qianru possibly really being on the bad guys' side. Although, the brownies saying that I was to be brought to her by name was fairly damning. Locksead had made such a switch from the leader of a relic thief gang to a solid upstanding guy that I'd been hoping he stayed that way.

But the odds weren't looking good.

"I think someone is holding the faeries. No proof, just a feeling." I was riding behind the other two, and I got the last part out as they both started to turn around.

"Can you tell what direction they're in? Wherever they are, the others should be." Alric had his hood up as he rode but I knew he was looking at everything we passed.

"Not really, but I'm fine with heading toward that… what's that?" What looked like a large ball was flying toward us. And badly. It kept dipping in the air, almost hitting the ground, then dragging itself back up again.

"Bunky and Irving!" Alric rose in his saddle. "They're tied together, but they're coming this way."

We rode to meet them as however they were tied, it wasn't good for flying. They started going down again not far from us but I got them with a spell and was able to lower them slowly. The constructs were easier to hurt than the faeries.

As we got closer, I saw Leaf, Crusty, and the black and white faery named Penqow all struggling within the ropes.

"Bads! Helps!" Leaf yelled while the other two kept chewing on the ropes.

Crusty held up a broken piece of rope.

"You're free." I smiled as she looked at the rope that she'd chewed through with wide eyes.

All three of us got off our horses and finished freeing Leaf, Penqow, and the constructs.

Alric picked up Bunky and looked him over, and Mathilda did the same with Irving. Both looked a bit battered but intact.

"Can you ask Bunky what happened?" Alric was one of the ones who understood him. Of course, as soon as the words left my mouth, all three faeries started talking at once. "Easy, girls, let him talk to Bunky."

Bunky made a few little gronks and buzzing sounds—echoed by Irving for emphasis.

Alric sat him down. Both constructs looked exhausted. "He says they were attacked as soon as they came out of the tunnel. All he can say is that they were bad people and they grabbed him and Irving with a magic-charged net. The faeries flew into a mist, which dropped them all, and the rest of our friends collapsed on their horses. Everyone is asleep, tied up, and waiting for us where that smoke is."

Along with obviously whoever grabbed them and was waiting for us.

"What do they want? Is anyone hurt?" I got back on my horse. I was grateful that Alric and Mathilda were out here with me, but those were some of my closest friends in there.

"Nons hurt. But bads take." Crusty decided she'd given Bunky enough time to speak. "We's didn't go sleep. We tie up."

"Why didn't you three get knocked out?" Mathilda set Irving down next to Bunky. We could pick them up when we had a plan, but for right now resting was the best thing for them.

"Dunno. They mad, tie us with them." Leaf grinned and pulled out a piece of twine from between her teeth. "Frees."

Her grin told me whose idea it was to chew themselves

and the constructs free. I'd like to know what knocked out the others but not these three, but that mystery would have to wait.

"Bunky said they didn't take the gold from Irving; they didn't do anything except trap them and tie them up." Alric looked off toward the smoke. "I could scout ahead and see what we're facing."

Mathilda and I both opened our mouths to protest, then shook our heads.

"I don't like that idea, but I get it. You are pretty sneaky." Knowing it was a good idea and being happy about it were two different things. Mathilda's unhappy nod told me she'd come to the same conclusion.

Alric rode back to me, reached over, and gave me probably the most passionate kiss anyone had ever received while sitting on horseback.

"If something happens while I'm gone, take off. We'll find you." He opened his cloak and Crusty and Penqow flew in. Leaf landed on me.

"We's protects!" All three faeries yelled at once with a few muted gronks of confirmation from Bunky and Irving.

I hoped nothing happened to any of us, but the odds of that were slim to none.

He trotted off toward the closest trees and was gone from view.

"Anyone else think sitting out here in the open is just asking for trouble?" Nothing was covering us and while I didn't see anyone, that didn't mean no one was around.

"Agreed." Mathilda got off her horse, picked up Bunky and Irving, and secured them on her horse. She took the reins and started walking to the tree line.

Leaf stayed on my shoulder. "This goods."

We didn't go far into the trees but it was better than being in the wide open.

"Any idea why these three faeries weren't affected by

whatever they used? Which, if they're connected with the others, was a form of varlick powder." At this point, I wanted to find all the varlick plants and destroy them. Nothing against them personally, but this powder was vile.

"No, and it would be good to find out. If they've built an immunity of some sort, we could expand on it." Mathilda placed Bunky and Irving back on the ground—both fell asleep immediately—then she dug through her pack. "I do have a small amount of the powder that I gathered at the last attack. Leaf? Can we test to see if this works on you?"

"Okays?" Leaf flew off my shoulder to land on Mathilda's horse.

I rode my horse a bit away from them. Granted, it had hit me when I was in my dragon form, but there might be a reason I collapsed last time.

Mathilda took out some of the powder and sprinkled it over Leaf.

We watched her as she wrinkled her nose, sneezed, then shook it off.

"I know she was knocked out with the rest of them and me when those brownies attacked. This powder is from that, right?"

"Yes." Mathilda looked to me with the pouch still in her hand. "I don't want to risk your changing, but maybe we could see? This could be important."

I got off my horse with a sigh. "Okay, but if I pass out, drop some water on me fast. I don't want to be out if things go bad all of a sudden." I avoided saying *which they will*. I stood in front of her with Leaf watching from behind her, and she dumped a handful of powder on me.

I sneezed. "Nope. Look, I'm fi—" Next thing I knew, I was sitting in the mud, Mathilda's water show had just ended, and a nice breeze quickly appeared. "That was fast! Should we test you? Maybe this is a weird variation

of the powder." Both Mathilda and Padraig believed the
people behind the powder were modifying it. "Although
I'm not sure about that water spell."

"I can show you. Don't worry about the wind. If I get
knocked out, just dump water and I'll do the rest." She
handed me the pouch. "Just a small amount should do."

Once I was certain I had the water spell going, and a
nearby shrub was now drenched, I shook the powder on
her.

And waited. Not even a sneeze.

She shook it off. "I felt nothing. You collapsed, which
means it's aimed at something specifically for your people as well as the faeries. If they knocked out our friends
and their horses, they've modified it again. But Leaf is
immune now."

We hadn't been speaking loudly, but both of us went
silent at the sound of a horse running toward us. I had
Rhyfel and my sword out, and Mathilda's staff was back
in place.

"Is okay. Friends." Leaf's whisper was loud enough
that if it hadn't been Alric and the other two faeries, we
would have been in trouble.

"Just us." Alric rode closer. "I found them. The smoke is
coming from a few ramshackle cabins grouped together.
Our friends are still unconscious and tied up in the middle of them. I saw five syclarions, two full-sized dwollers,
and a grimarian. They are just waiting for something or
someone. There was someone else inside one of the cabins speaking to one of the dwollers, but I couldn't hear
enough to know who they were."

"Waiting for us?"

He shook his head. "Hard to say. There were no scouts.
The two syclarions were dressed like the ones that
attacked us before and heavily armed. But not in a state
of alert."

Mathilda frowned. "They probably believe they have

all of us. I'd like to know how they were tracking that chawsia path. This is hours from the point we went in at."

"Do you think the syclarions were Paili?" I was so proud of how calm my voice was. And that I didn't jump on my horse and race north as fast as possible.

From the look of concern on Alric's face, I might have fooled myself but I didn't fool him. "I honestly don't know. But the ones who went after us in those ruins didn't have any of the Paili marks, and these were dressed like them."

"Which doesn't mean they aren't working for them." I took a deep breath. "Okay, whether they are Paili or not, we need our friends back. What's the plan?" Alric was much better at sneaky plans than me, and I was still stomping down my fear of the Paili.

"If we can wake up our friends, I think they can fight loose of the ties. Not to mention it doesn't look like the faeries are tied up at all."

"Nopes." Leaf had been behind me, but she, Crusty, and Penqow flew forward with their war sticks and wearing their war feathers. "No ties. But sleeps." She tilted her head and pulled out a familiar green and brown faery bag. "War kittahs? War puppy?"

Alric started to shake her off, but I had an idea. "Could your cats and puppy run a distraction without faery riders?" When they'd fought before, it had been with faeries on their backs. But this wouldn't be fighting—just running and causing mayhem.

Leaf, Crusty, and Penqow all chittered to each other for a few seconds, then Leaf nodded. "Yes. They runs fast."

"What if the cats and puppy all run into the camp, just on the edges, but enough to distract the people there. At the same time, Mathilda and I dump water on our friends; Leaf, Crusty, and Penqow get the faeries up and help free the others, and Alric fights whoever is left." Considering I didn't want to plan anything, this sounded good to me.

It also kept the fighting to a minimum—I hoped.

Alric smiled. "That might work. We're going to have to move fast, though. Getting our friends and their horses out of there isn't going to be easy; there won't be much time."

"We do!" Crusty raised her war stick and started to fly off.

"Not yet!" I didn't want to yell but I raised my voice. Leaf took off after her and brought her back.

Alric and Mathilda hammered out a few more aspects of the plan; for instance, the three of us would circle the cabins with a line of sight of our friends. We each would have a faery. Bunky and Irving both woke up and wanted to help, at least from what Leaf said. I wanted them to keep resting, but we couldn't leave them here. They were finally added to the three faeries and their rescue squad.

We went deeper into the woods so we could circle the cabins. Leaf kept wanting to open the faery bag she clutched in her tiny hand but held off when I'd tell her no. This wasn't a tricky plan, but the timing did need to be watched.

There was still no sign of scouts nor anyone even out this way as we went forward to our spots.

Alric had Penqow with him and watched for Mathilda and me to send our faery companions in the air once we were ready with our water spells.

The faeries insisted the cats and puppy were fine in their special bag, but we might need to let them out more often after this. Once Leaf opened the bag and lifted it up, the herd of cats and the puppy tore out and raced through the cabins. They did three laps before the people in the camp started after them. They were racing fast and if the meows and yips were any indications, they were having fun.

I let loose my water spell as Mathilda released hers on the other side of the camp. I might have been too enthusiastic with my spell as our friends did wake up, but I almost drowned them.

Padraig's spirit sword appeared in his hand and Covey went berserker. Foxy didn't need weapons either and ripped apart his ropes and those of Grillion. Welsy and Delsy freed themselves.

"Run!" Alric yelled as he raced toward a syclarion fighter who had turned back from the cat and puppy racing.

"Weapons!" Grillion darted into one of the structures.

"Damn it," Alric swore as the rest of our friends fought back as the people from the camp stopped chasing the cats and dog. The faeries all took off in the direction the cats and puppy had gone, and Grillion slowly came out of the structure. His raised hands were empty of weapons and he looked to be holding his breath.

Theria was directly behind him, holding a large knife to his throat.

CHAPTER THIRTY-SIX

I FROZE. THERE WAS no way I was taking a chance with Grillion's life. Theria was a brutal necromancer with more ways to destroy Grillion than I could imagine. Mathilda, Padraig, and Alric all stood down as well.

I hadn't counted on Foxy or Covey. Or for that matter, Welsy and Delsy.

A roar echoed across the camp, and Foxy slammed the dwoller and grimarian that he was fighting against trees and ran for Theria.

Covey beat him by seconds by throwing herself right at Theria. Welsy and Delsy yelled and charged forward, waving tiny swords. And half of the faeries grabbed Theria's knife hand and pulled.

Grillion bit him, Covey slashed him, and Foxy snapped his back. I stood there in shock, with Rhyfel crackling lightly. My dagger must have felt things were taken care of as he didn't try to reach out.

The rest of the attackers from the camp tore off and Alric, Padraig, and all four of the constructs went after them. Mathilda came over to us. Grillion was fine until he put his hand up to where the blade had been and came away with a tiny bit of blood. Covey caught him as he passed out.

She lowered him to the ground and shook herself out of her berserker stage. She pointedly looked to Theria on the ground. "Is he dead? How can we be certain?"

I was with her on that concern. Theria looked dead, but a necromancer of his apparent abilities? I wouldn't believe it until his body was destroyed.

Foxy stomped on Theria's chest a few times then grunted. "Think so. Is Grillion okay?"

Mathilda had a small white stick out and waved it under Grillion's nose. He jerked, coughed, and then sat up and looked around groggily.

"Wha…oh, him." He glared at Theria's body. "Thanks, everyone. That moment is going to haunt my dreams for a few decades." He rubbed his throat, but not where the blood had been.

The rest of the faeries came back into the camp, herding their racing cats. The puppy yipped around the edges of the cat crowd and seemed to think he was herding the cats as well. Leaf flew over and held up the green and brown bag, and the animals, along with a few faeries, hopped inside.

Garbage had come over to us when they got back, and I nodded to Leaf and the bag. "Why did some faeries go in?"

"We take turns. Plays with them." She peered down at Theria. "He go squish."

"Well, hopefully he's…folks? We have a problem." I'd glanced back at Theria when Garbage spoke. He wasn't just dead; he was oozing. I stepped away.

"What in the hells?" Grillion ran to the far end of the camp and looked ready to get on his horse and go much farther away, with or without us.

I couldn't disagree and scrambled back even farther. Theria's body was deflating and a foul orange-green ooze came sliming out of his clothing.

Mathilda and Covey also moved away quickly. Foxy moved closer and looked ready to investigate.

"Foxy, whatever that is, I don't think anyone should be

touching it." I had no idea what that was, but I knew it was nasty.

"Seen this before." He peered down, looking more reminiscent of Padraig or Covey with an interesting book than someone standing over a body turning to mush. "Back when I fought some of those mob goons while freeing Dogmaela and her family. Yup. It'll burn right through the floor and dirt." He looked up. "We should leave."

Alric and Padraig and their construct escorts came running back into the camp, and their swords vanished as they saw there were no more combatants to fight. We were still looking at Theria.

"Foxy and the others took out Theria, but now he's oozing." I stepped back a few more feet. I didn't think the dark orange-green stuff would come out this far, but I wasn't taking a chance. It was awful, even before Foxy's comment about it burning through things.

Padraig got there first and started swearing. "Mage spell. And a bad one. Run for your horses!" He and Alric stayed behind us. While neither one had their sword back, they both appeared to be prepping spells.

Everyone was almost to their horses, except Grillion, who was already waiting on his, when a popping sound came from behind us. Globs of green goo flew into the air, missing us by a few feet. I sprinted to my horse, escorted by a gronking Bunky and Irving. Welsy and Delsy jumped up with Covey, and we took off.

We'd been riding hard for a full three minutes and I was just about to ask if we could stop, when an explosion rocked the ground and shook the trees around us.

Alric had taken the lead and picked up speed once the shaking stopped.

Five minutes later, he slowed down. "Is everyone okay?"

The mass of faeries came tearing along the line of us, laughing and yelling. The rest of us were quieter but seemed okay.

"Did he just explode?" Grillion hooked a thumb over his shoulder in the general direction of the camp. The look on his face said he wasn't unhappy about Theria exploding.

"Go BOOM!" Garbage yelled and was echoed by all of the faeries.

"The thing back there exploded, yes." Padraig kept watching behind us. "But I don't know if it was Theria."

"We all saw him. You and Alric saw him. It looked like him." I had been close enough that I would swear that was him.

"Oh, it was—at that point. But necromancers are tricky. It felt like he swapped right before he died. Probably had his duplicate waiting and when Foxy, Covey, and the rest hit him, he cast his spell."

"I was watching him the entire time," Covey said. "He didn't vanish."

"We wouldn't have seen it if he was good enough." Mathilda reached in her bag and pulled out what looked like a tiny crystal ball. "Damn, that was what he did. This is showing a massive spike of ectoplasm. That was a thing, not Theria."

"How can we kill someone who can change out like that?" Grillion wasn't hysterical but close to it.

"It can be done. Just won't be easy. But he did give a major trick of his away, so now we know." Padraig looked too okay with the entire thing.

I wasn't happy about any of it, and according to him, there was an extremely good chance that Theria was still alive. That shouldn't make any of us happy.

"I want to know why they were holding you all. I'd think if Theria had been there, there would have been something going on in terms of torture." Alric rubbed the side of his horse's neck. All of the horses had run hard but they all looked glad to be away from the camp.

"What did they want?"

"We were knocked out the moment we came out of the tunnel, so not a clue. Maybe they were holding us to trap you three?" Covey was keeping a close eye on Grillion—he looked ready to bolt. She slowly nudged her horse closer to him.

Alric shook his head. "There were no scouts. They might have been expecting someone, but it wasn't us or anyone they'd have to fight. I think they thought all of us were together when they grabbed you and were waiting for whoever was giving orders."

"Someone worse than Theria?" Grillion shook a little at that.

"Probably," Alric continued. "They tied you all up where you fell, but they didn't separate you to see who they had."

"Tell me about it." Covey winced as she stretched. "I felt like an overstretched bit of dough when we woke up. A very wet overstretched bit of dough."

"Sorry about that. I might have been over-exuberant. Oh, and Bunky, Irving, Leaf, Crusty, and Penqow weren't knocked out—Mathilda's trying to sort that one out. Although I'm surprised that Welsy and Delsy were."

"We weren't," Welsy said.

Delsy nodded. "We played like we'd been affected, but then they tied up Bunky and the others. They looked ready to spell them, so we moved to distract them. Bunky and Irving escaped with the three faeries tied to them."

"We got zapped by the big guy who went gooey. Knocked us out by shutting down our systems. Siabiane might need to do some work when we get her back." Welsy wiggled his shoulders and the right one did seem loose.

Padraig looked up at the late afternoon sky. "I'd like to get a bit farther from whatever is left in that camp or who might be coming there. Alric and I took care of the ones we chased, and that explosion probably removed any survivors who were injured in the camp. But some-one is going to be looking for them."

"Head to Notlianda?" Earlier, Alric and Mathilda had sounded like we weren't that far and right now a city sounded wonderful.

Mathilda followed Padraig's sky-watching. "We'd get there after dark this time of year, not the best time for travelers to go in. I say we travel for a bit, then set up camp and go into Notlianda in the morning."

"I'd have to agree, as much as I'd really like a nice sturdy wall between us and that Theria." Grillion was calming down. "Going in once night starts to fall usually raises questions from the guards along the walls—ones we might not want to answer. Qianru's property is on the outer ring of the city, so we can get there quickly once the gates open in the morning."

"Walls? There weren't walls when I lived down here."

Padraig shook his head at Mathilda. "And how long ago was that? Things change, and if they've enclosed a large major city, I'd say things have not been changing for the better. Let's camp and go into the city in the morning."

A chill wind crossed our path but just made us ride faster. Even the faeries stayed quiet as we traveled.

The camp we set up was small and cold. Really cold. "I know the weather is opposite of the northern continent, but I imagined even winters in the south to be warmer than this." I had on two tunics, a vest, a jacket, and my heavy cape. I was still chilled.

Grillion looked around. He was in layers, too, and rub-bing his arms. "It's been getting colder since I came down here two years ago. But this feels worse."

"It was never like this when I lived here. It was warm and sunny almost year-round. One of the adjustments that Siabiane and I had to deal with when we adventured to the north was the change in weather." She looked at Padraig. "This can't be good, or a coincidence. This wind is coming from the south."

"Normally I wouldn't worry too much about weather patterns, but given the more recent sightings of creatures who should only live in the very far and frozen north, I'd agree something is going on. Something far south of us." Padraig watched the sky, but cloud cover blocked whatever he was looking for.

"But there isn't a land mass south of this continent." Covey's people were reptilian and she was slowing down. Alric gave her his thickest cloak.

"There wasn't. An island of ice had been reported about a year ago." Grillion shrugged. "Weather and strange islands aren't that interesting to most folks, so I ignored it."

"Add this to the list of things going wrong in the south. Shall we set up guards?" Alric looked toward the constructs. It was clear that all four had taken a beating in that camp. They were battered and moving slower than usual, and it was clear on his face that he wasn't certain about using them.

"We helps!" Garbage flew into his face. "Guards." She squinted over the campsite.

That wasn't a great idea. Having guards who could get distracted by a firefly or pretty leaf wasn't particularly safe. I was about to tell her no when Alric nodded.

"Thank you, Garbage. I think due to the recent event, we'll need a few guards. Could you set up your faeries to fly the perimeter of our camp? A bit into the tree line. Four at a time, spaced out? We'll keep our normal guard shifts. If anyone comes upon us, they'll see our guard but not your faeries." He nodded slowly, and she did the same. She liked the idea of being sneaky.

"But no playing around while on guard. This could be a dangerous job. Let us know if you find anyone. Don't let anyone through." I kept my face serious. Alric had a good idea by giving the faeries something to focus on, and hopefully some downtime would help the constructs.

"We guard!" She spun around and had her war feathers out of her bag and on before anyone could say no. The rest of the faeries did as well.

I shrugged when Alric looked my way. The faeries then went and had their own sorting discussion, and we set up our guard rotations. The fact that all four constructs, who normally were our extra guards, only made mild protestations that they could help told me they needed the downtime.

The conversation around the small fire was muted as everyone huddled under blankets and cloaks and kept their thoughts mostly to themselves. There were a lot of pieces that needed to be put together, but sitting outside wasn't the place to do it.

Alric brought over bowls of stew and sat next to me. "How are you feeling?"

"I'm building a list of things I hate. Grimarians. Theria and all necromancers. *Tir cudds*. Tjolia mountain dreks. And the frozen south. I know there are many more, but that list will start. Is there any hope for us to go back to Beccia and just live a quiet, normal life?"

My head was against his shoulder, so I felt his laugh as much as heard it. "Considering who and what you are, I seriously doubt there is a normal for you." He squeezed my shoulder. "But once we find out what Qianru is up to and get Siabiane and Lorcan back, I promise we can go back home."

I gave him a quick kiss. "Don't promise what you can't be sure will happen. But I appreciate the thought. Can we try to avoid any more Tjolia mountain dreks, though? I'm having nightmares about those."

"Deal."

We both finished our stew, just happy to be next to

each other for the few moments that peace and quiet remained.

Which lasted about ten minutes.

"Found! Look!" Garbage and twenty faeries came flying into the camp with two blanket-covered and stumbling beings walking in the middle of the swarm.

Everyone was on their feet with weapons and/or magic ready. The first prisoner stumbled and tripped, with the second falling over the first. The swearing sounded familiar.

"Girls? Can you uncover them?"

"Is dangerous!"

"We've got it. Just uncover them, please." My sword had vanished again and had not come back but Rhyfel was ready. He wasn't crackling at all, which confirmed my suspicions.

Finally, Garbage and her flock removed the covering.

Dueble was on the bottom and Nasif had fallen over him. Both were also tied with vines and had their mouths partially covered with leaves.

"Garbage! You know these two. It's Nasif and Dueble. Untie them." I ran forward to start freeing them but the faeries were faster and had all of the plant life removed immediately. I'd need to talk to them about that new skill as well, once things settled down. The vines they had used weren't like anything in this forest and I had no idea how they'd gathered them that quickly.

Garbage flew into both Nasif and Dueble's faces, then frowned as she recognized them. "Oops. Is sorry. Looking for bads." She then whistled and took her flock back into the woods.

I might have been a little too vehement about the faeries watching for the "bads."

I helped Nasif up, and Alric assisted Dueble. Nasif was a powerful elf and magic user. He had also become immortal, sending Alric and me forward to our time from a thousand years in the past. His partner was Dueble, a syclarion. His features were far less sharp than current syclarions as a thousand years ago his species was still dealing with what I'd done to it fifteen hundred years before. He was also immortal and a respected researcher. Rather, the other half of a fictitious name that they both used to publish academic papers. Syclarions as a whole weren't thought of well in the academic community.

"It's so good to see you both!" I hugged them as they looked around with an air of confusion.

"It's good to see you also, all of you." Nasif knew Padraig and Mathilda from long ago, although he and Dueble also saw them before the battle of the relics. They'd met Covey on the road a year ago. Nasif nodded to Grillion and Foxy as the only ones he didn't know. "I'm wondering why you're all here, though? Last communication that I had from Siabiane said the battle went well and things were settling down?"

We stepped back to the fire, and Mathilda poured hot tea for both. I noticed both Nasif and Dueble were dressed for the cold. We all started talking at once but nodded to Padraig to speak for us.

Both elven and syclarion faces were grim when he finished.

"That's not good news. Lorcan and Siabiane should have been impossible to take like that." Nasif shook his head.

Dueble sipped his tea and nodded. "And we've been digging just south of Colivith. I'd think we'd have noticed if there were something horrible going on there."

Covey laughed. "We're researchers. Many times we don't notice anything we aren't looking for."

Both looked ready to defend themselves, then shrugged and nodded.

"True. We have been working on some amazing finds. We might have been a bit narrowly focused," Nasif said.

"How and why were you here, though?" Not that I wasn't happy to see them. These two risked their entire existence to get Alric and me back to our proper time. But from the maps, we were a few days hard ride away from Colivith.

"We were summoned." Nasif winced. "And it was most likely a trap since it supposedly came from Lorcan. No idea why, but he claimed to be at a camp a bit east of here. We got the summons a few days ago and were almost there when a massive explosion shook the area. The camp was destroyed, so we were heading toward Notlianda when your faeries grabbed us. I have to say, they were fast. I couldn't even get a spell out and couldn't do anything once they had us secured."

Now I really needed to speak to the faeries about those vines. Nasif was a serious magic user and even tied up should have been able to free Dueble and himself with a spell or two. What did the girls have in those vines of theirs that they stopped magic? And how could we get some to use for ourselves?

"But now to know that Lorcan has been kidnapped... that is worrisome." Dueble was the quieter of the two, but I knew his mind was trying to find answers even as we spoke. A thousand years of pure researching left him with one of the sharpest minds in the world—along with Nasif.

"Why would Theria have called these two up to the camp, though?" Covey scowled.

"Theria was involved? Huge troll necromancer? Really nasty attitude?" Dueble paled significantly. It wasn't easy for dark-green scales to pale, but he almost turned white. "I think I should sit down." He didn't wait, just folded his legs under him and sat where he'd stood.

Nasif patted his friend's shoulder, then sat down also as the rest of us did. "We had a brief run-in with him down at our dig. He said he was paying gold coins for any gold jewelry we dug up. I told him to take off and said if he kept bothering us, I'd magically smelt any gold we found before he could touch it."

Dueble laughed but didn't look like he was getting up any time soon. "Then Nasif melted one of the gold coins for emphasis. It was wonderful."

"You'd never ruin an artifact." I hadn't spent much time with either of them—but they were serious researchers. My having to obliterate the relics that made up my staff had almost destroyed them—even though they agreed they were too dangerous to exist.

"Theria doesn't know that. He backed off," Nasif said.

"And tried something else by making you think Lorcan was calling for you." Alric shook his head.

"Better than that, they used a visage of Lorcan. But it didn't look like the enclave in the background and it was choppy. I should have known something was wrong."

That wasn't good. Most likely, the people holding him and Siabiane had tried to get Lorcan to reach out to them and when he refused, they made up their own version.

"Well, we would have come down to get you when we went to Colivith. But our first stop is Notlianda and seeing just what Taryn's former patron, Qianru, is up to." Neither had met Qianru and so Padraig gave a summary of her letters, visages, possibly being on the other side. Grillion jumped in with a few character observations of his current boss.

"She sent you a real Robukian? All of the pieces? Do you still have them?" Dueble was no longer as upset about Theria but he had the gleam of a researcher in his eyes now.

"They changed into a dagger." I took Rhyfel out of his sheath and held him out to Dueble and Nasif. "This is Rhyfel. He's a him, and the faeries can talk to him. He's saved us a few times." Soft green lines reached out to each of them. These lines seemed to be how Rhyfel learned about people and things.

"One actually changed." Nasif had his hands behind his back but looked ready to grab Rhyfel. "Do you know how rare that is? The rumors were rampant a few thousand years ago. Mages down here all wore the Robukian jewelry as a sign of status, but few were able to change it." He held his left hand out. "Hello there, Rhyfel. We'd like to be your friends."

Rhyfel paused, then sent a few more even lighter arcs their way. Then I put him away.

"This woman you are visiting in Notlianda, do you know where she got the Robukian? Having those and using a spelled letter to get them to you is impressive and a bit concerning if she is not on our side. How powerful of a magic user is she?" Nasif kept glancing toward Rhyfel's hilt but it was with complete fascination.

"Qianru isn't a magic user—not even slightly. She wasn't when she was up in Beccia, and I doubt it's suddenly changed." Alric handed over two bowls of stew. "Are there any serious and questionable magic users running around Notlianda? We're not sure which side she's truly on."

One too many confusions about loyalty on her end, and it was logical to question her. Not to mention her name being dropped as a point of contact for people trying to capture me. But I just couldn't see her as a criminal mastermind. Of course, I'd shown horrific judgment in prior boyfriends and patrons before—so maybe it was better to be cautious.

"None that we've noticed, but we don't come up here often," Nasif said. "Are you sure that Siabiane and Lorcan are in Colivith? Maybe she's working with people who grabbed them and are keeping them in Notlianda."

"We've got some information from a source that we need to get to Colivith. And a visage of Siabiane seemed to confirm that. Our source reinforced the need to get

there with some scrolls from the Library of Pernasi."
Covey said it calmly, but she watched both Nasif and
Dueble closely.

Yup, same drooling and bug-eyed response that everyone seemed to have at the mention of the scrolls.

"You have them…here?" Nasif looked into the darkening woods, as if Theria and a band of killers were ready
to attack. He was also looking around our possessions for
any indication of where they might be.

"The faery bags." Dueble smiled.

"Yes, we have some of the scrolls, not all of them, with
us. We also have several chests. Including one that was for
the Ceisiwr." Alric looked at me. "The thought is that
Taryn might be the Ceisiwr."

It had seemed far longer than just a month since they'd
dropped that idea on me, and I still didn't like it nor think
it was accurate. The Ceisiwr was mythological. A seeker
who would reunite what was missing and broken. Whatever that happened to be. During my first day of being
ill on the ship, Covey had regaled me with some tales
about the Ceisiwr. I'd explained from my sickbed, that as
the Ancient who lost her people, I already had enough
terms hanging on me and that someone else could be
Ceisiwr. She shook her head and gave up trying to talk
to me about it.

Nasif looked like he agreed with me. "Are you certain?
I mean, she does meet some of the criteria, yes, but *the*
Ceisiwr?"

"We're not sure. That was just speculation as to why the
chest came to her," Covey said.

"And nothing is coming out of those bags until we
are safe indoors." Mathilda narrowed her eyes at Nasif. "I
know how impatient you can be."

He laughed. "I've mellowed a bit over a thousand years,
but I agree. Although with those faeries standing guard,
I think we're safe."

The rest of the evening drifted into discussions of what Nasif and Dueble had found so far—mostly relics of Arlienia, the long-lost original homeland of the elves, along with items from an old civilization of syclarions as well as a few pieces from the Ancients. I drifted off while listening and staring at the fire until Alric shook me.

"You might want to get some rest. Foxy is on guard. Grillion and Covey are both asleep." He nodded to the sleeping forms.

I kissed him goodnight and stumbled to my bedroll. It was too cold to change clothes so I tumbled in with all of my layers of clothing on.

I briefly woke up when Alric came to his bedroll next to mine. The fire was dying, and I only heard Mathilda and Nasif talking quietly. I was just falling asleep again when we were invaded.

CHAPTER THIRTY-SEVEN

I ROLLED TO MY feet, seeing that Alric had done the same. He had his sword; mine was missing again but I had Rhyfel and a lot of annoyance at having my sleep taken from me.

The invaders were quiet, short, and gangly. Not rakasa or umbaji short. But more like teenager short. One of them moved close enough to the fire for me to see they were wearing livery. Specifically, really ugly livery. Speckled yellow on purple, with a badly drawn red chimera rampant. Qianru's livery. Having squads of houseboys was common among certain classes in the south. They were a combination of well-paid servants and students. Once they reached a certain age, they became journeymen in many areas of the community. When she'd come north, she'd brought some of them with her—and that horrific livery.

We were surrounded by houseboys now.

I held my hands up but didn't drop Rhyfel. "We're friends of Qianru's. Why are you attacking us?" As I spoke, I looked for my friend Tag. I'd met him through Locksead's relic thief gang, but he'd also been a former houseboy of Qianru. He'd joined her going south when she left. My eyesight wasn't great in the dark and they were moving around, but I figured he would recognize me and Alric. None of the ones I could see looked like

Tag, though.

"Look, we're friends with your mistress and we'd feel bad if we had to hurt you." Alric didn't raise his hands but looked around. "Grillion? Talk to them?"

Three houseboys pulled up Grillion. He was bound and gagged. "We found him. Qianru said to bring him back, along with any who were with him." The lead houseboy was almost as tall as me and broad-shouldered. Much taller than the others.

"This is ridiculous. We're friends with her. Locksead? Tag?" There was no reaction from the houseboys on the names, beyond a bit of muttering. They knew who I was asking for, but my friends weren't out there.

Mathilda came forward, holding herself like a royal matriarch. "We will come with you, young man. However, we will pack up our camp properly and not at a rushed pace. We respect your mistress, but any one of us could easily destroy you all." As she spoke, she raised her left arm and the main houseboy lifted a few feet off the ground. He didn't yell but appeared to be fighting that urge. "And you will untie our friend. He won't run. None of us will. You have my word." She moved her hand and the houseboy shook a bit. "Is that all understood?"

Considering the amount of magic and fighting abilities that faced them, the smart thing would be to back off. From the look on the face of the main houseboy as she lowered him, I didn't think that would happen. Sometimes youth and bravado were just stupidity in disguise.

He stood still for a few moments once his feet were back on the ground. Then gave a sharp nod. "Let the prisoner go free. We will do as they ask." He glared when a few of the houseboys complained and they quickly shut up.

Grillion came to stand by Alric and me and kept his voice low as he turned away from the houseboys. "They're wearing her livery all right—no one could miss that. But I don't recognize any of them. Now, to be fair, she had been expanding her houseboys to bring in more fighters, young ones, but fighters nonetheless. But still—these don't look like them."

"I hope that your suspicions are wrong and that Qianru is on our side. And that these are her houseboys and not a ruse." It wouldn't be that difficult to duplicate the livery and trick us. I glanced back where the group of houseboys had clumped together, talking softly. Either they had more people in the woods around us, or they weren't worried about us trying to escape. "But was that a great idea on Mathilda's part?" She, Covey, and Padraig were gathering their things and going about putting them on their horses.

Foxy glared at the houseboys. They all moved farther away from him.

"There wasn't going to be an easy way around this situation, not without a lot of damage to the houseboys. And they are mostly kids." Alric had our things packed and loaded on the horses in a flash. "And this way, we can get inside without talking to the guards. There's no way this group came out of the town gates."

Good point on his part. If Notlianda was as locked down as Grillion said, they wouldn't let a group of houseboys out and about at night.

Alric darted to the far side of the fire and came back with four blanket-wrapped bundles. "The constructs are still out, but I think the houseboys shouldn't see them." He handed one to me, Grillion, and Covey, keeping the last for himself.

"Where are Nasif and Dueble?" For being a fierce syclarion, Dueble was definitely not a fighter. But Nasif was. I didn't want to cause notice by looking around extensively but I didn't see either of them.

"They left not long after you went to sleep." Mathilda

came over to us. "They needed to get the things they'd left when the faeries grabbed them. I left a spell warning tied to Nasif. As long as they get back within the hour, it will explain what happened to us and where we went."

I also hadn't seen the faeries since I'd been woken up and was getting concerned when the larger houseboy held up a closed basket.

"By the way, we didn't mention before, but we have your flying friends. They are unusually fond of chocolate. Shall we go see my mistress now?" His voice cracked in a few places; he was younger than he looked.

And sneakier, too.

Rhyfel crackled from his sheath. I was figuring out that he reacted to my feelings of anger or fear as much as he did external threats. "You'd better not hurt them in any way. My dagger is fond of those faeries—violently fond. The results won't be good for any of you if they are hurt. Even if Qianru meant no harm." I held up Rhyfel and marched closer to the houseboy and smiled when he flinched. It was at Rhyfel, not me, but I'd take what worked. My friends wanted to use the houseboys to get us inside Notlianda without causing notice. I was fine with that as long as no one I cared about was threatened.

The houseboy held his ground but nodded slightly. "As long as you all come with us, we won't let anything happen to them."

I let Rhyfel crackle once more, the green almost touching the houseboy's cheek, then stepped back and put him away. "Then let's go." I got on my mare and adjusted the sleeping construct on my lap. I was pretty sure I had Bunky, as I heard little gronking noises, but I didn't want the houseboys to see them so I couldn't check.

Padraig and Alric walked, leading their horses, not riding them. I was going to get off my horse and join them, but Alric shook his head.

"We're down in case there is an issue that can't be

addressed on horseback. I don't think we can count on you to be rational when it comes to those faeries." He flashed a grin. "Safer that it's Padraig and me."

I frowned but stayed on my mare. He had a point. He liked the faeries, but if something did go wrong, he and Padraig would do a better job of taking care of things without getting too caught up. And they were far less likely to turn into a dragon if pushed too far.

We followed the houseboys through the woods, but all of them stayed ahead of us in either a show of bravado or realizing they were outmatched. A laugh hit me as I recalled a similar scene months ago. Qianru had been kidnapped and her houseboys tried to ambush us. This group was far more fighter-ish than that first batch, who'd seemed more frightened of their own weapons than us. But there was still a lot of uncertainty coming from the boys leading us.

"Those of you on horses will need to duck." A younger houseboy had dropped back to walk alongside us.

Just in time, too. There was a narrow arch with a low beam. The horses would have to duck a bit as well. I leaned over my bundle of fabric-covered construct as we went through.

The town wasn't as impressive as I'd expected, judging by the height and thickness of the outer walls. Then again, it was night and the torches were spread wide through this section, leaving large clumps of darkness. Farther toward the center, there appeared to be a closer layout of torches, leaving it bright and cheery. Out here, there were just enough to not trip.

We went down a narrow road, which eventually widened out. The building we approached looked like it had been an elegant farmhouse and the wall grew up around it. An additional twenty houseboys gathered in the dim lights with swords ready, watching us. Ironically, the livery wasn't as horrifying in the odd torchlight.

We stopped, but the houseboys with us continued toward the other group. The city itself didn't look to be under siege, but this place appeared to be expecting one.

The lead houseboy stepped back to us. "Our mistress asks if you'd all come in. You will be safe here."

Foxy scowled from the top of his horse. "I'll be staying out here, if you don't be minding. And I won't be happy if anything happens to my friends." He set his massive sword across his lap and was about as moveable as that boulder of Tjolia mountain dreks that I'd left behind.

The lead houseboy narrowed his eyes, his hand tightening on his sword, then wisely shook it off. Foxy was scary-looking when he wasn't pissed, let alone now. "We will let your friends tell her that." He turned, nodded to the rest of us, and marched inside, sure we'd follow.

The wicker basket of chocolate-passed-out faeries guaranteed that I would. I was off my horse, had my still-dozing Bunky tucked in his blanket on the saddle, and was ready to march forward when Alric, Padraig, and Grillion stepped in front of me and followed the houseboy. Grillion was in the middle of them and didn't appear happy about being first in the line of fire. I did notice both Alric and Padraig had a hand on Grillion's shoulders. Probably a good idea.

"You're impressive, but they're less likely to cause an issue." Covey jumped down next to me.

True. But I followed quickly behind them, with Covey at my side. Mathilda was drifting behind us, most likely conjuring some spells in case things went bad.

The houseboys stayed in two lines as we walked inside. My sword hadn't appeared, but I kept my hand on my dagger.

The front room was massive and glaringly white. That alone would have told me this was Qianru's place, if the three-foot-tall portraits of her scattered along the walls hadn't done so. It looked like a larger version of her ostentatious home on the Hill in Beccia. Rather, that one had been a reflection of this one. Like in the Beccian home, she had relics all over. While there were some impressive pieces from what I could see on my march through, I knew she'd have her best pieces in a display farther into the house. She enjoyed showing others her artifacts but her expensive ones were more secure.

The lead houseboy—if we were going to be here for any time, I'd be getting some names—stopped and motioned to Grillion with his free hand. "She would like Grillion to come in alone." A wide doorway showed a long white hallway. Knowing Qianru, she had a more formal greeting area back there.

Covey and I stood behind and to the side of Alric, Grillion, and Padraig. Mathilda had come inside the house but was staying near the front door. None of us budged when the lead houseboy gestured again.

Padraig drew himself up and looked down at the houseboy. "He's not going in without all of us. Please tell your mistress that Padraig, Alric, and Mathilda of the elves, along with Covey and Taryn, are awaiting her."

There was a rumbling among the houseboys who surrounded us, but the leader simply nodded and went down the hall. With my basket of faeries.

Rhyfel stared crackling, and I agreed with him. We were getting the girls back, regardless of which side Qianru was on.

"Taryn?!" Qianru's yell echoed down the hall, but I wasn't sure if it was happy or not. There was a bustle of fabric and soon a short, hawk-faced woman came down the hall. Deep black hair combined with her beak-like nose always reminded me of the Watcher birds used by the ruin guards in Beccia. She was wearing yards of stiff white fabric, lots of jewels, and her usual haughty attitude. But she was smiling as she bustled forward.

"Padraig! I had no idea all of you were coming down

here." She glanced my way. "I believe I tried to get *some-one* not to come because it was dangerous."

Padraig took her hands and smiled as if it were a royal reception in the palace. "It is good to see you again, my friend. We have missed your presence in the enclave. Unfortunately, much has changed and we had no choice but to come south."

Only Alric held Grillion now, but Grillion wouldn't face Qianru.

"I'd feared that Grillion was lost." There were a few layers of meaning in Qianru's words, and I still wasn't sure what side she was on.

"You sent him north with Fealk and Hass. Two followers of the Dark, it appears." Alric kept his words and face emotionless. "Two *late* followers." They'd both been killed by Theria after getting him free of the Beccian jail.

I'd figured that we'd find out more about her loyalties before such pronouncements, but my beloved Alric obviously felt differently.

I tightened my hand on Rhyfel's hilt and watched Qianru carefully.

She looked slowly at all of us, giving a slight nod to Mathilda, who still hadn't moved from the door. "We need to talk." She turned toward the lead houseboy. "Crailit, I need you and your crew to go back outside and stand guard with your men. The rest of you, follow me. Please."

The *please* was rare and seemed to come out with some force.

"I will stay here, if you don't mind." Mathilda's smile was tight and indicated she didn't care whether Qianru agreed or not. I also noticed no one had said anything about Foxy.

"And I'm not going anywhere without my faeries." I was ready to tackle Crailit if need be. He wasn't going outside with my faeries.

"Feistier than before, but agreed. Crailit, give her the basket." If Qianru was embarrassed at having used knowledge of the faeries against them, she didn't show it.

Crailit stepped toward me and handed me the basket. Then turned and marched out of the room with the rest of the houseboys following behind.

Qianru gave a short nod and then turned to go back down the hall. A dark man, hiding behind a work of art, stepped out with a smile once she left. At first, I thought maybe he'd been hiding from her, then realized that he'd been hiding from us.

"It's good to see you all." Locksead looked like a criminal because he was. But he'd filled out since I'd last seen him and appeared more relaxed. Even though he'd been standing in wait with a sword to see if we would attack Qianru. "I'll also wait out here. There are things happening tonight and we're not sure how it will go." He reached forward and shook Alric's forearm in greeting. Alric had run with him off and on for a few years in disguise as an unscrupulous relic thief.

Alric shared the greeting but grabbed Grillion when he tried to move away. "It's good to see you. Please grab Grillion if he tries to run?"

Locksead patted Grillion on the head. "You got into it this time, didn't you? I told you not to take that job." He looked back to Alric. "He won't run." Then he went to stand by Mathilda guarding the door, and we went down the hall.

I peeked into the basket and the faeries were all in one chocolate-covered pile. Either Qianru would let me wash them out in her restroom or kitchen, or I'd do it in the middle of her house. That I didn't have great control over my water spell would just make the results more entertaining.

Qianru led us through a smaller waiting area filled with elegant yet sumptuous chairs and wide bookshelves.

Obviously, the outer room was for show, but this was where she spent more of her time. Then she kept walking and went into a much smaller office. She seemed nervous until we were all in and she'd shut the door.

"I have spells for privacy on this room, but since I'm not sure where the man who did them for me has gone, might one or two of you magic users do an additional spell?" She kept her voice at a level we could barely hear. She didn't trust this room at this point and she looked frightened.

Even when we'd had to rescue her from being Jovan's prisoner, she had looked angry, not scared. That wasn't the case now. Something had her terrified.

Both Alric and Padraig cast low-level spells of concealing. The hiding spells worked better with more magic users as they could interweave the layers and leave the concealment appearing subtle.

Qianru let out a breath. "Thank you. Do you have the Robukian? I sent it to you in hopes it would stay up there and be safe. Grillion as well. But since that didn't happen, I do hope you brought it with you." She'd tossed one of her normal imperious glares my way as she spoke, but it didn't stick.

"He changed." I held up Rhyfel but didn't hand him over. It was looking like she was on our side, or at least was worried about some badness down here. But she had sent the pieces to me. "I wouldn't recommend touching him; he's got a bite." I made sure to let my mixed feelings about Qianru flow through to the dagger. He picked up on the annoyance and crackled away.

Qianru stumbled backward. "That wasn't expected. Okay, I can see the tension in your eyes, so I will tell my tale quickly and you can judge my actions." Her recovery was swift and she was back to looking like a judgy bird of prey.

"About four months ago, I was accosted by a pair of

hilstrike mages. Nasty people. I wouldn't recommend meeting them. They knew of Taryn and some powers that she might possess. They wanted me to help stop her." She laughed and rolled her eyes. "They implied you were responsible for the Ancients being lost and that they and their companions could stop you. Long story short, after they badgered me for a week, I sent them off."

"Can you describe them? These hilstrike mages?" Padraig's voice was soft and comforting, and I thought I might have felt a soothing spell coming from him. "Hilstrike mages usually don't announce themselves."

Which was true. The hilstrikes were a class of dark magic users and came from all walks of life. The ones I'd mostly run into were grimarians, but they could be anyone.

"I have...*had*"—she gave a watery smile and patted her chest— "a friend. He was the one who spelled the Robukian into my notes and got the visages of me to you. That exhausted him, by the way. He knew what the hilstrikes were when they first approached me and stayed hidden but watched them. I'm afraid something had happened to him as he's been gone a week now. That's not like him."

I had a feeling there was more than just friendship between this unnamed mage and Qianru, judging by the unshed tears in her eyes.

"Can we know his name? Likeness? We have places we must go and might find news of him." Padraig was working on keeping her calm.

Good idea. I'd never seen her this close to the edge.

"His name was...is...Klin. He's half-elven and half-human. A good and decent man. Tall, slender, long blond hair. A ready smile and a strong hand." She held up a small rendering of a handsome blond elf. Then she pulled out a delicate piece of embroidered fabric and dabbed at her eyes.

I'd already put Rhyfel away but didn't know about reaching out to comfort Qianru or not. She'd always been unique, but I'd never seen her this thrown off. Even when the elf she had believed was helping her, Jovan, turned out to be a necromancer and mass murderer.

"There is something wrong in Notlianda. I knew that even before Klin vanished."

"How did you know to send your houseboys after Grillion if you thought he would stay up north?" That seemed more than a little odd. Especially if she didn't have a magic user on hand to help her.

"Grillion was spotted in town. Not by my people, mind you, but I'd spread tales of him going north for me for a month or so, so when people that I socialize with told me they'd been seeing him this week, I knew I needed to bring him in. Someone saw him leaving town right before gate closing, so I snuck my houseboys out after him. Locksead gave Crailit the chocolate for the faeries in case he'd brought some back." She tilted her head. "Were all of you in town with him?"

Grillion had been avoiding her but looked up now. "We just came here; I haven't been in town since I rode out with Fealk and Hass." He quickly spilled out all that happened when they got to Beccia and ended with the fact that he could have been left to rot in jail. He repeated that part twice and he was holding her responsible for it. He'd been afraid of her before, but he wasn't now.

Qianru stayed silent for longer than I'd expected, then sat down. "Please, all of you sit. This is worrisome news." She waited until we all took seats; I held the basket of passed-out faeries on my lap. It was easier to leave them like this right now and at least I had them.

"I hadn't known about Hass and Fealk having alternative plans nor being members of the Dark. Along with increasing my houseboy fighters, Klin recommended hiring more workers who could fight. Locksead interviewed them for me, then Klin and I made the final choices. Locksead hadn't liked Fealk or Hass but he couldn't say why."

"But Klin did." Grillion was still scowling but it had lessened a bit. "I had no idea Klin was a heavy magic user, but I recalled him supporting those two."

"Klin didn't know what they were!" Qianru jumped to her feet, reaffirming that he'd been more than just a friend. Her taste in male companions might be worse than mine had been before I met Alric. It would be close between us. Qianru looked around at the various sympathetic faces around her. Grillion wasn't sympathetic but the rest of us were. She'd fallen for Klin and while he'd warned her of danger in the town, he might have been at the center of it.

Padraig shook his head when Grillion looked ready to push the matter. Grillion folded his arms and sat back in his chair.

"Now, he might have been tricked. We believe that Fealk and Hass were murdered by a nasty troll necromancer named Theria. And the other person they were supposed to rescue was actually a changeling masquerading as Domniall, Siabiane and Mathilda's necromancer brother. He exploded once we captured him, but I'd say the entire focus of that had been to get Theria out of the Beccian jail for some nefarious reasons."

"But why was he up there anyway?" She turned to me and her eyes widened. "You. Were those hilstrike mages right about you? But...how? No offense, but you do appear extremely ordinary."

I wasn't going to say anything; there still wasn't enough proof that we could trust Qianru. And I couldn't think of a safe way to answer the question.

"There are things about our Taryn that cannot be discussed at this time. But she is mostly an ordinary woman."

Padraig was so working the charm in here.

"Klin told me to send you the Robukian. Rather, he had me write the letter and he spelled the pieces into it. He knows who you are." She narrowed her eyes as she studied me, as if she could break through to my real self by will alone.

"But your letter said for me to come down immediately. It was only in code you said otherwise."

"That was Klin. He was afraid that things could fall into the wrong hands and that the code, and the visages we sent, would keep you and the Robukian safely in the north. I might not understand why those hilstrike mages wanted you, but I had no intention of handing you over."

"Right now, Taryn isn't our concern," Alric said. "Siabiane and Lorcan have been kidnapped, we believe by hilstrike mages. There is also a small group of Paili out and about, looking for us it would seem, and Theria's goons, who grabbed most of our group earlier today. We came here to see about the Robukian, but we need to move on quickly. Who do you think is causing a problem in Notlianda?" There was a lot more we wanted to find out about her, but asking her directly if she was the drop-off point for captured dragons might not go over well.

I noticed he didn't mention that he'd also been taken and neither he nor Padraig were saying much about our trip down here. I certainly wasn't planning on telling her what and who I was and how that played into everything. Even if she was on our side, that was just too risky.

"I'd say it's people who are working with the Dark, and possibly in league with the hilstrikes who are infiltrating Notlianda. The Dark has been a growing problem for the last twenty years, but hilstrike mages never showed themselves until more recently. They have no fear of being found out. Even the empress doesn't move against them." Qianru faced the others but she kept sneaking glances my way when she thought I wouldn't notice.

I didn't want to wake all of the faeries at this point—

not inside this small room—but I wouldn't object if one of them shook off their stupor early. Having a faery stare at her would make her back off about me for at least a while.

Covey watched Qianru like she would one of her students who might be contemplating cheating. "There were also some false Dark members up north a bit in a small village we passed through. And someone brought in some Tjolia mountain dreks as well."

Qianru had been leaning back before Covey's announcement, but almost jumped out of her seat as Covey finished. "Tjolia mountain dreks?" She got to her feet, beating down the floofy skirts she wore, and stomped to a massive landscape picture. Which turned out to be a board with notes and diagrams on the backside. "You're certain? Of course you are. That makes three known sightings of those things. I don't need to tell you that they don't belong here." She scribbled on her notes. "Where did you see them?"

I looked to the others but they nodded. "It was the village of Hassi." I doubted Larisona planned on keeping it a secret since she was making the ones I shoved into a boulder into a warning sign.

Qianru dropped back into her seat. "Oh no. One of my men moved up there to be closer to family a few months ago. I do hope he wasn't injured. When this is settled, maybe Locksead can ride up and see how he is."

"What was his name?" I knew the odds were long, but it wasn't a big village. And there were a lot of connections going on down here.

"Dhalin. A quiet, humble man. Worked hard and kept to himself." She stopped and looked around. "Oh, no. Was he hurt by the dreks?"

"Sadly, yes, he was. He was killed, actually." Padraig schooled his face for just the right amount of sorrow but said nothing about Dhalin's true connections. And it was true, Dhalin had been the first victim of the drek. It could have been that Qianru knew he was one of the Dark, but she wasn't that good at hiding her feelings.

"Oh, that poor man. He'd been here but a short time, but worked hard to keep this place running."

"Did your friend Klin hire him also?"

"He did. Klin was so helpful in bringing on good help. Even if he misjudged those two Dark followers. Can't say I'm sad about them being gone."

It was going to be ugly if and when we told her what Dhalin really was and that most likely Klin was part of the Dark, or maybe a hilstrike mage, as well.

"When those hilstrike mages visited you those months ago, did they specifically say what they wanted with Taryn?" Alric was seated next to me, and it seemed like he'd moved a bit closer to me.

"Nothing beyond that they had to stop her. I heard about the relic battle afterward, so maybe they were concerned about Taryn's ability to find those relics?" That steely-eyed stare rested on me again. "You were at the battle they were destroyed at, yes? I know most of the important actions were done by the valiant Flarinen and his elvish knights, but it was never clear how the relics were destroyed."

She adored Flarinen. Fortunately, he was just pompously annoying and as far as we could tell, not evil. I gave a somber nod. "We were there, but in a small capacity. The relics appeared to have been caught in a magic crossfire." The others had come up with that tale earlier but this was my first time to use it. It worked for me. And if you considered that I destroyed the relics in my dragon form with both physical strength and magic, then they were destroyed by a magical crossfire of sorts.

"I don't know why they wanted to find you then." She turned from me and my non-interesting self and faced the others. "Since you are here, I do hope you'll help sort out what has happened to Klin and what is happening in town."

"And who is walking around looking like me." Grillion was still obviously annoyed that he could have ended up rotting in a Beccian jail but now had another irksome issue to focus on. One I agreed on.

CHAPTER THIRTY-EIGHT

THERE WAS A lot of careful discussion and no answers. We were all watching what we told Qianru and while she agreed things were going on, she couldn't imagine why someone wanted to appear to be Grillion.

Toward the end, I felt some stirring in the basket I still held. Garbage, Leaf, and three more faeries were stirring. "What do?" She gave me her one-eyed glare as she climbed over the others and out of the basket. "Bird lady!" She didn't fly to Qianru but did wave at her. Her wings were still droopy, so I guessed the effects of the chocolate hadn't completely vanished. Not to mention her wings had chocolate smears on them.

"They gave you chocolate and you all passed out. I told you not to take chocolate from strangers." I'd warned them after some evil folks working with Locksead trapped them with it almost a year ago. And they didn't listen. I knew their love of the stuff overwhelmed what little common sense they had.

I looked over to where Qianru, Grillion, and Padraig were discussing someone pretending to be Grillion. "Do you have a washroom nearby? I'd better wash them off." Faeries usually fell asleep while eating chocolate, so not only would it help them wake up, but getting any residual chocolate off them would keep them from passing out again.

She nodded toward the door. "The guest washroom is next door to this office." Then she turned back to their discussion. I wasn't fond of being discounted, but in this case, it was a good thing. She valued me for finding the Ancient relics and with those destroyed, I was now back to being no one of importance. I would be happy if more people felt that way in the world.

More of the faeries were moving around when I dumped them all in the basin. "Garbage, you too. We're not sure what's going on here and I need all of you alert." I poured water from a large pitcher over them.

"Tea?" Crusty climbed out of the pile of soggy faeries, looking hopeful.

"Not that alert. No one ever needs you that alert. If someone offers you tea and you don't know them, say no." I couldn't imagine any advantage to a bunch of hyper-tea-charged faeries, but one never knew. They'd probably listen to that as well as they did the admonishment about the chocolate.

"Got grabbed." Garbage was soaking but fully awake now. And pissed. "Was going to tell you about extra guy. Then yums, then basket."

"Extra guy? What extra guy?" There had been a bunch of extra guys—the houseboys. But while she usually ignored names, she was good at differentiating between a group and a person. Usually.

"Guy with us. Grill. Saw second one." She hunched her shoulders and pantomimed someone sneaking. "Then change." She pointed her fingers upward from her ears.

"You saw someone who looked like Grillion sneaking through the woods near our camp and he changed into an elf?" That was extremely not good. There were other elves down here but I had a sinking feeling this was Qianru's not-so-missing friend, Klin.

"Yup. Then yums." She sighed but it wasn't clear if she was sighing that there wasn't more chocolate or that the chocolate had stopped her from telling me about the second Grillion.

Who was I kidding? She was sighing at no more chocolate.

I finished rinsing off the faeries and then used one of Qianru's fancy towels to dry them off. That was the least she owed us.

I was still wondering about a few things, though. If Klin was one of the bad guys, one of the assorted evil groups that were roaming about, why have Qianru send something as priceless as the Robukian up to me? Even if he didn't think it would transform into anything, those pieces were still incredibly valuable. And then why have her say to come down, but spell the letter to say the opposite?

And why pretend to be Grillion?

"Why face?" Leaf flew over after playing in the towel.

"Just thinking, sweetie. There's a lot of things going on and we're not sure what or why." And now I was confiding in a faery for help.

"Is you." Crusty flew up as well. She had been rolling like a mad thing in the towel but still managed to look slightly damp.

"What's me?" I reached for the towel but dropped my hand. Knowing Crusty, she liked being soggy.

"You center." She started drawing a circle with some water that was on the counter. She put a huge blob, which looked vaguely dragonish in the middle, then a bunch of lines all around it. "You." She tapped on the blob to reinforce her point. Then was transfixed by the water movement.

Garbage had been supervising the others but came over and nodded at Crusty's work. "Yup. Always after you. Even before you were you."

The hairs on the back of my neck rose at her words, and I had no idea what they meant. "What do you mean?

When we were living in Beccia before I remembered who I was?"

"Noes. Before born. We no born, just appear long ago. You born. Wanted you before born." The seriousness of the looks on the three faces surrounding me and the effort Garbage was making to speak clearly were disturbing.

I took a deep breath. "Some bad people, who might be after us now, or at least related to them, wanted to get me before my mother gave birth to me?" I figured that was too complicated for them.

All three nodded. More faeries came around us and they nodded as well. They all looked slightly sad too.

"Bads make *them* go away. Want you go away too," Penqow said.

Before I could ask who *them* were, Crusty, Leaf, and Garbage all started making designs on the ground. The lost and presumed dead nature spirits from the *tir cudd*. I leaned against the closed door and slid down. The game plan was to figure out what Qianru was up to and if she could be trusted, get our friends back, and then go home and live happily ever after. I really wanted the happily ever after.

Instead, things were getting worse. Had my parents been killed because of me as much, if not more so, than the fight between the Ancients and the syclarions?

Had my birth *started* the fight between them? I had no one to ask since my parents were dead and the rest of my people were lost in time. Thanks to me.

"This is bad." I dropped my head onto my knees.

"Will be okay." Garbage patted my hair. Soon all of the faeries were patting my hair and crooning like I was an injured animal.

Crusty crawled under my arm and kissed my cheek. "We stop. No take you." There was a fierceness in her voice I'd never heard before.

I gave myself another thirty seconds of wallowing in fear and pity, then took a deep sigh and lifted my head. "As long as all of you help me."

"We's do's!" All of the faeries yelled at once.

I was touched by their sincerity. They would keep me safe.

That what they needed to keep me safe from was something connected to before I was born didn't make me happy. But it was something I was going to have to deal with after we found Lorcan and Siabiane. I'd tell the others about this lovely situation once we were away from Qianru.

My friends were probably wondering what was taking me so long. We still needed to find a place to sleep that would be out of the way but not on the other side of the wall. In the daylight, hopefully, we could find an inn. I wanted to spend some serious time crying on Alric's shoulder, undisturbed by everyone around us.

I tidied things up the best I could and opened the door. The faeries tore out and down the hall. Hopefully, Mathilda was still at the front door and could hold them off.

The rest of my friends were still in Qianru's office but the door popped open as I reached for the handle.

Alric was the first out. "Good news. Qianru has a converted barn we can stay in. Lots of room. We're getting our things… Are you okay?" He stepped back and looked down into my face.

I hugged him tightly. "I will be in a few years." Or I'd be dead or lost like those missing deities were. I didn't say that last part out loud. "I've got a lot to tell everyone. The faeries know more than we thought. But I'll share once we're someplace safe." It took me another moment to realize what he'd said. "Wait, we're staying here? With Qianru?" I couldn't say more because she bustled out of the door and down the hall, muttering about arrangements. Covey, Padraig, and Grillion came drifting out behind her. "Am I the only one thinking that's not the best idea?"

"I think Qianru was a victim," Padraig said. "She was tricked into doing much of what she did, including sending the faeries you sent with her back early. People are using her connection to you and the northern elves to manipulate things. But, because of that, this might be the safest place to stay in Notlianda. As long as we stay hidden for the most part. Grillion knows back ways through this town and can keep us out of sight as much as possible."

"But...shouldn't we be leaving for Colivith?" I wasn't sure who the *bads* were who wanted me dead or missing since before I was born, or where they currently were, but there was a good chance of a connection to this town.

"Someone was pretending to be Grillion for a reason, we need to find out why." Padraig started walking us down the hall and toward the front room. "We also need to find out who was trying to get to you and the enclave through Qianru. Besides, the people involved in Theria's camp will be around, and I don't think we want to be on the trail when they are."

I gave a brief nod. I couldn't argue with that, but Mathilda might. Siabiane was her sister and Lorcan was one of her oldest friends. She'd been fairly calm about both of them being kidnapped as we traveled south, but that wasn't going to last forever. Foxy might disagree as well since the sooner things were completed, the sooner he could get back to Amara.

"Excellent. I've had my houseboys set up the barn." Qianru came back down the hall, grabbed Padraig's arm, and swept him down the hall. "It's not been a barn in years though, never worry. It's for my guests. Come along and I'll show you as they ready it." She neatly cut Padraig from the group and escorted him through a side door.

Mathilda and Locksead were chatting quietly by the

door in the front room as the rest of us came in. I didn't see a faery in sight.

"Don't worry," Mathilda said as she obviously caught me looking around. "They went on recon to where we left our friends. I wanted them to know we were okay. I gave them a note." There must have been more information she had needed to give them. She'd already left a beacon for Nasif and Dueble, telling them where we went.

Locksead laughed and held out a small bag. "And I promised the faeries sugar once they came back after successfully giving the note to the right people."

"You know your faeries."

Locksead hadn't been a major fan originally, often the case with folks, but he must have warmed up to the ones Qianru came down here with.

"I had to learn." His smile dropped, and he nodded to Grillion. "I'm sorry I didn't realize how vile Fealk and Hass were. I didn't want her to send them with you, and I should have been more set about it. I'm glad you found Alric, though."

Grillion clasped Locksead on the shoulder. "I know and I appreciate that. It was Klin who ordered them to come along." The two drifted to the side and started a low-level venting of complaints against the missing Klin.

I peeked outside and waved to Foxy. He gave a brief smile and wave, then went back to glaring. That there was no one around to see the glare didn't bother him. "He knows we're staying here, right?" I shut the door but stayed near it.

"Yes, but since the stable section of the barn also has to be freshened up, he opted to wait out there with the horses," Covey said. "We might need one of you magic users to look at the constructs. None of them are recovering."

That wasn't good. Bunky and Irving seemed worse

off than Delsy and Welsy, but they'd all been functioning when we set up camp. What was draining them?

Another reason for going to Colivith sooner rather than later—we needed Siabiane and Lorcan to check the constructs. Bunky might have been created by my people thousands of years ago, but Siabiane understood him so well that she'd made the other three. She could fix them all once we got her back. Or so I told myself.

The faeries came zipping into the front room with a crumpled note. They dropped it into Mathilda's hands, then continued in a line to Locksead and his sugar. I wanted to ask them what they saw but all of them were extremely focused on the sugar.

Once they got their sugar, they went zipping through the house and then turned down the hall where Padraig and Qianru went to the barn and outside.

"I told them they needed to investigate the new quarters before anyone could move in. Figured it would cut down on any urges they had to travel about tonight." Covey smiled as they left.

Mathilda read the note three times before finally handing it to Alric. "They say they found a nearly dying elf. He'd been left past the remains of Theria's camp. He'd been lying there for at least a few days and they're stabilizing him. He doesn't have any marks indicating that he's with the Dark."

CHAPTER THIRTY-NINE

NEITHER DUEBLE NOR Nasif were healers, but both were multi-skilled and Nasif had some strong magic. If anyone could help this elf, those two would be it.

Alric finished reading the note, swore, and handed it to me. Covey read over my shoulder.

"That description sounds like Qianru's friend—Klin. But if he's been out there, then who has been pretending to be Grillion?" I raised my head to notice all of them looking at me in confusion. "Long story, but Garbage said before they were grabbed by the houseboys, they'd seen Grillion's duplicate in the woods and that the copy then changed into an elf. I assumed it was Klin." Sounded a little like over-assumptions on my part, but with what he'd caused, I wasn't certain I trusted this Klin fellow.

"Are they safe where they are? I can try to go after them." Alric looked like he already had the best way out of town mapped out in his head.

Mathilda took the note back from Covey. "No one is going after them. Nasif says they're safe and I'm going to believe them. We need to stay low for a bit and keep our going back and forth to a minimum."

I'd been thinking she wouldn't want to waste time here before getting down to trying to find her sister and Lorcan, but apparently, you didn't make it to a few thousand years old by being rash. Well, unless you cheated, like me. Since I didn't live through those twenty-five hundred years, I don't think they counted.

Padraig came back into the main room, minus Qianru. "I think you'll be happy; the place is nicely laid out. During summer, Qianru uses it as a travelers' inn." He went out the front door to lead Foxy and our loaded horses around as Garbage and her gang came in to get the rest of us.

First she flew to Covey and snapped to attention. "The place is secure. And comfy." She even saluted.

I didn't want to know where Garbage had learned military behavior.

"We shows!" The faeries darted around, herding us toward the back door. Alric gave me a shrug and we followed.

Tiny strings of glows lit the trail to what appeared to be a classic red barn. At least it looked like red but even with the glows it was too dark to be certain. There was a wider entrance toward the back and Foxy, Padraig, Grillion, and Locksead led the horses back there. I assumed at some point we'd get our packs and the constructs from the stables.

The barn itself was spacious and well laid out. A comfortable front room led to a kitchen and a row of bedrooms.

Qianru beamed as we came inside. "Each room has its own restroom. A trend that I'm certain will be sweeping the world once all these troubles die down. I am the trendsetter." Her face glowed at the thought of all the gold coins that would be coming her way. There was no doubt that Qianru was a relic collector, and unlike most of the rich folks up on the Hill in Beccia, she actually knew a fair amount about them. But she was also extremely money-driven.

A hall led to the stables and the troop of houseboys was

bringing everything in. Aside from the blanket-covered constructs. Foxy was carrying all of them and took them into the nearest bedroom. He shut the door when he came back out.

I wasn't sure if that much caution was needed, but right now we couldn't take the chance. Up until Siabiane started making them, the only constructs in the world had been the chimera, and until a year ago, they'd been nothing but myths.

Qianru had little more to add to her tale from earlier but continued to hang around until all of us started yawning.

"Ah, yes, I will be off then. Feel free to use the kitchen, but I will be having my chef make a full breakfast tomorrow. I shall see you all at eight." With a wave to Locksead, she turned and left.

"It's very good to see you all, even if you seem to be bringers of troubling times. But if I don't join her for her nightcap, she will get cranky, and we can't have that, now can we?" He nodded and followed her out.

Grillion shut the door behind him with a thoughtful look. "It's odd to be here. I almost feel like I should go back to my old room in the main house and not travel on with you folks."

"You could do that, you know. It would be understandable if you stayed here once we leave," Mathilda said.

Grillion looked around the room and even Foxy gave him a small smile. He wasn't a magic user or the best fighter, but he had heart. I'd support his choice, but I admitted to myself that I'd miss him if he stayed here.

"If you folks don't mind, I'd like to stay through to the end—whatever it turns out to be. I'll tell Qianru in the morning."

The faeries all flew by, patted him, then zipped into the stables.

"I'm still trying to sort out us being here, although a

few days of not being chased, hunted, or attacked would be nice." I winced and hoped that I hadn't just jinxed us. Qianru and Locksead both said things were going wrong in Notlianda, and her friend Klin was missing, but maybe it wasn't related to us.

I ignored the laughter in my head.

"I'd like us to try to put together the pieces; there are too many people after us for them not to be related." Padraig came out from the small kitchen with a few tea-pots and mugs.

Watching the faeries fly in and out of the stables reminded me of their startling proclamation. "Oh, and I might as well bring it up now—with my luck, it's part of why we're being hunted." I quickly told them all of what Garbage and the others had told me. I wasn't the only one not happy about it.

Covey carefully put down her mug. "That ties into your being the Ceisiwr. The seeker is known before they come into the world. Sorry."

She knew I didn't agree with me being the Ceisiwr, the seeker who would fix everything. That's a pretty big job title. And one really would think someone like that wouldn't lose her people in a fit of fear and anger. I just shrugged. "I'm more concerned about whether the fight between my people and the syclarions that took my parents was motivated by who I am. Which, knowing that they wanted me dead or trapped before I was born, doesn't explain why or who I am supposed to be." That was annoying. The faeries couldn't give me answers they didn't have.

"The why is probably that they also think you're the Ceisiwr," Mathilda said. "There have been a lot of myths about that being, and not a lot of concrete evidence to support it."

The rest of the evening went back and forth with debates on my status, Qianru's missing friend, Theria and his goons, the Paili, the hilstrikes, and whoever those knights had been. Covey and Grillion had an ongoing debate but in either case, they weren't good.

We triple-checked that all the doors were locked, and Padraig and Alric set up a concealment spell, then we started opening faery bags. I had to call the girls back into the front room since Crusty had a bag with the jewels. None of the others had seen them, but I wanted them to now.

"Is mine?" Crusty clutched the bag tightly. The fact she added a question mark to her sentence indicated she knew she couldn't keep them but was going to hang on as long as she could. She did technically steal them, but I'd made it clear she wasn't keeping them.

"No, you were guarding them for me. But now everyone needs to see them." I quickly amended my comment. "Only the people in this room, understood?" I had no idea where the stones were going to end up, but if they stayed with Crusty, I didn't want her flying around showing them to strangers. And that was a serious risk with her.

"Fine." She flew down to the table we'd sat around, landed, and emptied the jewels out in the center of the table. "Pretty." She patted them.

The green one had changed me when I was already having some physical transformation issues. I wasn't taking a chance touching any of them until Padraig or Mathilda cleared them.

"Where's the other rock? The one who spoke of me?" I hadn't put the two things together, but when we were hiding in the ruins to the north, Crusty showed me a rock with my name on it as well as a scattering of scrolls that were connected to a battle to the south from long ago. Including drawings of a giant dragon construct. The rock in question had been spelled before I was born, yet contained images of me as a child.

I hadn't had the time, nor the ability at the time, to search through them. But adding what was in those scrolls and rock to what the faeries said about people looking for me before I was even born, I think they needed to be looked at. Not to mention there was a pessimistic side growing in my head. If I didn't survive this trip, the others needed to know what was happening.

Crusty gave the most long-suffering sigh that had probably ever come from a four-inch-high being. Then she crawled into her tiny black bag and pushed out the rock with my name on it, a bunch of scrolls, and two ale bottles. I had a feeling the last items weren't for me, although sitting in a nice pub with a bottle did sound wonderful.

"She found the rock and scrolls in the ruins we hid in. I can't touch the rock; it has images imprinted in it. These scrolls might be interesting, though." Of course, the first three scrolls I picked up consisted of two crop lists and a merchant list for fabric to have gowns made.

Crusty patted her pretty stones, then rolled one of the bottles to the side where the other faeries were. More clinking ensued and soon they had many sealed ale bottles.

"What about this one?" I lifted the second one she'd taken out to give it to them but they all shook their heads.

"You needs. Keep. Drink all." Garbage sounded like she was a doctor prescribing healing medicine.

I was not going to argue and kept the bottle near me.

Alric looked at the rock while most of the others looked at the gemstones. I noticed that no one was touching anything. Well, until Covey decided to sort the scrolls. As far as I could tell, and judging by the lack of reaction as she sorted, they weren't set up with magical tricks.

The same couldn't be said for the jewels and stone.

Alric finally picked up the rock but shrugged. "Nothing's happening—" His words were cut off as he was flung across the room.

CHAPTER FORTY

———◆———

FOXY GRABBED ALRIC as he flew past and put him back on his feet as if it were nothing.

Alric shook his head. "I should have expected that."

The Taryn rock had settled down after flinging Alric, and he told us what he saw as he'd held it. None of the images were of me, or at least he didn't see any children. But he did see an extremely old elven village, but not more than that. It might just show the past in general, not my past specifically. I wasn't ready to test that theory at this point.

Foxy nodded but seemed distracted as the rest of us looked over the stones and scrolls. "If folks don't be minding, I'm going to my room and talk to Amara. I have the constructs with me; they'll be safe." He hadn't been happy since we came inside the town walls and still looked out of sorts. With a nod good night, he went to his room and shut the door.

Grillion had been keeping an eye on the jewels but looked up. "Is he okay? This town isn't that bad."

"I think he didn't cope well with being grabbed with-out a chance to fight back like all of you were. Foxy never fought much in Beccia but it was because even the drunks knew better to take him on. He's just adjusting." Or so I hoped. I still wished there was a way to send him back to Beccia. He was taking a huge risk coming down here with the Klipu mob on his tail. But I knew how stubborn he was.

The others nodded and went back to sorting scrolls and peering at the jewels. I opened my bottle of ale. I would have shared, but there was only one bottle. I did offer some to Alric but he just gave me a stunning smile and shook his head. I knew I loved him.

Everyone turned their focus on the jewels. "Crusty thinks they're all magic but not sure what they do. She wasn't affected by them when she took them, but the one I touched messed with me and changed me in the ruins. There must have been a purpose for them to be embedded in the walls where they held Alric."

Padraig found a stick and was carefully moving the stones with it. "Never can be too careful with spelled gemstones. The art of using them for magical receptacles is almost completely lost now. It wasn't common even when I was young. You can see a bit of the setting left behind, as well as the materials used to put them in the wall."

Mathilda held her hand over them, then pulled it back with a frown. "How strong are those faery bags? I can't tell what the stones do, not without touching them, which I'm not up to yet. But there is something powerful within. Something attached to them that is leaving a trail." She peered closer but kept her hand back. "I think they are being tracked."

"Garbage? Can you come here for a moment?" The girls had been drinking but no singing, dancing, or bottle diving had ensued yet so she should still be able to answer questions.

"Yesss?" She drew it out as she twisted around to keep an eye on the other faeries and their bottles.

"Can your faery bags block magic?"

She shrugged. "Somes. Not that." She pointed to the gems and the Taryn stone.

Damn it. "People can find us with magic through those?"

"Yeah. Not good." She turned completely back to look at the ale bottles.

"Sweetie? Is there any way to make it so that magic can't get through?" The problem with the faeries was that their minds worked so differently than everyone else. It wasn't that they didn't care about issues; they just didn't know they were issues.

"Skunkwallow!" she yelled.

I wasn't sure if that was something to use or a name until a light-purple faery came stumbling over.

"Needs secret bag." Garbage held out her hand and the other faery reached into the tiny pouch on her overalls and pulled out a silver bag. The faeries had given one of those to Alric, Siabiane, and me when the Robukian started creating more pieces and the faeries weren't happy about it. The new silver bag went to Garbage and then to me.

Skunkwallow grinned, then tore off back to the drinking faeries.

"Theres. No follow." Garbage patted my cheek and ran back and jumped in a bottle of ale. I couldn't blame them. Although they usually had fun, this trip was hard on them too.

"Okay. Looks like, according to our expert, they will be safe in this bag. Is it okay to look at them a bit before we put them in there?" I peered at them closely. Eight stones, all cut beautifully and all looking like they'd just been polished. "Why are there lines of gold on the backs and sides? I know they were pulled out of settings, but gold shouldn't do that, should it?"

"We should be safe with them inside this barn. There are layers of protection, but once we leave this building, we could be found. They'll need to stay in that bag after tonight." Padraig used his stick to roll over a sapphire the size of my fist. Gold streaking. "It's almost as if they were removed from their settings by melting them off."

"Why would someone melt them off? Aren't there better ways to remove jewels? They destroyed the jewelry to get the stones?" I wasn't a jeweler nor a thief but it seemed like a wasteful way to do it.

"That crown we found in the *tir cudd*...how many empty settings did it have?" Covey was studying a yellow amfire, a rare stone that glowed from within and came from the far desert lands.

"Eight. I think." I glanced over to Foxy's shut door. Even if it wouldn't be rude to bug him if he was talking to Amara, which it would be, Irving was still unconscious. He'd swallowed the crown along with the rest of the jewelry when we were still in the *tir cudd*. Getting anything out of him wouldn't happen until he woke up and wanted to let us have it. When he'd swallowed my relics, you couldn't even see them inside his mouth, and he didn't have a stomach that we knew of. No one was sure where the relics had gone. "Not sure when we can get it back, though."

"I forgot about Irving," Padraig said. "But those stones look too large to have fit on that crown, at least from what I briefly saw of it."

"Not to mention that it was intact and not melted down."

"It could still be the same crown. The crowns and regalia of the very old empires were said to be indestructible. They might have melted it, released the gems, and it reformed on its own again." Mathilda shrugged. "Oddness among royal possessions is not unheard of. I do wish we could test our theory, though." She sighed. "Well, since we can't do that, let's do a quick check on what they do before locking them back up in a bag. If they are stones of importance a full examination could take years."

Alric and Padraig made adjustments to strengthen their concealment spell. It almost felt like the walls and ceiling were pressing in now.

Mathilda nodded, rolled up her sleeves, and picked up the yellow amfire. *"Hello, Taryn, can you hear me?"*

I almost screamed as Mathilda's voice came into my head loud and clear. And her lips didn't move at all. "How did you…?" I watched as the same look of surprise crossed all of my friends' faces as she turned to each one in order. Mathilda even turned to the faeries, but there was no indication she got through as they continued drinking and playing in their ale.

"I thought that it might enhance communication." She put the gemstone down gently. "In the old symbols of divination stones, the amfires were supposed to increase interaction between minds."

Covey used an extended claw to push aside a deep purple stone. "Jainl? Aren't they supposed to influence strength? I never looked into star or stone reading much as it seemed to be mumbo jumbo. But what if the stone divination readings done by mystics were based on these actual stones? Let me check something." She grabbed the stone. "I feel the same." Still holding the stone, she went to the chair Alric sat on. And easily picked it and Alric up with one hand.

She and Alric looked equally shocked. Luckily, both of them had great balance and reflexes as she set him back down without a problem.

Grillion's eyes were huge as he looked from Covey to Alric and back to the stones. "Those are the sacred stones of the *llyn canfyddydd*." He shook his head. "Don't ask me how to spell that and I probably ruined the pronunciation. But when I was a kid, we had an old man in the village who would tell us the best stories. He said his grandfather passed them along from his great-grandfather and back through time. Our village was poor so we didn't have much, but he made us all feel like kings and queens. According to him, those stones were first used to create peace all around the world. Not just in one town, kingdom, or land. *All over.* Then darkness came, peace fell, and the stones were lost." His eyes got a dreamy look as he gazed down at the pile and sighed. "Those stones are what led me to the life of a relic thief."

Alric shook his head. "You wanted to find them to bring peace...by stealing them?"

"What?" Grillion looked around the table sheepishly. "Nah. I loved the tales but didn't think they were real. But they made me realize there were treasures everywhere. And I have always argued if the original owners are long dead, how can it be thieving? Just because another group of people moves in to claim them doesn't mean they are theirs."

He had a point. The rulers of Beccia locked down their ruins and strictly controlled who was allowed to dig there. Even though the elves were back in our world, they couldn't take things from their own homes of long ago unless it was cleared by the Antiquities Commission. There had been some angry words thrown around at that, so I doubted it would hold for long.

"I'd say the likelihood of them being the basis for stone divination reading is strong." Padraig took hold of the sapphire. "This one should be..." He vanished and then appeared ten feet away from us next to the far wall. "The one that deals with space and distance." He popped out again and emerged out of the air at the end of the hall for the bedrooms. He pulled up the edge of his shirt and dropped the sapphire into it. "And that will be enough of that. But I think we have our answer as to what they are." He walked over to us and rolled the stone back with the others without letting it touch his skin.

I didn't know about divination stones any more than I knew the fortune cards or the star positions. I liked what was in the ground that I could find, and pieced together stories of the past that way. But it did look like Crusty had found the original stones that were the basis of the divination gemstones. "Does this mean that somewhere there's a magical deck of cards that does what all those fortune cards say they do?" I'd had my cards told once, and it was a disturbing experience. I didn't like the idea that there might be a real deck behind the mumbo jumbo. But paper couldn't last the way rocks and stones could. Right?

"No, of course not." But Mathilda's smile was too forced. She might not know if there was a deck or not, but she was disturbed by these stones enough to think there might be.

Padraig, Covey, and Mathilda all made notes about the rest of the stones, then Padraig used his stick to push them all into the silver bag. Even believing there were enough protections on this building to keep them and us safe, I know I felt better when the ties on the silver bag were tied. I was shocked when Padraig handed the bag to me.

"Shouldn't one of you carry it?" I took the bag gingerly.

"You or your faeries should keep them," Padraig said. "They found them, and I believe they are tied to the Ceisiwr. The word *canfyddydd* is an old word for *finder*. *Llyn* means *the ruler*. Until we can study them more, we won't know for certain that's what these stones are. But this is looking more and more like it's related to you."

I had a feeling deep inside that he was right. But I was trying extremely hard to ignore it. I had no idea until now what *llyn canfyddydd* meant. Knowing didn't make things much better. I weighed the bag in my hand as I debated. The faeries were capricious, reckless, and not always forthcoming about information. They would still be the safest bet for these stones. They also were all quite drunk and most were extremely soggy. I tucked the small bag inside my clothing. "For now."

"I think we need to find out why those mages had those stones in the walls of that chamber. Do you recall anything about that room?" Mathilda turned to Alric.

Alric shook his head. "Only that I couldn't fight back at all in there. There was a power like I've never felt coming from those walls—something beyond the Jhea spell. They might have had me tied up, but they didn't need to. They'd been mostly keeping me in another cell, but they knew you were coming and moved me there. They didn't care what I heard as they planned to kill me the moment you came through the door. Those stones might have been intended to work against you more so than me."

"And why they specifically haven't followed us if they knew we took them? That's another question," Covey said. "They expected us to try to get Alric back; they were using him as bait to bring in Taryn. Yet they didn't keep after us once we cleared their forest with Alric, Taryn, and the jewels. Why?" She hadn't fully retracted her claws from handling the stones so her finger drumming on the table was loud. With a grin, her claws retracted.

"Turf lines were being drawn." Grillion had been focused on the stones until the silver bag vanished. "When Fealk, Hass, and I went up north…the knights, the syclarions, and whatever it was in that place where Alric was taken—they would fight among themselves, then settle down and invisible lines were drawn. They didn't seem to worry much about us, but Fealk was also the one to speak to them as we rode through the various areas."

That wasn't good. Fealk had been a follower of the Dark. Had he flashed the tattoo on his arm to gain passage? Were all of the segments part of the Dark? Or just working with them?

Covey started pacing and looked to be going into her professor mode. Sometimes a scary proposition. "There could be a master plan, which would indicate there is but one actual group behind the others. Having smaller groups each controlling their own turf, but still with a common goal is brilliant. They may not realize they are being so well controlled." She shook her head. "My bet is the Klipu mob. These types of turf delineation are classic for them. Almost impressed that they have expanded to most, if not all, of a continent. Most likely those mage fights that destroyed the villages that Jadiera's crew told us about were part of the process."

Silence followed but confusion showed on Grillion's face and probably mine. Everyone else was thinking their own thoughts, but it looked like Covey was right in her theory from the grim looks of agreement that I saw.

It was hard to decide if a bunch of bad guys after you under one flag was better or worse than the same bunch under their own flags. Really, it wasn't that hard. If everyone was on their own, there was a good chance of infighting and the hope they'd knock down their numbers. They'd already gone through that and were now stronger because they weren't fighting each other so they could focus on whatever the big plan was.

"How hard is it going to be to get back north when we're ready?" My voice was stronger than I felt, and I was being positive about our getting Lorcan and Siabiane back, and Foxy doing what he needed to do with the mob without all of us dying.

And I knew in my gut that we could succeed on all of those fronts and still be unable to get back home.

"I think we'll be fine. With my sister and Lorcan along, we'll find…" Mathilda trailed off with a sigh. "I don't know why I feel the need to protect you." She shook her head. "You're an Ancient—you can handle it. The fact is, I've wondered about that the farther south we go. The

attacks in Hassi village made me think more about it.
Being followed through those gems was probably con-
tributing to the issue, but I've felt like our enemies are
closing in around us the farther south we go. Tightening
a noose. Even those birds that took flight along with the
sceanra anam against Taryn—murlin being used like that
wasn't uncommon, but it hasn't been done in probably a
thousand or more years."

Padraig watched Mathilda, then smiled. "To simplify, I'd
say we're going to have a hard time getting back north."

Considering that was all I wanted to do once we got
Siabiane and Lorcan back, his words hit hard. "That
wasn't what I wanted to hear, but at least I know." I
looked around and took a deep breath. "So, what's next?"
I was proud at how I kept my voice from shaking. It now
felt like everything was between us and Beccia, and we
weren't even to Colivith yet.

The plan to come to Notlianda to find out about
Qianru's actions and which side she was on was mostly
complete. She'd been used, she didn't know much, and
she was on our side. Mostly. But now we had to deal
with Klin and whoever was pretending to be Grillion.
Plus whatever weirdness Locksead felt was happening in
town.

"I think tomorrow we should have some of us wait
here for Nasif, Dueble, and their injured elf if he survives.
Some will need to see what the tone and feel of the town
is but stay low, don't cause notice. And Grillion needs to
be seen around town, a lot," Padraig said.

"I'm following on the first two, but why should he
be seen if the rest of us are trying not to be?" I wasn't a
strategist, but that's why I had friends who were.

Alric smiled. "So that whoever was pretending to be
him—and if what the faeries saw was correct, was also
pretending to be Klin—would have to change things up.
And whoever they'd been dealing with might approach

the real Grillion instead.'"

Grillion looked around the room, then shook his head. "Wait, if this other-me is really evil and powerful, wouldn't he be working with other equally evil people? And you want them to come to *me*?"

"I'll be with you, Grillion. Just a slight glamour like the one I used to use in Beccia when we ran together." Alric winced. "Minus the hair color."

When I'd first met Alric, he'd worn a magic glamour to appear as a human instead of an elf. Long ago in his youth, his father magically blocked his ability to glamour his white-blond hair. He'd been badly dying it black when we met. Thank goodness that had stopped.

Covey grinned. "I'll follow you both. My people aren't common this far south, so I'd be noticeable. Unless I don't want to be. I can be an extra set of eyes and backup protection."

"Padraig, Taryn, and Foxy will stay here. I'll take Lock-sead for a tour of the town, and the rest of you find out who is pretending to be Grillion." Mathilda got up from the table and stretched. "Let's sort out particulars in the morning. It's been a long day."

The faeries were settling down into their happy, drunken stupor. No wild shenanigans this time; they all seemed melancholy and some had already crashed, asleep on the chairs and sofas in the main room. As was sometimes the case, there seemed to be more than twenty-three. At some point, I'd work on getting an answer from Garbage as to how many faeries were with us.

The others rose as well, and we all trooped off to our rooms. Alric and I shared one room, but both of us were too tired to do anything beyond cuddling together after a few sleepy kisses.

CHAPTER FORTY-ONE

———◆———

" INS! NEEDS INS!"
The noise finagled its way through to my brain far too early in the morning. I burrowed deeper into Alric's side.

"They'll just find a way in on their own." He ruffled my hair but didn't move.

"Which begs the reason why they haven't." The faeries could go through walls and doors when they wanted to. Sometimes. I thought about calling them, then got out of bed instead. I didn't want to encourage random popping into bedrooms. I opened the door to have the bulk of our extended flock fly over me. And in some cases into me.

"Guests! Friends!" Garbage looped around my head then back out into the hall. The rest of her group followed. Then they flew back to us.

I couldn't see anyone in the main room but the room curved to the side of the hall. I trusted the faeries enough to know if we'd been under attack, they wouldn't have said "friends." "Go wake the others. We'll be out shortly." I wanted a quick shower and fresh clothes, and the way Alric was looking through his pack, he did as well.

The faeries did one more lap, just in case we were going back to bed, then zipped out the door.

Once ready, we went out to the living room to find Padraig and Mathilda talking quietly with Nasif and

Dueble. There was no sign of an extra elf, living or dead.

"I'm glad you're both safe. What happened to the elf you found?"

"He's safe, but you have had all the excitement. They told us what your faeries found." Nasif held up his hand. "But to answer your questions," he nodded as the rest came out of their rooms, even Foxy, "the elf we found is still alive, it is Klin, and he had been attacked about four days ago. Qianru and Locksead identified him when we brought him here and she sent for her private healer."

"What attacked him?" Alric asked as he buckled on his sword. That hadn't been in the room until a second ago.

I wished my sword was as well behaved.

"We're not sure," Dueble answered. "My guess is an animal. A large one, possibly with tusks."

"You mean a drek?" I'd been looking forward to breakfast but that feeling was quickly vanishing. The appearance of three of those things was a fluke; the ones traveling with them in the chawsia I mentally ignored since they had been together. But now another one attacked someone? They couldn't be ignored no matter how much I wanted to. Or I just had to try harder.

"That's my guess." Dueble looked even less happy about that guess than I felt.

"Excuse me, since I've never faced one of those things before, but shouldn't Klin have been killed?" Grillion looked around the room.

"He should have been," Padraig said. "And this could have been one of the group that was sent to Hassi village a few days ago. The timing would be right. He was attacked and then someone opened a chawsia path and sent them to Hassi. About the same time."

"They didn't kill him but killed that Dark elf and almost killed Alric?" I felt a phantom pain in my side where that creature's claw had stabbed me. I knew I was completely healed but it ached right now. "Maybe this Klin person called the dreks, sent them on the chawsia path, and got paid back by an attack as they were leaving." I hadn't met Klin but I wasn't happy with him. I also knew what kind of a fighter Alric was. That Alric would have been killed by that thing if I hadn't intervened, yet this Klin survived a drek encounter didn't seem right.

"It is questionable that someone survived a drek attack. But he was grievously injured. And he'd been moved to that location, so someone other than the drek knew what happened to him," Dueble said.

"And the faeries saw the fake Grillion turn into what we now believe was a fake Klin." I held up my hand as a thought hit me. "Garbage?" She flew over. "Can you go into the main house and look at the injured elf? Just you. I need this to be your job. You must stay quiet and don't hurt anyone. Just tell us if that is the same elf you saw the fake Grillion turn into."

"I's do." She turned to the rest of the faeries. "I's has job. Yous stay." They didn't look like they cared, but most of the faeries nodded.

I was about to tell Garbage to be careful not to be seen when she tore through the front door.

A moment later, she came back the same way. "Is not him. That one broken."

I took a deep breath. Faeries could be absolute in definitions sometimes. "If he wasn't beat up, would he look like the elf you saw?"

She tilted her head, wrinkled her nose, and squinted into the air. "Yes. Was *him*," she pointed to Grillion, then toward the main house. "Then that him. But no squished." She flew back to her flock. "We goes. Things!" All of the faeries tore off through the door.

"You have no control over them, do you?" Nasif laughed.

"Never have and never will. I hope no one needs them because I have a bad feeling they're off stalking something in the woods. I saw war feathers coming out as they took off." We'd gotten confirmation about Klin; that might be the best we were getting for the day from them.

A knock came from the front door, and Covey opened it. Locksead was loaded down with food and was followed by two houseboys, also loaded. "Qianru suggested you might be more comfortable eating in here. Since we have the injured one in the main house." He set the food down. The two houseboys did the same, then left when he nodded.

"Can you stay for a bit?" Padraig nodded toward the open door.

Locksead shut the door. "What's wrong?"

"We think that not only was someone pretending to be Grillion, but they were also appearing as Klin. Someone changing from Grillion to Klin was seen yesterday." Padraig didn't say it was the faeries but it was better that way. "At that time, we believe the real Klin was in no shape to go anywhere, as you've seen."

"What? A glamour? Can someone change that fast?" Locksead wasn't a magic user, but as the former leader of a gang of thieves, he'd had plenty working for him in the past.

"No." Mathilda helped spread out the food on the table. "Even the strongest magic users would have a problem with a change that quickly since they would be doing two distinct glamours."

"A changeling?"

That was not a word I'd wanted to say or hear for a long time. The most recent event with them had been one pretending to be Domniall, a nasty necromancer elf, and brother to Siabiane and Mathilda. Changelings were complete chameleons and with enough supporting spells could copy magic as well as appearance.

"That's what I'd suspect," Padraig said. "They were always more populous down here than in the north."

"And the one that exploded in Lorcan's study admitted he was part of the Dark." Alric helped with the food and we all sat down.

It was almost lonely without the faeries or the constructs, but much calmer.

"On a different subject, should something be done about the constructs? Are they showing any life at all?" It could be argued that the mechanical beings weren't alive, but I thought of them as being alive. And I knew my friends did as well. I no longer wanted to wait until we got Siabiane back to revive the constructs.

Foxy had started in on the breakfast with a huge plate full of food. "I heard noises coming from all four. And I had Amara sing to them last night." He looked embarrassed. "I figured it always helped make me feel better, so maybe?" He shrugged.

Mathilda patted his arm. "I say it couldn't hurt and given Amara's unique status, it might help. Let's eat, then finalize our new plans."

Grillion's eyes lit up until he saw Alric and Padraig shaking their heads.

"Sorry, Grillion. You, Alric, and Covey are still going out to see if you can get people to come to you as this changeling," Alric said.

Grillion waved a bit of toast in the air as he swallowed the piece he'd just eaten. "But if they know he was a changeling, wouldn't they be able to tell that I wasn't one?"

Covey shook her head. "Since we have no idea who is working with this changeling, there's no way to know if anyone in town knows what he is. Also, the changeling might show up where you are also. That's why I'm still going. You won't notice me, but I'll be there." Her grin was all berserker and no professor. She really didn't like changelings and had taken it personally that we had let one explode in Lorcan's study without her having a chance for a go at it.

"Gah." Grillion's mouth was full of eggs this time, so no real words came out. But the emotion was there. He didn't like being dangled out as bait.

"Since the main reason the rest of us were staying here was to wait for Nasif and Dueble, should we all be going out?" I hoped that without those blasted jewels calling out to people about us, we might be okay.

"No. I think it's still best if the three of us stay here. Nasif and Dueble could go out on recon, though. Assuming that there are syclarions in town?" Padraig watched them both. Grillion needed to be seen to try to gather information on this changeling—those two didn't have to. Because of the mess of time travel and who they both were, they'd mostly stayed hidden for the thousand years between their time and this time. Dueble especially wasn't fond of going out in public.

"There are some, but if you don't object, I'd like to stay here and catch up with Taryn." Dueble smiled. "I'd also like to see if I can help with the constructs."

We did have a lot to catch up on; the last time I'd seen him, I thought I was just a confused human named Taryn. While he knew who I really was now, we hadn't talked about it. He was a comforting person to talk to. We'd just have to wait until Locksead left with the others. There was no way anyone in Qianru's household should know what I really was. We were pretty sure she was on our side, but that could change in an instant if she knew what I was. Friendship would only go so far against the fame and fortune of discovering a real Ancient.

"I would like to join in the expedition, if you don't mind." Nasif finished his breakfast and threw up his hood. "Should I get a real disguise or will this do?"

Padraig and Mathilda tilted their heads together, then Padraig spoke. "If he's not in disguise, we might have another piece of bait. Theria worked hard to try to get him and Dueble to work for him. If he's near here, he might come to try to speak to him."

"But I'd say on that chance, *I* should have a bit of disguise." Mathilda patted herself and her appearance became more like a younger version of her sister. "He's seen me twice now and we don't want him sorting out where he's seen me before. If I'm with Locksead and Nasif, hopefully, he won't make the connection."

As much as I wanted to stay and just catch up with Dueble, the idea of my friends going fishing for evil changelings and necromancers didn't sit well with me. "You know, I could—"

"No."

They didn't shout it but having Alric, Covey, Padraig, Foxy, Nasif, and even Grillion all cutting me off at the same time was a bit annoying. Dueble didn't say anything but nodded in agreement.

"It was just a thought. And all of you better be extremely safe."

We finished eating and they got ready to leave. The only ones glamoured were Alric and Mathilda, but I knew Covey would find her way to blend into the background.

Alric was the last out, and he grabbed me for a passionate goodbye kiss.

I finally pulled back with a sigh. "You kiss as good as my elf boyfriend, but don't tell him." It was odd seeing human features where his elven ones should be. But it was still him.

"We'll check in if we find anything," he said and left. Locksead had gone out arm in arm with Mathilda, with Nasif looking bookish on her other side.

Foxy brought out the constructs and put them on the sofa. All four just looked asleep. If you could fall asleep in mid-action, that was.

I walked closer to them. "Do we really think this is

the result of what was done to them in that camp? Why did it wait so long to disable them?" It could be that the shutdown caught them so fast that they stopped in mid-action. Or it could be something else that happened to them when we had set up our own camp. Something we missed.

Padraig and Dueble came forward as well, each picking up a different construct.

"You could have a point, but we didn't notice anyone," Padraig said. "And if someone spelled the constructs, why wouldn't they have hit all of us as well?" He gently removed a small panel on the upper part of Welsy's back then looked up. "Siabiane told me about these access areas."

Dueble watched Padraig carefully, then did the same thing to Delsy.

"What if someone disabled them for a reason? If they were after us but wanted to take them out of the picture first?" The constructs had taken some hard hits from Theria and his people, but they were recovering. Something else might have happened.

"And the houseboys' arrival cut off their attack?" Padraig nodded. "Could be. We might owe Qianru thanks if that's the case." He held a glow over the interior of Welsy. "All I'm seeing in here is a lack of power." He looked over to Dueble, who nodded.

"I'm seeing the same. I'm not completely sure what should be here but everything looks intact; it just has no power for it to work."

Both Foxy and I stepped back when Padraig nodded toward Irving. I knew there was no way that I wanted to mess inside there. It took them a bit longer but they found his hatch as well—and the same results.

Padraig stood over Bunky and shook his head before turning to me. "I have no idea how we look inside one of these. I know you have odd things happen when you touch him directly, but you might be our only chance to get him back."

I took a deep breath and stepped closer. Touching Bunky always brought me a slam of images, all from my people. It wasn't nice, though; they uncomfortably flooded my brain. "Somebody might want to stand behind and catch me if I get flung. It's happened before."

Foxy stepped behind me immediately. "Never you fear."

I smiled at him, then put both hands on Bunky. Nothing happened for a few moments, then the flood of images hit me. I wanted to let go, but unlike all the other times, these were coming slow enough that they didn't wreck my brain. It felt like my seeing the images was giving them and Bunky strength. The longer I held on, the stronger Bunky felt under my hands. I felt his purr before I heard it. "He's back!" I fell backward as the images grew fast enough to disorient me and was held up by Foxy.

Bunky blinked his eyes, then gave a soft gronk and fluttered his tiny wings. I knew the wings were too small to actually be what kept him flying, but seeing them move was a great thing.

He started lifting about a foot in the air, then noticed his construct friends on the sofa. He hovered over the other three constructs, almost sniffing. Then he raced to the door, raced back to me, gronked, and went back to the door.

"He said he knows how to fix the others; we all need to follow." Padraig shrugged. "I understand him."

Great. Everyone understood Bunky but me. But as annoying as that was, at least we knew what he was doing.

My sword popped into being, which always nerve-racking. I buckled both it and Rhyfel on as we ran for the door.

Dueble stayed near the other three constructs. "I'll stay here if you all don't mind. I'll watch these and relay where you've gone. Um, where *are* you going?"

Bunky spun around the room, gronking.

"Back to our camp. At least to start. He has a few areas we need to go." Padraig had his sword on, and Foxy had his massive sword.

I opened the door to let Bunky out and then ran after him.

CHAPTER FORTY-TWO

PADRAIG RAN OUT after me, with Foxy jogging behind. Dueble waved at us and then shut the door.

Bunky zipped back twice before we got to the wall. The entrance he was using appeared to be the one the houseboys had brought us in through, well-hidden enough that I wouldn't have known where it was. Still, having this kind of passageway, hidden or not, defeated the purpose of having a massive wall around the city. Bunky was much larger than the faeries but that didn't help as much as I would have liked while following him. I thought I was keeping up but he vanished once we got on the other side of the wall.

I skidded to a stop and luckily so did the two behind me. "Am I just missing him, or did he vanish?"

Padraig had the best eyes of all of us but by the way he scowled as he looked around, I had a feeling he didn't see Bunky either.

Loud gronking up ahead gave us an idea of where he was. Padraig took the lead this time. While he was fast, he was easier to follow.

Bunky tore into the clearing we'd camped in, then zipped back out, chasing something. It looked like an upright person, not an animal, but it was far enough ahead that I couldn't be sure.

Foxy's eyes were better than mine as he raced past me

toward the left. Padraig kept going forward, so I stuck with him.

Bunky went higher and followed Foxy's turn to the left. I finally got a good look at who we were chasing: a tall woman in a dark cape. A familiarly vague-looking woman.

I couldn't catch up to Padraig or Foxy, they both ran faster than me, but I knew what I saw—the woman who'd appeared twice as a visage. Once to give me the chest of scrolls from the Library of Pernasi. The second time in the ruins we hid in while I changed shapes. But why was she running? She could just pop out at any time if she was a visage.

Unless she wanted us to follow her. I wasn't certain whose side she was on, so there was no way to tell if following her was a good idea or not. But as the only way I could share that with Padraig and Foxy would be to yell it, I had no option but to keep following.

They started slowing down, and Bunky flew back to me, gronking. As one of the few people who couldn't understand him, that wasn't helpful.

Foxy and Padraig stopped in a clearing. I ran in, with Bunky flying overhead.

"Where'd she go?" I looked around. "I'm pretty sure she's the visage who keeps popping up." I pulled out Rhyfel as the hairs on my arms stood up and the air grew cold. Unlike last night by our fire, it was warm and sunny right now. Yet I was freezing. Padraig and Foxy didn't show it, but I felt it.

"She was ahead of us, but then…" Padraig stopped and walked forward into the trees. "There's a grave back here. With an extremely old tombstone on it."

Foxy, Bunky, and I followed. The stone was so worn it was impossible to read. Bunky buzzed closer, then gronked.

Padraig listened as he made a few more gronks. "He

says that's who we were chasing. She's who messed up the constructs."

"A dead person? Like long, long, ago dead? I saw her—she's using a visage." The chill in the air increased until I was about to run back to Qianru's place on my own.

"Visage, ghost, the two are really quite similar." The voice came from behind me and far too close.

I jumped, screamed, and held an extremely crackling Rhyfel pointed at a ghost. "How are you…who are you?"

Padraig stepped closer, and I noticed that along with his sword, he had his hand cupped for a spell. "What are you? Ghosts don't exist."

Not completely true; Lorcan had been turned into one when his evil brother killed him to take his place. He'd recovered—his brother hadn't. But still, it didn't seem very common.

"Ah, Padraig. Yes, I know all of your names." The ghostly image was more lifelike than the previous two times. It looked like an elven woman with long, dark hair. "There is more to this world than you have seen in your study." She faced Foxy. "Or your pub. Please be careful when you face the mob. Amara would not be happy if you were lost. Making goddesses, even former ones, angry is never a wise idea." Then she turned to me. "And the seeker who wasn't. You muddled things up, but that was part of the prophecy—if you believe in those things." She shrugged.

I folded my arms and glared. "Who are you and why are you messing with us?" Ghost or not, I wasn't in the mood to deal with her.

"Fine. My name is Zaelian. I lived on this very spot a few thousand years ago. Long before Notlianda is what it is and where it is now. But I also lived near Colivith for many hundreds of years. I lived in the lost city of Pernasi and was the head librarian. Before they attacked us and I, like so many, was killed."

"You were killed in Pernasi, but buried here?" Padraig banished his sword but still had a spell ready in his hand.

"My body was brought back home after Pernasi fell. I wouldn't give up the secret location where we'd hidden many items from the library. So a nasty hilstrike mage cursed me. I am forced to roam the land." She held out her arms. "And here I am. I can travel but my form gets weaker the farther I go. I didn't think I could break the curse until a few months ago or so. My time might be off. Time doesn't matter when you're dead. But the strength that Taryn expanded into the world when she destroyed those relics was impressive and powerful. And gave me the clue on how to break the curse holding me. If Taryn breaks into the hidden place in the ruins of Pernasi, I will be free."

I watched her while I tried to sort things out. There were so many questions in my head that I could spend a week and not get them all out. "If you're a ghost, how did you get that chest to me? And those scrolls, were they in this secret place that you need my help to break into?"

"She wasn't this untrusting before she found out who she was." Zaelian looked past me to Padraig.

"You knew who she was before?"

"I knew the Ceisiwr existed. Part of my studies was to find the one who would become Ceisiwr when they were young enough to be trained. Obviously, that didn't work. But I still followed you once in a while. Missed the entire issue with the syclarions and your people. Sorry."

"Do you know where my people are?" If this woman had been ghosting around all this time, maybe she knew something.

"I'm sorry, child, I don't. The rest of the scrolls and items in the locked chamber might have some help for you. But I can't promise that. I still have some magic, so I was able to get that chest to you. It had been my own and not in our locked chamber."

"Why did you attack our constructs? You need to fix them." Foxy had been silently watching but he stepped forward now.

Bunky added an unfriendly gronk.

"I needed to slow you down and keep you out of Notlianda. There are things about to happen that none of you should be involved with and were blocked from my ability to see until yesterday. Had it worked, you all would have just dozed off for a few days. The event would be over and you could focus on getting down to Colivith. But my job was cut off when those ill-clad houseboys arrived." She sighed. "I can fix the constructs." She became far more solid, eventually looking as real as any of us. "Let's be on our way. My plan to keep you out of things has failed and maybe your construct friends can help when the mess hits. I can't keep this form up for long, so please move quickly." She started walking briskly, refusing to answer any more of our questions.

She went directly to the secret walkway in the wall, even though the gate wasn't much farther and wide open. We stayed behind her.

"Is this safe? Can she be what she says she is?" I jogged alongside Padraig, with Foxy behind us. Bunky was staying extremely close to Zaelian and gronking to himself as we went.

"I have no idea. In all my studies, I never heard of someone who did what Lorcan's brother did to him, let alone a ghost hanging around for thousands of years."

"It was three thousand, two hundred, and fifteen years, to be more exact. And I have extremely good hearing." She didn't slow down or turn as she spoke.

We were out of the wall and almost to the barn when yelling came from the center of town. Zaelian started swearing and picked up the pace. She stopped at the door.

"I appear more solid this way and I can move some things in this form, but I'm not wasting that energy on your front door. I also don't wish to go back to my ghost form and back again—that change exhausts me but it is the only way that I can go through solid objects. I need to save your constructs and we're running out of time." She stood directly in front of the door, tapping her foot.

I knocked to let Dueble know we were coming in and then opened the door.

Zaelian went through the door and ran to the constructs.

I shook my head when Dueble looked ready to stop her. "She's helping us. We think." I looked outside right before Foxy shut the door. "What's the yelling about?"

"Oh, not much," Zaelian said as she worked on Irving's panel. "The changelings are trying to take over the town. Blah. They do that every few hundred years, but I didn't want you and your companions caught up in it. It can get bloody and shouldn't have happened for at least a few more years—something provoked the changelings deliberately. Your little friend is ready." She pulled back, and Irving blinked and flew into the air. She quickly fixed Delsy and Welsy, then dusted her hands and stood up.

"Thank you. We think." Both Welsy and Delsy narrowed their eyes.

Before they could add to that, a minor explosion came from somewhere in town.

"Our friends are out there. How bad is this going to get?" I believed in my friends, but changelings could be tricky.

Zaelian scowled. "Not good, but you can't go out there and risk yourself."

"What? Why? I'm not letting them get hurt or worse." I ran to the door but it wouldn't open.

"I need you to get me free." The tone in her voice was flat.

The only side she was on was hers.

"Look, you might have forgotten what it was like being

a living being, but if you don't let us out to help our friends, I will never help you." I got closer to her. "Did you know my people can blow ourselves up? We can, and I will, if you don't let us go."

CHAPTER FORTY-THREE

I IGNORED THE STARTLED reactions from my friends as I stared down Zaelian. Alric and the others could be facing hordes of changelings right now. This wasn't the time to fuss around. "I will do it. You'll never be free."

Zaelian was taller than me and used that height to enforce her glare. Then she stepped back. "Don't do that. You can go fight those nasty changelings. But you're on your own. I can't help you." The last of her words were lost as I, Padraig, Foxy, the constructs, and even Dueble tore out the door.

It wasn't hard to see where the trouble was. Plumes of various colored smoke were coming from what looked to be the center of town.

"Any plans, or just racing in?" Padraig didn't pass me but did run alongside.

"I hadn't gotten that far. And before you ask, not talking about my people's ability to explode. Maybe later." Honestly, I didn't know much—just that I could do it if I had no other choice. That was something we needed to look up in some scrolls somewhere.

"Mind if I take lead?" Padraig smiled.

I was running full out and he was jogging. Elves.

"Go ahead." I motioned for him to take over and he led us down a series of back alleys.

Yelling and sounds of sword fighting could be heard

better now, but I didn't see anything.

Until we came bursting out of the last alley and into the town square.

Dozens of people were fighting but there was no sign of magic being flung about. There was also no way to tell who was a changeling or not.

Aside from the fact that not far from us, two Grillions were fighting. One was clearly a changeling—just no idea which one.

Alric, still in his human glamour, was near the Grillions, and Covey was smacking around people near them. I didn't see Mathilda, Locksead, and Nasif, but they were here somewhere. Padraig and I ran toward the Grillions, who seemed to be oddly equally matched. Dueble and Foxy took off to the left.

We were outnumbered but I didn't think this type of open free-for-all was good for the constructs. All four had stayed with Padraig and me, but the brownies would get stomped and the flyers would be too noticeable. I pulled off to the side, a small pathway between shops, and gestured for them to come over. Padraig stayed with me but he was watching the Grillions.

"I need the four of you to go back and protect the barn. And Qianru." She had more than enough house-boys, but I needed a reason to get these four out of here. "And keep an eye out for the faeries." They weren't here, and I hadn't seen them when we met Zaelian, but they were somewhere in war feathers. That made me nervous.

"We can stay and help," Welsy and Delsy said at the same time.

But I saw how they looked at the crowd. They weren't up for it but didn't want to admit it.

"I know, but we need our base protected."

Padraig turned and nodded solemnly. "We do. You'd be doing us a great favor."

Bunky dove down near my head, gronked, then led

them back out of the center of town.

"How do we know which is the real Grillion?"

The fighting was moving off to the left, but the Grillions, Alric, and Covey were all still in a group, along with a few extra fighters.

"There's a spell, but it won't make any of them happy." Padraig looked over. "There's no way I can just hit the Grillions with it."

"Oh, for crying out loud. Living beings are so fussy." Zaelian might have said she was staying out of it, but she was now in her more transparent form right next to me. "If I do this, I will wink out for a bit. You need to get to Colivith as soon as possible. Promise me you'll use a chawsia path to get there." She was watching the crowds and flexing her fingers.

"Agreed," Padraig answered for us, which was fine by me.

I'd helped with those paths, but I'd never done one on my own.

I thought Zaelian was muttering spell words in preparation for her spell. Nope. She was swearing to herself. She briefly became solid, then a spell flowed from her, hitting everyone in the town's center. Then she vanished.

"I don't think that did anything...oh." The Grillion closest to Alric exploded. The other one screamed, jumped backward, and fell.

One by one, the fighters poofed. And people screamed. Covey looked around for more to fight when the changeling she'd been fighting exploded. Luckily, none of the explosions were big, so there wasn't a lot of gooeyness around. But it was still pretty gruesome.

There were three people in the center of the fighting who'd looked to be elves but were transformed into changelings. They didn't explode. But they watched in horror as the rest of their people exploded.

"You will rue this day! Who cast this spell?" the tallest of the three yelled out over the crowd of confused townsfolk.

The people of Notlianda didn't want the changelings to take over; that's why they were fighting back. But they also didn't look pleased with the explosions.

The changeling looked like he was sniffing the air, then looked directly at Padraig and me. "You will die." He stared at all of us, then he ran off.

We hadn't cast it; Zaelian had, then conveniently vanished. That wasn't to say that if Padraig or Mathilda had cast it instead the results wouldn't have been the same, but I had a feeling Zaelian played fast and loose with anything not directly related to her getting to leave this plane of existence.

A lot all happened at once. Covey growled and attacked the two remaining changelings. Five townsfolk turned their swords toward Padraig and me, even though they'd just been fighting changelings a moment before, and a thousand faeries in war feathers came swooping into the town center.

The faeries weren't alone and were followed by a massive pack of sceanra anam and murlin—all working together. So much for my idea they might have come from different groups.

The faeries spun around to face their adversaries but even with so many faeries, I questioned their ability to defeat them all. And I'd sent Bunky back to the barn, so I couldn't get him to call for reinforcements. Where had the faeries found so many and why had they provoked them? It might have been just a chance encounter but them leaving in war feathers and coming back under attack seemed to rule that out.

"We have to help them!" We had our own issues as the townsfolk closest to us were still debating fighting us or not.

Padraig stepped in front of Dueble and me, holding

out his sword. "We're not changelings. Why would you attack us?"

"You brought their wrath down on us!"

"You weren't trying to fight them off?" I was lost; there were at least three or four townsfolk who were down and probably not getting up thanks to the changelings.

A large man near us, the leader it appeared, looked around. "We were. But that kind of magic is never good. Too many bad things are drawn to it. Things worse than them. That magic will bring them here."

Ah, they weren't talking about the wrath of the changelings, but other worse creatures. Great.

The faeries were flying around in aerial battles but the townsfolk didn't seem to even notice the murlin and sceanra anam flying overhead. I squinted as one of the murlin flickered. They weren't real?

Padraig continued to talk down the large man and his cohorts, Covey destroyed the two changelings who didn't flee, and I went behind a building and called my faeries.

They were in battle, but I knew that mentally offering them enough ale would work. Should work. Needed to work. Alric came after me and waited with his sword raised.

"Do you have a faery bag with you? One that's safe?" I hadn't planned what I was going to do once I got the faeries to me, but with Alric here an idea formed.

He glanced back at me oddly, then handed me a tiny black bag.

"Thank you. Keep everyone away." I called the faeries again, putting everything I could into it. I heard them first, then saw them as they tore toward me with their enemies behind them. I really hoped I was right in my guess. "Girls! In the bag!" I held open the faery bag and watched as all of them flew in.

The sceanra anam and murlin were right behind them.

CHAPTER FORTY-FOUR

I TIED UP THE bag and ducked down as the sceanra anam and murlin flew low over Alric and me. Then they vanished. I'd hoped that would be the case, but it was still startling.

Alric spun around but he was still keeping an eye out for any of the townsfolk coming for us. Either they didn't see us run this way, or they were busy fighting our friends.

"Where did they go?" He hadn't seen the faeries go into the bag.

I held it up. "The faeries are all in here, but I think the sceanra anam and murlin were illusions. They vanished as soon as I closed the bag."

"Those were some extremely real illusions. I felt them fly over us." He kept watching the sky above us. "I want to know who sent them, but there's no way to track that magic."

"I know. I think I'd better keep the girls in the bag for now, until we figure out what just happened and if the townspeople are going to lynch us all for Zaelian saving their lives." I tucked away the faery bag and noticed my hand was shaking. My mind might have thought those birds and sceanra anam were illusions, but my body hadn't.

"How did you know?" He wasn't watching the town center as closely as before, but I knew he was listening to them.

"I have no idea. One did seem to flicker. Beyond that, they felt *exactly* like the ones that came after us when I was up flying about. Exactly the same. It was too weird and if I was wrong…" I shook my head. "Not sure what I was going to do if I was wrong. But I think I need to sit down." The adrenaline crash was hitting me hard.

I found a short bench and dropped down to it. "How are things out there?"

"From what I saw before, Covey killed two of the changelings but one escaped. The townspeople are sort of settling down but I think that Zaelian gets her wish; we should get out of here quickly. If there are more change-lings, they could come back. And the townspeople might help them go after us."

I took a deep breath and got back on my feet. "Let's go find our friends then." They were all together and had moved to where Padraig and Dueble stood watching the townspeople mostly go about their business. Covey still looked wild about the edges, Grillion looked ill, and Mathilda, Locksead, and Nasif looked like they'd been out for an afternoon stroll.

The townsfolk had backed off but the man who had approached us earlier was talking very animatedly to a large group and kept looking our way.

"We might want to go back to the barn. Quickly." Alric nodded to Padraig.

"Are the faeries okay? Where did those birds and crea-tures go?" Grillion still looked pale, but his concern for the faeries was touching.

"The faeries are fine. And the others are gone." It looked to me like more people were joining the crew glaring at us. "Grillion? Can you get us back to Qianru's without people seeing us? I think we need to leave." Yes, some of those people might know that Locksead and Grillion worked for Qianru, but I was hoping they didn't think of it until after we were long gone. Qianru could take care of them.

He glanced over to where I was looking, ducked his head, and darted down an alley. "This way."

We all followed, and I noticed that Locksead was ducking a bit too. And keeping to the middle of our group. Good idea.

We got back to the barn intact and unspotted—at least, no one stopped us. The constructs took their guarding orders seriously and were waiting for us.

"We were fighting down a side road, but I saw that spell. What did you use on the changelings? That wasn't anything I'd seen." Mathilda shook off her glamour once we got inside.

"It wasn't us." Padraig looked to me to tell the tale, but I was still shaking from the faeries, sceanra anam, and murlin situation. I gestured for him to tell it.

Mathilda looked the most shocked at his summed-up telling. "I recall that name. Pernasi fell long before either me or my sister was born. But that name is something familiar." She closed her eyes.

"Who is she?" Grillion had gotten over his trauma faster than I would have expected.

Mathilda opened her eyes. "That's what I'm trying to recall. But it's just out of reach. I'll think of it at some point. What happened to the faeries and those things?"

I pulled out the faery bag. "The girls are in here; the others were an illusion." I wasn't sure about letting the faeries out since I had no idea what had created the illusion, nor how deadly it could have been. I'd learned long ago that just because you can't see something didn't mean it couldn't kill you. I was applying the reverse of that to these illusions.

"I think we—" Padraig's comment was cut off at a sharp knocking on the front door. Alric stepped behind the door with a spell ready and Padraig opened it. And was shoved back by Qianru.

"What have you done? People are asking my houseboys about you. Did you really blow up a bunch of change-lings? Not good, not good." She shook her head and she stomped around. "I don't have time for this. Klin will live but he's not awake yet and needs peace." She glared at me. "Something that won't happen right now. How quickly can you leave?"

"We were coming to tell you we will be leaving immediately. I believe Grillion will be staying on with us." Padraig's smile was a bit forced, but we'd had a busy morning.

Locksead stepped forward. "Me too. I'll be back, but I need to get some dirt under my boots." He nodded to Alric. "I'll just be a second."

Alric nodded, so they must have spoken of it at some point. No one seemed terribly surprised at Locksead joining us. I liked him, and he was a good fighter and sneaky as well. I had a feeling we'd need that.

Qianru looked around in a state of shock. "Who will take care of me?"

Grillion sighed and rattled off ten names. "And that's not even mentioning the houseboys. You'll be fine. Where's Tag gone?"

"I suppose you are right; I will make do with but a few guards." She held her dramatic pose for a moment. "As for Tag, some woman hired him away from me a week after you left. A tall, dark-haired elven woman. Had a job for him in Colivith. Led him away immediately. You simply can't get good help these days." With a nod to all of us except Grillion, Qianru marched out of the barn.

Grillion shut the door behind her.

I would have liked to ask more questions about Tag. He was a good kid. But Qianru wasn't in the mood and probably couldn't tell us anything else. Besides, I had a gut feeling who convinced him to go to Colivith: Zaelian.

We all ran for our rooms and gathered our things as soon as Qianru stomped off down the walkway. Welsy and Delsy went to the stables to get the horses ready, and Bunky and Irving hid out front in the shrubs in case anyone approached. I would have liked my faeries to be out there with them, but we didn't have time for dealing with whatever attacked them.

"Aren't the townsfolk going to notice us riding out of here? Even that secret way in the wall isn't a secret." I secured my pack on my horse.

Locksead was back with his pack and horse. Dueble didn't look terribly happy as he sat on his horse, but Nasif stayed near him. The constructs had come to the stable once we were ready.

"That's why we're not going out that way. Taryn's going to cast a chawsia path to Colivith." Padraig smiled as if he'd just announced I was going to make pancakes for breakfast.

"I can't do one of those." I waved my hands in the air in a bad approximation of the tunnel. "Why don't one of you do it?"

Padraig shook his head. "Because our magic signatures are all over that town, even Nasif's. There were magic balls…not spell breakers, but gathering ones. Expensive and not common in the north, but someone is watching the magic usage in this town closely. A powerful mage can follow us through it. The tracking only lasts a few hours, but I don't think we have time for that to wear off."

Alric came to my side. "I know you can do it." The looks on all of my friends' faces echoed his words.

"Did you all see what I did to a chawsia path back in Hassi? It wasn't good." I was becoming more comfortable with my magic—again. But this could go bad. Very bad.

Locksead opened his mouth to ask about it but Grillion quickly shook his head. I knew he'd probably tell him later.

"You weren't trying to build one, you were trying to close one. I'll walk you through it." Padraig's smile was at full strength now.

We heard yelling, and Locksead stuck his head out of a side door. "Whatever you're doing, make it fast. The town guards are in a standoff with Qianru. She'll stall them some, but she will back down eventually."

Padraig and Alric talked me through the spell. I wanted one more practice run. Then the yelling from outside got closer and the door to the front room of the barn shattered. Or that's what it sounded like from out here.

"Now!" Alric yelled, and I threw the spell.

Once it was up, Padraig motioned for me to go through. The caster could be first or last but having me in the front was more for my protection. Unless, of course, I landed us right in the middle of a prison. Or Dark training center. I shook my head. No. We were going to Colivith. To a nice, big, open area outside of it. Bunky and Irving flew alongside my horse and me as we ran through the tunnel. I didn't look back, but it sounded like my friends were behind me.

The tunnel started shaking, and I focused on holding in steady and the spell putting us out where we wanted. A splotch of grass and sky appeared in front of us, so I bent down over my mare and encouraged her to run faster. We ran out of the tunnel with everyone behind us. Padraig shut it as soon as he came through.

I looked around but had no idea where we were. There weren't any large cities around, and Colivith was supposed to be huge. And I was pretty sure it wasn't on an island.

CHAPTER FORTY-FIVE

"DAMN. WHERE ARE we?" Locksead looked around the area. It was a large meadow, with slivers of frost in the scrubby grass. Big enough for us, maybe even me in my dragon form, but not a lot else. Rocky beaches surrounded us and dropped into cold-looking water. Past the water was either very low clouds or heavy mist. There were dark shapes but no idea what they were.

"I have no idea." I slowly looked around.

"There aren't islands south of Colivith. Nor anywhere down here." Mathilda scowled at the mist, then held out her hand. "Or there weren't." She waved her hand and the mist pulled back, revealing a collection of small islands and a rocky shore a distance away. She released it and the mist flowed back. "I'm not sure how, but that was the southern point of the continent in the distance. Colivith is a few miles inland."

"What in the…" Grillion didn't finish his statement but looked as confused as Locksead. They'd both been living here long enough to know if some islands had suddenly appeared.

"I told you not to have me cast the spell." I folded my arms. "Now look what I've done." I wasn't a water fan, and that water looked freezing. I hadn't seen any ships in the water during our peek at the other islands and continent. "Are these islands natural?" This one looked real, but islands didn't just plop into the ocean. They needed volcanos and time.

We had some food and water, but not enough to last long here. I rubbed my arms as a freezing wind brushed over the island. I had a feeling that even with magic, we'd all freeze to death before we ran out of food.

Padraig and Alric were off their horses and looking at the shore and the water. Welsy and Delsy were looking as well, although they seemed focused on the scrubby plant life.

"Not southern plants." Welsy shook his head in disapproval.

"No, these are tundra. Who would do such a thing?" Delsy held up a piece of grass. "Completely out of place."

Siabiane would be glad to know that their gardening instincts were still intact.

"Someone created this and is changing the weather down here." Mathilda stayed on her horse but was looking more concerned by the minute. "But why? One of the first tenets of magic is that you can't change the weather. The repercussions could be horrific."

Covey prowled around the island and then got back on her horse. "How are we getting off this? I'm thinking another one of those tunnel spells?"

"I don't think I could do another right now." I didn't think I could do anything except maybe find a nice place to sleep. I rubbed my arms and grabbed another cloak I had stuffed in my pack. It was a good thing the faeries were in their bag; they didn't fare well in extreme cold. The sun was out, at least it appeared to be so through the mist. But this place would freeze us all at night.

"No, Taryn can't cast another one, not for a while anyway," Nasif said. "Something is disrupting the larger magics, so any of us would have trouble right now. Chawsia paths are usually far more stable than they've been as of late." He took a few steps away and looked at the rocks. "I had no idea that these were down here. There were rumors, but we're used to ignoring most of the outlandish ones."

"Let me take another look." Mathilda raised her hands and the mist lifted again. This time everyone was expecting the other islands, so we were watching them.

"We're closer to the coast than I thought, so that's good."

"What's on that island nearest to us?" Unlike this one, it was huge and massive shapes were roaming around.

"Licten beasts." Alric squinted. "And damn it, Tjolia mountain dreks."

"At least we know where they're getting them from." Grillion didn't sound any happier about that than I was. The mystery of where they were coming from was solved—the issue of why and how they were there wasn't.

"So someone is using a chawsia path to get them off and on that island? Wouldn't that take a lot of power?" I was trying very hard not to look over to the island in question.

"It would be extremely difficult to do that from an island that size. They would need to get them to the continent before opening a path." Nasif glared at the island as the mist drifted down over it again. "And it would be noticeable to any strong magic users in the area. We might have been focused on our dig, but I would have felt that much heavy magic being used at once. They have another way."

I looked around the icy water that surrounded us. "What? Swimming? I don't think licten beasts or dreks are swimmers." I hoped not; on the second appearance, that island was far closer than I thought.

"Tunnels." Welsy and Delsy echoed each other. "They have massive tunnels."

"Under the ocean? Granted, we're not in the deep ocean, but still." I was having a hard time imagining something that big under us.

Mathilda shrugged. "This entire situation is impossible. The power needed to make these islands, change the weather to suit the inhabitants, and not have it be picked up by other magic users is massive. An underwater tunnel would be workable, and less noticed by magic users. I noticed there were two small islands between us and the shore this last time I raised the mist. I have a feeling the islands are connected by shorter tunnels under the water."

"Those things could come here, then." Foxy had been silent but seemed far more relaxed about making his pronouncement than I was at hearing it.

"They could, but I would think the creators need a way to keep their beasts where they want them." Mathilda walked back toward the center of our little island. "That being said, we probably want to get moving quickly. Look for anything that could be a passageway."

The island had appeared small when we got here, but having to find a secret entrance seemed to increase its size.

Welsy and Delsy finally found it. "This patch of ground is false." They stomped on a section that looked to me like everything else. But the elves and Foxy all nodded—they had better hearing than I did.

It took a few minutes, but we managed to force the passageway open. Creepy, dark, and damp. Lovely. Alric sent a few glows down and we found the direction for the coast. We were all inside when the rumbling started.

"Run!" Padraig and Alric had stayed in the back.

We picked up speed even though the horses obviously didn't like the closeness of the tunnel. But if it was large enough for Tjolia mountain dreks, it was big enough for them. I swallowed as I realized that might be what was causing the rumbling.

We came out on the next island and slammed the doorway behind us closed. It looked like that was a security measure; the underwater tunnels all ended at the next island. Welsy and Delsy found the new one just as a series of grunts and yells came from our old island.

"I thought those drek things masked sound?" Grillion asked.

"They do when they're near their prey. Masking sound takes an effort for them so they won't waste it. I suggest we move quickly." Mathilda rode into the new tunnel and we followed.

There were actually two more islands that we hadn't noticed on our path to the shore, but eventually we got to the continent.

Foxy rolled boulders over the way we'd just come out. "Probably won't stop them but might slow them down."

The island we'd just left was now visible even without Mathilda holding back the mist. Three dreks and five licten beasts came onto the island and roared. The fact the dreks made everything silent when they hunted was terrifying. But their roars weren't much better.

"I think we need to get out of here fast," Padraig said.

"But won't those things just rampage around here? Even if they don't get to Colivith, they could destroy nearby villages." I didn't want those things following us, but it wasn't fair to lead them to innocent people.

"We need to crush that exit, make it impossible for them to get out. Foxy's boulder will help keep it closed, but they could get through." Alric turned to me with a thoughtful look. "Someone larger might be able to stomp it closed."

"Seriously? You want me to transform so I can squish something?" I glared and then shrugged. He made a good point. "Fine." I got off my horse and handed her reins to Alric. "You all probably want to move back." I almost started to shift, then ran over to Alric and handed him the bag of faeries. I had no idea what having them with me during the change would do, and I wasn't up to finding out.

The change this time was quick and felt smoother. I walked over to the boulder Foxy had rolled over and stomped. I was going to move it but it might help crush the tunnel. I tamped the ground a few times, then added a bit of the push spell for good measure. The ground caved in.

"That enough?" My voice sounded like me, just louder. Padraig and Mathilda got off their horses—none of the four-legged animals seemed to want to come too close— and checked the ground.

"Nicely done," Mathilda said once she'd put her hand on the smashed dirt. "The tunnel is collapsed in such a way their only option is to turn back. Whoever built these will most likely be able to redirect the final tunnel, but it'll take some time."

I shook myself back into my human form, and Alric handed me back the faery bag. It was nice being able to do that without sprouting antlers, spikes, or anything else extra. "I added a bit of my push spell as well."

"That does seem to be a good one for you." Mathilda tilted her head. "I wonder why? Most magic users do have a few go-to spells, but that's been yours since you regained your ability and came out of being a magic sink. It's an unusual one."

"I have no idea. But it has been helpful."

"Would you people please hurry up?" Zaelian popped up next to me, startling me and my horse. "I need you to get into the secret chamber and let me free. But, you apparently will need your two missing magic users. Something I didn't see before. This is exceedingly vexing." She looked around, realizing everyone was staring at her—or at least the ones who hadn't met her yet were staring at her. "Oh. Hello. I'm Zaelian. Dead, former head librarian of the Library of Pernasi. I'm a ghost. And I need you all to move fast, as some people are coming and I think they might have ill intent. Follow me!" She took off as I would have thought a ghost would travel, floating along but at a good speed.

"Best to follow her," Padraig said as he nudged his horse to follow.

I didn't see or hear anyone else coming, but the woods were thick enough to hide them if they were far enough away.

Zaelian seemed to flicker in and out as she flew deeper into the woods, but Padraig kept following her. We rode for a good half hour before she paused, looked around, and then turned sharply into an even thicker clump of trees.

I hoped that since she needed Lorcan and Siabiane to help get her free of this existence, she was going to stick with us and help us plan to get them out. Instead, she led us to a cave. Granted, it was far from where we'd shut down the tunnel, but I didn't see anything like a city nearby. Maybe she wanted to plan here?

"Okay, now get them out and let's be on with this." She hovered in front of the cave, looking impatient.

"Lorcan and Siabiane are in a cave?" I peered inside. Yup, looked like a standard cave.

"And that troublesome child, Tag. I had him keeping watch for me as I can't always control when and where I appear. They grabbed him a few days ago. I can see he and your friends, but can't manifest enough to free anyone. Nor cast any spells, and that is worrying along with being annoying." She gestured toward the cave mouth. "Go along now. Free them. Let's get things moving."

Padraig shook his head. "It's not that we don't believe you, but who would hide prisoners in an abandoned cave? I can even smell that various animals have been living in it recently."

Zaelian looked angry, then spun toward the cave. "No,

that's not a…hmmm." She drifted around a bit, almost fading out completely. When she came back, she was somber. "I've been around for over three thousand years. I finally find a way out and instead I'm wasting out of existence. Damn it. They are destroying the spells around the chamber where we hid the library items. Since I'm tied to the chamber, the more they destroy, the more they damage me. If the seal collapses without the right person behind it, I get left to fade away. My memories won't go with me to the afterlife." Her voice was calm, but the look on her face wasn't. She was terrified.

Mathilda approached her. "We still have time. Relax and focus. You know where our friends are. Or this Tag person—do you have memories of him that you can grab onto to lead you?"

"You are very wise for one so young," Zaelian said. "Let me ground myself."

A few moments later, she grinned. "Oh, you are even wiser than I thought. And I wasn't that far off. Just the wrong cave." She took off, floating quickly through the woods.

I was still having trouble with the idea that instead of a dungeon, our friends had been left in a cave. But I changed that thought when we grew closer. It was a cave but obviously one built by hands, not made by nature. And ten heavily armed and armored guards—syclarions, dwollers, elves, and humans—all stood watch.

CHAPTER FORTY-SIX

WE PULLED BACK out of sight as soon as we saw them. They were still far enough away, and there were enough trees here that there was a chance that they didn't see us. Yet. It was difficult to know for certain, plate armor looked the same to me, but these looked a bit different than the knights who'd chased us further north.

Zaelian drifted around us. "I can check to make sure this leads to where they are held. I don't think they're in the cave, but this leads to the dungeon they are in." She vanished before any of us could say no.

Padraig took a deep breath but stayed silent. All of us had weapons at the ready.

Zaelian popped back a few moments later. "That is the one. You'll have to get through those guards, plus the other five inside. This is a good time, though; it looks like many of them are gone elsewhere. When I popped in after they kidnapped Tag, there were dozens of guards milling about."

Considering that she'd first tried to lead us to an animal lair, I wasn't sure I believed her. But I also couldn't think of a reason why anyone would have that many guards on a cave unless it led somewhere important.

Padraig, Alric, Covey, and Foxy would take the lead and work on drawing the guards away from the mouth of the cave. Grillion, Mathilda, and Locksead would be the second wave and come from the left, also pushing the guards away. Dueble, the constructs, Nasif, and I would be the ones sneaking in and hopefully taking out the remaining guards.

Mathilda held up her hand before we moved into place. "Taryn, when you are ready to go in, let the faeries out of their bag."

"What? What if those illusions come back? What if they *can* hurt people?"

"I think we want that, actually. And no, they can't hurt anyone directly. The faeries and the illusions will cause a lot of ruckus. Distractions are a good thing sometimes."

I wanted to ask more questions, first of all—who set those illusions after the faeries. But we didn't have time. This was a trust in Mathilda moment. I nodded and pulled out the bag that contained the faeries.

The first group of my friends took off, followed by the second. Once they were engaged and drawing the guards away, I opened the bag and let a hundred, war feather-clad faeries loose. Garbage flew over to me.

"What do?"

"Can't explain, but we need you to distract those guards. And…" The sceanra anam and murlin appeared, as expected. "Those are illusions."

"Knows." She grinned and let out a war cry. "Attacks now!" Then she took off.

I didn't have time to worry as Dueble, Nasif, the constructs, and I all ran inside the cave mouth. We'd left our horses hidden in the trees but Alric assured me they'd be fine.

Everyone I was with had better night vision than me, so I wasn't too surprised when Dueble threw a spell packet at a guard I hadn't seen yet. The spell bag exploded in the guard's face and she slumped to the floor.

"I don't need my own magic." Dueble grinned as we kept running.

The next guard hadn't been caught as unaware and so I stepped in with my sword and Rhyfel. Rhyfel seemed very happy at having someone covered in metal to play with and sent green arcs that covered his armor. That guard might not have been dead when we jumped over him, but he was twitching badly.

Nasif took out the next two guards, and the four constructs took out the final one. We'd been running for a bit and it still looked like a cave, not a dungeon. I was starting to slow down when a wave of depression slammed into me like a wall. I almost dropped to my knees and saw everyone else doing the same. Even the constructs. Another damn Jhea spell.

I tried to sing my lullaby, but the sense of pointlessness was so bad I couldn't draw a deep enough breath to sing. We all fell to the floor. Even Rhyfel's sparks couldn't get through to me, and he tumbled out of my hands.

"We save!" The faeries sounded like they were miles away, but I was too depressed to care. Nothing mattered.

Then Crusty slammed into the side of my head, singing. Normally faery singing was bad enough to be used for torture, but she was singing my lullaby. Soon dozens of faeries filled the chamber, all singing. The song was pure hope and filled the area.

I picked up Rhyfel and got to my feet to see the others doing the same. "Whatever you do, girls, don't stop singing." I added my voice to their song and felt the spell within growing stronger. Still singing, I ran down the way we'd been heading.

The path ended in a dungeon with five cages. Lorcan, Siabiane, and Tag were lying on the ground in three of them—still breathing but otherwise not moving. The other two cages were empty except for scattered bones which I refused to look at for long.

"No guards?" Nasif cast a spell of revealing but nothing appeared. "They must think that Jhea spell will stop any escapes. Keep singing. We'll get them out."

The cages were solid, but between Nasif, Dueble, and the constructs, they freed our friends. I kept singing and helped get the cages open. Lorcan and Siabiane stirred, which was good, but there was no way to know how long that massively powerful Jhea spell had been running.

I wanted to see where the other corridors went. Whoever grabbed my friends was at that other end, and I wanted to have a few words with them. But we could only hold off the Jhea spell, not break it.

Still singing, with Nasif carrying Siabiane and Dueble carrying both Lorcan and Tag, we ran back up to the cave entrance.

The murlin and sceanra anam were circling as if waiting for us to come out. Mathilda stood behind them. There was no sign of the guards or the rest of our friends. "Oh, shoo. You're done now. Go back to your owner." The murlin and sceanra anam vanished. Alric and the rest came riding back without any of the guards.

"Do you know where they came from?" I moved my jaw about; it was nice not to be singing anymore.

"I have some suspicions, but they aren't an issue right now." She ran to Nasif and her sister. "Is she…"

"They're all alive, just been trapped by the strongest Jhea spell in the world." I knew more had been done to them, they had bruises and marks, but this wasn't the place to deal with it. My friends had taken care of the guards, but there had to be more coming.

"Come on, I found a safer cave." Zaelian had vanished during the fight but was back now, even if a bit more wispy-looking than before. I got on my horse and Alric, Padraig, and Locksead all took our unconscious friends on their saddles. Once all on horseback, we raced after our ghost.

We road for another twenty minutes before Zaelian stopped again. This cave didn't smell of recent animal residents and wasn't a made one. Hopefully, it was far enough and hidden enough that no one could find us for a bit. Something had called the rest of the guards away and there was no way to know when they would be back.

Siabiane, Lorcan, and Tag were all made comfortable on as many blankets as we had and Mathilda looked over all of them. Tag looked the best but he'd been captured less than a week ago.

Once Mathilda checked all of their vitals, she went back to Siabiane. Nasif had some medical knowledge so he went to Lorcan. Alric and I went to Tag.

"There's not much we can do until they come out of this stupor." Mathilda brushed Siabiane's face. "I'm just so glad we have them." She had been strong up until now but tears slid down her face. "All of them. I'm sorry your young friend was exposed to this."

There were still over a few hundred faeries and they were still in war feathers. They'd stopped singing the lullaby but were now crooning a lower tune. Highs and lows mingled together as they settled around our injured friends.

First, Siabiane started crying. Then tears came from Lorcan and finally Tag. Siabiane opened her eyes and hugged her sister so tightly I thought she might crush her. Lorcan hugged Nasif and then Dueble. Tag grabbed me, then released me and wiped away his tears.

"You saved us. You actually saved us. How many years?" Siabiane pulled back from her sister and looked around.

"Years? You've been gone two months." Padraig spoke when Mathilda looked too choked up to do so.

"No. That can't be right. I felt the passage of time. The loss and despair as the world fell to darkness." Lorcan looked around. "But you all look the same?"

"It's really only been two months," Alric said. "The world hasn't fallen. And the people we are up against have some seriously strong power backing their Jhea spells."

Tag looked around. "I was only there two months? It felt like years."

Zaelian popped up next to him. "You, my lad, were only gone a few days. And I am so sorry you went through that." She looked down at him with an almost fondness, then looked away

We filled Siabiane, Lorcan, and even Tag in what had been going on. They were hungry and thirsty, but once the residual effects of the spell faded, they were in much better shape than I feared. I'm sure the multitude of faery kisses being bestowed on all three didn't hurt.

Lorcan tilted his head and watched Zaelian. "You say that you were the last librarian of Pernasi? Who was the mage in charge of the library when it fell?" He wasn't glaring but he also didn't look like he believed her.

Zaelian returned the look but hers was more of a glare. "I remember your name now. You were some magic using high mucky in the north." Zaelian was still fluctuating in terms of transparency, but focusing on Lorcan seemed to be keeping her more solid. "The mage who died to keep our secrets hidden was named Jilian. He was a good man and died before I did so he didn't get cursed to roam. They thought of that little bit as I was dying and there was no one left to torture."

Lorcan watched her for a few more moments, then relaxed and nodded. "Well met. I am sorry you are still here."

"Me too. But with Taryn's help hopefully we can end that." She looked around the cave. "Could you magic users put a shield over the cave mouth? I've got a bad feeling we were followed."

Alric shook his head, but he and Mathilda quickly put up a shield. "We were careful as we ran. We're not as far away as I would like, but no one followed us." Alric was a damn good tracker and he knew how to hide tracks just as well.

"They have powers…" Zaelian faded out completely then came back looking frightened. "They are sending things after you. Horrible soulless knights and monsters."

"Dreks?" Grillion had stayed out of things after being introduced to our rescued friends. But he was paying attention now.

Zaelian's eyes misted over. "No. Nor those running armored beasts. These are something else. Something that I can't see." Her eyes came back to normal. Well, what was normal for her anyway. "Trolucs. The term is in my mind, whoever is controlling them is thinking it. But it's not one I know." She sounded personally affronted about that.

Other people knew the word though. All of the magic users except me jumped to their feet and ran for the cave mouth at the term.

"What are they and why do you all look ready to blow holes in something?" Alric, Padraig, Mathilda, Nasif, Lorcan, and Siabiane all had spells ready and were watching the shielded cave mouth.

"Is there any way out of this cave besides this?" Alric aimed his question at Zaelian but didn't look back toward her. Or me. "Taryn, ready the strongest spell you have. Rhyfel will help too. If someone has set Trolucs on us, we're in for a fight. The soulless knights you felt would be working with them and are just as bad."

"There's no other way out. I was looking for a place to hide so your friends could recover…I wasn't thinking." Zaelian's fear was clear, but I had a feeling that it was more because she was losing parts of herself—including the part that would have figured we'd be followed when she found this place.

"It's not just your fault, we all should have been more careful." Padraig took a position near the cave mouth but I couldn't hear anything approaching.

"Is bads? We gets!" Garbage and her faeries had been sitting silently along a wall. Before anyone could stop them they raced out of the cave. Hopefully, Alric and Mathilda's shield worked better on whatever was after us than it did on the faeries.

"Damn it, they have no idea what they're after. Neither do I." I didn't want to distract the others, but if we were being attacked, I needed to know if it was something I might need to go full dragon for. Not that I was looking forward to it, but I was thinking we might be running out of options.

"Trolucs are another transplant from the north. Large cats with massive fangs. They are usually tied to a powerful mage." Mathilda gripped her staff. She didn't add to the soulless knights part—the term itself was terrifying on its own.

Foxy, Covey, Dueble, Grillion, Locksead, and Tag had stayed back when the magic users moved forward. But they now grabbed weapons. Except Tag. Like Siabiane and Lorcan he didn't have weapons. Unlike them, he also didn't have magic.

Locksead grabbed a pair of daggers from his pack and handed them to him. "Stay back as much as possible."

Tag nodded but didn't move back.

The silence from outside the cave was eerie. Even more so since I knew there were a hundred or so faeries out there. I didn't hear a single war cry.

CHAPTER FORTY-SEVEN

T HE CONSTRUCTS HAD been silently watching but after a few minutes, all four came to me.

"We can go see what is going on", Welsy said.

Delsy nodded. "Bunky is worried about the faeries."

"So am I. But even you four aren't impervious to spells." I glanced over to Zaelian who seemed to be arguing with herself. She'd taken out all four constructs without much difficulty, the risk was too great that someone else could do the same.

"No, but I think I can make them more protected." Dueble glanced over to Nasif. "This is a good time to test it. If Siabiane and Taryn don't mind."

Nasif stepped away from the cave mouth a shook off the spell he'd readied. "Agreed."

Siabiane turned slightly but nodded. "I trust you two. We're blind in here."

"Me as well." I assumed they were asking me because of Bunky. But if the faeries were in danger, he'd go after them regardless. A better chance at his survival was welcome.

I watched, but both Nasif and Dueble move so quickly, as they darted between the constructs, I wasn't certain what they'd done.

"They are ready," Nasif stepped back.

"Zaelian? Do they seem harder to get to than before?"

I turned around, but she was gone. "Zaelian?"

"She might have gone out to view those coming after us." Dueble patted Bunky on the head.

None of us mentioned the other option—she'd said if the protections around the secret holding of the library were breached incorrectly, she'd vanish. Not good for her or us.

"Okay, we'll drop the shield to let the constructs out." Alric watched all four carefully. "You are only doing surveillance. No fighting. Look for the faeries and whoever else is out there. Then come right back."

Bunky and Irving gronked, Welsy and Delsy nodded. With a nod to Padraig and Mathilda, Alric dropped the shield. The constructs raced out, and the shield went back up.

I didn't like fighting, not at all, but waiting was almost worse. Even though all four constructs came running back less than ten minutes later.

Alric dropped the shield then raised it again.

Welsy and Delsy ran to Siabiane. "An army is coming. Hundreds of knights. Many with massive cats. They are on foot." Both of them spoke at the same time then sat down.

"How far were they?" She looked closely at both.

"Ten minutes at their pace." Obviously, the constructs had been moving faster than that.

Bunky and Irving flew about Alric gronking rapidly.

He held up his hand. "Slow down, I can't understand you."

They repeated it slower, and the ground started shaking.

"Damn it. They say the faeries are in nets and that those knights have a lot of magic. They might have been ten minutes away before, but they aren't now."

Now that I knew what it was, the shaking and deep thudding sounds were horrifying. Those knights were making that much noise without being on horseback?

"Options?" Lorcan still looked weak but he'd been a leader of elves for centuries.

"We can't defend this cave against that many, our only way out is to fight," Padraig said.

No one even debated it and we got into formation. Locksead and Foxy stayed near the center with Grillion and Tag as none were magic users. Covey refused to go anywhere but the front and as she was in full berserker mode, no one argued.

Rhyfel crackled with almost glee, and my sword felt like it joined in. "I'm not leaving the faeries." I kept my voice steady but wanted to make sure I was clear. The odds of us getting out were bad, but I wasn't leaving the girls. Nets didn't hold them for long unless there was some heavy magic behind it.

Alric gave me a quick kiss. "You won't be alone."

Then we all got on our horses and Alric dropped the shield.

The plan was to go out ahead of the attackers and find a better place to defend.

Two problems—the knights and their trolucs were right past the edge of the cave and all of our horses were immediately magicked out from under us. I hoped the animals were sent somewhere safe, but all of us were left scrambling to our feet.

We were surrounded by a few hundred knights in full armor. The first two rows had massive snow cats on leashes. Their heads were the size of small boulders and filled with upper and lower fangs and a row of sharp teeth. Their paws were the size of my head. I was glad the horses were gone now, those trolucs would have slaughtered them.

A row of thirty knights stepped around the ones with the trolucs and raised their swords. Great. Instead of being slaughtered at once, they were just going to send waves in.

"Bunky, I need you and the other constructs to get the faeries." I thought I saw a few tall pikes with odd nets hanging from them in the back of the crowd. "Get them out."

Bunky gronked and he and the brownies slipped away. Irving flew over to me and hacked up the crown. If the knights knew what it was, they gave no indication. The thirty closest to us were clearly waiting for some command to attack, but hadn't moved once they got into position.

Siabiane was next to me. "That's definitely the canfydd crown. But why does he want...Taryn? Put on the crown." Her voice became urgent.

"What?" I looked from her to the crown to the rest of my friends. "What good would that do? Not to mention it doesn't have the stones." No idea why they hadn't attacked us yet, but I doubted those knights and their feline killing machines were going to let me dig out the faery bag and the magical gems.

The thirty knights began stepping forward. Alric and Padraig sent spells their way only to have the magic flung back at them. I swore the trolucs grew a bit in size when that happened.

I picked up the crown as the fighting started. Covey was the first to attack but claws weren't great against armor. Soon all of my friends except Siabiane were fighting for their lives.

The army of knights and trolucs watched.

"You have to change and put it on." Siabiane grabbed my arm. "Now." She let go and joined the fight.

Damn it. The crown would be too small once I changed. Maybe wearing it on an arm would help. All of my friends were losing as I changed and hung onto the crown.

The change was fast this time and the crown had

grown. I put it on my head and roared.

The knights and trolucs charged forward, and all of my friends were already down on the ground.

I swung my tail and sent a dozen knights and trolucs flying into the air. But there were too many to take them on like this. The crown spoke to me, to deep inside my soul. It showed me how to use my abilities those I knew of and those new to me. I gave another massive roar and pushed out with magic, energy, and anger. The knights all died where they stood and the trolucs vanished.

Power like I'd never felt before flowed through me. This was right. It was what I was meant to be. Images flooded my mind. All of my people—my real people—paying me homage as I ruled the world. All of the world. Lands I'd never heard of would follow me.

"Taryn! Take the crown off!" Alric stood below me. "Take it off. You won."

There was panic in his eyes that I didn't understand. I'd destroyed those against us. We were safe. He should be glad for me.

"You have to take it off. Please." He put his hand on my front leg and I almost shook him off in anger.

What was happening to me? A massive flock of faeries surrounded us, all humming the lullaby. I wasn't under a Jhea spell. I felt great...I felt...this was wrong. A wave of sickness at what I'd done hit me.

"Taryn, please!" Alric was frantic now.

I reached up, removed the crown, and shrunk to my human size.

"What did I do?" I kicked the crown away, but Irving swooped down and ate it before anyone else could get it. Or I could destroy it. The feelings of power still echoed in my head. I slumped to the ground and found myself held tightly by Alric and surrounded by faeries.

"You cries." Crusty patted my cheeks before I realized what I was doing.

"Is okay." Garbage and Leaf came and started patting me as well.

"The knights are all dead but the trolucs have vanished." Padraig stayed back but he couldn't have gotten too close with the faery swarm surrounding me anyway.

"I sent them home." I was still crying and confused but that I knew. "They didn't have a choice in this fight and wanted the snow. Our horses are coming back too." I had felt that as I took off the crown. They'd been relocated just as I'd relocated the trolucs. I know knew the spell and how much massive power it took to cast it.

"We need to get away from here," Mathilda looked battered but the worst part was the fear and worry in her eyes as she looked at me.

The horses reappeared and I was helped onto mine. I wasn't physically hurt, but the feelings I'd had when I destroyed the knights sat in my soul.

We weren't able to travel quickly, and Alric and Grillion rode in the back to obscure our trail. Covey, Mathilda, and Foxy all tried to talk to me but I couldn't find the words. I'd become a monster that had nothing to do with my dragon form.

Padraig led us into an abandoned barn and we settled in with as many magic shields up as possible.

Zaelian reappeared looking confused and nearly transparent. "I thought I'd just left you. I was pulled away but saw who had taken your friends. Who was behind it. It was the imperial palace in Colivith. The empress of the southern lands, all of the southern lands, was behind this. It appears she's preparing to declare war." There was a tremble in her voice I'd not heard before.

"With the north?" Alric asked.

"With the rest of the entire world."

THE END

DEAR READER,

Thank you for joining me on another adventure with those faeries and the people who travel with them. As always, I appreciate you for coming along on the newest escapade. The next book in this series will be out in 2022.

If you want to keep up on the further adventures of any of my characters, make sure to visit my website and sign up for my mailing list.

http://marieandreas.com/index.html

You can also sign up on Amazon to follow me and they will keep you updated.

https://geni.us/NZ6jX0o

If you enjoyed this book, please spread the word! Positive reviews are like emotional gold to any writer. And mean more than you know.

Thank you again—and keep reading!

ABOUT THE AUTHOR

MARIE IS A multi-award-winning fantasy and science fiction author with a serious reading addiction. If she wasn't writing about all the people in her head, she'd be lurking about coffee shops annoying total strangers with her stories. So really, writing is a way of saving the masses. She lives in Southern California and is owned by two very faery-minded cats. She is also a member of SFWA (Science Fiction and Fantasy Writers of America).

When not saving the masses from coffee shop shenanigans, Marie likes to visit the UK and keeps hoping someone will give her a nice summer home in the Forest of Dean or Conwy, Wales.